I'd Die for You

BY F. SCOTT FITZGERALD

NOVELS

The Love of the Last Tycoon (*Unfinished*)

Tender Is the Night

The Great Gatsby

The Beautiful and Damned

This Side of Paradise

STORIES

Bits of Paradise
uncollected stories by F. Scott and Zelda Fitzgerald

The Basil and Josephine Stories
edited and with an introduction
by Jackson R. Bryer and John Kuehl

The Pat Hobby Stories
edited and with an introduction by Arnold Gingrich

Taps at Reveille

Six Tales of the Jazz Age and Other Stories
with an introduction by Frances Fitzgerald Smith

Flappers and Philosophers
with an introduction by Arthur Mizener

The Stories of F. Scott Fitzgerald
a selection of 28 stories, with an introduction
by Malcolm Cowley

Babylon Revisited and Other Stories

The Short Stories of F. Scott Fitzgerald
edited and with a preface by Matthew J. Bruccoli

FSF's French driver's license, 1931.

F. Scott Fitzgerald

I'd Die for You

AND OTHER LOST STORIES

Edited by Anne Margaret Daniel

SCRIBNER

LONDON NEW YORK TORONTO SYDNEY NEW DELHI

First published in Great Britain by Scribner,
an imprint of Simon & Schuster UK Ltd, 2017
A CBS COMPANY

1 3 5 7 9 10 8 6 4 2

Simon & Schuster UK Ltd
1st Floor
222 Gray's Inn Road
London WC1X 8HB

Simon & Schuster Australia, Sydney
Simon & Schuster India, New Delhi

www.simonandschuster.co.uk
www.simonandschuster.com.au
www.simonandschuster.co.in

A CIP catalogue record for this book
is available from the British Library

Hardback ISBN: 978-1-4711-6470-5
Trade paperback ISBN: 978-1-4711-6471-2
eBook ISBN: 978-1-4711-6472-9

Printed and bound by CPI Group (UK) Ltd, Croydon, CR0 4YY

that is
Steward
Ou
'orest
isation.
er.

Contents

F. Scott Fitzgerald, Cannes, 1929.

Introduction

. . . it isn't particularly likely that I'll write a great many more stories about young love. I was tagged with that by my first writings up to 1925. Since then I have written stories about young love. They have been done with increasing difficulty and increasing insincerity. I would either be a miracle man or a hack if I could go on turning out an identical product for three decades.

I know that is what's expected of me, but in that direction the well is pretty dry and I think I am much wiser in not trying to strain for it but rather to open up a new well, a new vein. . . . Nevertheless, an overwhelming number of editors continue to associate me with an absorbing interest in young girls—an interest that at my age would probably land me behind bars.

—F. Scott Fitzgerald to Kenneth Littauer,
editor of *Collier's* magazine, 1939

After his sensational start as a professional writer in 1919, F. Scott Fitzgerald was increasingly stereotyped as a writer of what he himself had dubbed "the Jazz Age." Readers, and editors, anticipated from him standard romances, poor boys wooing rich girls, parties and glamour and glib flappers. When he tried something different, in a darker and deeper historical decade, and as a mature man who had lived through much pain, Fitzgerald found it very difficult to break out of this early stereotype. The young writer surrounded by campus life at Princeton (*This Side of Paradise*) becoming part of a new, golden couple (*The Beautiful and Damned*) and then the creator and chronicler of the Jazz Age (the story collections of the 1920s, and *The Great Gatsby*) gives way straight to *The Crack-Up* in most literary biographies and readers' conceptions of Fitzgerald. He wanted, as he put it, to "open up a new well, a new vein." Unfortunately, only a very few appreciated what he was trying to do.

These stories are about divorce and despair; working days and lonesome nights; smart teenagers unable to attend college or find a job during the Great Depression; American history, with its wars, its horrors, and its promises; sex, with marriage thereafter—or not; and the wild, bright vitality and grinding poverty of New York City, a place Fitzgerald truly loved and understood in all its possibilities, shallowness, and ugliness. They show him not as a "sad young man" growing old, and trapped in the golden days of his own recent past, but at the fore of Modern literature, in all its experimentalism and developing complexities.

* * *

> F. Scott Fitzgerald, graying and chunking up, is reputedly one of the most difficult authors from whom editors may wangle stories these days. He is the literary symbol of an era—the era of the new generation—and editors continue to want stories of flask gin and courteous collegiates preceding ladies through windshields on midnight joy rides. The public has acquired this Fitzgerald taste, too. But Fitzgerald has taken an elderly and naturally serious turn. Mellowed is the term. He wants to write mellowly, too. And if they won't let him he won't write at all. So there.
> —O. O. McIntyre, "New York Day by Day" column, 1936

Contemporary editors of popular, mass-market magazines at the time were not philistines, of course. However, there were good reasons for them to shy away from what Fitzgerald was writing by the mid-1930s; some of the stories are dark and stark. Only one editor fully saw the merits of what Fitzgerald was trying to do and published him consistently—Arnold Gingrich, of *Esquire*, a novelist himself. Fitzgerald sold the brilliant Pat Hobby stories to *Esquire* for $200 or $250 apiece in the two years before his death. (This was a low price to Fitzgerald, but not for a writer during the Depression; and not if you consider its relative worth, when according to the 1940 U.S. Census the average annual income was just over $1,000.) Gingrich encouraged Fitzgerald to turn his fine chronicles of a failed, drunken, Irish-American screenwriter into a novel. But even Gingrich wouldn't go for some stories; Fitzgerald wrote about young men worrying over venereal disease and having gotten sixteen-year-olds pregnant, and *Esquire* said no thanks.

Most of these stories are from the days when America, and the world, was in the Great Depression. Fitzgerald's fortunes, so high just a few years before, had fallen with the country's. He was often sick, often broke, and anxiously shuttling between the Baltimore area—where he and Zelda had settled with their daughter, Scottie—and a string of health resorts in the North Carolina mountains. After a breakdown in Europe in 1930, Zelda was hospitalized in February 1932 at the Phipps

Psychiatric Clinic of Johns Hopkins Hospital in Baltimore. For the rest of Fitzgerald's life, and hers, Zelda would be in and out of costly private clinics and hospitals; the pressure Scott put on himself to earn enough money to pay for these was immense. From early 1935, Fitzgerald's own health was a concern to him, too, and despite his fear of a recurrence of the tuberculosis with which he'd been diagnosed as a young man, he complicated matters by smoking and drinking to excess.

However, the first story in this collection, "The I.O.U.," comes from Fitzgerald's earliest days as a writer; and the last complete ones, "The Women in the House" and "Salute to Lucy and Elsie," from a stint in Hollywood in 1939 when he had quit drinking and was eagerly working on a new novel, published after his death as *The Last Tycoon*. There is writing from every stage of his well-chronicled career—the youth reveling in bright days and nights of success and celebrity; the husband and father at thirty suddenly plunged into a world of doctors and hospitals because of his wife's illness; a struggling man in poor health himself, looking for that new vein to open up for his own writing; and, above all, a professional writer who never failed to take inspiration and energy from the American landscape and personalities around him. That hunger never ended for F. Scott Fitzgerald, and these stories show it.

*   *   *

Is there any money in collections of short stories?
—Fitzgerald to his agent, Harold Ober, 1920

Short stories were, from the first, Fitzgerald's bread and butter. When Princeton's president, John Grier Hibben, wrote him to complain of, among other things, the characterization of a shallow university and its students in his story "The Four Fists" (1920), Fitzgerald replied, "I wrote it in desperation one evening because I had a three inch pile of rejection slips and it was financially necessary for me to give the magazines what they wanted."

To give the magazines what they wanted: that was Fitzgerald's brief as a young writer, and he continued in this very lucrative mode through the 1920s. He sold his work for money and was acutely aware of that fact and of how much he could make, quickly, with short stories, as opposed to waiting until he had enough of a novel complete to consider serialization. He and his family lived well, but after the immense success of his first two novels, *The Great Gatsby* (1925) did not sell well, and he needed money. Fitzgerald's discouragement over *Gatsby*'s lukewarm reception helped to keep him writing short stories for the *Saturday Evening Post* and spurred him to turn to work on screenplays in Hollywood as the Jazz Age ended. Fitzgerald was walking the tightrope between art and commerce, and did it as well as any writer of his generation.

He was also quite aware of what was his best writing and what was, as he termed it, hack work. Fitzgerald never lied to himself, or anyone else, about the difference between his commercially successful and his imaginatively satisfying stories. He was delighted when the two categories coincided, when stories he valued, like "Babylon Revisited," "Winter Dreams," "The Rich Boy," and the stories about Basil Duke Lee, sold for a high price. He always wished the ones he himself thought best would sell better. "I am rather discouraged that a cheap story like The Popular Girl written in one week while the baby was being born brings $1500. + a genuinely imaginative thing into which I put three weeks real entheusiasm [sic] like The Diamond in the Sky ["The Diamond as Big as the Ritz"] brings not a thing," he wrote to his agent, Harold Ober, in 1922. "But, by God + Lorimer, I'm going to make a fortune yet." George Horace Lorimer, the Yale graduate who edited the *Saturday Evening Post* from 1899 to 1936, paid Fitzgerald well for his writing: a fortune, in fact, for a young writer. In 1929 the *Post* began to pay him $4,000 per story, the equivalent of over $55,000 today. Yet Fitzgerald chafed under the golden chains, telling H. L. Mencken in 1925, just after *Gatsby* was published:

> My trash for the *Post* grows worse and worse as there is less and less heart in it—strange to say my whole heart was in my first trash. I thought that the Offshore Pirate was quite as good as Benediction. I never really "wrote down" until after the failure of the Vegetable and that was to make this book [*Gatsby*] possible. I would have written down long ago if it had been profitable—I tried it unsuccessfully for the movies. People don't seem to realize that for an intelligent man writing down is about the hardest thing in the world.

To his editor Maxwell Perkins at Scribner, in the same year, he was blunter and briefer: "The more I get for my trash the less I can bring myself to write."

Fitzgerald always considered himself a novelist, though he was a superb writer of short fiction—not a more humble form of writing than the novel, just briefer. His short stories, loved and well-known, stand alone, but they were often a testing ground for him, a place for rough drafts, an initial space for ideas and descriptions, characters and places, elements of which would find their way into his next novel. The ledger of his life and writings, which Fitzgerald kept until 1938, lists many stories in the "Record of Published Fiction" section as "stripped and permanently buried." That "stripping" process is readily visible in his tear sheets and on magazine copies of the stories he published, where Fitzgerald revised, redacted, and indicated passages that later appeared in *The Beautiful and Damned, The Great Gatsby,* and *Tender Is the Night.*

The stories in this collection, most of which are from the middle and late 1930s, feature lines that will be familiar to those who have read Fitzgerald's working papers (published as *The Notebooks of F. Scott Fitzgerald* in 1978) and *The Love of the Last Tycoon,* his final novel, left unfinished at his death.

* * *

Is there money in writing movies? Do you sell scenarios?
—Fitzgerald to Harold Ober, December 1919

The pull and possibilities of Hollywood, and of writing scenarios and screenplays for movies, were a lure for Fitzgerald from his earliest writing days. In September 1915, when he was a sophomore at Princeton, the *Daily Princetonian* ran an advertisement that read: "Special Notice to Students Who Fail / Motion Picture Studio Work opens an almost immediate field for substantial earnings to young men who possess some natural ability." This equation of motion picture work and failing was writ large for Fitzgerald from his first time in Hollywood. Though several of his stories and two of his novels were made into movies in the 1920s, he did not like them—he and Zelda thought the 1926 film version of *The Great Gatsby,* now lost, was "rotten." Nonetheless, in January 1927 the Fitzgeralds settled at the Ambassador Hotel in Los Angeles for three months while Scott worked on a screenplay, made to order, for Constance Talmadge. Talmadge, nicknamed "Brooklyn Connie," was a major silent star trying to break into talkie comedies. At first, he and Zelda enjoyed meeting and socializing with movie stars, but it soon wore thin. The screenplay was rejected, and the Fitzgeralds headed home to the East. Zelda reported that Scott "says he will never write another picture because it is too hard, but I do not think writers mean what they say[.]"

She was right. Those unremarkable sales and mixed reviews for *The Great Gatsby* changed Fitzgerald as a writer. He threatened a future course of action almost immediately, writing to Perkins from Europe in the spring of 1925:

In all events I have a book of good stories for the fall. Now I shall write some cheap ones until I've accumulated enough for my next novel. When that is finished and published I'll wait and see. It if will support me with no more intervals of trash I'll go on as a novelist. If not I'm going to quit, come home, go to Hollywood and learn the movie business.

In 1931, Fitzgerald went back to Hollywood, again for the money, for another miserable few months that proved creatively fruitless and personally taxing. *Tender Is the Night*, the novel he had been working on, remained unfinished. And this time, Zelda was not with Scott in Los Angeles; she was at her parents' home in Montgomery, Alabama, on the verge of a breakdown that would send her into a hospital the following spring. However, her judgment, in writing to her husband in Hollywood in November 1931, could not be sounder: "I'm sorry your work isn't interesting. I had hoped it might present new dramatic facets that would make up for the tediousness of it. If it seems too much drudgery and you are faced with 'get to-gether and talk-it-over' technique—come home, Sweet. You will at least have eliminated Hollywood forever. I wouldn't stay and waste time on what seems an inevitable mediocrity and too hard going."

Though he failed—again—in Hollywood in 1931, Fitzgerald, needing money—again—returned there for good in the summer of 1937. The third time was not the charm. In the title story of this collection, we see his view of the movie business—the inherent corrosiveness and the danger to individual creativity. Arnold Gingrich had warned Fitzgerald, in 1934, not to go back, and told him why in no uncertain terms: "It would be awful to see you piss away your talent in Hollywood again and I hope it won't come to that. Because, regarding the written word like a musical instrument, you are the supreme virtuoso—nobody can draw a purer finer tone from the string of an English sentence—and what the hell has the written word to do with Hollywood?"

As Fitzgerald wrote to Perkins shortly before he left for the West Coast, with cold self-knowledge and prescience, "Each time I have gone to Hollywood, in spite of the enormous salary, has really set me back financially and artistically. . . . I certainly have this one more novel [*The Love of the Last Tycoon*], but it may have to remain among the unwritten books of this world." Fitzgerald's bills were large, for everything from his own living expenses to Zelda's private sanitarium near Asheville, North Carolina, to Scottie's schools. And the contract from Metro-Goldwyn-Mayer was large, too—$1,000 a week for his work as a script doctor. The last few of his stories were written in the time he could borrow from work on the screenplays of others—screenplays it was mind-numbing to read, and on which his dismissive comments survive in the margins. The Hollywood work discouraged and literally sickened him, and his lack of enthusiasm for the place is evident in the weakness of his screenplay scenarios. Yet that MGM contract saved Fitzgerald when he was deeply in debt, and he found the material for *The Love of the Last Tycoon* there. He was happy when he died, working hard on that "one more novel," but the psychic and creative costs of selling his talent and time were immense, and surely contributed to that novel remaining unfinished.

* * *

Fitzgerald thought some of the stories in *I'd Die for You* were excellent, and was deeply disappointed, for personal more than financial reasons, to have them rejected by editors wanting him to write jazz and fizz, beautiful cold girls and handsome yearning boys. He was a professional writer from his college days, laboring over draft after draft, and regularly continuing to revise even after a story or book was published. His own copy of *The Great Gatsby* has changes and notations made in his hand that extend from the dedication page to those now-epic concluding paragraphs.

Fitzgerald wanted the hard work he put into writing his stories to be rewarded. He wanted these stories to be published. He tried to have them published. However, most of them come from a decade in his life when he no longer wanted to be edited. Early in his career, he had not minded the changes so much; sometimes editors made them without his knowledge, which angered him later, and sometimes he held his ground when it mattered. He complained in 1922 of the "reams of correspondence" he had to have with Robert Bridges, the editor of *Scribner's Magazine*, "over a 'God damn' in a story called <u>The Cut Glass Bowl</u>" (but his phrase the "God damn common nouveau rish" stood). In the 1930s, Fitzgerald was increasingly uncompromising about deletions, softenings, sanitizings—even when one of his oldest friends and a consummately professional agent, Ober, asked him to make revisions; and even when Gingrich, whose support of the Pat Hobby stories kept Fitzgerald both solvent and published, asked. He preferred to let the stories lie in wait. The right time might have come during his lifetime, if he had only lived longer.

No one chronicled his hardest times better than Fitzgerald himself, in his self-excoriating and confessional essay collection *The Crack-Up* (1936). The reevaluations he was making show in these pieces: a man trapped in an asylum desperate for a way out in "Nightmare"; a writer changing career course in "Travel Together"; a cameraman and a movie star thinking through the limits of their success, and wanting more, in "I'd Die for You."

In several of the stories in this collection, Fitzgerald explores new opportunities available to women during the 1930s—and the limits on those opportunities: Mrs. Hanson, the traveling saleswoman of "Thank You for the Light"; teenagers such as Lucy and Elsie having sex; Kiki's apparent affairs in "Offside Play." The traditional marriage plot is under siege; "Salute to Lucy and Elsie," for example, leaves a nuanced mix of approval and contempt for the new generation's freedoms; and the film scenario "Gracie at Sea" alternately mocks and endorses them.

That four of these stories feature nurses and doctors in leading roles connects all too clearly to the Fitzgeralds' lives during this period. The "medical stories"—"Nightmare," "What to Do About It," "Cyclone in Silent Land," and "The Women in the House"—borrow some of their grim detail from what happened on the way to the crack-up, and Fitzgerald's, and Zelda's, continuing illnesses thereafter.

"I'd Die for You," the collection's title story, which Fitzgerald also called "The Legend of Lake Lure," stems from his sad days in the salubrious North Carolina mountains. He went there for his health; fearing a recurrence of tuberculosis, he hoped the fresh air would help cure him—and cure Zelda. From 1935 until 1937, with trips back to Baltimore, where he, Zelda, and Scottie had tried to live in the early 1930s, Fitzgerald spent most of the time at a variety of North Carolina hotels. When he was solvent, he stayed at resort hotels, including the Lake Lure Inn, Oak Hall, and the Grove Park Inn; when he was broke, he lived in motels, ate canned soup, and washed out his clothes in the sink. When he had the time, health, and capacity to work, Fitzgerald was quite literally writing for his life. "I'd Die for You" comes from that time and those places.

Despite Fitzgerald's own preoccupations and anxieties, some stories are the antithesis of autobiographical. Rather than wondering about the forces operative in his own life, Fitzgerald takes inspiration from, and perhaps refuge in, thinking and writing about the larger forces affecting American culture and history, from Depression-era poverty to questions of race and civil rights, and regional customs, perspectives, and culture. Sometimes, to be sure, those public and historical matters melded with the personal and private for Fitzgerald. As he was leaving the South, and his Alabama-born wife, for Hollywood in 1937, Fitzgerald was thinking hard about history and family. The genesis for a Civil War tale, presented here in two complete drafts with very different plots, came from his father's story of a cousin strung up by his thumbs in rural Maryland. "Thumbs Up" and "Dentist Appointment" are full of brutality and torture, hard deeds and hard words—offering a sharp contrast to the romantic rewrites Fitzgerald was adding at the same time to the screenplay of *Gone*

With the Wind. These stories jarringly explore key moments in one of the most significant times of American history, and wonder at the myths that had arisen from it, while also showing Fitzgerald's questioning of what sort of connection family history had given, or forced upon, him as a writer to larger historical moments. They also question originality and creative sources; retelling, or perhaps exorcising, a bedtime story one has heard as a child, versus a writer wanting to find something new.

"Ballet Shoes," "Gracie at Sea," and "Love Is a Pain" are in the form of screenplay proposals, or scenarios. Others read as if Fitzgerald had set out to write a marketable screenplay, and reshaped it into what he would rather be working on—a short story, or a novel draft—instead. For example, "The Women in the House" reads at first like a bright Golden Age romantic comedy, designed for William Powell and Carole Lombard. Then keen descriptions come into play, and a dark shadow falls across the plot: the handsome adventurer hero is dying of a heart condition that, tragically, mirrors Fitzgerald's own. Can he still, in good conscience, court the beautiful movie star he loves? Twists enter the story that no movie studio would have approved, like a nurse criticizing past patients who were "dope fiends" and a male film star who is possessed of an uncanny "extraordinary personal beauty" and a large marijuana patch. The story sears and blisters Hollywood's vanities, falsities, and greed, but literally delivers a bed of roses, in one of Fitzgerald's classically beautiful, but not quite redemptory, endings. He not only mocks the love and romance plot Hollywood profited from, but serves up a knife-sharp parody of what editors wanted from him, and has fun doing it.

"Gracie at Sea," "Ballet Shoes," and "Love Is a Pain" are certainly imperfect as short stories, but that is what they are trying hard not to be. "Ballet Shoes" was written for another ballerina, but Fitzgerald felt that Zelda's passion and training for ballet would help him "deliver something entirely authentic in the matter, full of invention and feeling"—and this makes the scenario revealing biographically. Fitzgerald returned to "Gracie at Sea" five years after starting it; his revision is included here for comparison. "Love Is a Pain" is notable for being "an original" by Fitzgerald; his own idea for a whole movie, and not simply his treatment of a story by someone else.

* * *

I think the nine years that intervened between <u>The Great Gatsby</u> and <u>Tender</u> hurt my reputation almost beyond repair because a whole generation grew up in the meanwhile to whom I was only a writer of <u>Post</u> stories. . . .

It's odd that my old talent for the short story vanished. It was partly that times changed, editors changed, but part of it was tied up somehow with you and me—the happy ending. Of course every third story had some other ending but essentially I got my public with stories of young love. I must have had a powerful imagination to project it so far and so often into the past.

—Fitzgerald to Zelda Fitzgerald, October 1940

The imagination driving the stories of *I'd Die for You* is acutely powerful. Their quality is uneven, and Fitzgerald himself knew this, as is evident from his correspondence. Some were very clearly written for cash, and, though radiant lines and phrases and characters are there, they feel hasty and flawed. Debt and hard times wounded him irrevocably in the mid-1930s; the pain and honesty of what he wrote to Ober in May 1936 sounds out in the stories from these days:

This business of debt is awful. It has made me lose confidence to an appalling extent. I used to write for myself—now I write for editors because I never have time to really think what I <u>do</u> like or find anything to like. Its [*sic*] like a man drawing water out in drops because he's too thirsty to wait for the well to fill. Oh, for one lucky break.

Yet as he said to Zelda, about what the *Post* wanted of him and what he was no longer willing to do, "As soon as I feel I am writing to a cheap specification my pen freezes and my talent vanishes over the hill." Whether Fitzgerald was writing to suit himself or someone else's expectations, all these stories, taken together, show his increasing creative freedom, exploring of possibilities, and, often, heady resistance to producing what was expected of "F. Scott Fitzgerald," or to following traditional rules or demands. Editors and readers didn't want young people having sex on a cruise ship? Didn't want soldiers to be tortured during a war? Didn't want people threatening to commit suicide? Or drinking and drugs in the Hollywood hills? Or graft and payola in college sports? Too bad. Sometimes he was willing to revise. Sometimes, and particularly in cases where he was spending his talent seeking Hollywood approval—as in "Gracie at Sea"—Fitzgerald's lukewarm feeling about what he was doing is plain. But sometimes, and increasingly as the 1930s went on, Fitzgerald refused to submit to the expectations of those surprised to find in him a broad streak of realism, or a progression into the bleakness and broken styles of High Modernism, or just plain something they thought ugly.

The fineness and precision, the lapidary phrases and elegant language we associate with Fitzgerald's earlier prose, remain in the best of these stories as well. In Fitzgerald's writings from the first to the last there continued to be humor both bright and dark, a fascination with beautiful people and places and all things, a delight in what the moonlight or dappled sunlight could do to a mood, and an affection for both his readers and his writing. Even when he despaired of ever regaining his popularity during his lifetime, Fitzgerald knew how good he was, and still could be, telling Perkins, in the spring of 1940,

> Once I believed . . . I <u>could</u> (if I didn't always) make people happy and it was more fun than anything. Now even that seems like a vaudevillian's cheap dream of heaven, a vast minstrel show in which one is the perpetual Bones. . . .
> But to die, so completely and unjustly after having given so much. Even now there is little published in American fiction that doesn't slightly bare [sic] my stamp—in a <u>small</u> way I was an original.

Although Hollywood was, as he always knew it to be, bad for his craft as a writer in most ways, it was not entirely negative for Fitzgerald. In these stories there is often a compelling strain of the cinematic, where long scenes of description without dialogue seem like visual images on a screen: a man running, breathing harder and harder, up the stairs at Chimney Rock, looking for a girl, in "I'd Die for You"; an ambulance crashing in slow motion, its occupants emerging shaken and bruised to see a school bus full of screaming children in flames, in "Cyclone in Silent Land." Skillful or innovative sequences like these offset, or atone for, other moments, such as the baby crawling up a harp in "Gracie at Sea," where Fitzgerald's talents are compromised or downright abused. He wrote to Zelda in April 1940, "I have grown to hate California and would give my life for three years in France," but the month before he had told her, "I write these 'Pat Hobby' stories—and wait. I have a new idea now—a comedy series which will get me back into the big magazines—but my God I am a forgotten man." Those new ideas, comic and not tragic ones, would make him remembered again. Through it all, through the difficulties and alcoholism and sickness, Fitzgerald kept on writing, and trying to reflect what he knew and saw. The true Fitzgerald hallmark of these stories is their capacity for hoping.

Anne Margaret Daniel
January 2017

Editorial Note

The versions of the stories printed here are the last surviving ones on which it can be determined Fitzgerald worked. I have incorporated his handwritten changes to typescripts or manuscripts, placing in brackets phrases and passages lined through in uncompleted revisions. For example, the copy of "Offside Play" supplied to me by the Trustees of the Fitzgerald Estate predated one in the Fitzgerald Papers at Princeton. The texts were identical, but the Princeton copy bore Fitzgerald's revisions in pencil, including the instruction on the first page: "Change to Princeton" (indicating that he wanted the location of this story to be changed from Yale to Princeton). The change was never made in the text of the story itself, but his intention should be known. Likewise, I have followed his stated preferences in cases where variant versions of a story survive. For example, Fitzgerald agreed to cut "The Women in the House" into a far shorter story called "Temperature," but did not like the result and insisted in his letters that the longer original be offered for publication. Based on this, I have reproduced "The Women in the House" in its June 1939 version here. Where there is evidence of a substantially different version of a story having been drafted that does not now survive, such as the two pages from "Salute to Lucy and Elsie" focusing on the girls and their families, I have noted this.

"Day Off from Love," while unfinished, is a section of a short story that reveals a moment of Fitzgerald's creative process. Many examples of what Fitzgerald called "false starts" and what are obviously drafts of incomplete stories survive. Some run to twelve or fifteen pages before they fade out or stop abruptly. Others are as short as a paragraph or two. No other incomplete or fragmentary efforts are included. On some of these manuscripts or typescripts, Fitzgerald has marked his intention to save individual lines. One of these starts, titled "Ballet School— Chicago," was identified in 2015 as the beginning of a novel; it is not, being instead an abandoned story. Fitzgerald wrote ideas in several paragraphs or pages for Pat Hobby stories, and for many movie scenarios, to which he never returned. Three stories that Fitzgerald is known to have completed have since disappeared: "Recklessness" (1922), "Daddy Was Perfect" (1934), and "They Never Grow Older" (1937) are discussed in his correspondence but have not, so far, been found.

Almost a hundred years have passed from the composition of the earliest of these stories until today. As many things mentioned in these stories are unfamiliar to readers now, the annotations are designed to situate the reader, explain what Fitzgerald meant, and, where relevant, add details about his connection to a particular event or situation or person. In the headnotes, I have drawn upon Fitzgerald's correspondence to outline a story's compositional history. The typists working on these stories were various and their styles not consistent. In some cases, I worked from carbon copies upon which commas and periods are indistinguishable. Rather than creating a diplomatic transcription, I have standardized punctuation for the sake of the contemporary reader. I retain Fitzgerald's frequent use of the em dash—a trait he shares with Modern writers he admired, such as James Joyce. Where he underlines for emphasis or to indicate a quotation, or sets off a book title in quotation marks, I have italicized, as was the case in the final typeset publication of his writings. In my headnotes to each story, I have tried not to reveal crucial plot details. However, to avoid any spoilers, please read the stories themselves first.

AMD

FSF, 1921.

Fitzgerald wrote "The I.O.U." in 1920, when he was only twenty-three. All the sparkle and wit of his earliest writing is here, in the wake of *This Side of Paradise* and its success. On the surface, the story is a happy satire of a new business with which he had just become familiar—the publishing world. Even as a young man and writer, though, Fitzgerald was never light. The story is set in a post–World War I world of disappointment and death, and there are thoroughly modern notes of poking fun at books of self-help, spiritual communication, and bodice-ripping romance. The setting is midwestern, with a start in Manhattan—that is to say, two of Fitzgerald's home places.

This story is crucially concerned with the commercial aspect of publishing, at a time when Fitzgerald was making a great deal of money for his own writing. And he evidently wrote it for *Harper's Bazaar*, which did not print it. On June 2, 1920, when the Fitzgeralds had just moved to Westport, Connecticut, he told Harold Ober that he would be dropping off a finished draft for Ober to send to Henry Blackman Sell, editor of *Harper's Bazaar*: "I am also leaving 'The I.O.U.' This is the plot that Sell particularly wanted for *Harps. Baz* and which I promised him. I think it is pretty good." By July, however, it had gone on to the *Saturday*

Evening Post; said Fitzgerald, "If 'The I.O.U.' comes back from the *Post* I wish you'd return it to me as I think I can change it so there'll be no trouble Selling it." He was beginning *The Beautiful and Damned* at just this time, though, and was concentrating hard on his second novel, letting Ober know in the same letter that "there will probably be no more short stories this summer." This story was lost in the shuffle of Fitzgerald's first fame. "The I.O.U." remained the property of the Trustees of the Fitzgerald Estate until 2012. Yale University's Beinecke Library purchased the manuscript and typescript that year for $194,500.

The I.O.U.

The above is not my real name—the fellow it belongs to gave me his permission to sign it to this story. My real name I shall not divulge. I am a publisher. I accept long novels about young love written by old maids in South Dakota, detective stories concerning wealthy clubmen and female apaches with "wide dark eyes," essays about the menace of this and that and the color of the moon in Tahiti by college professors and other unemployed. I accept no novels by authors under fifteen years old. All the columnists and communists (I can never get these two words straight) abuse me because they say I want money. I do—I want it terribly. My wife needs it. My children use it all the time. If someone offered me all the money in New York I should not refuse it. I would rather bring out a book that had an advance sale of five hundred thousand copies than have discovered Samuel Butler, Theodore Drieser and James Branch Cabell in one year. So would you if you were a publisher.

Six months ago I contracted for a book that was undoubtedly a sure thing. It was by Harden, the psychic research man—Dr. Harden. His first book—I published it in 1913—had taken hold like a Long Island sand-crab and at that time psychic research had nowhere near the vogue it has at present. We advertised this new one as being a fifty heart-power document. His nephew had been killed in the war and Dr. Harden had written with distinction and reticence an account of his psychic communion through various mediums with this nephew, Cosgrove Harden.

Dr. Harden was no intellectual upstart. He was a distinguished psychologist, Ph.D. Vienna, LL.D. Oxford and late visiting professor at the University of Ohio. His book was neither callous nor credulous. There was a fundamental seriousness underlying his attitude. For example he had mentioned in his book that one young man named Wilkins had come to his door claiming that the deceased had owed him three dollars and eighty cents. He had asked Dr. Harden to find out what this deceased wanted done about it. This Dr. Harden had steadfastly refused to do. He considered that such a request was comparable to praying to the saints about a lost umbrella.

3

For ninety days we prepared for publication. The first page of the book was set up in three alternative kinds of type and two drawings each were ordered from five sky-priced artists before the jacket par excellence was selected. The final proof was read by no less than seven expert proof-readers lest the slightest tremble in the tail of a comma or the faintest cast in a capital eye should offend the fastidious eyes of the Great American Public.

Four weeks before the day set for publication huge crates went out to a thousand points of the literate compass. To Chicago alone went twenty-seven thousand. To Galveston, Texas, went seven thousand. One hundred copies apiece were hurled with sighs into Bisbee, Arizona, Redwing, Minnesota and Atlanta, Georgia. The larger cities having been accounted for stray lots of twenty and thirty and forty were dropped here and there across the continent as a sand-artist fills in his nearly completed picture by fine driftings from his hand.

The actual number of books in the first printing was three hundred thousand.

Meanwhile the advertising department were busy from nine to five six days of the week, italicizing, underlining, capitalizing, double-capitalizing; preparing slogans, headlines, personal articles and interviews; selecting photographs showing Dr. Harden thinking, musing and contemplating; choosing snapshots of him with a tennis racket, with a golf stick, with a sister-in-law, with an ocean. Literary notes were prepared by the gross. Gift copies were piled in stacks, addressed to the critics of a thousand newspapers and weeklies.

The date set was April 15th. On the fourteenth a breathless hush pervaded the offices and below in the retail department the clerks were glancing nervously at the vacant spaces where the stacks were to rest and at the empty front windows where three expert window dressers were to work all evening arranging the book in squares and mounds and heaps and circles and hearts and stars and parallelograms.

On the morning of April 15th at five minutes to nine Miss Jordan, the head stenographer, fainted from excitement into the arms of my junior partner. On the stroke of nine an old gentleman with Dundreary whiskers purchased the first copy of *The Aristocracy of the Spirit World*. The great book was out.

It was three weeks after this that I decided to run out to Joliet, Ohio, to see Dr. Harden. This was a case of Mohammed (or was it Moses?) and the mountain. He was of a shy and retiring disposition; it was necessary to encourage him, to congratulate him, to forestall the possible advances of rival publishers. I intended to make the necessary arrangements for securing his next book and with this in mind I took along several neatly worded contracts that would take all disagreeable business problems off his shoulders for the next five years.

We left New York at four o'clock. It is my custom when on a trip to put half a dozen copies of my principal book in my bag and lend them casually to the most intelligent looking of my fellow passengers in the hope that the book may thereby be brought to the attention of some new group of readers. Before we came to Trenton a lady with a lorgnette in one of the staterooms was suspiciously turning the pages of hers, the young man who had the upper of my section was deeply engrossed in his and a girl with reddish hair and peculiarly mellow eyes was playing tic-tac-toe in the back of a third.

For myself I drowsed. The New Jersey scenery changed unostentatiously to Pennsylvania scenery. We passed many cows and a great number of woods and fields and every twenty minutes or so the same farmer would appear sitting in his wagon beside the village station, chewing tobacco and gazing thoughtfully at the Pullman windows.

We must have passed this farmer ten or fifteen times when my nap was suddenly terminated by the realization that the young man who shared my section was moving his foot up and down like a base drummer in an orchestra and uttering little cries and grunts. I was both startled and pleased for I could see that he was much moved, moved by the book he clutched tightly in his long white fingers—Dr. Harden's *Aristocracy of the Spirit World*.

"Well," I remarked jovially, "you seem interested."

He looked up—in his thin face were the eyes that are seen in only two sorts of men: those who are up on spiritualism and those who are down on spiritualism.

As he seemed still rather dazed I repeated my inquiry.

"Interested!" he cried, "Interested! My God!"

I looked at him carefully. Yes, he was plainly either a medium or else one of the sarcastic young men who write humorous stories about spiritualists for the popular magazines.

"A remarkable piece of—work," he said. "The—hero, so to speak, has evidently spent most of his time since his death dictating it to his uncle."

I agreed that he must have.

"Its value of course," he remarked with a sigh, "depends entirely on the young man being where he says he is."

"Of course." I was puzzled, "The young man must be in—in paradise and not in—in purgatory."

"Yes," he agreed thoughtfully, "it would be embarrassing if he were in purgatory—and more so if he were in a third place."

This was rather too much.

"There was nothing in the young man's life which pre-supposed that he might be in—be in—"

"Of course not. The region you refer to was not in my thoughts. I merely said it would be embarrassing if he were in purgatory but even more embarrassing were he somewhere else."

"Where, sir?"

"In Yonkers, for instance."

At this I started.

"What?"

"In fact if he were in purgatory it would only be a slight error of his own—but if he were in Yonkers—"

"My dear sir," I broke out impatiently, "what possible connection is there between Yonkers and *The Aristocracy of the Spirit World*."

"None. I merely mentioned that if he were in Yonkers—"

"But he's not in Yonkers."

"No, he's not." He paused and sighed again, "In fact he has lately crossed from Ohio into Pennsylvania."

This time I jumped—from sheer nervousness. I had not yet realized at what he was driving yet I felt that his remarks hinted at some significance.

"You mean," I demanded quickly, "that you feel his astral presence."

The young man drew himself up fiercely.

"There's been enough of that," he said, intensely. "It seems that for the last month I have been the sport of the credulous queens and Basil Kings of the entire United States. My name, sir, happens to be Cosgrove P. Harden. I am not dead; I have never been dead, and after reading that book I will never again feel it quite safe to die!"

II

The girl across the aisle was so startled at my cry of grief and astonishment that she put down a tic instead of a tac.

I had an immediate vision of a long line of people stretching from 40th Street, where my publishing house stands, down to the Bowery—five hundred thousand people each one hugging a copy of *The Aristocracy of the Spirit World*, each one demanding the return of his or her $2.50. I considered quickly whether I could change all the names and shift it from my non-fiction to my fiction. But it was too late even for this. Three hundred thousand copies were in the hands of the American Public.

When I was sufficiently recovered the young man gave me a history of his experiences since he had been reported dead. Three months in a German prison—ten months in a hospital with brain fever—another month before he could remember his own name. Half an hour after his arrival in New York he had met an old friend who had stared at him, choked and then fainted dead away. When he revived they went together to a drug-store to get a cocktail and in an hour Cosgrove Harden had heard the most astonishing story about himself that a man ever listened to.

He took a taxi to a book store. The book he sought was sold out. Immediately he had started on the train for Joliet, Ohio, and by a rare stroke of fortune the book had been put in his hands.

My first thought was that he was a blackmailer but by comparing him with his photograph on page 226 of *The Aristocracy of the Spirit World* I saw that he was indubitably Cosgrove P. Harden. He was thinner and older than in the picture, the mustache was gone but it was the same man.

I sighed—profoundly and tragically.

"Just when it's selling better than a book of fiction."

"Fiction!" he responded angrily, "It *is* fiction!"

"In a sense—" I admitted.

"In a sense? It *is* fiction! It fulfills all the requirements of fiction: it is one long sweet lie. Would you call it fact?"

"No," I replied calmly, "I should call it non-fiction. Non-fiction is a form of literature that lies half-way between fiction and fact."

He opened the book at random and uttered a short poignant cry of distress that made the red-haired girl pause in what must have been at least the semi-finals of her tic-tac-toe tournament.

"Look!" he wailed miserably, "Look! It says 'Monday'. Consider my existence on this 'further shore' on 'Monday'. I ask you! Look! I smell flowers. I spend the day smelling flowers. You see, don't you? On page 194, on the top of the page I smell a rose—"

I lifted the book carefully to my nostrils.

"I don't notice anything," I said, "possibly the ink—"

"Don't smell," he cried, "Read! I smell a rose and it gives me two paragraphs of rapture about the instinctive nobility of man. One little smell! Then I devote another hour to daisies. God! I'll never be able to attend another college reunion."

He turned a few pages and then groaned again.

"Here I am with the children—dancing with them. I spend all day with them and we dance. We don't even do a decent shimmee. We do some aesthetic business. I can't dance. I hate children. But no sooner do I die than I become a cross between a nurse girl and a chorus man."

"Here now," I ventured reproachfully, "that has been considered a very beautiful passage. See, it describes your clothes. You are dressed in—let's see—well, a sort of filmy garment. It streams out behind you—"

"—a sort of floating under-garment," he said morosely, "and I've got leaves all over my head."

I had to admit it—leaves were implied.

"Still," I suggested, "think how much worse it could have been. He could have made you really ridiculous if he'd had you answering questions about the number on your grandfather's watch or the $3.80 you owed as a poker debt."

There was a pause.

"Funny egg, my uncle," he said thoughtfully, "I think he's a little mad."

"Not at all," I assured him, "I have dealt with authors all my life and he's quite the sanest one with whom we've ever dealt. He never tried to borrow money from us; he never asked us to fire our advertising department, and he's never assured us that all his friends were unable to get copies of his book in Boston, Massachusetts."

"Nevertheless I'm going to take his astral body for an awful beating."

"Is that all you're going to do?" I demanded anxiously. "You're not going to appear under your true name and spoil the sale of his book, are you?"

"What!"

"Surely you wouldn't do that. Think of the disappointment you'd cause. You'd make 500,000 people miserable."

"All women," he said morosely, "they like to be miserable. Think of my girl—the girl I was engaged to. How do you think she felt about my flowery course since I left her. Do you think she's been approving my dancing around with a lot of children all over—all over page 221. Undraped!"

I was in despair. I must know the worst at once.

"What—what *are* you going to do?"

"Do," he exclaimed wildly, "Why, I'm going to have my uncle sent to penitentiary along with his publisher and his press agent and the whole crew down to the merest printer's devil who carried the blasted type."

III

When we reached Joliet, Ohio, at nine o'clock next morning I had calmed him into a semblance of reason. His uncle was an old man, I told him, a misled man. He had been fooled himself, there was little doubt of it. His heart might be weak and the sight of his nephew coming suddenly up the path might finish him off.

It was, of course, in the back of my mind that we could make some sort of a compromise. If Cosgrove could be persuaded to keep out of the way for five years or so for a reasonable sum all might still be well.

So when we left the little station we avoided the village and in a depressing silence traversed the half mile to Dr. Harden's house. When we were within a hundred yards I stopped and turned to him.

"You wait here," I urged him, "I've got to prepare him for the shock. I'll be back in half an hour."

He demurred at first but finally sat down sullenly in the thick grass by the roadside. Drying my damp brow I walked up the lane to the house.

The garden of Dr. Harden was full of sunshine and bosomed with Japanese magnolia trees dropping pink tears over the grass. I saw him immediately sitting by an open window. The sun was pouring in, creeping in stealthily lengthening squares across his desk and the litter of papers that strewed it; then over the lap of Dr. Harden himself and up to his shaggy, white-topped face. Before him on his desk was an empty brown envelope and his lean fingers were moving busily over the sheaf of newspaper clippings he had just extracted.

I had come quite close half hidden by the magnolias and was about to address him when I saw a girl dressed in a purple morning dress break stooping through the low-branched cluster of apple trees that made the north end of the garden and move across the grass toward the house. I drew back and watched her as she came directly up to the open window and spoke unabashed to the great Dr. Harden.

"I want to have a talk with you," she said abruptly.

Dr. Harden looked up and a section of the *Philadelphia Press* fluttered from his hand. I wondered if it was the clipping that called him "The new St. John."

"About this stuff!" continued the girl.

She drew a book from under her arm. It was *The Aristocracy of the Spirit World*. I recognized it by the red cover with the angels in the corners.

"About this *stuff!*" she repeated angrily, and then shied the book violently into a bush where it skimmed down between two wild roses and perched disconsolately among the roots.

"Why, Miss Thalia!"

"Why, Miss Thalia!" she mimicked, "Why you old fool you ought to be crocked off for writing this book."

"Crocked off?" Dr. Harden's voice expressed a faint hope that this might be some new honor. He was not left long in doubt.

"Crocked off!" she blazed forth, "you heard me! My Gosh, can't you understand *English*! Haven't you ever been to a *prom*!"

"I was unaware," replied Dr. Harden coolly, "that college proms were held in the Bowery and I know no precedent for using an abbreviation of the noun crockery as a transitive verb. As for the book—"

"It's the world's worst disgrace."

"If you will read these clippings—"

She put her elbows on the window-sill, moved as though she intended to hoist herself through and then suddenly dropped her chin in her hands and looking at him level-eyed began to talk.

"You had a nephew," she said. "That was his hard luck. He was the best man that ever lived and the only man I ever loved or ever will love."

Dr. Harden nodded and made as though to speak but Thalia knocked her little fist on the window-sill and continued.

"He was brave and square and quiet. He died of wounds in a foreign town and passed out of sight as Sergeant Harden, 105th Infantry. A quiet life and an honorable death. What have you done!" Her voice rose slightly until it shook and sent a sympathetic vibration over the window vines. "What have you done! You've made him a laughing-stock! You've called him back to life as a fabulous creature who sends idiotic messages about flowers and birds and the number of fillings in George Washington's teeth. You've—"

Dr. Harden rose to his feet.

"Have you come here," he began shrilly, "to tell *me* what—"

"Shut up!" she cried. "I'm going to tell you what you've done, and you can't stop me with all the astral bodies this side of the Rocky Mountains."

Dr. Harden subsided into his chair.

"Go on," he said, with an effort at self-control. "Talk your shrewish head off."

She paused for a moment and turning her head looked into the garden. I could see that she was biting her lip and blinking to keep back the tears. Then she turned and fixed her dark eyes on him again.

"You've taken him," she continued, "and used him as a piece of dough for your crooked medium to make pie out of—pie for all the hysterical women who think you're a great man. Call *you* great! Without any respect for the dignity and reticence of death? You're a toothless yellow old man without even the excuse of real grief for playing on your own credulity and that of a lot of other fools. That's all—I'm through."

With that she turned and as suddenly as she had come walked with her head erect down the path toward me. I waited until she had passed and gone some twenty yards out of sight of the window. Then I followed her along the soft grass and suddenly spoke to her.

"Miss Thalia."

She faced me, somewhat startled.

"Miss Thalia, I want to tell you that there's a surprise for you down the lane—somebody you haven't seen for many months."

Her face showed no understanding.

"I don't want to spoil anything," I continued, "but I don't want you to be frightened if in a few moments you get the surprise of your existence."

"What do you mean?" she asked quietly.

"Nothing," I said. "Just continue along the road and think of the nicest things in the world and all of a sudden something tremendous will happen."

With this I bowed very low and stood smiling benevolently with my hat in my hand.

I saw her look at me wonderingly and then turn slowly and walk away. In a moment she was lost to view beyond the curve of the low stone wall under the magnolia trees.

IV

It was four days—four sweltering anxious days—before I could bring enough order out of the chaos to arrange any sort of business conference. The first meeting between Cosgrove Harden and his uncle was the most tremendous nervous strain of my life. I sat for an hour on the slippery edge of a rickety chair preparing to spring forward every time I saw young Cosgrove's muscles tighten under his coat sleeve. I would make an instinctive start and each time slip helplessly from the chair and land in a sitting position on the floor.

Dr. Harden finally terminated the interview by rising and going upstairs. I managed to pack young Harden off to his room by dint of threats and promises and wrung out of him a vow of twenty-four hours silence.

I used all my available cash in bribing the two old servants. They must say nothing, I assured them. Mr. Cosgrove Harden had just escaped from Sing Sing. I quaked as I said this but there were so many lies in the air that one more or less made little difference.

If it hadn't been for Miss Thalia I would have given up the first day and gone back to New York to await the crash. But she was in such a state of utter and beatific happiness that she was willing to agree to anything. I proposed to her that if they would marry and live in the west under an assumed name for ten years I would support them liberally. She jumped for joy. I seized the opportunity and with glowing colors painted a love-bungalow in California with mild weather all the year around and Cosgrove coming up the path to supper and romantic old missions nearby and Cosgrove coming up the path to supper and the golden gate in a June twilight and Cosgrove and so forth.

As I talked she gave little cries of joy and was all for leaving immediately. It was she who persuaded Cosgrove on the fourth day to join us in conference in the living-room. I left word with the maid that we were on no account to be disturbed and we sat down to thresh the whole thing out.

Our points of view were radically divergent.

Young Harden's was very similar to the Red Queen's in *Alice in Wonderland*. Some one had blundered and some one had to suffer for it right away. There had been enough fake dead men in this family and there was going to be a real one if some one didn't look out!

Dr. Harden's point of view was that it was all an awful mess and he didn't know what to do about it, God knew, and he wished he were dead.

Thalia's point of view was that she had looked up California in a guide-book and the climate was adorable and Cosgrove coming up the path to supper.

My point of view was that there was no knot so tight that there wasn't a way out of the labyrinth—and a lot more mixed metaphors that only got everybody more confused than they were in the beginning.

Cosgrove Harden insisted that we get four copies of *The Aristocracy of the Spirit World* and talk it over. His uncle said that the sight of a book would make him sick to his stomach. Thalia's suggestion was that we should all go to California and settle the question out there.

I got four books and distributed them. Dr. Harden shut his eyes and groaned. Thalia opened hers to the last page and began drawing heavenly bungalows with a young wife standing in the doorway of each. Young Harden hunted furiously for page 226.

"Here we are!" he cried, "Just opposite the picture of 'Cosgrove Harden the day before he sailed showing the small mole above his left eye' we see the following: 'This mole had always worried Cosgrove. He had a feeling that bodies should be perfect and that this was an imperfection that should in the natural order be washed away.' Hm! I have no mole."

Dr. Harden agreed.

"Possibly it was an imperfection in the negative," he suggested.

"Great Scott! If the negative had failed to photograph my left leg you'd probably have me yearning all through the book for a left leg—and have it joined to me in chapter twenty-nine."

"Look here!" I broke in. "Can't we reach some compromise. No one knows that you are in town. Can't we—"

Young Harden scowled at me fiercely.

"I haven't started yet. I haven't mentioned the alienation of Thalia's affections."

"Alienation!" protested Dr. Harden, "Why, I have paid her no attention. She detests me. She—"

Cosgrove laughed bitterly.

"You flatter yourself. Do you think I was jealous of your old grey whiskers? I'm talking about her affections being alienated by these descriptions of me."

Thalia bent forward earnestly.

"My affections never wavered, Cosgrove—never."

"Come Thalia," said Cosgrove somewhat grumpily, "they must have been slightly alienated. How about page 223. Could you love a man who wore floating underwear. Who was—who was filmy."

"I was grieved, Cosgrove; that is I would have been grieved if I'd believed it, but I didn't."

"No alienation?" His tone expressed disappointment.

"None, Cosgrove."

"Well," said Cosgrove resentfully, "I'm ruined politically anyway—I mean if I decided to go into politics I can never be president. I'm not even a democratic ghost—I'm a spiritual snob."

Dr. Harden's face was sunk in his hands in an attitude of profound dejection.

I interrupted desperately, talking so loudly that Cosgrove was compelled to stop and listen.

"I will guarantee you ten thousand a year if you will go away for ten years!"

14 • F. Scott Fitzgerald

Thalia clapped her hands and Cosgrove seeing her out of the corner of his eye began for the first time to show a faint interest.

"How about after the ten years are up?"

"Oh," I said hopefully, "Dr. Harden may be—may be—"

"Speak up," said the Doctor gloomily. "I may be dead. I sincerely trust so."

"—so you can come back under your own name," I continued callously. "Meanwhile we'll agree to publish no new edition of the book."

"Hm. Suppose he's not dead in ten years?" demanded Cosgrove suspiciously.

"Oh, I'll die," the Doctor reassured him quickly. "That needn't worry you."

"How do you know you'll die?"

"How does one know anyone will die. It's just human nature."

Cosgrove regarded him sourly.

"Humor is out of place in this discussion. If you'll make an honest agreement to die, with no mental reservations—"

The Doctor nodded gloomily.

"I might as well. With the money I have left I'll starve to death in that time."

"That would be satisfactory. And when you do, for heaven's sake arrange to have yourself buried. Don't just lie around the house here dead and expect me to come back and do all the work."

At this the Doctor seemed somewhat bitter and then Thalia who had been silent for some time suddenly raised her head.

"Do you hear anything outside?" she asked curiously.

I *had* heard something—that is I had subconsciously perceived a murmur—a murmur growing and mingling with the sound of many footsteps.

"I do," I remarked, "odd—"

There was a sudden interruption—the murmur outside swelled to the proportions of a chant, the door burst open and a wild-eyed servant rushed in.

"Dr. Harden! Dr. Harden," she cried in terror, "there's a mob, maybe a million people, comin' along the road and up toward the house. They'll be on the porch in a—"

An increase in the noise showed that they already were. I sprang to my feet.

"Hide your nephew!" I shouted to Dr. Harden.

His beard trembling, his watery eyes wide, Dr. Harden grasped Cosgrove feebly by the elbow.

"What is it?" he faltered.

"I don't know. Get him upstairs to the attic right away—put leaves over him, stick him behind an heirloom!"

With that I was gone, leaving the three of them in puzzled panic. Through the hall I rushed and out the front door onto the screen-porch. I was none too soon.

The screen-porch was full of men, young men in checked suits and slouch hats, old men in derbys and frayed cuffs, crowding and jostling, each one beckoning and calling to me above the crowd. Their one distinguishing mark was a pencil in the right hand and a notebook in the left—a notebook open—waiting, virginally yet ominously portentous.

Behind them on the lawn was a larger crowd—butchers and bakers in their aprons, fat women with folded arms, thin women holding up dirty children that they might better see, shouting boys, barking dogs, horrible little girls who jumped up and down shouting and clapping their hands. Behind these in a sort of outer ring stood the old men of the village, toothless, musty-eyed, their mouths open, their grey beards tickling the tops of their canes. Over behind them the setting sun, blood red and horrible, played on three hundred twisting shoulders.

After the burst of noise that succeeded my appearance a silence fell—a deep hush pregnant with significance—and out of this hush came a dozen voices from the men with notebooks in front of me.

"Jenkins of the *Toledo Blade!*"

"Harlan of the *Cincinnati News!*"

"M'Gruder of the *Dayton Times!*"

"Cory of the *Zanesville Republican!*"

"Jordan of the *Cleveland Plain Dealer!*"

"Carmichael of the *Columbus News!*"

"Martin of the *Lima Herald!*"

"Ryan of the *Akron World!*"

It was weird, uncanny—like some map of Ohio gone mad with the miles refusing to square and the towns jumping about from county to county. My brain quivered.

Then again the hush fell. I noticed a commotion in the middle of the crowd, a sort of wave or eddy floating down the center like a thin line of wind blowing through a wheatfield.

"What do you want!" I cried hollowly.

Like one voice came the response from half a thousand throats.

"Where is Cosgrove Harden!"

It was out! The reporters swarmed about me, pleading, threatening, demanding.

"—kept it pretty close, didn't you—almost didn't leak out—pays to pay bills—won't he give an interview—send us the old faker—"

Then that strange eddy in the field of people suddenly reached the front and died out. A tall young man with yellow hair and stilt-like legs emerged dynamically from the crowd and dozens of willing hands propelled him forward toward me. Up to the porch he came—up the steps—

"Who are you?" I shouted.

"Name's Elbert Wilkins," he gasped, "I'm the fella that told."

He paused and his chest swelled. It was his great moment. He was the immortal messenger of the Gods.

"I recognized him the day he came! You see—you see—" We all swayed forward eagerly,—"I got his I.O.U. for three dollars and eighty cents he lost to me at draw-poker, and *I want my money!*"

I am a publisher. I publish any sort of book. I am looking for a book that will sell five hundred thousand copies. This is the season for novels with a psychic turn. If possible I would prefer something by a fervent materialist about a wealthy clubman and a dark apachess—or something about love. Love is a sure thing—it takes a living man to love.

Zelda Fitzgerald, self-portrait
as ballerina in the moon, 1927.

"Nightmare" is, as Harold Ober's accompanying note indicates, "[v]ery improbable of course but well told." It is a fantasy set in a mental institution, a story of family connections (there are several brothers who are institutionalized together, and a father-daughter team of doctors), as well as having a boy-gets-girl plot.

By 1932 Fitzgerald knew all too well what even the most exclusive, and progressive, private mental institutions were like. Zelda had first been hospitalized in Europe in 1930, and from February until June 1932 was a patient at the Phipps Clinic in Baltimore. The question of who is, and who is not, "crazy" is at the heart of "Nightmare"—how sanity is defined, and how much depends upon who is doing the defining. Surely it is wish fulfillment, too, for Fitzgerald to imagine the salvation of someone sane from duplicity and disaster.

"Nightmare" was rejected by *College Humor*, *Cosmopolitan*, *Redbook*, and the *Saturday Evening Post*, all magazines that had regularly and eagerly published Fitzgerald's work. The very rejections of this story make it interesting today; in 1932, this was not what readers expected under the byline "F. Scott Fitzgerald," and therefore not what editors wanted. Times were bleak enough, and he was "meant" to be the writer one wanted to read for moonlight and money. Part of the plot turns on wealth, to be sure (the brothers have money, and the doctor in charge of the hospital wants it), but the descriptions of patients and their care did not appeal to editors wanting flappers and fun from Fitzgerald. He wrote sadly, but resignedly, to Ober in April 1932, "Nightmare will never, never sell for money, in any times." In June 1936, Fitzgerald said that he still had the story with him, but had "stripped" it "and used almost all of the best lines from it in *Tender Is the Night*." The typescript of the story, with changes in pencil by its author, remained in family hands until it was sold at Sotheby's in New York on June 15, 2012.

NIGHTMARE

By

F. Scott Fitzgerald

May I say in the beginning that I don't believe this ever happened: it is all too grotesque and I have been unable to find the exact locality where it took place or to identify the people by their real names. But here is the story as I heard it.

In a pleasant section of New Hampshire, on a hill that is white in the winter and green in summer, four or five houses stand near each other. On a spring afternoon all the doors and windows of the largest and most elaborate house are thrown open toward the tennis courts; often the sound of a violin and piano drifted out upon the summer air. There

There is movement in the reception room downstairs as if a house-party were taking place. Walking the length of the terrace you might see through the French windows people playing in the billiard room, or other people listening to the spirited

Nightmare

(Fantasy in Black)

May I say in the beginning that I don't believe this ever happened: it is all too grotesque and I have been unable to find the exact locality where it took place or to identify the people by their real names. But here is the story as I heard it.

In a pleasant section of New Hampshire, on a hill that is white in the winter and green in summer, four or five houses stand near each other. On a spring afternoon all the doors and windows of the largest and most elaborate house are thrown open toward the tennis courts; often the sound of a violin and piano drifts out upon the summer air. There is movement in the reception room downstairs as if a house-party were taking place. Walking the length of the terrace you might see through the French windows people playing in the billiard room, or other people listening to the spirited strains of Suppé's *Light Cavalry*, or further on a group with embroidery in hand—all of them on a certain June day are intent on some pastime, save for a tall girl in white who stands in the doorway looking out toward the New Hampshire mountains with an expression of rapturous discontent.

There was conversation in the salons—some of it in a merry mood. A tall, sheep-like gentleman, standing in a group of three, remarked in a guarded voice:

"Now there's Mrs. Miller playing bridge. If I could just slip up behind her with a good pair of scissors and snip off half a dozen of those mousy curls they'd be fine souvenirs and she'd be much improved."

The other two men were not amused at his fancy. One of them made a contemptuous remark in bad Spanish and regarded the speaker sullenly—the third paid no attention but wheeled sharply as the group was joined by a fourth.

"Well, well, Mr. Woods—and Mr. Woods—and Mr. Woods," said the new arrival jovially, "What gorgeous weather."

The three Mr. Woods—they were brothers, aged perhaps thirty-five,

19

forty and forty-five—agreed with him. He was a dark stout man with flashing brown eyes and black hair and a hawk-like face that somehow blended with his forceful, soft-flowing voice. He was a dandy and rather more sure of himself than anyone in the room. His name was Vincintelli and his birthplace Milan.

"Did you enjoy the music that Mrs. Sachs and Mr. Hepburn have been giving us?" Vincintelli asked.

"I was just saying—" began the eldest Woods brother, but broke off.

"You were just saying what?" asked Vincintelli, quietly yet sharply.

"Nothing," said Mr. Wallace Woods.

Vincintelli looked around and his eyes lingered for a moment on the young woman in the doorway. Instinctively he felt dissatisfied with the physical attitude she had assumed—somehow standing in the doorway like that betrayed the fact that her mood was centrifugal rather than centripetal—she was drawn toward the June afternoon, the down-rolling, out-rolling land, adventurous as an ocean without horizons. Something stabbed at his heart for his own mood was opposite—for him she made this place the stable center of the world.

He made a parallelogram of the rooms, rather more rapidly and nervously than was his wont, speaking a greeting here, dropping a joke or a joviality there, congratulating the amateur musicians, and then, passing close to Kay Shafer who did not turn to look at him, he arrived again in the vicinity of the Woods brothers who still stood together in a group.

"You should mix around more," he chided them, "You shouldn't be such an exclusive triumvirate."

"Yo no quiero," said the second Woods brother, rapidly and contemptuously.

"As you know I do not speak Spanish well," said Vincintelli calmly, "we could communicate so much better in English."

"Yo non hablo Inglese," asserted Mr. Woods.

"On the contrary you speak excellent English, Mr. Woods. You are an American born and bred, like your brothers. We know that, don't we?" He laughed, confidently, firmly, and took out his watch. "It's two-thirty. We must all go to our schedules." As he turned briskly it seemed to be a sort of signal, for the people in the room, singly or in pairs, bestirred themselves and slowly drifted from the room.

"Train leaving," chanted the youngest Mr. Woods, "New York, New Haven and Hartford—for Pelham, Greenwich, South Norwalk, Norwalk!" His voice suddenly grew louder until it resounded through the room, "West Point! *Larchmont*! NEW HAVEN! AND POINTS BEYOND!"

A nurse skipped quickly to his side.

"Now Mr. Woods." Her trained voice indicated disapproval without exasperation, "we mustn't make quite so much noise. We're going to the carpentry shop where—"

"*Train leaving at Gate 12*—" His voice had sunk to a plaintive but still sonorous cadence as he walked obediently with her to the door. The other brothers followed, each with a nurse. So also, with a sigh and a last glance outdoors, did Miss Shafer. She stopped, however, as a small short-legged man with a shield-shaped body and beaver whiskers hurried into the room.

"Hello, father," she said.

"Hello, my dear," he turned to Vincintelli, "Come to my office immediately."

"Yes, Professor Shafer."

"When are you leaving, father?" asked Kay.

"At four." He hardly seemed to see her and she made no effort to say goodbye; only her young brow wrinkled a little as she glanced at her watch and went on out.

Professor Shafer and Dr. Vincintelli went to the Professor's office in the same building.

"I will be gone three or four days," said Professor Shafer, "Here are some last points for you to note: Miss Katzenbaugh [says] she wants to leave and since she's not committed we can't stop her—until her sister arrives from New York detain her on one pretext or another. It is clear paranoid schizophrenia, but when they refuse to commit what can we do?" He shrugged his shoulders and glanced at his paper. "The patient Ahrens is suicidal; watch him closely and remove all small objects from his room. You cannot be too careful—remember the golf balls we found in Mr. Capes at the autopsy—also, I think we can regard Mrs. O'Brien as well and discharge her. Talk to her and write to her family."

"Very well, Professor," said Vincintelli writing busily.

"Move Carstairs to 'the Cedars.' When there is a full moon he meows at night and keeps people awake. Finally, here are some prescriptions and routine notes that will explain themselves. There—" he sat back in his chair, "I think that is all. Is there anything you would like to ask me?"

Vincintelli nodded thoughtfully.

"About the Woods brothers," he said.

"You are always worried about the Woods brothers," said Dr. Shafer impatiently. "It is not a case that permits of much interesting prognosis. Their progress has been steadily down-hill."

Vincintelli nodded in agreement. "Today," he said, "I tried bringing them over to lunch. It was a failure—the brother who imagines himself a train announcer was shouting when he left."

Professor Shafer looked at his watch. "I must leave in ten minutes," he said.

"Let me recapitulate," said Vincintelli, "their history. The Woods brothers are rich and prosperous stockbrokers; the eldest, Wallace, breaks down on the day after the market crash in twenty-nine and is sent here with his pockets full of ticker-tape. He develops a mania for cutting off people's hair, and we have trouble every time he gets hold of a pair of shears. There was the unfortunate incident of Mrs. Reynard's wig—not to mention the time he tried to get at your facial hair with a nail scissors."

The professor passed his hand uncomfortably through his beard.

"The second brother, Walter, was in charge of the Foreign Bond Department. He broke down after the revolutions in South America and came here with the delusion that he could speak nothing but Spanish. The third brother, John, who specialized in railroad securities, was all right until the fall of 1931 when he fainted one day and woke up under the impression that he was the train announcer in the Grand Central Station. There is also a fourth brother, Peter, who is quite sane, carrying on the business."

Professor Shafer looked at his watch again. "That is all quite correct, Dr. Vincintelli, but really I must leave you. If there is any special change of treatment you would recommend for them, we can take it up on my return."

He began tucking papers into his briefcase, while Vincintelli regarded him rather glumly.

"But Professor—"

"It seems to me that we should conserve our interest for cases more promising than those of the Woods brothers," and with that Professor Shafer hurried out.

While Vincintelli still sat there, a moody dissatisfaction in his eyes, a small red light glowed on his desk and Miss Shafer came into the room. The doctor stood up.

"Is father gone?" Kay asked.

"You can still catch him, I think."

"It doesn't matter. I just want to report that the press is broken in the book-bindery."

He stared at her with open admiration.

"To look at you," he said, "it is hard to believe that you are a full-fledged doctor."

"Do you mean that to be a compliment?" she asked indifferently.

"Yes, a compliment to your youth. To be a doctor—there could be no higher calling. But to be a psychiatrist—" A light of exaltation came into his eyes, "that is to be among the peers, the samurai of the profession. And when some day you will see arise the splendid towers of our Institute for Psychiatric Research, which will parallel the Rockefeller Institute—"

"I think," said Kay Shafer slowly, "and have thought for some time, that you yourself are in the early stages of manic-depressive psychosis." As he stared at her she continued, "And I think that I will soon develop symptoms myself if I don't get out of here. I should think father would see I haven't any gift for it."

Kay was twenty-three, with a tall graceful form apparent even under her rather severe white dress. She had brown eyes with active light in them and a serious face shot through with sudden moods of amusement. She was serious today, though, as she continued.

"What may be a fine place for a neurotic young doctor with exalted ambitions may not be a fine place for a girl with an interesting nose."

A month ago Vincintelli had asked her to marry him and she had refused him with confirmatory laughter. Instinct warned him that it was not yet time to try again, but he kept anxiously remembering her pose of flight by the window.

"That's because you haven't yet been able to view your work professionally," he suggested in a don't-worry-little-girl tone. "If you see someone badly afflicted it depresses you—a natural feeling in a layman but not suitable to a nerve specialist. They are merely cases—even their sufferings have a different quality than ours. They suffer perhaps more but not as normal human beings suffer. It's like reading into a plodding horse the sensibilities of an educated person."

"It seems much the same to me," Kay admitted. "I know that father can't agonize over every case he treats, but it has made him hard. I simply say with all humility that I'm not fitted for the work."

He came over and stood beside her, even put his hand tentatively on her bare forearm, but immediately withdrew it as if he sensed some hardening of the pores.

"Let me help you, Kay. If your life was joined to—"

He was interrupted by a click from Professor Shafer's desk as the red light came on. Impatiently he moved away from Kay and called "Come in." It was the Professor's secretary.

"Mr. Peter Woods is here from New York, doctor."

"Mr. Peter Woods—oh, yes," Vincintelli straightened up; his features relaxed their intensity and an expression of genial urbanity had settled on his face as Mr. Peter Woods came into the room.

He was a tall young man of about thirty, with pleasant mien and manner, and the rather harassed face of one who bore heavy responsibilities.

"Dr. Vincintelli?" he said, "I understand that Professor Shafer is away."

"Come in, Mr. Woods—I'm very happy to meet you. I'm sorry the Professor's gone, but since I've occupied myself particularly with your brothers I hope I'll be a satisfactory substitute. In fact—"

Peter Woods collapsed suddenly into the armchair beside the desk.

"I haven't come about my brothers, Dr. Vincintelli, I've come about myself."

Dr. Vincintelli gave a start, and turned quickly to Kay.

"That will be all, Miss Shafer," he said. "I will talk to Mr. Woods."

Only then did Peter Woods notice that there was another person in the room, and seeing that a pretty girl had heard his avowal he winced. Meanwhile Kay was studying him—certainly he was the most attractive looking man she had met since leaving medical school, but she was examining more carefully the flexing of his hands, the muscles of his face, the set of his mouth, searching for the "tension" which in its medical sense is one of the danger signs of mental troubles.

"I will see Mr. Woods alone," repeated Dr. Vincintelli.

"Very well."

When she had left the room, Vincintelli, his features sympathetically composed, sank back into Professor Shafer's arm chair and folded his hands.

"Now, Mr. Woods, let me hear about it."

The young man drew a long breath, then he too sat back in his chair concentrating.

"As you may know, I'm the youngest member of the firm," he began. "Perhaps because of that I am less inclined to worry than my brothers, but frankly the stock-market crash didn't bother me much. We were so rich in 1929—I didn't think anybody ought to be as rich as we were. As things got worse I felt like hell about it but still I didn't feel like my brothers did—and when they collapsed, one by one, I couldn't understand it. It didn't seem justified by the circumstances."

"Go on, go on," said Dr. Vincintelli, "I understand."

"What bothered me personally was not the hard times—it was my brothers. Ever since Walter broke down a year ago I've lived with the idea that there was hereditary mental trouble in the family and it might hit me. That was all until last week."

He drew a long breath.

"I came home from work last Friday to the penthouse where I live alone at 85th Street. I had been working very hard—I'd been up all

night the night before, smoking a lot. As I opened the door on all that
big silence I felt suddenly that the time had come—I was going insane."

"Tell me all about it," Dr. Vincintelli leaned forward in his chair. "Tell
me exactly what happened."

"Well—I saw—I saw—"

"Yes," said Dr. Vincintelli eagerly.

"I saw rings and circles before my eyes, revolving and revolving like
suns and moons of all colors."

Dr. Vincintelli sank back in his chair.

"Is that all?"

"Isn't that enough?" asked Peter Woods. "I'd never seen anything like
that before."

"No voices?" demanded Dr. Vincintelli, "No buzzing in your head?"

"Well, yes," admitted Peter, "some buzzing, like a hangover."

"No headaches? No feeling that maybe you weren't who you thought
you were? No feeling that you wanted to kill yourself? No terrible fears?"

"Well, I can't say I had any of those—except the last—I had a terrible
fear that I was going to go crazy."

"I see," said Dr. Vincintelli, pressing his fingers together. There was
a moment's silence—then he spoke up in a crisp decided voice. "Mr.
Woods, the wisest thing you ever did in your life was to come voluntarily
and put yourself under our care. You are a pretty sick man."

"My God," groaned Peter Woods, "Do you mean I may be like my
brothers?"

"No," said Dr. Vincintelli emphatically, "because in your case we're
going to catch it in time."

Peter Woods buried his face in his hands.

It was the custom for such patients as were not under restraint to dine
rather formally with the staff at a long table in the pleasant dining
room—when they sat down Kay Shafer found herself sitting opposite
Mr. Peter Woods.

Over the whole assemblage brooded a certain melancholy. The doctors kept up a sort of chatter, but most of the patients, as if exhausted
by their day's endeavor or depressed by their surroundings, said little
but concentrated on their food or stared down into their plates. It was
the business of Kay as of the other doctors to dissipate as much of this
atmosphere as possible.

As she sat down she smiled and spoke to Peter Woods and he looked
at her with a rather startled expression. After a minute he addressed a
casual remark about the weather to Mr. Hughes, the patient sitting on

his left, but receiving no answer he lowered his eyes and made no further attempt at conversation. After a minute Mr. Hughes spoke up suddenly.

"The last one to finish his soup," he said, "is a rotten egg."

No one laughed or seemed to have heard. The cadaverous woman on Peter Woods' right addressed him.

"Did you just arrive?"

"Yes."

"Do you play polo?" she asked.

"Why, a little."

"We must play soon—perhaps tomorrow."

"Why, thank you very much," he said, looking surprised.

The woman leaned toward him suddenly.

"My heavens, this fish!"

Peter Woods looked down at his plate; there seemed nothing the matter with the fish.

"Why, it seems very nice."

"Nice?" She shook her gaunt head. "Well, if you think it's nice all I can say is you must be crazy."

Kay saw him wince, look again at the fish, poke it reticently with his fork, even inhale it unobtrusively as if he thought his own judgment had become fallible.

Mr. Hughes spoke up again.

"The last one who finishes—" but Kay felt that this had gone far enough. She leaned forward and said to Peter Woods in a clear crisp voice that cut across Mr. Hughes' remark:

"Do you know New Hampshire, Mr. Woods?"

"I've never been here before," he answered.

"There are some fine walks and climbs around here with beautiful views," Kay said.

"Dullest scenery in North America," muttered the horsewoman, sotto voce.

Kay continued her conversation until Mr. Hughes interrupted.

"As a matter of fact I am a doctor," he said irrelevantly, "one of the best doctors in the country." He cast a look of jealousy at Dr. Vincintelli at the head of the table. "I wish they'd let me take charge of this place for about a week. I had a clinic of my own that makes this one look like a poor-house."

He stared at his plate sadly.

"What was the matter?" Peter Woods asked with an effort. "Did it fail?"

"It failed," said the doctor despondently, "Everything failed. I had to come here."

"That was too bad."

"Yes," agreed the doctor absently, and then, "And I know why it failed."

"Why?"

"Plot—I had powerful enemies. What do you suppose they used?"

"What?" asked Peter Woods.

"Mice. Filled the whole place with mice. Mice everywhere. Why, I used to see mice—"

Again Kay interrupted him.

"Now, Doctor Hughes, mustn't tell Mr. Woods about that right now."

The man sunk his voice to a whisper but Kay heard.

"She hates me," he said. "Can't stand it if I talk about mice."

"Like horses?" the woman patient asked Peter Woods.

"Yes, I do."

"Rode all my life but was thrown from a horse three years ago." She hesitated. "But still keep my own stable. Only six now—three hunters that you'll like. Show them to you tomorrow."

The conversation was interrupted by the sound of moving chairs. Dr. Vincintelli rose and the table rose with him. Kay drew a long breath of relief. She had, to a certain extent, adjusted herself to the irrationalities and delusions of the patients, but tonight had been difficult and she had seemed to see it all through the eyes of the newest arrival. She liked him—she hoped that his brothers' fate was not going to overtake him. It was all very depressing and it strengthened her desire to get away.

About nine-thirty when the patients had retired and she was starting across the grounds to her home, Dr. Vincintelli called after her and caught up with her.

"What did you make of Woods?" he asked. "I purposely placed him opposite you."

Kay considered.

"Why, I can't say I noticed anything. He seemed rather tired and rather embarrassed. Mr. Hughes and Miss Holliday were particularly annoying and absurd and after dinner that alcoholic Chetwind kept asking him how he'd like a highball."

"I suppose they were showing off for a newcomer."

"Well, it was a nuisance," Kay said.

The doctor was silent for a minute.

"It's a much more serious case than it appears," he said suddenly.

"Do you think so?" she asked, rather anxiously.

"I talked to him a long while this afternoon. Already he has certain delusions. He will follow the same course toward paranoid dementia that his brothers followed. He's already receding from reality." His tone changed, became almost elated. "But it's wasteful to talk shop on a night like this."

She was so absorbed in the tragedy of Peter Woods that she hardly knew when he took her arm—realized it only when he said her name in a tender voice. Then she broke sharply away from him.

"Kay, I want to tell you—"

"Be quiet!" she cried. "Even if I cared for you, which I don't, I'd scarcely be in a receptive humor just after hearing a thing like this."

"But can't you make your work and your personal life into two separate—"

"I can't become a monster overnight. Excuse me, I want to be alone."

She ran on suddenly and left him standing there. Her eyes were full of tears for the unpreventable sadness in the world.

II

My schedule, thought Kay next morning, reads like a debutante's date list—"see the dancing teacher—see the portrait painter—see the milliner"—except that the dancing teacher, the portrait painter and the milliner are no longer practicing their professions.

For a moment, standing by the summer window, she forgot them all and the same vague nostalgia for something she had never known had rushed over her. She wanted to be in a boat going to the South Seas, in a town car going to a ball—in an aeroplane going to the North Pole. She wanted to stand in a shop full of utterly useless and highly ornamental jim-cracks—ivory elephants—Algerian bracelets, ear rings, yes and nose rings—and say, "I'll take this, I'll take this, I'll take this." She wanted to buy out the cosmetics department of a drug store, and talk about trivialities to men who would think of her as decorative rather than competent.

Instead she had to see Mr. Kirkjohn the dancing teacher. Mr. Kirkjohn was a pleasant man in many respects—his only fault was his ambition. Mr. Kirkjohn wanted to go to Paris and walk down from the Arc de Triomphe to the Café de la Paix. A harmless enough aim in itself, but during his stroll Mr. Kirkjohn wanted to be entirely unclothed. Failing Paris, Mr. Kirkjohn wanted to be entirely unclothed wherever he was—unless he was alone, when he did not care. Kay's visits to him were short and unfrequent, for no sooner did he see her than he reached for his tie.

There were other calls, none of them cheerful pastimes save one to a young girl who was cured and was going home. Kay envied her—

already she was talking about the clothes she was going to buy and the trip abroad she was going to make this fall.

"You'll visit me, Doctor, won't you?" the girl asked. "You've done more for me than anyone here."

"My dear, I wouldn't know what to say to your friends. I've talked science to doctors and baby talk to patients for so long that I've forgotten how to chatter. Write me a letter with all the new slang in it. I don't know anything later than 'Oh, Yeah?'"

There were several other visits—then she took out her roadster and started for the village five miles away. It was a gorgeous morning and she sang as she drove.

> Leaves come tumbling dow-wn overhead
> Some of them are brown, some are red
> Beautiful to see-ee, but reminding me-ee
> Of a faded summer lu-uve—

Suddenly she stepped hard on the brakes—the well set-up man walking down the road had looked up as she passed and to her astonishment she recognized Mr. Peter Woods.

She stopped the car twenty feet beyond him and in the minute during which he came toward her she thought quickly. He had no suitcase and it was obvious that he had simply walked out of the clinic. He must be taken back and if he should prove obdurate she could do nothing alone. The road was lonely, deserted. Should she drive on to the village and phone back to Dr. Vincintelli or should she try persuasion? Her heart beat fast as he came alongside.

"How do you do," he said, lifting his hat.

"Why, Mr. Woods, how do you happen to be here?"

"I simply walked out," he admitted with a smile, "I couldn't stand it any longer."

"Without seeing Dr. Vincintelli? Really, you should have talked over any such decision with him. It really isn't fair to the clinic, you know, Mr. Woods. Jump in and I'll turn around and we'll drive back and talk to him."

He shook his head.

"I have taken a dislike to Dr. Vincintelli, and, frankly, to the clinic. The atmosphere doesn't seem to me very restful."

"Nevertheless, Mr. Woods, it's not the thing to start off like this on the road."

He gave her what she thought was an odd look.

"But you're starting off like this on the road."

"That's entirely different," said Kay, tartly.

"I don't see why. Up to four o'clock yesterday I was responsible for my actions—I came here voluntarily for treatment, but if I'd stayed a few more hours I wouldn't have been responsible for anything."

She looked at him closely. He seemed to be in a mild and pleasant mood, but remembering what Dr. Vincintelli had told her the night before, she kept the car in gear and her foot on the accelerator.

"Besides," he said, smiling, "you haven't told me what you're doing here."

There it was, the cloven hoof, the irrational remark.

"Our cases are different, Mr. Woods," she said firmly. "I am not sick. Did anyone tell you I was?"

"No one has mentioned you to me." He smiled. "I admit you don't look sick but I believe it is characteristic of mental trouble to assert that one is perfectly well. Now *I know* I am as yet utterly sane—and yet—"

"Mr. Woods," interrupted Kay, "you are doing something you will regret. Why not stay at least until my—until Professor Shafer returns Monday. The rest can do you no harm."

"Rest!" He laughed ironically.

"—and will almost surely do you good. You are in no condition to travel."

"I'm going by automobile. My chauffeur is still waiting for orders in the village."

"You are in no condition to travel by automobile."

Again the odd look, the odd remark.

"Then why are you in condition to travel by automobile?"

This time she did not contradict him but it was saddening to note that spot of darkness, a spot that often widened until it obscures the whole mind. Yet she was somehow not afraid of him now.

"You can be cured, Mr. Woods, and you can be cured here. Our treatment, our plant, is modeled upon the most modern usages in Europe." She realized that she was quoting from a circular. "You ascertained that or else you wouldn't have sent your brothers here. If the clinic doesn't prove suitable to you, Professor Shafer will be the first to advise that you go elsewhere."

"It will be too late."

"Never. I'm sure you can be saved."

"Have they saved you?"

She made her voice softer and more persuasive.

"Mr. Woods, just to oblige me, get in the car."

"Ha-ho," he sighed, considering. "If I do, it will be largely for the privilege of sitting beside you. I think your pretty face was the only thing that kept me sane last night at table."

She hated to admit it, but the compliment pleased her.

"Get in. And we'll go back and I'll take you to the carpentry shop."

"Why should I want to go to the carpentry shop?"

"It's called ergotherapy—occupational, you know. We no longer believe in repose, you see."

"Dr. Vincintelli told me to repose—it was like being told to grow three inches."

"That was merely temporary. You'll have some vocational occupation assigned to you—something you like."

"What's yours? Driving a car?"

"Get in, Mr. Woods."

"If I do it will be the first really crazy thing I've ever done."

She was thinking that by now they must have discovered his absence and sent out a posse. They had no legal right to detain him by force unless he was a public menace, but Dr. Vincintelli would try to overtake him for purposes of persuasion.

Peter Woods suddenly made a gesture of indifference and got into the car.

"You're more attractive than Vincintelli," he said, "and rather more sane than anybody I've met."

"Thank you." As she started off a car flashed in and out of sight on a neighboring hill and she recognized it as being from the clinic—Vincintelli at last! On an impulse she couldn't explain to herself, she turned up a side road that circled back to the clinic.

"Are you married?" asked Peter Woods suddenly.

"No."

"Why don't you marry? That would probably solve all your problems."

"Possibly—but marry whom?"

"Wait until I'm well and marry me."

She looked at him gravely.

"Do you ask every girl that on first acquaintance?"

"I've never asked anyone that before. And—" he admitted, "I probably wouldn't now if I wasn't in this state of nervous despair. But I looked at you back there on the road and you looked so lovely and clean and straight. I couldn't believe" He broke off. "I suppose it's partly that white dress that makes you look like a nurse—something trustworthy and secure."

Kay was annoyed.

"If there's one thing I'd never marry a man for it would be that he wanted a nurse. I could only consider a proposal from someone stronger than myself."

"Let them get me well," he said grimly. "I'm not weak—it's just impossible to fight unless you know your faculties are all right."

On his face for a moment, as his own words reminded him of a fact from which he had momentarily escaped, was an expression of such anguish as to make her heart swell with pity. He was, save for his sickness, exactly the sort of man she would like to marry. She felt a strong physical attraction in him. But she remembered his brothers and froze back into her professional attitude as they drove in at the clinic gate.

"I don't think Dr. Vincintelli is here," she said, "suppose we walk around and look at the work-shops. They're very pleasant and cheerful."

"All right," he said resignedly. "But don't expect me to jump for joy when I see them."

He admitted the beauty of the place—it might have been a country club with a caddy house and some bungalows around it. "The Beeches" and "The Cedars," houses for hopeless cases, were separated from the other buildings by a fringe of trees. The workshops were three—a carpentry shop buzzing with activity, a book-bindery and a cottage for bead-work, weaving and work in brass. The faces of the patients were sad and they toiled slowly, but the sun was cheerful in the windows, and the bright colors of the stuffs they handled gave an illusion that all was well. Watching them Peter Woods made one of his unmotivated remarks:

"Why aren't they in white like you?"

As they issued forth Dr. Vincintelli's car drove up at the main entrance. He was frowning and in haste; as his quick roaming glance fell upon them he started and stood motionless. Then he came toward them and Kay saw that he was angry.

"Really this is very irregular," he said to her.

"In what way?" she responded coldly.

"I thought I'd made it plain to Mr. Woods," he smiled perfunctorily at Peter, "that he was to remain by himself for the present."

"It was my fault," said Peter Woods. "I got horribly bored. Lure of the great outdoors and all that."

"It really won't do in your condition. You must obey orders, my dear sir, or I won't answer for the consequences."

"All right," said Peter wearily. "I'll try it for another twenty-four hours. Do I go to my cell at once?"

"I'm going with you. I'm changing your arrangements a little."

Peter looked at Kay and smiled.

"Enjoyed seeing the place," he said. "If I stay we can string some beads together or something, what about it?"

"Fine," she answered lightly.

But her heart was heavy for him, as, handsome and in the full prime of life, he walked with Dr. Vincintelli across the sunny yard.

III

Dr. Vincintelli spoke to Kay after lunch. He was still annoyed and only her position there kept him from venting it on her.

"I don't think you quite understand this case of Mr. Woods," he said. "I thought I told you that I had recognized definite paranoid symptoms. For the moment I want to observe him in complete isolation."

"You didn't tell me that," she responded. "I found him on the road. I was simply introducing him to the regime all the patients follow."

"That regime did not succeed with his brothers," he said sharply. "I have other ideas."

She granted him that. He did have ideas—several text books of his on diagnosis and prognosis were standard, and were translated into many languages. Her father had every confidence in him, yet Kay could not like the man, and whenever he was drawn toward her she shrank back with repulsion.

Save for a daily round in which she alternated with two other doctors, Kay was not often in those more melancholy buildings where the human mind had faded down and disappeared, leaving only a helpless shell. But two days later her turn came and she went to "The Cedars" to see and hear reports on the sad and hopeless cases. Approaching a door where a woman patient had previously lived she took out her key but the infirmarian shook his head.

"That's an isolation case, Dr. Shafer. Orders are that he's not to be disturbed by anyone."

"Who is it?"

"It's Mr. Peter Woods."

"What?" She was unable to understand why he had been brought here. "Let me see him."

"It's against orders."

"Never mind," she said firmly. "Dr. Vincintelli's orders do not apply to doctors."

Reluctantly he opened the door and entered before her as if to protect her from attack. As they went in a man sprang up from the low couch, which was the only article of furniture in the room. His face was so distorted with rage that she scarcely recognized the pleasant young man of two days before.

"So it's you," he shouted. "This is what you got me back here for! What are you, a stool pigeon? Well, they've got me crazy now, damn them, raving crazy—if ever I get my hands on that Vincintelli I'll choke him to death, the—"

"You'd better get out," said the infirmarian.

"Get out!" cried Peter Woods. "Get out! Get *out!*"

It was horrible—in vain Kay called on her professional training for support but she could not divorce herself from the human element in this case. There was some sympathy between herself and this man that was not obliterated or impersonalized, even after seeing him as he had become. With a tremendous effort she steadied herself.

"Listen to me, Mr. Woods." She kept her voice from trembling. "I want you to talk to me calmly. I want to know what has happened to put you in this state."

He laughed wildly.

"You do, eh? Well, you won't. I'll talk to somebody that's sane. It's like them to send you here—I suppose they think I'll talk to you because you're crazy. You tell that dirty dog, Vincintelli, to come here and I'll break every bone in his body—"

The sight of the guard seemed to madden him further, but the man was forewarned and as Peter Woods moved he stepped backward blocking Kay out of the door which he hastily slammed.

Dr. Vincintelli was standing just outside.

"I hope you are now satisfied, Miss Shafer," he said coldly. "And as long as I am in charge here I must insist that my regulations be obeyed."

Her eyes filled with tears, not at Vincintelli's remark, for she hardly saw him, but because of the plight of the anguished soul behind the heavy door.

"I have a telegram from your father," Vincintelli continued, "He wants you to join him immediately in New York in order to accompany a female patient up here."

"Very well," said Kay in a dead voice.

She felt like a traitor—she saw Peter Woods as he walked quietly along the road toward freedom, she saw him voluntarily entering her car and coming back to this horror. In spite of the fact that she stood in awe of her father, she resolved, on her way to the station, to ask him to look into the wisdom of Dr. Vincintelli's treatment. During the six months that she had been an interne in the clinic she had never failed to sense the sickness of a person by any one of a hundred small indications—perhaps in this case she was drawing on her subconscious experience, for she had lived since childhood in this atmosphere. That was the trouble with this case, it didn't *feel* right. Until this afternoon it had seemed to her something that would yield quickly to treatment.

With a certain discouragement at the fact that she was not sufficiently experienced to trust her own judgment, she recapitulated what she had seen.

1. It was against Peter Woods that his three brothers were insane.
2. It was in favor of Peter Woods that he had come voluntarily to the clinic.
3. It was in favor of Peter Woods that he had been logical and tractable even in his discouragement.
4. It was against Peter Woods that he made curious and unmotivated remarks.

What were those remarks? She reconsidered them. There was his tendency to suppose that sane people were insane, for instance that she was insane. He had made several assertions to this effect; he had never addressed her as "Doctor" but always spoken to her as if she were a patient. This afternoon he had called her a "stool pigeon," implying that she was a patient currying favor with the authorities by inducing him to return to the clinic. Finally, there was his curious remark in the work shop: "Why don't all the patients dress in white like you."

The car came to a stop in front of the station and as if the action of the brakes jarred awake a stray elf of intuition in her mind, she sat suddenly upright.

"I wonder," she said aloud, and then, "Good God!"

It was impossible, impossible, and yet she remembered a moment in Dr. Vincintelli's office just before Peter Woods arrived, and then other moments in the past few months came tumbling into her memory. Her voice was almost hysterical as she cried to the chauffeur:

"I'm not leaving on this train. I've forgotten something. Turn around and drive back as fast as you can."

She wondered if she were making a fool of herself—she even wondered if her action was entirely rational, but she knew that she must go.

Twenty minutes later she went quietly into "The Cedars" and directly to Peter Woods' room. Silently she opened his door with her pass-key. The room was empty.

She located the infirmarian in charge.

"Dr. Vincintelli prescribed a hydro-therapatical treatment," the man said, "for the next eight hours."

"Did the patient submit quietly?"

"I can't say he did, Dr. Shafer. He was pretty excited. It took three of us."

Kay knew what he meant. Peter Woods, the banker, was buckled securely in a sort of hammock which in turn was submerged in a warm medical bath. It was a treatment often used to good effect in cases of extreme nervous agitation.

"I see," she said. She started off as if to leave the building, but went instead by another corridor to the baths. Again her pass-key opened a door to her, and she was in a cork-walled chamber with a single tub—in it reclined the well-trussed figure of Peter Woods.

He was smiling, even laughing, hilariously, irrepressibly, and for an awful moment she wondered whether the laughter was maniacal.

"You seem in a more cheerful frame of mind," she ventured.

"I can't help myself. It's too damn absurd—I was thinking if my office force could see me now. It's all so utterly fantastic, like the Spanish Inquisition that there's really nothing to do but laugh." The smile was fading from his face and an expression of wrath was coming into his eyes. "But if you think I'm not going to make that fellow pay for this—"

"Now please," she said hastily, "I want you to give me your calm attention for a minute. Will you?"

"Do you expect me to get up and walk away?"

"Did Dr. Vincintelli at any time tell you how the patients were dressed?"

"Why, yes," he said wonderingly. "He said you all wore white to remind you that your best nurse is yourself."

"And the doctors and nurses?"

"He said they just dressed like ordinary people so that the patients wouldn't have the sense of being in a hospital. What of it?"

Every illogical remark he had made was explained—he had taken the nurses and doctors for patients, the patients for the staff. She saw him shiver inside the wet mummy case.

"Isn't it true?" he demanded. "What is true in this crazy place? Are all the doctors crazy or all the patients sane—or what?"

"I think," said Kay thoughtfully, "that one of the doctors is mad."

"How about me? Am I sane?"

Before she could answer she turned at a sound behind her—Dr. Vincintelli stood in the open door.

"Miss Shafer." His voice was low and intense. His eyes were fixed on hers. "Miss Shafer, come here to me."

He retreated slowly before her, and she followed. He had a certain power of hypnosis which he used occasionally in treatments, and she saw that he was exerting it on her. Her will seemed to cloud a little and she followed him out step by step until he closed the door upon Peter Woods' wild roar.

He seized her by the elbows.

"Listen to me, you little fool," he breathed. "I am not crazy. I know what I am doing. It is you who are mad—you who are standing in the way of something that will be a monument to your father and a blessing to mankind forever. Listen." He shook her a little. "A month ago the three insane Woods brothers came to your father *voluntarily* and said they wanted to will him all their money for research work."

"But of course he refused," said Kay indignantly.

"But now all is changed!" he cried triumphantly. "This is the fourth and last and there are no heirs. No one is wronged—we have our Institute, and we will have reared a monument for which humanity will bless our name forever."

"But this man is sane!" Kay exclaimed. "As sane as I am."

"You are wrong. I see signs that you do not see. He will break, like the others, in a week, in three days, perhaps before your father returns—"

"You devil!" she cried. "You're mad—you're driveling—"

There was a sudden interruption—the buzzing of bells, doors banging and the appearance of excited nurses in the corridors.

"What is it?"

"The three Woods brothers—they've disappeared!"

"Impossible!" cried Vincintelli.

"Their windows have been sawed with files from the carpentry shop."

The veins grew large as worms on Vincintelli's forehead.

"Get after them!" he shouted furiously. "They must be on the grounds. Sound the alarm in the main building—"

He had forgotten Kay—still crying orders, he rushed down the corridors and into the night.

When the corridor was empty Kay opened the door of the bath-room, and quickly unbuckled the straps that held Peter Woods.

"Get out and get dressed," she said. "We're leaving—I'll run you away in my car."

"But they've locked up all my clothes somewhere."

"I'll get you a blanket," she said, and then hesitated. "That won't do—the police will be watching the roads tonight and they'll take us both for lunatics."

They waited helplessly. But outside there were voices calling here and there through the shrubbery.

"I've got it," she cried. "Wait!"

Straight to the room of Mr. Kirkjohn across the hall she fled, and opened the door. Scented and immaculate he stood before his mirror, brushing his hair.

"Mr. Kirkjohn," Kay said breathlessly, "take off your clothes!"

"What?" Then, as he comprehended, a quiet glow of satisfaction spread over his face.

"Take off everything, and throw it to me."

"With pleasure, dear lady," he said.

Coat, vest, tie, trousers, shoes, socks—she caught them all and gathered them up in a pile.

"Dear lady, this—" his hand was on the top button of his union suit, "is the happiest day of my life."

With a little shriek Kay shut the door.

Half an hour later, the throttle pressed down to the floor of the car, they were still speeding along the roads of New Hampshire through the summer night. There was a moon and the universe was wide and free about them. Peter Woods drew a deep breath.

"And what made you think that in spite of everything I was sane?" he demanded.

"I don't know." She looked demurely at the stars. "I suppose it was when you asked me to marry you. No girl could believe that a man who proposed to her could be entirely crazy."

"And you won't mind being a little saner than me."

"But I'm not—darling." She hurried over the word she had never used before. "I'm in the grip of the greatest lunacy of all."

"Speaking of being in the grip of anything," he said, "when you get to those next trees why not stop the car?"

IV

The three elder Woods brothers were never found. However, an unconfirmed story reached me some months ago that the announcer at a certain terminal in New York has a peculiar intonation that makes Wall Street men start and mutter—"Now where have I heard that voice before?" The second brother, Wallace, has conceivably fled to South America, where he can make himself understood. As for the tale itself, it was told me by the first barber in the Elixer Shop, Scranton, Pennsylvania. Check up on it if you like—the barber I mean is a tall, sheep-like man with an air of being somewhat above his station.

Scott and Zelda with their storied car, "The Rolling Junk,"
in *MOTOR* magazine, 1924.

"What to Do About It" centers on a young male doctor. Dr. Bill Hardy
is "irreverent," to put it mildly, as he copes with both hypochondriacs
and the truly ill. It is a boy-gets-girl tale made strange and fantastical,
and surely cinematic, by the intersections of medicine and a madcap,
gangster-derived plot.

Fitzgerald sent "What to Do About It" to Harold Ober in August
1933. The *Saturday Evening Post*, always the first port of call for Fitzgerald's stories for many years by then, thought the story "not satisfying,"
while *Cosmopolitan* found it "too subtile." None of the magazine editors
knew quite what to think of the boy, Ober's own favorite character in
the story and the originator of the title phrase.

In the summer of 1936, Ober suggested that a revised version of
the story could go out for consideration again, but Fitzgerald replied
he could "scarcely remember the plo[t]" and sent "Thank You for the
Light," which he'd just finished, instead. The surviving typescript of
"What to Do About It" remains the property of the Trustees of the
Fitzgerald Estate.

WHAT TO DO ABOUT IT

by

F. Scott Fitzgerald

The girl hung around under the pink sky waiting for something to happen. She was not a particularly vague person but she
was vague tonight: the special dusk was new, practically new,
after years under far skies; it had strange little lines in the
trees, strange little insects, unfamiliar night cries of strange
small beasts beginning.

--Those are frogs, she thought, or no, those are grillons--
what is it in English? --those are crickets up by the pond.

--That is either a swallow or a bat, she thought; then
again the difference of trees--then back to love and such practical
things. And back again to the different trees and shadows, skies
and noises--such as the auto horns and the barking dog up by
the Philadelphia turnpike...

The dog was barking at a man at whom it presently sniffed;
finding nothing either hostile or ingratiating, he nosed around
and wanted to play. The man was on his way to meet the girl,
though as yet he was unaware of it; he continued to sit in the
middle of the dirt lane and try to wrest a 1927 tire-look of
its prey.

"Get away, you animal!" he exuded, and muttering unwilling-

What to Do About It

The girl hung around under the pink sky waiting for something to happen. She was not a particularly vague person but she was vague tonight: the special dusk was new, practically new, after years under far skies; it had strange little lines in the trees, strange little insects, unfamiliar night cries of strange small beasts beginning.

—Those are frogs, she thought, or no, those are *grillons*—what is it in English?—those are crickets up by the pond.

—That is either a swallow or a bat, she thought; then again the difference of trees—then back to love and such practical things. And back again to the different trees and shadows, skies and noises—such as the auto horns and the barking dog up by the Philadelphia turnpike . . .

The dog was barking at a man at whom it presently sniffed; finding nothing either hostile or ingratiating, he nosed around and wanted to play. The man was on his way to meet the girl, though as yet he was unaware of it; he continued to sit in the middle of the dirt lane and try to wrest a 1927 tire-lock of its prey.

"Get away, you animal!" he exuded, and muttering unwillingly he returned to the lock, which was an excellent job of steel and ingenuity and had only half yielded to his inadequate chisel.

He was not a burglar—he was a doctor and this was his car and had been for some months, during which the "rubber on it" in salesmen's jargon had endured beyond modest expectations. Turning into the lane from the main road he became aware that the rubber had yielded gently to the pressure of time, thus accounting for the inaccuracy of the steering wheel. This he had noticed immediately after leaving the hospital.

"The old boy could have come in his sedan," he muttered, "He's getting lazy. In most businesses they'd send him to the minors—in ours we endow them."

From overhearing this bellyache an interested observer might have deduced that Doctor Bill Hardy belonged to the latest and most irreverent of generations. He was little less than tall, and standardly welded, rather like the 1927 tire lock, and his thoughts in this moment of recu-

41

peration were inspired by the fact that his boss, the distinguished Doctor C. H. L. Hines, had delegated to him the most unpleasant of duties—to visit, console and administer to a chronic female hypochondriac of a certain age, on an evening when he had important business of his own.

He was too good a doctor to have confused duty with personal pleasure but in this case the line between the two was drawn very close: there was the woman in a southerly suburb of the city who must be called upon, consoled, or at least got rid of with tact, and there was this woman in the mansion at the lane's end who needed nothing yet considered that she did, but who poured twenty-five dollars fortnightly into Doctor C. H. L. Hines' coffers for the reassurance that her heart was not stopping and that she had neither leprosy nor what she referred to as "the bubonic." Usually Dr. Hines did the reassuring. This evening he had merely rolled to the telephone and mumbled, "Look, Bill, I'm about to begin dressing for an engagement m'wife'nI've looked for'd to for ages. Go out see what you can do with the damn—with Mrs. Brickster."

Bill adjusted the chisel and the gong—it was a curious thing he had found under the seat that he thought of as a gong because it gave out a ringing sound—and struck a discouraged blow. To his surprise the lock yielded: he was so inspired by his own mechanical, or archaeological, achievement that ten minutes later he was able to roll down the lane to face his case. Shutting off the motor and backing out of the car he confronted the girl.

Confronted is exact: for on her part she noticed his arrival with merely a hopeful surprise. She was eighteen with such a skin as the Italian painters of the decadence used for corner angels, and all the wishing in the world glistening in her grey eyes.

"How do you do—I'm Doctor Hardy, Dr. Hines' assistant. Mrs. Brickster phoned—"

"Oh, how do you do. I'm Miss Mason, Mrs. Brickster's daughter."

The red dusk was nearly gone but she had advanced into the last patch of it. "Mother's out but is there anything I can do?" she asked.

"Is there anything I can do," he corrected her.

She smiled a little. "Well, I don't think I know you well enough to decide that for you."

"I mean tonight—is there anything I can do tonight?"

"I couldn't even tell you that, Dr. Hines—"

"No. I'm Dr. Hardy, Dr. Hines' assistant."

"—excuse me, Doctor Hardy. We give a cup of coffee in the kitchen and what small change is in the house."

Bill realized in the course of this last that all was not according to Aristotelian logic. He reconsidered, began again;

"I was called from this house, Miss Mason, to treat your mother. If she has been taken away—"

"Father took her away."

"Oh—I'm sorry—what was the matter?"

"She found that the Chicago Opera Company was doing *Louise*."

"Oh I see," Bill agreed. Yet he *didn't* see, for in the thickening dusk the girl was dazzling his vision a little, "You mean she can't stand *Louise*—I know; I had an aunt who could never—"

"This is getting sadder and sadder, Dr. Hines—"

"No. Hardy, Dr. Hines' assistant."

"—excuse me, Doctor Hardy. But when aunts begin to appear in the picture you wonder just what are we driving at! Mother went *toward Louise*, not away from it. But she left rather suddenly with father carrying his cuff buttons. I've just come home after some years away and just met my new father and I'm trying to get adjusted. If somebody in the house is sick I don't know who it is. Mother said nothing about it to me."

"Then your mother isn't sick? She didn't phone Dr. Hines? It's all a mistake?"

"She didn't seem sick starting for the opera."

"Well, suppose—well, suppose we give it up." He looked at Miss Mason once more and decided not to. "I mean suppose we check up. I'll give you the address of a physicians' exchange and you phone and see if they received such a call. I won't even take coffee or small change— I'll wait out here in the car."

"All right," she agreed. "It'd be better to straighten out the situation."

. . . When she appeared on the verandah some minutes later she had an envelope in her hand.

"Excuse me, Dr. Hines—you were perfectly right. Mother *did* call the doctor—"

"My name is Hardy."

"Well—let's not start that over again; she called up whichever you two is which; I'm sorry to seem discourteous, but for all I know you might be a racketeersman."

He kept his laugh secret as he said:

"That leaves us where we were before—unless your mother expects me between the acts at the opera."

She handed him the envelope.

"I found this on the hall table going out—addressed to Doctor—" —stopping herself in time she said gently while he took the letter to his headlights, for it had grown too dark for the sky's light. ". . . I hope it clarifies matters."

Dear Doctor

I really called you about the boy, as I am again growing interested in domestic affairs, as you suggested, and it is very successful. But my husband and I thought it would be better for me to go out so, I went out, especially as there was an opera I especially wanted to see. Or we may go to a movie. Almost anything to get one's mind off myself, as you suggested. So sorry if I have caused you any trouble.

Sincerely

Anne Marshall Mason Brickster

P.S. I meant to stay and tell you about the boy but my husband felt I should get away. He told me he stole the bluga. I don't know what the bluga is but I'm sure he shouldn't do it at his age.

A.M.M.B.

Bill switched his car lights from dim to white; by the new brilliance he looked at the letter again—it read the same; the boy had stolen the bluga, the woman wanted something done about it. For the first time a dim appreciation of the problems which Dr. Hines was called upon to face, and to which he himself was to succeed, brought a dim, sympathetic sweat to his temples. He turned abruptly to the girl.

"Now, when did you miss the bruga?"

"What bruga?"

No go.

"The brunga?"

She edged away, faintly but perceptibly, and Bill covered himself by telling all:

"Here: your brother has evidently taken something that doesn't belong to him. Your parents want to see the why and wherefore of it. Can you make out this word?"

Their heads were close together under the light, so that his brisk blond sidelocks scratched her cheek while a longer tenuous end of gold silk touched him materially in the corner of his eye, but really all over.

"I can't help you out," she said after a moment.

"I feel I should investigate," he suggested.

"All right," she agreed. "His light's still on."

She led the way through a hall adorned with the remnants of slain game. "Will you see him down here?" She paused at the foot of the stairs—"or in his boudoir?"

"Let's go up," Bill suggested; he had a lingering hope that the bruga might be triumphantly snatched up from under a pillow, and the whole situation cleared up by that moral lecture carried in the knapsack for instant production. The Loveliness led the way upstairs like a beacon that afterwards upon the verandah might illume the problems of a young doctor—or some such matter.

There seemed justification for the beginning of his hope, the solution of the mystery, when, promptly upon their entrance into a presumably lighted room they were plunged into blackness. Miss Mason wielded the switch: whereupon Bill stared at a boy of thirteen clad in a pajama top that feebly covered an undoffed union suit, upon a bed blatantly uninhabited, yet used, and upon a book still quivering from its hasty transition under the pillow.

"That must be the igloo," he thought. His mind had now transformed the object sought-for into North Arctic form; but as he reached deftly under the pillow beneath the boy's hostile stare, and snatched a glance at the book in bringing it out he found it to be a faint blue volume entitled "EX-WHITE-SLAVER,"—the authorship being identified with touching modesty as "by *a Man Who Still is one.*"

He put it down coolly, as if it existed for him only in the sense that a copy of, say, *My Forty Years in the Fountains of Tivoli* can be said to exist in the memory of a guest, and remarked;

"Well, how're *you*, young man?"

But the young man had long given up dealing with such palaver. He looked disgustedly at Bill, back at his sister, back at Bill: then treated them both to what, in the euphemistic tradition of their great-grandparents, might have been termed The Robin.

But Bill was of stern stuff; he seized the boy by his shoulder, lowered him firmly to the sheet and announced: "If you want to play that game you'll find I'm bigger than you."

The boy, reaching the surface of the sheet unresistingly, looked up at him with uncommunicative eyes and answered:

"What you goan do about it?"

This was a question. Bill was good at certain subjects but something told him this wasn't one of them. He glanced at the girl, but he found in her glistening eyes the age-old look of one who says: "In a man-managed world I've got to be told where I am being led before I agree to go there or not." Bill sat down beside the bed and descended to conversation which, marred by pauses, stammers and total stops would have been reported as follows by an adequate court stenographer.

"What do you like?"

"Me?"

Pause while boy looks over doctor.

"What do you like?" the doctor asked again.

"I like books," says the little boy in an unconvinced voice.

"I like books too."

"If you don't mind," the girl interrupted as she saw the beginning of the tranquil and parental flow, "I'll go about some things I must do."

Bill felt that the door behind her shut rather quickly. He wished now that he had gone away when he discovered that Mrs. Brickster was out—he was no psychiatrist, nor was he a moralist—it was as a scientist that he considered himself. He had enough confidence to have dealt sensibly with a sick woman in an emergency—but with a glance at the patient some forgotten revulsion for boys of thirteen arose upon his head like the crest of a rooster and he thought angrily: and I'm not a detective either.

But he kept his temper and offered to the young man in the purest syrup:

"What games do you like?"

"Oh, all right."

"No, but which ones?"

"Gangster's the only game I like."

"Well, that's fun."

Like Diamond Dick Bill thought, but something prompted him to ask:

"Who do you like to win—the gangster or the police?"

The boy looked at him scornfully:

"Mobsmen, naturally. You half-witted?"

"Don't get rude again!"

"What you goan do about it."

"I'm going to—"

Another dream of his childhood recurred to Bill; this was just like being a pirate anyhow . . .

"What books do you read?" he kept the same control of his face as though he were going over the boy's body with a stethoscope.

"I don't know, now."

"Do you see pictures?" He saw the boy's face light as if he saw a way out, "Gangster pictures?"

"They don't allow me much." But the new tone was too smug to be convincing, "They don't allow us and the other rich boys to go to anything except comedies and kidnapping and things like that. The comedies are the things I like."

"Who? Chaplin?"

"Who?"

"Charlie Chaplin."

Obviously the words failed to record.

"No, the—you know, the comedies."

"Who do you like?" Bill asked.

"Oh—" The boy considered, "Well, I like Garbo and Dietrich and Constance Bennett."

"Their things are *comedies*?"

"They're the funniest ones."

"Funniest what?"

"Funniest comedies."

"Why?"

"Oh, they try to do this passionate stuff all the time."

"This what?"

"Oh, this looking around."

"Like what?"

"Oh, you know. This uhm—like on Christmas."

Bill started to delve into that but he remembered the still unsolved matter of the igloo and thought better of it. It seemed more prudent to return to books.

"What books have you got?" he asked.

The boy looked at him attentively.

"Hey, you're not a heel, are you?"

Bill considered quickly whether he was or wasn't a heel.

"No," he conceded himself.

"Well—" The boy rose in bed, "I got two kina kinds. I got that one about the four girls named Meg who fall down the rabbit hole and that—and I got a lot like that." He hesitated. "And I got some books of my own."

"Can I see them?"

The boy considered.

"What you goan do about it?"

For the third time Bill considered, and finally answered:

"Nothing."

"Lift up the end of the mattress then."

Bill lifted. Afterwards he debated with himself whether he counted ten or twenty. The ones he remembered were: *The Facts of Love*; *War and Peace, Volume I; Prize Short Stories of 1926; Psychiatry, its Permutations in Eighty Years; Fifty Popular Secret Stories of the World's Fair of 1876.*

The boy's voice cut soft and sharp over Bill's meditation upon the *cache*—"You a heel maybe then. You've seen them. What you goan do about it?"

"Take out your tonsils probably," said Bill; he ducked out of the way as the mattress slammed down, the event being obviously prompted by approaching footsteps.

"It's all all right with me, old boy," Bill said, "I haven't—"

"Old stuff—"

He stopped at the appearance of his sister, to whom he was unused and who vaguely frightened him.

"Mother and father are home," she announced to Bill, "you want to see them downstairs?"

"You'd make a good doctor's assistant," he said.

"I lived with a doctor for three months."

Bill breathed deeply, as she continued, "His wife became very ill. You know not *gravement* but *chronicquement*. I like doctors."

The little boy was concentrated upon whether or not he had been betrayed as Bill followed her out of the room, looking backward and beginning two trial sentences; but on a last glance at the boy's incorrigible expression he finished with: "I won't give you away but I'd like to talk to you some more," adding at the door: "At least I won't tell any of your friends that you talked to me confidentially."

He had done his best but he had never felt clumsier than in the minute of following Miss Mason through the long hall and down the stairs. At their ending he bucked up for he was projected into the scene he had imagined.

An obviously silly, but not quite persecutable, woman stood at the entrance to the main room, for which no adequate name has yet been found in the Republic; she stood there waving him breezily into a study; there they displaced a husband who was being signalled to go away by that hand which was not occupied at the moment in encouraging Bill forward.

"I knew who you were," said Mrs. Brickster, "I recognized you from Dr. Hines' prescriptions. He describes *every*thing so well. This movie tonight, he could have described it as well as a reviewer." He relaxed as he refused her proffered highball and said in a professional voice:

"Now, Mrs. Brickster, what seems to be the trouble?"

She began:

"Of course the thing commenced with a twitching . . ."

And she ended two hours later with:

". . . probably you're right, it was just the strain of my daughter coming home."

She had worn out the false force of her nervous fatigue suddenly and she turned against him.

"And as you're leaving, Doctor, could I beg you to remind Dr. Hines that when it's him I want it's him I want." The telephone rang and, still talking, she picked it up. "—in future I expect the principal not the assistant—yes, he's here . . . at 6632 Beaming Avenue . . . very personal and urgent and mention Ellis S. to him." She pronounced the words as individual discoveries of villainy and said as she rang up: "I hope you discover no more trouble there, Doctor, than you have found here."

And as the door closed in back of him a few minutes later Bill wondered indeed if he was now to confront difficulties more sinister than those he had left behind.

He rested a minute on the verandah—resting his eyes on a big honeysuckle that cut across a low sickle moon—then as he started down the steps his abstracted glance fell upon a trailer from it sleeping in the moonlight.

She was the girl from foreign places; she was so asleep that you could see the dream of those places in the faint lift of her forehead. The doctor took out his watch—it was after three. He walked with practiced dexterity across the wooden verandah but he struck the inevitable creaky strip and promptly the map of wonderland written on the surface of women's eyebrows creased into invisibility.

"I was asleep," she said. "I slept."

As if he had told her to wait here for him. Or as if the hair that had brushed his forehead had said stay to him; but she seemed too young to play with so he picked up his satchel and said, "Well, I must—" and left, remembering that he had been a long time in the house and that all the time the girl had been asleep.

II

He drove rapidly for he had far to go—from a spot north of the city, through the city itself, to a colony of suburban houses a dozen miles south: the message on the phone had sounded frightened—perhaps this was not the night to break things off. But his thoughts were still concentrated on the scene from which he drove away to an extent that minutes and miles raced past and it was with surprise that he found his car before the familiar house on the familiar street.

A light burned inside the house; a sedan stood in front of it; as Bill stepped from his own car the door of the sedan opened and a burly figure emerged from it.

"Are you a doctor?" said the figure advancing toward him. "Do you happen to be the doctor who's a personal friend of Mrs. Dykes?"

"Yes—is she sick?"

"No. But I'm Mr. Dykes. I got home today from Den—from Honolulu."

So this ghost had materialized at last—and materialized indeed, for in the bright moonlight he seemed eight feet tall with long, prehensile arms. Bill took a preparatory step backward.

"Don't worry—I'm not going to slam you—not yet. Let's get into your car and have a little talk before we go in the house."

"What is this?" Bill demanded, "A hold up?"

The man laughed—formidably.

"Something like that. I want a couple of your signatures—one on a check, and the other on a letter you haven't written yet."

Trying to think fast Bill got into the car.

"A letter to who?" he asked.

"To my wife. You were pretty smart, weren't you, not to write her a letter—I've turned the house upside down looking for one."

"Look here, Mr. Dykes—I've known your wife only a month and professionally."

"Oh yeah? Then why is a picture of you plastered right beside her dressing table?"

Bill gave a spiritual groan.

"That's her affair," he explained, "I happen to know she got it from a classmate of mine in medical school who's married to a friend of hers. I didn't give it to her—"

"I see, I see," the big man interrupted scoffingly, "And you're not the man she wants to marry—with me away in Den—in Honolulu. And I like to come, don't I, and find my wife has taken up with one of the medical boys? And I'm going to take it lying down like a sap? You're going to pay off, and you're going to give me evidence I can get a divorce on. And you're going to like it."

Bill was not going to like it at all, but he was in a position that, as he cast about in his mind, seemed at its mildest somewhat circumscribed. Whether his reaction to what happened next was relief or terror he could never afterwards decide, but at the sharp order "Stickum up!" from the rumble seat both men jumped forward as if they had been pricked. But even in the split second before a figure appeared on Bill's side of the car there was something faintly familiar in the voice. Then the voice said:

"You didn't know he had one of his rod men along, big boy. Just step out so there won't be any blood on the upholstery. *Quick!*"

Trembling piteously the large man fumbled at the handle, and in this moment Bill identified his savior. It was that boy. And at the classic word: "Scram!" he recognized something vaguely recognizable about the instrument which was causing Mr. Dykes to retreat, to stumble to get up and then to tear down the street at the gait of a likely pacemaker. Being closer to the instrument Bill had identified it as something *like* a revolver and yet not quite a revolver. By the time Mr. Dykes' heels were faint in the distance he identified it as that mysterious piece of steel which he still thought of as The Gong.

III

The boy got into the car and Bill, somewhat shaken by the heavy grasp of events, turned and started toward the city.

"That guy certainly was yellow," remarked the boy with satisfaction.

"Yes, he was," said Bill, rather automatically, as his professional habits began to reassert themselves, "What I'd like to know is what you were doing here."

"I just came for the ride," said the boy airily.

"Can't you ride in the daytime?"

"For your ride. I was pretending to take you for a ride. All the time we were on the road I had a gat pressed so close to your back—"

"Oh, cut it out, cut it out," said Bill ungratefully, "I don't like that kind of talk."

"Oak. But no spill-over to the parents, see? Or I'll tell what I saw—wolfing that guy's Jane away from him when he was in Den—in Hula-hula. How'll that sound to the fair you left on the verandah?"

"The who?" Once more Bill was startled, yet he rode easier to it as he became more accustomed to the shocks.

"Don't think I didn't see that last look around. How'd she like to hear about this—"

"You don't know what you're talking about," Bill argued, "You wouldn't understand this situation if I explained every detail to you."

"Explain it to her then."

On second thought Bill decided he wouldn't; he very definitely wouldn't care to have to explain it to her; he could at least get some hold on this incorrigible boy.

"I'm going to begin your education here and now," he announced. "First place I sympathize with you—to some extent. Certainly it's better to be a fighter than one of these softies brought up full of tender feelings about themselves. And you can pick your cause—there's good and bad fighting, and a lot in the world to fight for; your beliefs, your honor, your family and—I mean, you'll find out later there is a lot you'll decide is worth fighting for. At present confine yourself to the defense. This crime stuff doesn't touch you—you oughtn't even to think about it. You ought to be just like older people and put it out of your head—"

He was becoming convinced minute by minute that he didn't know what he was talking about himself, and he stole a side glance to see if the boy had noticed the fact.

But the boy had dozed—some time back he had dozed.

IV

It was false dawn when they turned into the lane: on the outskirts of the acres Bill awoke his protector.

"We're here. Now the thing is to hope to God you haven't been missed—and to try to get you in without anybody seeing you."

Sluggish from his night's operations the future criminal stared blank at Bill.

"Wake up!" said Bill impatiently, "It's practically daylight."

"What you goan do about it?"

"I'm going to assume you have enough common sense to get in without being noticed."

"The French girl would."

"Would what? What French girl?"

"I mean my sister." The boy pulled himself together visibly. "You know—the fair. She just got back from France or somewhere. She'd let me in."

This project had the effect of bringing Bill almost up to normal.

"How would you wake her up?" he asked.

"I'll think of some way."

"Just to be sure of that I'll come along."

Through the new trees, the new quivering life, the new shadows that designed new terrain on the old, through the sounds of different strange insects, they traversed the lawn and stopped under a window.

"Now what?" Bill whispered.

"That's her room—and the window's open."

Bill went through a hasty mental review of the classical ways in which one assaulted a sleeping house.

"We could throw pebbles up," he suggested doubtfully.

"No—we throw in one of these flowers. You know how frails are—if a stone sails in they put up a yelp—if it's a rose they think there's the Prince of Wales at last."

The first rose missed; the boy missed; then Bill made two perfect throws which cleared the sill. The acoustical result was inaudible below and they waited breathlessly.

"Try another—" began the boy, then paused as a tender trusting face appeared at the window and tried to focus sleepy eyes upon whatever should be below.

There were moments of whispering that could only be reproduced by one of the fabled mimics employed on the radio. After the face disappeared the boy turned to Bill disgustedly: "You see, they're all alike. Half they understand and half they miss. Just half, that's all you can ever expect. She's going to dress herself up in clothes, as if we were going to take her downtown to business."

Miss Mason, however, dressed herself up in clothes remarkably quickly and remarkably well, opening a side door to them seven minutes later. After seeing her Bill decided he could better explain matters without any comment from a third party, so, taking advantage of a yawn detected on the boy's face he pointed sternly inward and upward. The boy winked once, started to open his lips, found his unspoken word changing irresistibly into a new yawn, gave up, and disappeared.

"Now Miss Brickster—" began the doctor and stopped.

"Miss Mason," she corrected him. She countered, "I bet I can half guess already what happened. My brother stayed in the rumble seat; I saw him climb into it just before I went to sleep myself."

—What an illusion that they only get half of it, Bill thought. That devil doesn't know everything. Why, this girl—

"Don't tell your parents on him," he said, "I've come to like him. I don't want him to get in trouble."

"Dr. Hardy."

"Yes, Miss Mason."

"I've been home from Europe two months and I've seen so many strange things happen here that I wouldn't dare open my mouth about anything that wasn't my business."

—Just the wife for a doctor in every way, he thought.

"Miss Mason."

"Yes, Doctor."

"Miss Mason—naturally under the circumstances I haven't been able—" He passed his hand over the new stubble of his beard, "—to complete my toilet. So I'll ask you to—"

"Yes, doctor."

"—say goodnight or good morning."

"Certainly, I understand."

"—with the privilege that tomorrow—or today—when I come back to see your mother—"

"Yes, doctor."

"—of saying good afternoon."

"That would be a pleasure."

"Goodnight, Miss Brickster."

"Goodnight, Dr. Hines."

V

Bill arrived at the office in a state of irritation caused not only by loss of sleep but by indefinable objections to his situation that he lacked the alertness to analyze. One of them, though, he was sure of; it was that Doctor Hines never arrived till noon any more and that fact threw double harness, sometimes fire-horse harness, upon his assistant. Bill saw no justification for this growing laziness of a man in his middle forties.

—Maybe I'm just sore because I'm late myself this morning. Maybe I'm trying to switch it off on him.

Thus he tried to stay within bounds of equity, but as Dr. Hines arrived at the moment when Bill was regarding a mass of twenty obligations and twenty messages he lost his temper.

"It's hard for me to do all this detail and keep reading," he implied fairly faintly but fairly audibly.

Dr. Hines looked at him surprised, then fell back into vacuous placidity.

"But in these times," he spoke with the imitation heartiness that he used for patients, "—it's good to have anything to do at all, ha-ha." He arrested the last "ha" on what he read in Bill's face.

"I mean it, Doctor Hines. I don't know why you don't get down here and I don't care, but it's damned unjust considering the percentage I take. I suggest you get to bed earlier at night."

Dr. Hines' eyes widened; his lower lip dropped.

"All right," he said, piling up his resentment, "But have you forgotten I picked you up as a raw interne and brought you into the practise that I had built up in this city—" He paused to blow and Bill said patiently:

"I admit that," suddenly he added an afterthought that had been passed up to him from below the night before, "What are you going to do about it?"

"I'll tell you what I'm going to do about it and I'll tell you quick." Dr. Hines paused at this moment and, being no fool himself, examined his conscience and blew but with less wind, "I'm going to—"

He suddenly realized he was going to do nothing about it. After a big start he had let himself grow soft over a long period; lately he had handed over everything difficult, even his personal secrets, to Bill Hardy. With Bill no longer there the very structure of the firm collapsed. Dr. Hines simply sat and stared at the younger man.

Bill guessed the older man's thoughts; he realized that he had gotten his point over, and granting his senior enough time to recuperate and preserve his dignity he retired; tossing the most necessary directions about the afternoon to the competent Miss Weiss as he went out the door.

He drove quickly north, and as he drove he thought, or concluded a thought he had been thinking for the last fatigued hours, that the little boy was fighting a battle with realities on his own, that there would eternally continue to be Mrs. Bricksters, that romance was for children and work and danger for men, and the best he could hope was that at day's end something softer and different would be waiting at the turning of a lane.

It was only afternoon then, but Bill thought he saw just that across the shrill early afternoon with an entirely new opera of insect sounds and the trees' shadows thrown a new way. He was not absolutely sure he saw it; then he was suddenly sure.

In a few minutes he said:

"I've got something to tell you. Unfortunately very quickly, because there seems to be a lot of stuff I've got to do at the minute—"

"Awll–ll right," said the little boy sitting with them, "Awll–ll right—" And without even being told, "I can always take orders from a big shot— I'm gone." And amazingly he was.

Bill looked after him with a faint touch of regret that he probably would never find out what the Bluga was and how it was that people looked at each other on Christmas. Then he turned to the girl.

"Look," he began, "You are so beautiful—practically unearthly. You—"

"Yes."

"You have everything a girl could have—" He hesitated. "In short—"

And as she knew he'd be a long time, since he had said "in short," she decided to speed up things.

"What are you going to do about it?" she asked.

Become impatient of all the explaining that seemed to be demanded in this household Bill Hardy took matters into his own arms and began a practical demonstration.

FSF mugs in a photo booth.

Fitzgerald and the young Baltimore-based writer, and later actor, Robert Spafford (1913–2000) collaborated on the movie treatment "Gracie at Sea" after Fitzgerald met George Burns and Gracie Allen in Baltimore in 1934, when they were on tour.

The scenario, or screenplay synopsis, is a short story in form, thoroughly characterized and thought out. "Gracie at Sea" tries hard to be the sort of farce that Burns and Allen were already becoming known for—that is to say, with Burns the straight man, and Allen the "dumb Dora"—but Fitzgerald couldn't keep himself from real fiction writing. When George is described in the first paragraph as "a fundamentally lonesome and self-obliterating man," it's clear this isn't just a cinematic "vehicle which will carry [Burns and Allen's] stuff[.]"

Fitzgerald was upset that he'd spent the time on a screenplay that did not sell. He wrote to his cousin Ceci Taylor, late in the summer of 1934: "Everything here goes rather badly. Zelda no better—your correspondent in rotten health + two movie ventures gone to pot—one for Gracie Allen + Geo. Burns that damn near went over + took 2 wks' work + <u>they</u> liked + wanted to buy—+ Paramount stepped on. It's like a tailor left with a made-to-order suit—no one to sell it to." When he was based in Hollywood at the end of the decade, Fitzgerald revised this screenplay synopsis one more time for a potential new cast. His revision is included in the explanatory notes to this story.

GRACIE AT SEA

by

F. Scott Fitzgerald
and
Robert Spafford

The general idea of offering this story for
George Burns and Grace Allen is dependent upon the thesis
that farce and comedy do not hold attention over half an
hour - and at the same time that there is great material
in their personalities for full length pictures.

For the first half hour of pure farce, one
laughs, for the second half hour one is amused; and for the
third half hour one wants to hit the comedians on the head.
Chaplin realized this when he decided to make longer pictures, as in Tilly's Punctured Romance and The Kid, etc.,
and took a good deal of his purely farcical personality out
of the picture to make way for counter means such as: Pathos
of the Kid himself, to make way for this general principle,
which has been well known to writers of light comedy for many
years.

On this assumption, the authors who submit this
story have tried to intersperse a vehicle which will carry
George Burns' and Grace Allen's stuff, with touches of sentiment and emotions which are common to all and will arouse,
we hope, the same feeling of recognition which has previously
greeted only their farcical endeavors. The idea was first
offered to George Burns in person and interested him enough
so that he encouraged us to go on.

Herewith follows suggested story:

Gracie at Sea

The general idea of offering this story for George Burns and Grace Allen is dependent upon the thesis that farce and comedy do not hold attention over half an hour—and at the same time that there is great material in their personalities for full length pictures.

For the first half hour of pure farce, one laughs, for the second half hour one is amused; and for the third half hour one wants to hit the comedians on the head. Chaplin realized this when he decided to make longer pictures, as in *Tilly's Punctured Romance* and *The Kid*, etc., and took a good deal of his purely farcical personality out of the picture to make way for counter means such as: Pathos of the Kid himself, to make way for this general principle, which has been well known to writers of light comedy for many years.

On this assumption, the authors who submit this story have tried to intersperse a vehicle which will carry George Burns' and Grace Allen's stuff, with touches of sentiment and emotions which are common to all and will arouse, we hope, the same feeling of recognition which has previously greeted only their farcical endeavors. The idea was first offered to George Burns in person and interested him enough so that he encouraged us to go on.

Herewith follows suggested story:

Gracie at Sea
by F. Scott Fitzgerald
and Robert Spafford

Poor George, at this moment on the basis of a small inheritance, had been just about to quit work as publicity man and retire to the country, when his boss called him into his office to speak of a case that had a strange and fascinating interest for George, for George was a fundamentally lonesome and self-obliterating man. In himself, he encouraged those qualities which contributed to the satisfaction of others and got his pleasure in that success rather than in any advance on his own part. Because of this very quality, he was considered the best publicity man in Manhattan, and perhaps that is why his boss had asked him to take this peculiarly difficult and intricate case.

In brief, the case, as the head of the agency explained to poor George, was to go into the environment of the rich and solve a strange situation that had arisen there.

It seemed that a Mr. Augustus Van Grossie, long identified with yacht racing in America, had an unusual situation with his two motherless children—that the elder daughter must be married before the younger daughter. And behold, the elder daughter was a mass of mistakes. Pretty enough, she, nevertheless, always gave herself away by some awkward blunder of speech or conduct, so that the correct young people of her environment fought shy of her. Therefore, since she could find no suitor it seemed that neither of the sisters would ever get married.

The task requested of the publicity agency was to send the most competent man that they had down to Newport to see if during the sequence of the cup races, Gracie's carefully, if unsuccessfully manoeuvered gifts could be exploited to the extent of marrying her off. This was a last possible expedient on the part of her father.

At first George objected vehemently. He had already picked out his little cottage where he would enjoy his small patrimony in making plants into onions instead of onions into orchids. But his professional instincts re-asserted themselves. The task fascinated him and off he went.

On the train, he was still baffled at his own weakness. Nevertheless, he had with him a typewriter, all of the data on the cup races and all he could dig out of newspaper morgues about the Van Grossies and their traditions. At the moment when he was thinking of turning back, he saw upon a satchel which was being deposited together with his own bag in the wrong place across the aisle the name of Gabrielle Van Grossie. With instinct for rising to such a situation he crossed the aisle and under the excuse of clearing up the confusion of the baggage, introduced himself as a friend of her father's who was going down to see the races and had been invited to stay in her house. Gabrielle, or Gay as she soon explained to him her nick-name was, sounded gay like her name and looked much more young and impetuous than her whole name would indicate.

During the ride, George managed to draw out from her innocence a few facts about the family with whom he was going to spend his next week—one of which was that she felt a vast impatience with the tradition which made it necessary for her sister Gracie to marry before her self. He guessed with his trained prescience that maybe she had a lover for whom she yearned and that this tradition forbade their union; and yet that she did not blame Gracie for it, but only the spirit that moved her father.

At about this same moment, the young man who, unknown to George, was the object of this young girl's affection, was visiting the, as yet, unlaunched competitor to represent America in the cup races of the following Saturday. He was a fine young man in every way and a great favorite of Mr. Van Grossie's, who hoped that sooner or later he might fall in love with the elder daughter, Gracie. They were looking at the yacht, from a technical standpoint. Little did they know what strange function it was to fulfill in both their lives during the next week.

And about an hour after the twilight that brought George into Newport, another scene was taking place which was equally to affect the destinies of the people concerned.

A girl in the garden of the enormous Van Grossie villa at Newport was feeding a pool of avid gold fish. She had finished her last throw of the proper food from a container and was saying good-bye to her favorite gold fish—a large mouthed and particularly taciturn specimen. But as she turned away, there was a curious answer. She turned back. "What did you say, Noah?"

Noah made no answer. "Oh, you silly thing!" she said, and turned away again.

Then she heard the strange cry the second time. She turned back and laughing, said, "Noah, I bet you say that to all the girls." But laughing out loud as she did, she nevertheless could not neglect the fact that the unexpected sound which had attracted her attention came from a little inlet some distance away, off toward a little patch of woods. It was a curious sound. It was a sound that had been for a long time in Gracie's heart—even though she did not recognize it. It was a sound of something new and unfound and fascinating, and she stopped in her tracks looking up at the sky for a moment, upon the chance that it might be a bird that she had never heard before. Yet she knew in that same heart that it was not a bird, and a minute later found her following a repetition of that sound to its source.

Its source was a dark arbor in the corner of the inlet, its source was the sea. Its source was God knows where. To be more specific, its source seemed to be from a small, very broken, utterly unseaworthy-appearing little dory in which was a laundry basket and turned out to be a little boy who even in the fast growing darkness caused her to snatch him out of the dory and nurse him with cries of delight. The child had probably come from some derelict tramp steamer, but Gracie was not thinking of it in those terms at the moment. She was merely delighted and started up through the little woods.

At the other end of the little woods another scene which would have surprised Mr. Van Grossie was taking place. Little Gay, scarcely off the train, was rushing off into the woods to keep an appointment with Mr. Van Grossie's hand-picked candidate for Gracie's hand. In a bower in the woods, the two met and embraced passionately, while in the big house George was getting more explicit details of his assignment.

The millionaire and the publicity agent strolled down through the gardens. As they reached the edge of the little woods, the same cry that Gracie had heard some minutes earlier reached both their ears. "What was that?" said Mr. Van Grossie, but George, in this new environment, was giving no opinions. He wanted to use his own judgment and while he knew very well the direction from which the cry had come, he wanted to pause a minute and consider. Again the cry sounded. This time he said to himself; "Well, if that isn't the cry of a baby, I never heard one" and "look here" he said to his host, deliberately pointing the way in an opposite direction, "you go down that direction and investigate and I will go this way." No sooner had the older man, considerably puzzled, started off in the indicated direction, than George darted toward the sound. In an instant he had come upon the young girl he had met on the train, a strange young man and an elder girl carrying a baby in a wash basket. The two pairs of human beings had evidently just come in contact, and being no laggard in intruding upon strange situations, he introduced himself into the general excitement which followed upon the discovery of the baby.

The advices of what to do about it were various, but George, seeing for the first time the girl he was to publicise and hoping for more story and more mystery, agreed that the baby should be concealed from her hard boiled father for the time being and given over to the charge of an old nurse, and it was obvious that Gracie had decided immediately to adopt the child.

Thoughtfully, George went in search of Mr. Van Grossie, thinking that he would be more able to make up his mind about Miss Gracie next day.

And well he might, for the next day, he saw Gracie in her natural element.

She had been commissioned to christen her father's boat, and from far and near people assembled upon the ways to watch and applaud. It seemed a sure-fire stunt to George who did not see how she could possibly go wrong. But Gracie's talent for going wrong re-asserted itself, for at the moment that she was to smash the bottle on the bow, and the boat was to slide down the ways, she stopped her swing, holding the bottle aloft, to wave to the crowd. The boat began to move and the hurriedly completed swing which she had directed toward the bow missed fire, swinging Gracie around in an acrobatic circle. Nothing defeated by this, she took a mere second in the arms of sympathizers to murmur "Where am I" and then set off in a mad run, with skirts flying, in pursuit of the boat sliding rapidly down the ways. Just as the yacht slid into the water Gracie arrived at the end of the ways. Nothing daunted she reached the boat only by a daring leap through mid-air in esthetic pose—and attained her aim at the sacrifice of sinking gently into the bay. George made a quick dive and brought her to the surface, but with the idea recurring to his mind even at his first reappearance on the surface, that he had a difficult venture. His task as a publicity man was to show that Gracie was a mature and gracious, and accomplished woman. The papers the next day said nothing of the incident except for sly remarks, but the implication was enough to make him grind his teeth and decide that next time, things would not be as heretofore.

He decided that perhaps since most musicians were considered eccentric, any curious departure from convention on Gracie's part in that line might be excused. So he decided that he would concentrate to the best of his ability on rehearsing Gracie for a hard number. It happened that was one of his many accomplishments and he was careful to call rehearsal in the morning several days before the event. It was held in the drawing room of the Van Grossie mansion. The baby had still been kept under the supervision of a confidential nurse, but Gracie had dared upon this occasion to sneak it into the music room for rehearsal. George played the piano and found that Gracie had certain talents. He concentrated therefore on her following his own piano accompaniment. Gracie, however, was torn between her supposed love of music on the harp and her interest in the child playing about her on the floor. When the baby decided to climb up the slanting slope of the harp, she obligingly began to tip the harp, all unknown to George, so that the baby would have something more solid to climb and George at the piano, all unknowing, kept on playing and admonishing and advising her without sensing what made an increasing series of extraordinary discord. He got madder and madder, while the child got more and more interested as it found it could climb. So did Gracie. Correspondingly, her interest in the music decreased. Her harp had now tilted so that Gracie was practically underneath it at a dangerous angle and playing it as no known instrument had ever been played, her body slanting dangerously backward.

Finally, still looking at his score on the piano, he said, thinking that he is being heard: "Now," he said, "we will try to get the finale with a big crescendo of harp and piano." At that moment, the crash that he had commanded arrived, but in an entirely different form, and turning around, he saw the harp, Gracie and the child sprawled upon the floor. As he picked them up one by one, Gracie, the child and the harp, talking all the time, he kept up a continual bawling-out to the effect that Gracie did not care about serious music, during which time Gracie was thinking only of whether the child had been possibly annoyed in the fall from the harp. Finally, he turned to her, and in one sharp line of abjugation which he thought would wither up any one who had seriously studied music, said; "Look what you have done to your Bach." Gracie felt at the baby's diapers. Feeling at his wet diapers, she said, "I didn't do it, he did it himself."

George was still shaking his head in doubt the next morning when he had embarked in a foursome on the golf links with the two sisters and Gabrielle's devoted Dick. Unfortunately his problem was complicated by the fact that Gracie was no golf player any more than she was a christener of boats. His own idea was to bring them all together and dispose of the situation of the baby, but there were two particular points about Gracie's claim that precluded that. While Gabrielle and Dick went ahead in an intimate twosome and descended into one sand-pit, there would always be Gracie in another sand-pit far behind, and he was continually rushing everywhere as a liaison officer between two trench systems, trying to keep the party as one. It was not that Gracie hit the ball so badly, but that a large caddie she had hired held in a large bag that she had somewhere found, a young male child who continually absorbed her attention. As near as he could make out in his impassioned abjurations to Gracie, she was teaching the child to count in accordance with her own score, and it was only because of the aforesaid predilection of the younger couple for the privacy of the dunes that he was able to bring them together at all and discuss with any intelligence what plans should be made for the future of the child. Perhaps, he thought, the whole situation would be beyond his abilities, but he was indefatigable, and in carrying out his new plan the next day he had mustered everything he knew about publicity into the picture.

It was to be a beauty contest, and Gracie was to win the prize. Moreover, it was to be a fully publicised beauty contest and he had taken careful thought. Society reporters from all over New England and New

York were present to take notes. Photographers were there in scores. Gracie, with the help of her sister, had been carefully instructed in her role; her competitors had been chosen with equal care from among the wall flowers and past debutantes in the vicinity, so that when Gracie won, no one would find any special injustice in the choice. The judges were hand-picked, but;

George had failed again to count on Gracie. When one of the entrants in the contest asked Gracie to fix her number on her back, Gracie obligingly did so. Gracie reversed the number "6" so that it should read "9," and a few minutes later Gracie's old trusted nurse, bringing up Gracie's adopted baby, allowed her to play with Gracie's number and reversed it so that it on the contrary read 6 instead of 9. Orders had been given that number 9 should win the contest.

So George, after this parade before the impassioned cameras, issued bulletins about the charming Miss Van Grossie's triumph—and then a few minutes later saw the cup provided for presented to the girl who wore mistaken the reverse number 9 instead of to Gracie who should have won it except for the upside down conditions of the numbers on their respective backs.

The story has gone off by telegraph to New York and by this time the society columns have managed to give it the wrong headlines with slight hints of the right story. It is too good a story again to be missed by social gossip columnists and George again had cause to wonder why he ever called himself a publicity agent since his attempts in this case have been rewarded by constant failure. He still had trumps in his hand to play, however and:

He banked everything on that night of the musicale. George and Gracie entered the room, she leaning on his arm as she swept majestically across the floor to the temporary stage at the end of the room. This was George's final trick and he was about to push Gracie into prominence as the world's greatest harpist.

He made a formal speech of presentation which Gracie acknowledged sweetly. Amid many bravos, George announced the first selection and with him as accompanist, Gracie started a tentative glissonde on the harp strings. She got off to a beautiful start but ended up in a terribly sorry chord. Quite unperturbed and with George prompting and keeping time, she swung on with the composition. Suddenly the baby peeked out from behind the piano where he had been in hiding. The child was old enough to realize that George Burns considered him a nuisance and so he tried to keep out of George's sight. He kept edging his way closer and closer toward Gracie, until finally just as Gracie reached a difficult passage, the baby ran out from its hiding place and managed to trip and fall head and shoulders through the harp strings.

That, of course, ended the musicale; Gracie bowing her way out and pushing the harp before her, she managed to keep the child unseen by anyone but George. Once outside the room it was obvious to both George and Gracie that a safe hiding place would have to be found for the child. When she managed to extricate the baby from the harp strings, she and George ran down to the boat house and into the store room, where they put the baby to sleep for the night on a jib sail which was stretched out horizontally to air. George and Gracie sat down alongside while they waited for the child to go off to sleep. Before the child finally closed its eyes, both George and Gracie were leaning back against the wall, dozing off themselves. They were awakened roughly the next morning when they were discovered by Mr. Van Grossie. As they opened their eyes they saw him angrily lifting the child into his arms and starting off down across the lawn evidently intending to dispose of the child, in some way of his own. Gracie and George took a short cut hurriedly to the dock where they found Dick and Gabrielle waiting to go out to the sailing yacht. George captured the little dory and hid it under the wharf and he sat in it making notes on his typewriter. Gracie explained hurriedly to the young lovers that the situation could be clarified if they would only claim that they were married and the baby was theirs. As Mr. Van Grossie came rushing on the scene with the baby in his arms, he was confronted by this false situation. On learning that Dick and Gabrielle seemed to be married, he was extremely disappointed but before he had a chance to vent his rage the "get ready" gun had been fired by the Race Committee. Mr. Van Grossie philosophically took the attitude that there was no use crying over "spilt milk." He shoved the baby into Gracie's arms and then dragged Dick and Gabrielle out to the racing yacht in the motor launch, calling back to Gracie to come on out with George as soon as he showed up. With Mr. Van Grossie out of sight, George re-appeared over the side of the pier. He and Gracie jumped into the one remaining motor boat and started for the races.

Gracie and George had both become much excited because of all the confusion and tension which pervaded the air just a moment or so before the historic races. Gracie sat in the stern holding the baby with one arm and steering with the other, while George sat in the bow, his typewriter resting on an air cushion on his knees. They had gotten about twenty feet from the wharf when the launch suddenly capsized and broke in half. George's half sank very slowly, his typewriter floating out of his reach on the air cushion. The baby, who had managed to climb onto another one, was also floating gleefully as Gracie's half of the boat, which had the motor and the propeller, sped in crazy circles around him. The baby was amused and delighted when George's portion of the boat filled with water and sank to the bottom. George was swimming frantically and treading water as he chased his floating typewriter. Gracie was unable to stop the boat for the minute but finally, as it completely filled with water, she ran it into the dock and was dumped unceremoniously into the water. The loss of the motor boat forced them to take the only remaining craft which happened to be the small battered dory. George and Gracie climbed aboard and with Gracie at the oars they went to the rescue of the floating baby and typewriter—and continued on among the numerous sight-seeing craft that milled about the contending yachts. Gracie rowed up just in time to tie onto the back of her father's boat as the starting gun was fired. In the ensuing confusion, as Gracie and George tried to scramble aboard the yacht, the baby was stranded and it was not until after the yachts had started that Gracie was suddenly horrified to remember that the baby was still in the trailing dory. The Van Grossie boat was in the lead and Gracie and George were struggling to effect the rescue of the baby, who sat laughing and clapping his hands as the dory rocked and swerved in the yacht's wake. Gracie suddenly decided that she needed a good length of rope to do the trick so with George still watching the child, she ran up the deck until she found at the base of the main mast the sort of rope she needed.

However, this rope was fastened to a marlin's pike at the base of the great mast. Nothing daunted and not at all worried, or aware of the fact that that particular rope was the one which held the main sail up in place, Gracie struggled until she was able to pull out the marlin's pike, determined on getting that rope. As the spike finally came out, the huge main sheet tumbled down practically smothering the boat; and the rival boat swept by triumphantly to victory.

After a moment signs of life began to appear from under the canvas which covered the deck like a blanket. Dick and Gabrielle appeared from under one corner and embraced each other happily. Near the foot of the mast, an indistinguishable hump raised up and called out just as though nothing had happened, "Oh, Georgie, where are you?" From somewhere near the stern came George's distracted and discouraged response, "Right here, Gracie." She extricated herself from the sail and ran back to join him. George decided that it would probably be politic to remove Gracie from the scene with the utmost dispatch. As he helped her down into the dory occupied by the baby he announced: "I think, Gracie, that for the benefit of mankind I had better make you my eternal problem." Gracie giggled happily as she sat down at the oars; "Oh! George, you *do* say the *nicest* things." George's face, with his usual pained expression, was bent over his typewriter as he tapped out his final press release as the dory headed back to shore. As the small boat fades off in the distance, George was busily writing: "VAN GROSSIE HEIRESS SOON TO ANNOUNCE MATRIMONIAL EXCURSION WITH —————"

FINIS.

FSF and Carmel Myers, 1927.

"Travel Together," the saga of a screenwriter with writer's block, slumming for inspiration on a southern train with a gang of railroad hoboes, reads at first like something entirely new. But by the second page of the typescript there is a "pretty girl of eighteen," Chris Cooper becomes an accidental hero, and we are in Fitzgerald's world. The possibilities of travel and its different modes, and the pleasures and perils inherent in getting around, always fascinated Fitzgerald—think of cars, and the way they are represented in *Gatsby*. Here, freight trains cross desert and scrublands; the "nineteen wild green eyes of a bus" full of "dozy passengers" shine through the dark. There are grace notes that are by now standard for his stories: a woman who, like Jay Gatsby, changes her name and creates herself anew, but can't escape her past; a diamond as big as, if not the Ritz, the Hope. Yet that feeling of novelty lingers in the screenwriter already wanting to escape from Hollywood and write plays; the girl who is resourceful enough not to need a man's help, but accepts him for her own reasons.

Fitzgerald sent the story to Harold Ober in January 1935, and Ober liked it. Fitzgerald immediately wanted to "get a version together to offer the movies." On March 4 Ober offered "Travel Together" to *Cosmopolitan*, telling its editor, Bill Lengel, that the price was $1,500 and that the story ought to get $2,000. Little correspondence thereafter survives about "Travel Together," as Fitzgerald's letters to Ober from February 19 to December 30, 1936, were removed from the Ober files. Ober himself wrote a note on the file folder: "where are Scotts letters to me for above period one letter from Scott Oct 5 1936." (Some have emerged at auction, including one sold at Bonham's in December 2015, dated September 10, 1936, in which Fitzgerald refers to the "Crack-Up" stories in *Esquire* as "emergency things," done because the *Post* was not accepting his stories or was asking for revisions.) On June 5, 1936, Ober wrote to Fitzgerald, "*College Humour* has asked us for a story of yours. I find we have here four unsold ones, which we might show him. They are, TRAVEL TOGETHER, NIGHTMARE, WHAT TO DO ABOUT IT and ON YOUR OWN of which I believe TRAVEL TOGETHER is the best of the lot. Since *College Humour's* outside price is $500 and since these are all old stories you may not wish to have them offered. Will you drop me a line about this?" A letter from Fitzgerald to Ober, dated June 19 and sold at Sotheby's in 1982, contains Fitzgerald's refusal. The Ober card files note that "author may rewrite."

"Travel Together" shows Hollywood on Fitzgerald's mind, and the rejection of it by Chris Cooper, his screenwriter character, in the end. The story itself conforms to the trajectory the moviemakers want—a hobo film too sad that needs a love interest. However, Fitzgerald's ironic delivery of the goods with the romance of Judy and Chris still was not enough to sell the story. Fitzgerald comes back to the idea of being a playwright, something at which he had had great success in college, and then failed terribly at in 1923, when his comedy/satire *The Vegetable* flopped during Atlantic City tryouts. In 1937, he wrote to Max Perkins, "I am thinking of putting aside certain hours and digging out a play, the ever-appealing mirage." He never did.

TRAVEL TOGETHER

by

F. Scott Fitzgerald

When the freight stopped next the stars were out,
so sudden that Chris was dazzled. The train was on a rise.
About three miles ahead he saw a cluster of lights, fainter
and more yellow than the stars, that he figured would be
Dallas.

In four days he had learned enough about the shipments to be sure that in Dallas there would be much shunting of cars billed to that point. If he decided to go on
he could catch up with the freight before morning. And after
the inactivity -- except when he had held on to rods all
night -- the hiking one mile or so sounded like luxury. An
Arabian Night luxury.

He stretched himself, breathing deep. He felt good,
better than he had for years. It wasn't a bad life if you
had food. By the starlight he saw a few other figures emerge

Travel Together

When the freight stopped next the stars were out, so sudden that Chris was dazzled. The train was on a rise. About three miles ahead he saw a cluster of lights, fainter and more yellow than the stars, that he figured would be Dallas.

In four days he had learned enough about the shipments to be sure that in Dallas there would be much shunting of cars billed to that point. If he decided to go on he could catch up with the freight before morning. And after the inactivity—except when he had held on to rods all night—the hiking one mile or so sounded like luxury. An Arabian Night luxury.

He stretched himself, breathing deep. He felt good, better than he had for years. It wasn't a bad life if you had food. By the starlight he saw a few other figures emerge cautiously from other cars and, like himself, breathe in the dry Texas night.

That reminded Chris immediately of the girl.

There was a girl in the caboose. He had suspected it this morning at Springfield with the sight of a hurriedly withdrawn face at a window; when they laid over an hour he had seen her plain, not twenty feet away.

Of course she might be the brakeman's wife, and she might be a tramp. But the brakeman was a gnarled old veteran, ripe for a pension rather than for a pretty girl of eighteen. And a tramp—well, if she was *that* she was different from the ones he had so far encountered.

He set about warming up his canned soup before starting the hike into town. He went fifty yards from the tracks, built himself a small fire and poured the beef broth into his folding pan.

He was both glad and sorry that he had brought along the cooking kit; he was glad because it was such a help, sorry because it had somehow put a barrier between him and some of the other illegitimate passengers. The quartet who had just joined forces down the track had no such kit. Between them they possessed a battered sauce-pan, empty cans and enough miscellaneous material and salt to make "Slummy." But then they knew the game—the older ones did; and the younger ones were catching on.

Chris finished his soup, happy under the spell of the wider and wider night.

"Travel into those stars maybe," he said aloud.

The train gave out a gurgle and a forlorn burst of false noise from somewhere, and with a clicking strain of couplers pulled forward a few hundred yards.

He made no move to rise. Neither did the tramps up the line make any move to board her again. Evidently they had the same idea he did, of catching it in Dallas. When the faintly lit caboose had gone fifty yards past him the train again jolted to a stop. . . .

. . . . The figure of a girl broke the faint light from the caboose door, slowly, tentatively. It—or she walked out to where the cindery roadside gave way to grass.

She gave every impression of wanting to remain alone—but this was not to be. No sooner had the four campers down the track caught sight of her than two of them got up and came over toward her. Chris finished the assemblage of his things and moved unobtrusively for the same spot. For all he knew they might be pals of the girl—on the other hand they had seemed to him a poor lot; in case of trouble he identified himself with the side on which they weren't.

The things happened quicker than he had anticipated. There was a short colloquy between the men and the girl who obviously did not appreciate their company; presently one of them took her by the arm and attempted to force her in the direction of their camp. Chris sauntered nearer.

"What's the idea?" he called over.

The men did not answer.

The girl struggled, gasping a little and Chris came closer.

"Hey, what's the idea?" he called louder.

"Make them let me go! Make them—"

"Oh, shut your trap!"

But as Chris came up to the man who had spoken he dropped the girl's arm and stood at a defiant defensive a few yards away. Chris was a well-built, well-preserved man just over thirty—the first tramp was young and husky; his companion existed under rolls of unexercised flesh, so that it was impossible to determine his value in battle.

The girl turned to Chris. The white glints in her eyes cracked the heavens as a diamond would crack glass, and let stream down a whiter light than he had ever seen before; it shone over a wide beautiful mouth, set and frightened.

"Make them go away! They tried this before!"

Chris was watching the two men. They had exchanged a look and were moving now, so that one was on either side of him. He backed up against the girl, murmuring, "You watch that side!" and catching his idea she stood touching him to guard against envelopment. From the corner of his eye Chris saw that the other two hoboes had left their fire and were running up. He acted quickly. When the stouter and elder of the tramps was less than a yard away Chris stepped in and cracked him with a left to the right of his chin. The man reeled and came up, cursing but momentarily repulsed, and wiping his chin with a long rag which he took from some obscure section of his upholstery. But he kept his distance.

At that instant there was a wild cry from the girl: "He got my purse!" —and Chris turned to see the younger man making off twenty feet, to grin derisively.

"Get my purse!" the girl cried. "They were after it last night. And I've *got* to have it! There's no money in it."

Wondering what she would have in her purse to regret so deeply Chris nonetheless came to a decision, reached into his swinging bundle and, standing in front of the girl, juggled a thirty-eight revolver in the starlight.

"Pull out that purse."

The young man hesitated—he half turned, half started to run, but his eyes were mesmerized on the sight of the gun. He stopped in the moment of his pivot—instinctively his hands began to lift from his sides.

"Get that purse out!"

He had no fear of what the kid had in his pocket, knowing that the police or pawn-shop would long have frisked them of all weapons.

"He's opening it in his pocket!" the girl cried, "I can see!"

"Throw it *out!*"

The purse ajar fell on the ground. Before Chris could stop her she had left him and run forward to pick it up—and anxiously regarded its contents.

One of the other pair of hoboes now spoke up.

"We didn't mean any harm, brother. We said let the girl alone. Dint I, Joe?" He turned for confirmation, "I said let the girl alone, she's in the caboose."

Chris hesitated. His purpose was accomplished and—he still had four cans of food . . .

. . . Still he hesitated. They were four to one and the young man with a sub-Cromagnon visage, the one who'd stolen the purse, looked sore enough for a fight.

As bounty he extracted a can of corned beef and one of baked beans from his shrunken sack and tossed them.

"Get along now! I mean get along! You haven't got a chance!"

"Who are you? A tec?"

"Never mind—get going. And if you want to eat this stuff—then travel half a mile!"

"Ain't you got a little canned heat?"

"For you to drink? No I guess you got to make your own fire, like you did before."

One man said in sing-song: "Git along, little doggie" and presently the quartet moved off beside the roadbed toward yellow-lit Dallas.

II

Crossing the two starlights there obtruded the girl.

Her face was a contrast between herself looking over a frontier—and a silhouette, and outline seen from a point of view, something finished—white, polite, unpolished—it was a destiny, scarred a little with young wars, worried with old white faiths . . .

. . . And out of it looked eyes so green that they were like phosphorescent marbles, so green that the scarcely dry clay of the face seemed dead beside it.

"Some other tramps took about everything else I had when I got off in St. Louis," she said.

"Took what?"

"Took my money." Her eyes glittered for him again in the starlight, "Who are you?"

"I'm just a man. Just a tramp like you. Where are you going?"

"All the way. The coast—Hollywood. Where *you* going?"

"Same place. You trying to get a job in pictures?"

The marble of her face was alive, flashing back the interest in his. "No, I'm going—because of this paper—this check." She replaced it carefully in the purse. "You going to the movies?"

"I'm in em."

"You mean you been *wor*king in them?"

"I've been in em a long time."

"What are you doing on this road, then?"

"Lady! I didn't mean to tell this to anybody, but I write them—believe it or not. I've written many a one."

She did not care whether or not he had but the very implausibility overwhelmed her.

"You're on the road—like me."

"Why are you on the road?"

"For a reason."

He took a match out of his rucksack—and simultaneously his last can of soup knocked against him.

"Have a bite with me?"

"No thanks. I've eaten."

But there was that wan look about her—

"Have you eaten?" he reiterated.

"Sure, I have . . . So you're a writer in Hollywood."

He moved around collecting twigs to start a fire for the last can of soup and he saw two pieces of discarded railroad ties. They were pretty big and he saw no kindling at first—but the train was there still. He ran to the caboose and found the brakeman.

"Well *what* kindling?" the old man grumbled, "You want to take the roof off my shack. What I'd like to know is what became of that girl? She was a lady—else I don't know a lady."

"Where'd you find her?"

"She came down to the yards without any money in St. Louis. Said somebody stole her ticket. I took her in—and I might of lost my job. You seen her?"

"Look, I want to get some kindling."

"You can take a handful," the brakeman said tentatively and then repeated, "Where is that girl—off with those rod riders?"

"She's all right." Out of his boot he slipped a card.

"If you ever come on a run to Hollywood come to see me."

The brakeman laughed, and paused:

"Well, anyhow you seem like a nice fellow."

Taking advantage of his good humor Chris loaded an arm with kindling.

"Don't worry about that girl," he said, "I won't let her get hurt."

"Say don't," the brakeman said at the door, "Don't. She was like my own daughter. I took her in here, but I didn't like the looks of that gang. Know? They didn't look nice. Know? Usually they look not so bad nowadays."

"Goodbye there."

—The couplings clanged. Meditatively Chris walked to where he had left her.

"Look!" she exclaimed.

The nineteen wild green eyes of a bus were coming up to them through the dark.

"Wouldn't it be good?—if we could."

"We can," he assured her, "I can take you all the way to Los Angeles—"

She doubted.

"You know sometimes I think you *have* got a position out there."

In the bus she asked him:

"Where'd you get the money to do this?"

The dozy passengers moved to give them seats.

"Well I'm making up a picture," he said.

Still she didn't know whether to believe him or not, but it was a somewhat weary face for a young man, and must have worked some time.

"What are you writing now?" she asked.

"This. It's a picture I've got in mind. It's about hoboes—"

"And you're going to try to sell them the idea out in Hollywood."

"Sell them! It's sold. I'm getting data. My name's Chris Cooper. I wrote *Linda Monday*."

She seemed to have become tired and listless.

"I don't go much to the pictures," she said, "You've been mighty sweet to me." She gave him a side smile, half of her face, like a small white cliff.

"Damn, you're beautiful!" he said involuntarily, and then: "Who are you? You're somebody—" Again he had to lower his voice as a weary pair in front of them stirred.

"I'm the mystery girl," she said.

"I begin to think you are. You've got me guessing."

The bus slowed for its Dallas station. Midnight was rocking overhead. More than half the passengers disembarked, permanently or temporarily, among them Chris; the girl remained in her chair and, as she rested, a faint glow of pink stole back into her cheeks.

At the telegraph office Chris dispatched a wire to a celebrated woman upon a fine streamlined train westbound.

He returned to the bus and roused the girl from a half sleep to ask casually:

"Did you ever hear of Velia Tolliver?"

"Of course. Who hasn't? Isn't she the discovery of the year?"

"She's on her way to the coast. I wired her to get off at El Paso and I'd join her there."

But he was tired of showing off for a girl who obviously didn't believe him; and perhaps the baffled vanity in his eyes gave her the energy to say:

"I don't care much *who* you are. You've been good to me. You saved my check." Sleepily she clutched her worn purse containing the much folded check. "That's what I didn't want the tramp to get."

"You certainly seem to think it's valuable?"

"Well, did you ever hear of Paul Downs?"

"Seems to me I have."

"He was my father. That's his signature." Fatigue overcame her again and without further elucidation she dozed as they got in motion to cross the long Texas night.

The bulbs, save for two, were dimmed to a pale glow; the faces of the passengers as they composed themselves for slumber were almost universally yellow tired.

"Good night," she murmured.

Not till the next day when they paused at Midland for lunch did he say:

"You said your father's name was Paul Downs. Was he called 'Popsy' Downs? And did he own a string of coast-to-coast steamers?"

"That was father."

"I remember the name now, because he lent us an old eighteen-fifty brig we used in *Gold Dust*. When I met him he was throwing a nice little party—"

He shut up at the expression on her face.

"We heard about it."

"Who's we?"

"Mother and I. We were well off then—when father died, or we thought we were." She sighed. "Let's go back to the bus again . . ."

. . . It was another fine night when they drew into El Paso.

"You got any money?" he asked.

"Oh, plenty."

"Liar. Here's two dollars. You can pay me back some time. Go buy yourself something you need—you know—stockings, handkerchiefs—anything."

"You sure you can spare it?"

"You still don't believe me—just because I haven't got much cash in hand."

They stood in front of a window filled with open road maps.

"Goodbye then," she said tentatively, "And thanks."

Chris felt a pull at his heart. "It's just au revoir. I'm meeting you at the railroad station in an hour."

"All right."

She was gone before he realized it. She was only the back of her hair curling up around her hat.

On the way he thought what the girl would probably do—thought *with* her. He worried whether she would, after all, return to the station. He was sure she would walk, walk and look in windows. He knew El Paso and guessing the streets she would travel, he felt more than delight when he found her half an hour before the arrival of the train.

"So you're going along. Come to the ticket window."

"I've changed my mind. You paid all you should for me."

His feeling came to words:

"I'd like to pay a lot more mileage for you."

"Let's forget that. Here's your two dollars. I haven't spent any. Oh yes I did. I spent twenty-five, no—I spent thirty-five cents. Here's the rest. Here!"

"Talk nonsense, will you? Just when I'd begun to think you had some sense. Velia's train'll be in in a minute and she'll be getting off. She's the prettiest thing I ever saw. She's our choice for the girl tramp in the hobo picture."

"Sometimes I almost believe you're what you say you are."

Then, as they stood by the news-stand he turned to her once more—to see the snow melting as he looked at her. Her pink lips were scarlet now. . . .

. . . . The train came in. Velia Tolliver, looking exactly like herself, seemed much upset.

"Well, here we are," she said, "Let's have a quick one in the buffet, and we can wire Bennie Giskig to meet us in his car at Yuma. I'm tired of trains. Then I want to get back on board and go to bed. Even the porters looked at me as if I had lines on my face."

She looked curiously at the girl as they came into her drawing room ten minutes later.

"My maid got sick and had to be left in Chicago—and now I'm helpless. What's your name? I don't think I caught it."

"Judith Downs."

For a moment as Velia flashed a huge blue stone, bigger than an eye, upon them and then put it into a blue sack Judy wondered if she was going to be asked to take the place of the missing maid.

Chris and Judy went down to the observation car and presently Velia came back and joined them, obviously refreshed by a few surreptitious drinks, by way of making up for her maid's absence, so to speak.

"You're hopeless, Chris," she declared. "After you leave me in New

York and go off on this crazy trip and what do *I* get—I get a wire to get off the train and you show up with a girl!"

She wiped away a few vexatious tears and got herself into control.

"All right. Then I'll accept her—if you don't love me." She examined Judy more critically than heretofore. "You're—pretty dusty. Do you want to borrow some clothes? I got one trunk in my drawing-room. Come on."

. . . Ten minutes later Judy Downs said:

"No—just this skirt and this sweater."

"But that's just an old sweater. I'm almost sure I gave it to my maid a long time ago, and it just got mixed up in here. You won't? All right. Go along with Chris and have you a time. I think I'll just lie down for awhile."

But Judy had not chosen the sweater because it was old, but because on a tab at the back of the neck she had seen the name "Mabel Dychenik." And the check she carried so carefully in her purse read

Pay to the Order of Mabel Dychenik—$10.00

III

Back in the observation car, feeling fresher, Judy said:

"She was nice lending me this outfit. Who is she?"

"Oh, she began as a rural gold digger; she was just out of the mines when I picked her out of a ten-twenty-thirty. I even changed her name for her."

They sat late on the observation platform while New Mexico streamed away under the stars; and they had a quick breakfast together in the morning. Velia didn't appear until they reached Yuma. They all went to the little hotel to spruce up and wait for Bennie Giskig, who had wired that he would meet them there in his own car and carry them the intervening miles to Hollywood.

"Lots of variety in the trip anyhow," Chris said to Judy, "Easy stages— each one different from the last—it's been fun—with you."

"With you too."

And then suddenly it wasn't fun when Velia came out of the women's room wailing:

"I've lost my little blue bag I always have on my wrist—I mean what was inside it. My big stone—the only nice thing I have! My blue diamond!"

"Did you look thoroughly? Through all your bags?"

"My things are on the train. But I know it was in its own case and that was on my arm."

"Suppose it slipped out—"

"It couldn't," she insisted. "The case has a patent catch—it couldn't just open and close again."

"It must be in your baggage."

"Oh no!" With sudden suspicion she turned toward Judy, "Where is it? I want it back now!"

"*I* certainly haven't got it."

"Then where is it? I'll have you searched—"

"Be reasonable, Velia," Chris said.

"But who is she? Who *is* this girl? We don't know."

"At least come in the side parlor here," he urged.

She was on the edge of collapse.

"I want her searched."

"I don't mind," offered Judy. "I've only got the coat and sweater you lent me. I threw away the old dress on the train, it wasn't worth saving. And I couldn't very well have swallowed it."

"You see, she knows, Chris. She knows that thieves swallow the jewels they've stolen."

"Don't be absurd!" he said.

While the search was being conducted by the telephone girl under Velia's close supervision, Bennie Giskig, one of the supervisors of Bijou Pictures, drove up at the door. He encountered Chris in the lobby.

"Ah, good," he said, in the cocksure manner that Chris had come to associate with his métier, a manner sharply different from those who actually wrote and directed the pictures. "Good to see you, Chris. I want to talk to you. That's why I drove here. I am so busy a man. Where is Velia—I want to see her even more. Can we start right away—I have business back in Hollywood."

"There's a little trouble here," Chris answered. "Bennie, I found a girl for you. She's with us."

"All right. I'll look at her in the car—but we got to get started back."

"And also I've got the story."

"So." He hesitated. "Chris, I must tell you frankly plans have changed a little since we started on that. It's such a sad story."

"On the contrary, I've found it can be a very cheerful story."

"We can talk about it in the car. Anyhow Velia goes into another production first, right now, almost today—"

At this moment the latter, all upset and tearful and at a loss, came out of the coatroom, followed by Judy.

"Bennie," she cried, "I've lost my big diamond. You've seen it."

"So? That's too bad. It was insured?"

"Not for anything like its real value. It was a rare stone."

"We must start now. We can talk it over in the car."

She consented to be embarked and they set out for the coast up and over a hill and then down into a valley of green morning light with rows of avocado pear trees and late lettuce.

Chris let Bennie unburden himself to Velia about the immediacy of her picture—a matter which in her distraught condition she scarcely understood at all.

Then he said:

"I still think my story's better than that one, Bennie. I've changed it. I've learned a lot since I started on this trip. This story is called 'Travel Together.' It's more than just about hoboes now. It's a love story."

"I tell you the subject's too gloomy. People want to laugh now. For instance in this picture for Velia we got a—"

But Chris cut through him impatiently.

"Then I've wasted my month—while you've changed your mind."

"Shulkopf couldn't reach you, could he? We didn't know where you were. Besides you're on salary, aren't you?"

"I like to work for more than salary."

Bennie touched his knee conciliatingly.

"Forget it. I'll set you to work on a picture that—"

"But I want to write *this* picture, while I'm full of it. From New York to Dallas I was on the freights—"

"Who cares about that though? Now wouldn't you yourself rather ride along a smooth road in a big limousine?"

"I thought so once."

Bennie turned to Velia as if in good humored despair.

"Velia, he thinks he would like to ride the freights and—"

"Come on, Judy," Chris said suddenly, "Let's get out. We can make it on foot." And then to Bennie, "My contract was up last week anyhow."

"But we were going to renew—"

"I think I can sell this somewhere else. The whole hobo idea was mine anyhow—so I guess it reverts to me."

"Sure, sure. We don't want it. But Chris, I tell you—"

He seemed to realize now he was losing one of his best men, one who had no lack of openings, who would go far in the industry.

But Chris was adamant.

"Come on, Judy. Stop here, driver."

Absorbed in her loss to the exclusion of all else Velia cried to him: "Chris! If you find out anything about my diamond—if this girl—"

"She hasn't got it. You know that. Maybe I have."

"You haven't."

"No, I haven't. Goodbye Velia. Goodbye Bennie, I'll come up and see you when this play's a smash. And tell you about it."

In a few minutes the car was a dot far down the highway.

Chris and Judy sat by the roadside.

"Well."

"Well."

"I guess it's shoe leather and hitch-hike again."

"I guess so."

He looked at the delicate white rose of her cheeks and the copper green eyes, greener than the green-brown foliage around them.

"Have you got that diamond?" he asked suddenly.

"No."

"You're lying."

"Well then, yes and no," she said.

"What did you do with it?"

"Oh, it's so pleasant here, let's not talk about it now."

"Let's not talk about it!" he repeated astonished at her casual attitude—as if it didn't matter! "I'm going to get that stone back to Velia. I'm responsible. I introduced you, after all—"

"I can't help you," she said rather coolly. "I haven't got it."

"What did you do with it? Give it to a confederate?"

"Do you think I'm a criminal? And I certainly would have to have been a marvelous plotter. To've met you and all."

"If you are, you're finished being one from now on. Velia's going to get her diamond."

"It happens to be mine."

"I suppose because possession is nine points of the law—Well—"

"I *did*n't mean that," she interrupted with angry tears. "It belongs to my mother and me. Oh, I'll tell you the whole story though I was saving it. Father owned the Nyask Line and when he was eighty-six and so collapsed we never let him steam around to his west coast office without a doctor and nurse—he broke away one night and gave a diamond worth eighty thousand dollars to a girl in a nightclub. He told the nurse about it because he thought it was gay and clever. And we know what it was worth, because we found the bill from a New York dealer—and it was receipted.

"Father died before he reached New York—and he left absolutely nothing else except debts. He was senile—crazy, you understand. He should have been at home."

Chris interrupted.

"But how did you know that was Velia's diamond?"

"I didn't. I was going West to find a girl named Mabel Dychenik—because we found a check made out to her for ten dollars in his bank returns. And his secretary said he'd never signed a check except the night he ran away from the ship."

"Still you didn't *know*—" He considered. "After you saw the diamond. I suppose they're pretty rare."

"Rare! *That* size? It was described in the jeweller's invoice with a pedigree like a thoroughbred's. We thought sure we'd find it in his safe."

He guessed: "So I suppose you were going to plead with the girl and try to litigate."

"I was—but when I met a hard specimen like Velia, or Mabel, I knew she'd fight it to the end. And we have no money to go into it. Then, last night, this chance came—and I thought if I *had* it—"

She broke off and he finished for her:

"—that when she cooled down she might listen to reason."

Sitting there Chris considered for a long time the rights and wrongs of the thing. From one point of view it was indefensible—yet he had read of divorced couples contending for a child to the point of kidnapping. What was the justice of that—love? But here, on Judy's part, what had influenced her action was her human claim on the means of her own subsistence.

Something could be done with Velia.

"What *did* you do with it?" he demanded suddenly.

"It's in the mails. The porter posted it for me when we stopped in Phoenix this morning—wrapped in my old skirt."

"My God! You took another awful chance there."

"All this trip was an awful chance."

Now, presently, they were on their feet, walking westward with a mild sun arching up behind them.

"Travel Together," Chris said to himself, abstractedly, "Yes, there's the title of my script." And then to her, "And I have title on you to be my girl."

"I know you have."

"'Travel Together'," he repeated, "I suppose that's one of the best things you can do to find out about another person."

"We'll travel a lot, won't we?"

"Yes, and always together."

"No. You'll travel alone sometimes—but I'll always be there when you come back."

"You better be."

FSF at the restaurant
at Chimney Rock, summer 1935.

On September 23, 1935, Fitzgerald wrote from Baltimore to his friend Laura Guthrie (Hearne) in Asheville: "Send me the page of notes with the stuff about the Ashville [sic] flower carnival—I'm going to write one story here—I mapped it out today." Fitzgerald had finished two drafts of this story by mid-November 1935, referring to it, in a letter to Harold Ober, as the "Suicice [sic] Story." He was eager to have it sold, noting that he was in need of more money: "if I'd Die For You sells, it will change the face of the situation." A "suicide story" was unexpected from Fitzgerald, and particularly to readers used to his lighter fare of the 1920s. It is a deliberate effort to complicate and move on from the youthful romantic plots of his early short stories. Set among the natural beauty of the North Carolina mountains, the story is dark indeed. In the

87

richness of color and description, as well as the possibly dangerous and doomed Carley Delannux, there are many echoes of *The Great Gatsby*. One cannot read a phrase like "corruption in its wake" without recalling *Gatsby*. The motion picture plot superimposed on the love story, a cameraman in love with the star, is even reminiscent of the moving-picture director and his star at one of Gatsby's parties. Atlanta Downs and Delannux have their similarities, too, to Rosemary Hoyt and Dick Diver of *Tender Is the Night*.

Ober wrote Fitzgerald about the story's progress on December 13:

> I liked I'D DIE FOR YOU but I am afraid it is going to be difficult to sell. The *Post, American, McCall's, Cosmopolitan* and *Red Book* have declined it. Littauer of *Collier's* liked it but Chenery didn't. Littauer, who also reads stories for the *Woman's Home Companion*, has turned it over to the *Companion* and he thinks they might possibly be able to use it. One difficulty with the story seems to be the threat of suicide all the way through . . . *Cosmopolitan* thought the man who was hiding from the process servers was altogether too mysterious and didn't really come to life.

Fitzgerald refused to tone down the suicide threats. From a Baltimore hospital in January 1936, he replied to Ober, "If I'd Die For You hasn't sold you might as well send it back to me. I'm not going to touch it myself again but I know a boy here who might straighten it out for a share of the profits, if any." The "boy," Charles Marquis "Bill" Warren (1912–1990; best known as the creator of the television series *Rawhide* in 1959), had met Fitzgerald in Baltimore in 1933, and would later collaborate with him in Hollywood on a screenplay for *Tender Is the Night*, but Warren did not revise "I'd Die for You." Ober offered to send the story to *Pictorial*, a lesser publication, but Fitzgerald, as desperate as he was for money, did not want this. On January 29, he asked again, "I wish you would send I'd Die For You right back."

Shards of Fitzgerald's notes from his difficult Carolina days show him experimenting with the color-filled language that was already a hallmark of his prose, now turning it to darker, sadder ideas:

> Dull brown stale—where the dark brown tide receded the slate came it was indescribable as the dress beside him (the color of hours of a long human day—blue like misery, blue for the shy-away from happiness, "if I could [touch] that shade everything would be all right forever."

And:

For himself, like so many men who are shy because they cannot fit their world of imagination into reality, or don't want to, he had learned compensations—oh but once had it the blue-green unalterable dream, the ideal and the colors were off of the women who loved him for his celebrity or his money or his confidence[.]

During his time in North Carolina, Fitzgerald attempted suicide. Martha Marie Shank, his friend and sometime secretary who saved even the smallest fragments of paper on which he wrote thoughts and scenes, like those above quotations, reported these incidents—but so did Fitzgerald himself, to friends. In 1936, after *New York Post* reporter Michel, or Michael, Mok published a hatchet piece just in time for Fitzgerald's fortieth birthday, he took an overdose of pills. Writing to Ober in October, Fitzgerald recounted the story: "I got hold of a morphine file [vial] and swallowed four grains enough to kill a horse. It happened to be an overdose and almost before I could get to the bed I vomited the whole thing and the nurse came in + saw the empty phial + there was hell to pay for awhile + afterwards I felt like a fool. And If I ever see Mr. Mock [*sic*] what will happen will be very swift and sudden. Dont tell Perkins." To his old Princeton friend, and lawyer, John Biggs, Jr., Fitzgerald was also explicit: "I had had such a bad time in Carolina + came up [to Baltimore in 1935] for that Xmas + had fooled plenty with the thirty-eight."

Also haunting Fitzgerald was the near-constant threat of Zelda harming herself. When he roughed out a list of possible names for "Suicide Carley" Delannux, he put in a column next to them incidents from Zelda's life. Yet in April 1936, he wrote to Beatrice Dance, a woman with whom he had a brief affair in North Carolina, "The other day I took [Zelda] to Chimney Rock where her family used to come when she was a child. And in trying (unsuccessfully) to locate the boarding house where they had stayed, the cloud of tragedy seemed sometimes to lift. As I told you, sometimes one would never know she was ill." There was nothing so personal, or painful, in Fitzgerald's life that he could not turn it to art, perhaps in an attempt to comprehend it or lay it down, perhaps in a desire to master it and remake it into the nostalgic, even the beautiful.

Finally, the fate of young English actress Peg Entwistle (1908–1932) is behind this story. A stage actress who had success on Broadway as a teenager in the 1920s, Entwistle tried to make it in Hollywood and did not. She wanted to return to New York, but had no money to do so. On September 18, 1932, she climbed to the top of the letter *H* in the

Hollywood sign and jumped. She was just twenty-four. Her death was widely reported, and remains a key image of the corrosive effect of the film business on those who gravitated to it.

#2

"I'D DIE FOR YOU"

By

F. Scott Fitzgerald

Within a cup of the Carolina mountains lay the lake, a pink glow of summer evening on its surface. In the lake was a peninsula and on this an Italianate hotel of stucco turned to many colors with the progress of the sun. In the dining room of the hotel four moving picture people sat at table.

"If they can fake Venice or the Sahara--" the girl was saying, "--then I don't see why they couldn't fake Chimney Rock without sending us all the way East."

"We're going to fake it a lot," said Roger Clark, the camera man. "We could fake Niagara Falls or the Yellowstone if it was just a question of background. But the hero of this story is the Rock."

"We can be better than reality," said Wilkie Prout, assistant director. "I was never so disillusioned as when I saw the real Versailles and thought of the one Conger built in twenty-nine--"

"But truth's the foot rule," Roger Clark continued. "That's where other directors flop--"

The girl, Atlanta Downs, was not listening. Her eyes--

I'd Die for You
(The Legend of Lake Lure)

Within a cup of the Carolina mountains lay the lake, a pink glow of summer evening on its surface. In the lake was a peninsula and on this an Italianate hotel of stucco turned to many colors with the progress of the sun. In the dining room of the hotel four moving picture people sat at table.

"If they can fake Venice or the Sahara—" the girl was saying, "—then I don't see why they couldn't fake Chimney Rock without sending us all the way East."

"We're going to fake it a lot," said Roger Clark, the camera man. "We *could* fake Niagara Falls or the Yellowstone if it was just a question of background. But the hero of this story *is* the Rock."

"We can be better than reality," said Wilkie Prout, assistant director. "I was never so disillusioned as when I saw the real Versailles and thought of the one Conger built in twenty-nine—"

"But truth's the foot rule," Roger Clark continued. "That's where other directors flop—"

The girl, Atlanta Downs, was not listening. Her eyes—eyes that had an odd sort of starlight in them which actually photographed—had left the table and come to rest upon a man who had just entered. After a minute Roger's eyes followed hers. He stared.

"Who's that number?" he said. "I know I've seen him somewhere. He's somebody who's been news."

"He doesn't look so hot to me," Atlanta said.

"He's somebody, though. Blast it, I know everything about him except I don't know *who* he is. He's somebody it was hard to photograph—broke cameras and that sort of thing. He's not an author, not an actor—"

"Imagine an actor breaking cameras," said Prout.

"—not a tennis player, not a Mdvanni—wait a minute—we're getting warm."

"He's in hiding," suggested Atlanta. "That's it. Look, see how he's got his hand over his eyes. He's a criminal. Who's wanted now? Anybody?"

The technician, Schwartz, was trying to help Roger remember—he suddenly exclaimed in a whisper:

"It's that Delannux! Remember?"

"That's it," said Roger. "That's just who it is. 'Suicide Carley.'"

"What did he do?" Atlanta demanded. "Commit suicide?"

"Sure. That's his ghost."

"I mean did he try to?"

The people at the table had all bent slightly toward each other, though the man was too far away to hear. Roger elucidated.

"It was the other way around. His *girls* committed suicide—or were supposed to."

"For *that* man? Why he's—almost ugly."

"Oh it's probably the bunk. But some girl crashed an airplane and left a note, and some other girl—"

"Two or three," Schwartz interrupted. "It was a great story."

Atlanta considered.

"I can just barely *imagine* killing a man for love, but I can't imagine slaying myself."

After dinner she strolled with Roger Clark through the lakeside arcade past the little stores with the weavings and carvings of the mountaineers, and the semi-precious stones from the Great Smokies in their windows—until they came to the Post Office at the end and stood gazing at lake and mountains and sky. The scene was in full voice now, with beeches, pines, spruce and balsam fir become one massive reflector of changing light. The lake was a girl, aroused and alive with a rich blush of response to the masculine splendor of the Blue Ridge. Roger looked toward Chimney Rock, half a mile away.

"Tomorrow morning I'll try a lot of shots from the plane. I'm going to circle around that thing till it gets dizzy. So put on your pioneer's dress and be up there—I can maybe get some things by accident."

That was as good as an order, for Roger was in control of the expedition; Prout was only a figure head. Roger had learned his trade at eighteen as an aerial photographer in France—for four years he had been top man in Hollywood in his line.

Atlanta liked him better than any man she knew. And in a moment, when he asked her something in a low voice, something he had asked her before, she answered him with just that information.

"But you don't like me enough to marry me," he objected. "I am getting old, Atlanta."

"You're only thirty-six."

"That's old enough. Can't we do something about it?"

"I don't know. I've always thought—" She faced him in the full light. "You wouldn't understand, Roger, but I've worked so hard—and I always thought I wanted to have some fun first."

After a moment he said without smiling:

"That's the first and the only terrible speech I've ever heard you make."

"I'm sorry, Roger—"

But the habitually cheerful expression had come back into his face.

"Here comes Mr. Delannux, looking tired of himself. Let's pick him up and see if he'll give you a tumble."

Atlanta drew back.

"I hate professional heart-breakers."

But as if in revenge for her recent remark Roger addressed the advancing figure, asking for a match. A few minutes later the three of them were strolling back along the beach toward the hotel.

"I couldn't make out your party," said Delannux. "You didn't exactly have a vacation air about you."

"We thought maybe you were Dillinger," Atlanta answered, "or whoever it is now."

"As a matter of fact I *am* in hiding. Did you ever try to hide? It's awful—I'm beginning to see why they come out and give themselves up."

"Are you a criminal?"

"I don't know—and I don't want to find out. I'm hiding from a civil suit and as long as they can't serve the papers on me I'm all right. For awhile I hid in a hospital but I got too well to stay there. Now you tell me why you're going to photograph this rock."

"That's easy," answered Roger. "In the picture Atlanta plays the part of a mother eagle who doesn't know where to build her nest—"

"Shut up, idiot!" To Delannux she said: "It's a pioneer picture—about the Indian wars. The heroine signals from the rock and that sort of thing."

"How long will you be here?"

"That's my clue to go in," Roger said. "I ought to be working on a broken camera. Staying out, Atlanta?"

"Do you think I'd go in unless I had to—on a night like this?"

"Well, you and Prout be up on the rock at eight o'clock—and better not try to climb it in one breath."

She sat with Delannux on the side of a beached raft while the sunset broke into pink picture puzzle pieces that solved themselves in the dark west.

"It's strange how quick everything is nowadays," said Delannux. "Here we are, suddenly sitting on the shore of a lake—"

—He's one of those quick workers, she thought.

But the detached tone of his voice disarmed her, and she looked at him more closely. Plain he was—only his eyes were large and fine. His nose was bent sideways in a fashion that gave him a humorous expression from one angle and a sardonic one from the other. His body was slender with long arms and big hands.

"—a lake without a history," he continued. "It ought to have a legend."

"But it has one," she said. "Something about an Indian maiden who drowned herself for love—" At the look in his face she stopped suddenly and finished, "—but I'm no good at stories. Did I hear you say you'd been in the hospital?"

"Yes—over in Asheville. I had the whooping cough."

"What?"

"Oh, all the absurd things happen to me." He changed the subject. "Is Atlanta really your name?"

"Yes, I was born there."

"It's a lovely name. It reminds me of a great poem, Atlanta in Calydon." He recited gravely:

> *When the hounds of Spring are on Winter's Traces*
> *The mother of months in meadow or plain*
> *Fills the shadows and windy places*
> *With lisp of leaves and ripple of rain—*

A little later he was somehow talking about the war.

"—I hadn't been within miles of the line and I was very bored and had nothing to write home. I wrote my mother that I'd just saved the lives of Pershing and Foch—that a bomb had fallen on them and I'd picked it up and thrown it away. And what did mother do but telephone the news about her brave boy to every paper in Philadelphia."

She felt suddenly at home with this man yet utterly unable to imagine his causing any devastation in the feminine heart. He seemed to have none of that quality that was once called "It" about him, only an amusing frankness and a politeness that made him easy to be with.

After awhile people came out to swim, and their voices sounded strange in the dark as they experimented with the cooling water. Then there were splashing crawls, and after that their voices again, far away on the diving tower. When they came in and hurried shivering up to the hotel, the moon was showing over the mountains—just like a child's drawing of the moon. Behind the hotel, a choir was rehearsing in a negro church but after midnight it stopped and there were only the frogs and a few restless birds and the sound of automobiles far away.

Atlanta stretched, and in doing so saw her watch.

"It's after one! And I'm working tomorrow."

"I'm sorry—it's my fault. I've talked and talked."

"I love to hear you talk. But I must go, really. Why don't you have lunch with us at Chimney Rock tomorrow?"

"I'd like to."

As they said goodbye amid the ghostly wicker of the lobby Atlanta was conscious of what a nice evening she had with him—later, before she went to sleep, she remembered a dozen indirect little compliments he had given her—the kind that one could remember with a pleasant shimmer. He made her laugh and he made her feel attractive. Had he possessed the special quality of being "thrilling" she could even imagine some girl falling for him a little.

"But not me," she thought sleepily. "No suicide for me."

II

On top of Chimney Rock, which is a great monolith breaking off from the mountains like the spout of a teapot, about twenty persons can stand and look down at ten counties and a dozen rivers and valleys. This morning Atlanta looked down alone upon miles of green wheat and light blue rye and upon cotton fields and red clay and terribly swift streams capped with white foam. By noon she had looked at plenty of scenery while the airplane zoomed round and round the rock, and she was hungry when she descended the winding steps to the restaurant, and found Carley Delannux and a girl on the terrace.

"You looked nice up there," he said. "Sort of remote and unimportant—but nice."

She sighed; she was weary.

"Roger made me climb those steps three times *running*," she said. "I think it was punishment for sitting up last night."

He introduced his companion.

"This is Miss Isabelle Panzer—she wanted to meet you and since she saved my life I couldn't refuse her."

"Saved your life?"

"When I had whooping cough. Miss Panzer's a nurse—just *barely* a nurse—I was her first case."

"My second," the girl corrected him.

It was a lovely discontented face—if ever the two can go together. It was very American and rather sad, mirroring an eternal hope of being someone like Atlanta without either the talent or the self discipline that makes strong individuals. Atlanta answered some shy questions about Hollywood.

"You know as much about it as I do," she said, "—if you read the magazines. All I know about pictures is someone says to climb up a rock and so I climb up a rock."

They waited to order lunch, until Roger could arrive from the landing field at Asheville.

"The way I feel is all your fault," said Atlanta, looking reproachfully at Delannux. "I didn't get to sleep until four."

"Thinking about me?"

"Thinking about my mother in California. Now I need diversion."

"Well, I'll divert you," he suggested. "I know a song—do you want to hear it?"

He went inside and presently some chords drifted out with his voice.

I'd climb the high-est mountains—

"Stop!" she groaned.

"All right," he agreed. "How's this one—"

—I love to climb a mountain
And to reach the highest peak—

"Don't do it," she begged him.

Tourists were droning up from the highroad to the restaurant; Roger Clark arrived and they ordered luncheon on the terrace.

"I want to hear what Delannux is hiding from," Atlanta announced.

"So do I," Roger said, relaxing from his morning with a glass of beer.

"We come here and he picks us up—" Atlanta continued.

"You picked *me* up. Here I come to hide—"

"That's what we want to know about," Roger's tone was cheerful but Atlanta saw that he was regarding Delannux quizzically. "Have you got a bear after you?"

"My past is a sort of bear."

"We haven't got any pasts in pictures," said Atlanta, mollifying the turn of the conversation.

"Haven't you? It must be great to be that way. I've got enough past for three people—you see I'm a sort of survival from the boom days—I've lived too long."

"Sort of a luxury article," suggested Roger mildly.

"That's it. Not much in demand any more."

Underneath his light tone Atlanta detected a certain discouragement. For the first time in her life she wondered what it felt like to be discouraged. So far she had never known anything but hope and fulfillment. From the time she was fourteen there were always picture people coming into her father's drug store in Beverly Hills and promising to get her a test. And finally one of them had remembered.

Discouragement should be when you didn't have money or a job.

With Delannux on the hotel porch after dinner that night she asked him suddenly:

"What did you mean when you said you'd lived too long?"

He laughed but at her seriousness he answered:

"I fitted in to a time when people wanted excitement, and I tried to supply it."

"What did you do?"

"I spent a lot of money—I backed plays and tried to fly the Atlantic, and tried to drink all the wine in Paris—that sort of thing. It was all pointless and that's why it's so dated—it wasn't *about* anything."

Roger came out at ten o'clock and said somewhat gruffly:

"I think you ought to turn in early, Atlanta. We're working at eight tomorrow."

"I'm going right away."

She and Roger walked upstairs together. Outside her room he said:

"You don't know anything about this man—except that he has a bad reputation."

"What junk!" she answered impatiently. "Talking to him is like talking to a girl. Why, last night I almost went to sleep—he's harmless."

"I've heard that story before. It's a classic."

There were steps on the stairs and Carley Delannux came up. He paused on the landing a moment.

"When Miss Downs goes to bed the lights go out," he complained.

"Roger was afraid I'd got drowned last night," said Atlanta.

Then Roger said something utterly unlike himself.

"It did cross my mind that you were drowned. After all, you were out with Suicide Carley."

There was a hushed awful moment. Then Delannux made a lightning motion with his hand and Roger's head and body slapped back against the wall.

Another pause, with Roger half stunned keeping on his feet only with the aid of his back and palms against the wall and Delannux facing him, hands by his side clenched and twitching.

Atlanta gave a whispered cry:

"Stop! Stop!"

For another instant neither man moved. Then Roger pushed himself upright and shook his head in a dazed way. He was the taller and heavier of the two and Atlanta had seen him throw a drunken extra over a five foot fence. She tried to wedge herself between them but Clark's arm brushed her aside.

"It's all right," he said. "He was perfectly right. I had no business saying that."

She drew a breath of relief—this was the Clark she knew, generous and just. Delannux relaxed.

"I'm sorry I was so hasty. Good night."

He nodded to them both and turned away toward his room.

After a minute Clark said, "Good night, Atlanta," and she was standing alone in the hall.

III

"That's the end of Roger and me," she thought next morning. "I never loved him—he was only my best friend."

But it made her sad when he did not tell her when to go to bed the next night, and it was not much fun now on location or at meals.

Two days of rain arrived and she drove with Carley Delannux back into the hills and stopped at lost shacks trading cigarettes for mountain talk and drinking iron water that tasted of fifty years ago. Everything was all right when she was with Carley. Life was gay or melancholy by turns but it was at all times what he made it. Roger rode along with life—Carley dominated it with his sophistication and humor.

This was the season of flowers and she and Carley spent a rainy day fixing up a float to represent Lake Lure for the Rhododendron Festival in Asheville that night. They decided on a sailboat with a sea of blue hydrangeas and an illuminated moon. Seamstresses worked all afternoon on old-fashioned swimming costumes; and Atlanta turned herself into a stout bathing beauty of 1890, and they telephoned the little nurse, Isabelle Panzer, to be a mermaid. Roger would drive the truck and Atlanta insisted on sitting in front beside him. She was inspired to this gesture by the vague idea, peculiar to women in love, that her presence would cheer and console the other man.

The rain had stopped and it was a fair night. In Asheville their float took its place in the assembling parade—there had already been one parade in the afternoon and the streets were littered with purple pink rhododendrons and cloudy white azaleas. Tonight was to be Carnival, wild and impudent—but it was soon apparent that to plant an old world saturnalia in the almost virgin soil of the resort was going to be difficult; the gaiety was among the participants rather than in the silent throngs from the mountains, who gathered on the sidewalks to watch the floats move by in the shaky and haphazard manner peculiar to floats, with great silent gaps, and crowdings and dead halts.

They lurched along the festooned streets between a galley manned by those vague Neros and sirens that turn up in all parades and a straggling battalion that featured the funny papers. This last provoked comment from critical youth on the sidewalks:

"You s'posed to be Andy Gump?"

"Hey, you're too fat for Tillie the Toiler!"

"I thought Moon Mullins was s'posed to be funny!"

Atlanta kept thinking that Carley would have brought the scene alive to her somehow if only with mockery—but not Roger.

"Cheer up!" she urged him, "We're supposed to be jolly."

"Is this jolly? Are we having fun?"

She agreed that they weren't but she resented his lack of effort.

"Did you expect a million dollar super-film? You've got to *make* things fun."

"Well, you're doing your part all right—and the crowd is going to have a circus next time you move. Then the *whole* top of your bathing suit is going to fall off."

"Good Lord!" She grabbed at her back, and finding nothing, simply tipped over backward into the bottom of the float, rolling through the flowers until she could get space to pull the flimsy garment together. Above her and almost beside her were two figures—Miss Panzer on a rocky throne and Carley, holding a pitch-fork trident. While Atlanta patched the rip, she tried to catch what he was saying, but only fragments floated down to her. Then as she sat upright and hunched her back to test the adjustment she heard Isabelle Panzer say:

"You didn't tell me you loved me but you made me think so."

Atlanta stiffened and sat still as still, but his reply was lost in the explosion of a distant band.

"Didn't you know what I was risking," the girl continued. "When I was still a student nurse I sat in the solarium with you night after night and if the superintendent had come up I'd have been finished."

Again Atlanta could hear only an indistinguishable murmur from him.

"I know I'm just a small town girl to you. But all I want to know is why did you make me love you so?"

Now Carley turned his head and Atlanta heard his words plainly.

"Nevertheless it's a pretty high dive from Chimney Rock."

—then Isabelle again.

"I don't care if it's five thousand miles—if you don't love me there isn't any living. I'm going to climb up there and see how quick I can get to the bottom."

"All right," Carley agreed. "Please don't leave any notes addressed to me."

IV

Back in the seat with Roger, Atlanta stared out at the receding crowd, neglecting now to wave or to be gay. There was a faint drizzle in the air again and people were putting coats and papers over their heads; autos honked imperatively from parking spaces and the bands died one by one at the corners, their instruments giving out last gleams as they were cloaked against the increasing rain.

The Lake Lure party hurried from the float to their car—Atlanta got in front beside Roger. When they dropped Isabelle at her apartment, Roger asked her: "Don't you want to sit in back?"

"No."

They drove out of the city facing a splitting windshield in silence.

"I'd like to talk to you," she said finally, "but you're so cross with me."

"Not any more," Roger said. "I couldn't get that way twice."

"Well, something's happened that seems terrible and—"

"That's too bad," he interrupted sympathetically. "But since you'll be back with your mother in just a week now, you can tell her about it."

At his coldness Atlanta instinctively began a sort of emergency primping, wiping the clown's paint from her face, removing pads from her waist, shaking her wet hair wild and combing it to an aura around her head. Then bending forward into the faint dashboard lights she begged him:

"Let me ask you one thing."

"Not tonight, Atlanta. I haven't recovered from the shock."

"What shock?"

"The shock of finding that you're just another woman."

"I'm going to ask you one thing—did anybody ever really kill them-selves because they loved someone too much? I mean do you think so?"

"No," he said emphatically. "Why? Are you planning to kill yourself for Mister De Luxe?"

"Don't talk so loud. But listen, there have *been* people who've done that, haven't there?"

"I don't know. Ask one of the script writers back home—they'll tell you. Or ask Prout. Hey, Prout—"

"Don't start a row again!"

"Then let's don't talk."

The car passed Chimney Rock and pulled up at the hotel in a drip-ping quiet. They had been on the road an hour but it seemed only a minute to Atlanta since she had heard Isabelle Panzer's voice on the float. She was not angry—her feeling was one of overwhelming grief—and in the midst she felt perversely sorry for Delannux.

But when he asked in the lobby if everyone was absolutely deter-mined to go to bed—a question obviously aimed to her—she said hastily:

"I'm for the tub. I've never felt so uncomfortable."

But she could not sleep. For the first time in her life, for better or worse, she was emotionally wide awake, trying by turns to analyze her passion for the man, to argue him from her mind, to think what should be done. Had Roger not been concerned she would have gone to him and asked him—but now there was no one. Toward morning she dozed—to awake with a start before seven. One glance at a som-ber window told her there would be no work for a few hours anyhow, and her maid confirmed the fact on her arrival. Atlanta got listlessly into her bathing suit and went down to the lake for a dip, swimming on an unreal surface that existed between a world of water like mist and a drizzling firmament of air. She went up to the hotel and breakfasted and dressed, and then it was almost nine o'clock. Downstairs she read a letter from her mother, and for a moment stood with Prout on the verandah.

"Roger's in a bad humor," he announced. "He's got camera parts laid all over his bed."

"Maybe he's lucky to have something to do on a rainy day."

Presently she went into the lobby and asked the number of Mr. Delannux's room. When she knocked at his door and when he answered "Yes?" she called:

"Why don't you ever get up? Do you hide all day? Are you an owl?"

"Come in."

Inside the door she stopped. The room was full of luggage in disarray and Carley was in the process of helping a boy belt down a suitcase.

"I thought you'd be resting," he said. "I thought on a rainy day—"

"What are you doing?" she demanded.

"Doing?" He looked a little guilty. "Oh, as a matter of fact I'm leaving. You see, Atlanta, I'm safe now and I can go back to the great world."

"You said it'd be a week more."

"You must have misunderstood." She stood stock still in the middle of the floor as he went on talking. "You know when you knocked I jumped. You might have been the process server after all."

"You said you had a week more," she repeated stubbornly.

The negro boy shut the bag with a click. His eyes turned interrogatively toward Delannux—

"Come back in fifteen minutes," Carley said.

The boy closed the door behind him.

"Why are you going?" Atlanta demanded, "—without saying anything to anybody? I come in and find you with your bags all packed." She shook her head helplessly. "Of course it's none of my business what you do."

"Sit down."

"I will not sit down." She was almost crying now. "It even looks as if you did your packing in ten minutes—look at all those shoes. What do you think you're going to do with them?"

He glanced at the forgotten shoes on the wardrobe floor—then back at Atlanta's face.

"You were going without saying goodbye," she accused him.

"I was going to say goodbye."

"Yes—after you had all your bags in the car, and there was nothing to be done about it."

"I was afraid I'd fall in love with you," he said lightly. "Or you'd fall in love with me."

"You needn't worry about that."

He looked at her with a flash of amusement.

"Come here close," he said.

A small voice inside told her that he was trying some power of his on her, that he was just perversely playing. Then another and, it seemed, a stronger voice forgave him for that, made her interpret his command as a desperate cry of need.

He repeated:

"Come here."

—and she took a step forward.

"Come closer."

She was touching him and suddenly her face was reaching up to his. Then at the end of the kiss he kept her close with the pressure of his hands along her inside arms . . .

"So you see I think I'd better go away."

"It's absurd!" Atlanta cried. "I want you to stay! I'm not in love with you—honestly! But if you go I'll always think I drove you away."

She was so transparent now that she was not even ashamed—meaning him to see the truth underneath. "I'm not jealous of Miss Panzer. How could I be? I don't care what you've done—"

"I can understand Isabelle thinking she liked me—because she hasn't got anything. But you've got everything. Why should you be interested in a battered old wreck?"

"I'm *not*—yes, I guess I am." She had a burst of unusual eloquence. "I don't know just why—but all of a sudden you're just all the men in the world to me."

He sat down—his face was tired and drawn.

"You're young." He sighed, "—and you're beautiful. You've got your work—and you've got any man you want for the asking. Do you remember when I told you that I belonged to another age?"

"It isn't true," she wailed.

"I wish it weren't. But since it is, anything between you and me would be all dated—sort of mouldy." He stood up restlessly. "You think I could live in your nice fresh world of work and love. Well, I couldn't. We'd last about a month and then you'd be all bitter and dented—and maybe I'd care. And that might be tough for me."

He looked up and faced her helpless love.

"Can't you imagine somebody who'd had the best experiences in the world not wanting any more—not wanting love to be real love? Can you imagine that? I even resent your beauty because now I'm old—but once I had what it takes to love a girl like you—"

There was a knock at the door. Prout was there, his eyes darting from one to the other.

"It's clearing off outside," he said. "Roger told me to find you right away."

Atlanta pulled herself together. In the doorway she paused and told Carley:

"I'll be back in a minute. You won't go till I see you. You promise?"

"Of course."

"Then I'll be right back. You can drive me over to Chimney Rock."

A moment later, down in Roger's room, she was listening to his instructions like a woman in a dream. The minute he was finished she dashed back up the stairs and, with a quick knock, entered Carley's room.

But it was empty.

V

She hurried down to the desk, to be told that Delannux had paid his bill and gone out to the garage—perhaps had driven off by now. Breathlessly she sped out the door, down the drive through a light rain. She was outraged, furious with herself and him. She turned a corner . . .

—and there he was, talking to a mechanic in front of the garage.

She leaned against the damp rain on the garage door, gasping with her emotion.

"You said you wouldn't go."

"Seems I can't."

"You told me you'd wait."

"I have to. One of the washers took my car out for a joy ride, and broke a wheel. It'll take two days to get another."

Roger Clark's car was being driven out of the garage—Atlanta still had many things to say, but there was no time. All she could think of was:

"Women must come easy for you if you can do this. I don't think you like women—you pretend to, but you don't. That's why you can do what you want with them."

She heard Prout's "Halloo!" from in front of the hotel. That was her signal and she went quickly.

All day, as they worked, she planned and planned. But it was like a condemned criminal planning to escape, but always distracted from his schemes by the sound of keys turning in locks around him—or by the hope that reprieve would come from outside, with no effort on his part. Plans are difficult at such moments—Atlanta could only wait for an opportunity. Nevertheless, clouds of fragmentary possibilities were around her head. Perhaps Carley didn't have much money—maybe he would be glad of a chance in Hollywood. He had been a rich jack-of-all-trades—perhaps he could be placed as a specialist in an advisory capacity.

Or, failing this, she could go East and try for a big part on the stage, train with a famous teacher—there she would at least be in touch with Carley.

Her reasoning came to wreck upon the single rock that he did not love her.

But the full force of this didn't come home to her until she got back to the hotel in the evening—and found he was not there. Before the end of dinner she went to her room, and cried on her bed. After half an hour her throat hurt and no tears started unless she forced them; then she turned on her back and said to herself:

"This is what's called infatuation. I used to hear about it, how it was just love without any sense to it, and the thing to do was to get over it . . . But just let them try it . . ."

She was tired; she called her maid to rub her head.

"Don't you want to take one of those pills?" the maid suggested. "The ones that made you sleep when you had the fractured arm."

No. Better to suffer, to feel the full poignancy of the knife in her heart.

"How many times did you knock at Mr. Delannux's door?" Atlanta asked restlessly.

"Three or four times—then I asked downstairs and he hadn't come in."

—He's with Isabelle Panzer, she thought. She's telling him how she's going to die for love of him. Then he'll be sorry for her and think I'm just trivial—a little Hollywood pet.

The thought was intolerable. She sat bolt upright in the bed.

"Give me some of the sleeping stuff after all," she said. "Give me a lot of it—all that's left."

"You were only supposed to take one at a time."

They compromised on two and Atlanta sank into a doze, but waking now and then in the night, she was haunted by a dream—of Isabelle dead, and of Delannux hearing the news and saying:

"She loved me enough—so much that the world wasn't good enough for her afterwards."

Next morning found her with a hangover from the sedative—she had no energy for her usual dip. Dressing in a state of lethargy she rode to location without a thought, realizing that the others were looking at her with the concern reserved for people who are "upset."

She hated that, and contrived a more cheerful front through the morning hours, laughing at everything, though it seemed as if all of her was dead except her heart, and that was pumping her bloodstream around at a hundred miles per hour.

About four they went down to the restaurant for a sandwich. Atlanta was raising hers to her mouth when Prout made his unfortunate remark.

"Delannux got the wheel for his car," he said. "I saw it arrive when I went for the carpenter."

In a moment she was on her feet.

"Tell Roger I'm sick! Tell him I can't work to-day! Tell him I've borrowed his car!"

She dropped down the corkscrew to the main road at the speed of a roller coaster, and drew up at the hotel three minutes later—almost beside the bus from Asheville. And there, disembarking, dusty and hot and tired, was Isabelle Panzer. Atlanta caught up with her on the hotel steps.

"Can I speak to you a minute?"

Miss Panzer seemed taken back by the encounter.

"Why, yes, Miss Downs, I suppose so. I came to see Mr. Delannux."

"What does a minute more or less matter now?"

The two women sat facing each other on the verandah.

"You love him, don't you?" said Atlanta.

Isabelle broke suddenly.

"O God, how can *you* ask me that—when it's you he loves now—it's you he left me for—"

Atlanta shook her head.

"No. He doesn't love me either."

"Neither of you mean anything when you talk about love."

To be spoken to like that by a child—a girl who had endured less in all her nursing course than Atlanta had sometimes endured in a day.

"*I* don't know what love means?" she exclaimed incredulously.

She felt a sound in front of her eyes, like a miner's lamp exploding. Something must be done about the whole matter immediately—

And then Atlanta knew what to do: she must make words real at last, put into action all she had ever thought, dreamed, pretended, been ordered to do or tempted to do, justify all that was superficial or trivial in her life, find the way to supreme consecration and consummation at last. It was plain as plain.

Deliberately she went over to the other girl and kissed her on the forehead. Then she went down the steps, climbed into Roger's car, and drove off.

Chimney Rock restaurant was empty after the session of the day's traffic—and, as she had hoped, there was no sign of the picture outfit.

She left the key in the car and started to leave a note but she did not know any longer exactly what she had wanted to say—anyhow she had left her purse at home with the pen in it.

Her feet and legs were stiff from the day's climbing—well, she would leave her shoes behind like the evil queen in the *Wizard of Oz* who had been all burned up except her shoes. She kicked them to one side and put her foot experimentally on the first step—it was cool to her foot—it had seemed warm in the afternoon even through her soles.

As she began to climb she became increasingly conscious of the rock looming above. But maybe it would be like jumping into a basket of many colored skies.

VI

Roger came up on the porch less than five minutes after Atlanta had left. Isabelle was sitting there.

"Good evening," he said. "Waiting to see Delannux off?"

"Something like that."

—Why didn't she say anything? he wondered. Why did she sit like that? Was there a pistol in her handbag?

There was a bustle of departure in the lobby—in a moment Carley Delannux and baggage came out on the porch.

"Goodbye, Delannux," Roger said, without offering to shake hands.

"Goodbye, Clark." He seemed scarcely to notice Isabelle—a car stopped at the door and he went forward to meet the mechanic.

"How's the wheel?"

He broke off. "Excuse me, I thought it was someone else."

"This is Delannux," cried Isabelle suddenly.

There was a moment of confusion. Then the man who had come up the steps reached forward, tucked a white sheet in Carley's pocket and said:

"This paper is for Mr. Delannux. Don't bother to read it. I can tell you what it is. It's a *Capias ad Respondum*. That means I've got to take you North with me on a little matter of director's responsibility."

Carley sat down suddenly.

"So you got me," he said. "And in about four more hours you couldn't have served that paper."

"No sir—not after midnight to-night. The Statute of Limitations—"

"How did you find me? How did you even know I was in North Carolina?"

But suddenly Carley stopped, knowing very well how the process server had found him—and Roger realized too. Isabelle gave a broken little cry and covered her eyes with her hand.

Carley threw her an expressionless look, without even contempt in it.

"I'd like to see you alone," he said to the process server. "Shall we go up to my room?"

"All right by me, but I warn you I'm not for sale."

"It's just to arrange certain things about leaving."

When they had gone Isabelle wept on silently.

"Why did you do it?" Roger asked mildly. "It'll ruin him, won't it?"

"Yes. I guess so."

"Why did you want to do that?"

"Oh, because he was so bad to me, and I hated him so."

"Aren't you a little sorry?"

"I don't know."

He thought for a moment.

"You certainly must have loved him a lot to have hated him that much."

"I did."

He was terribly sorry for her.

"Don't you want to go and lie down in Atlanta's room for awhile?"

"I'd rather lie on the beach, thank you."

After he watched her depart he still sat there. She turned and called back to him.

"You'd better look after your own girl," she said. "She's not in the hotel."

VII

Roger sat alone rocking and thinking. He loved Atlanta, no matter how little she had given him to love lately.

—She's not here, he said to himself.

He sat there thinking and thinking, with a mind accustomed only to technical problems.

—She's a fool. All right then—I love a fool.

—Then I ought to go and find her because I think I know where she is. Or shall I sit on this porch rocking?

—I'm the only living human being that can take care of her.

"Let her go!"

"I can't—" He spoke aloud at last, saying what most men have said about a woman one day—and most women about a man: "I happen to love her . . ."

He got up and ordered a hotel car, hurrying a little as he got in with the sense that it might be too late. He drove quickly to Chimney Rock and up the mountain to the restaurant, as far as the car could go. As he began the climb a thought dogged his steps.

—Up toward nothing or perhaps toward a life of future misery and unhappiness, of other Carleys.

He stopped at a turning, and looked at the starlight, and started on again counting Eighty-one, Eighty-two, Eighty-three. After that he stopped counting.

When he reached the top at last he was frantic with worry. All his self control, all his restraint, all that made him a forceful person had left him as he mounted those last steps and came out into the open sky. What he had expected to see he could not have said.

What he saw was a girl eating a sandwich.

She was sitting with her back against one of the iron posts that supported the rail.

"Is this Roger?" she demanded. "Or do my eyes deceive me?"

He leaned against the rail, panting.

"What are you doing up here?" he asked.

"Enjoying the stars. I've decided to become an eccentric—you know—like Garbo. Only my stuff will be mountain tops. When we finish this picture I'm going to Mount Everest and climb—"

"Make sense!" he interrupted. "What did you come up here for?"

"To throw myself over, of course."

"Why?"

"For love, I guess. But I happened to have this sandwich with me—and I was hungry. So I thought I'd eat first."

He sat down across from her.

"Are you interested in anything that's happening down below in the mere world?" he enquired. "If you are, you might as well know that they got Carley."

"Who did?"

"The process server—the one that had been looking for him. It was a tough break. If he'd kept hid till midnight he couldn't have been served—Statute of Limitations, or something."

"That's too bad. How did it happen? How did they find where he was?"

"Guess."

"I can't—it wasn't you."

"Good God, no! It was the Panzer girl."

She thought a minute.

"Oh, so that's what she was waiting for."

There was silence for a moment on top of the rock.

"Why on earth did you think I'd do a thing like that?"

"I didn't after I thought. Excuse me, Roger."

"But I did have Mr. de Luxe looked up."

"What did you find out?" Her query was detached, impersonal.

"Nothing much—except there wasn't any girl who killed herself about him. A certain Josephine Jason he was engaged to found she had pleuro-cancer—that means the lining of the lungs are gone—and she crashed on purpose. You can't blame Carley."

"Oh, I'm so tired of Carley, Roger. Couldn't we let him alone for awhile?"

He smiled to himself in the darkness.

"What changed your mind—the sandwich?"

"No, I guess it was the rock."

"Too high for you?"

"No—it seemed somehow like *you*. After I got up on top it seemed as if I was standing on your shoulders. And I was so happy doing that, I didn't want to leave."

"I see," he said ironically.

"I somehow knew you wouldn't let me. I wasn't a bit surprised when you came up the steps."

He grabbed her hands and pulled her to her feet.

"All right," he said. "Come on. We'll go back to the hotel—I'm worried about the little Panzer—let's see where she is."

She followed him down the steps; at the bottom, as he dismissed the hotel car and they got into his, Atlanta said:

"No, it doesn't seem to matter about him any more."

"It matters about everybody."

"He can probably take care of himself, I mean."

When they reached the hotel and found what had happened—that Carley Delannux had somehow locked the process server in his room in a state of bruised coma and driven off, Atlanta said:

"You see? He'll be all right. Maybe they won't catch him this time."

"Won't *catch* him—they've caught him. If you're served with one of these writs and don't show up, you're a fugitive from justice. Anyhow, let Rasputin solve his own problems. I'm worried about what he left behind him—this girl. We didn't pass a car or a person between here and Chimney Rock—and there's no bus."

Atlanta guessed suddenly.

"She's on the lake. I chose Chimney Rock so she chose—"

But he was already running toward the boathouse.

They found her an hour later, drifting very quietly in the moonlight of a small cove. Her face upturned seemed placid and reconciled, almost as if surprised at their presence—in her hand, like Sesame of the Lilies, was clutched a bunch of mountain flowers—much as Atlanta's hand had clutched a sandwich half an hour ago.

"How did you find me?" she called from her canoe.

As the launch sailed alongside, Roger said:

"We wouldn't have—if I hadn't had some portable flares with me. You'd be drifting still."

"I decided I didn't want to go overboard. After all, I've got my certificate now."

Long after Roger had gotten her a taxi, and pressed on her the money to go back to her people in Tennessee for awhile—long after he and Atlanta became one of the many untold legends of Lake Lure, the best kind, and he had left her outside her door—he walked down through the arcade past the little shops of the mountaineers and up to the post office, where there was nothing beyond save the bottomless black pools that were rumored to hold black secrets of Reconstruction days.

There he stopped. He had heard in the lobby what he had not wanted Atlanta to hear to-night—that what was left of Carley Delannux had been picked up at the foot of Chimney Rock an hour ago.

It was sad that the season of Roger's greatest happiness was ushered in by this tragedy of another man, but there must have been something in Carley Delannux that made it necessary for him to die—something sinister, something that had lived too long, or had been too long dead on its feet, and left corruption in its wake.

Roger was sorry for him; he was a slow-thinking man but he knew that what was useful and valuable must not be sacrificed to that. It was good to think of Atlanta, who meant starlight to so many people, sleeping safely in a room a hundred yards away.

•

FSF on a mountain road in North Carolina.

This undated fragment, "Day Off from Love," written in 1935 or 1936, is a character study of men and women, of the sort Fitzgerald could do so very well. Set in the Southern Appalachians, it is about a young engaged couple, Mary and Sam. She has lived a lifetime already, before they met, and suggests they maintain a certain distance, taking a day off from each other every week as their wedding approaches. She rambles in the mountains and meets an older, worn, yet fascinating man who is rather like Carley Delannux in "I'd Die for You." But Fitzgerald, in "Day Off from Love," is more interested in the woman. In some important ways, Mary is a prototype for Cecilia in *The Last Tycoon*. Fitzgerald had long been dissatisfied with the way he wrote women characters, complaining to Max Perkins in December 1924, before *Gatsby*'s publication, that Jordan "fades out" and apologizing for Myrtle being "better than Daisy." Mary has a vividness, vitality, and self-knowledge that make one wish Fitzgerald had finished this story beyond a chapter-length sketch.

*The trouble is of course that
I forgot the real idea — this
is Nora, or the world, looking at me*

DAY OFF FROM LOVE

by

F. SCOTT FITZGERALD

On the afternoon they decided to marry they walked

through the wood over damp, matted pine needles, and rather

hesitantly Mary told him her plan.

"But now I see you every day," Sam mourned.

"Only this last week," Mary corrected him. "This was

because we had to find out whether we could be together

all the time and not--not---"

"Not drive each other mad," he finished for her,

"You wanted to see if you could take it."

"No," Mary objected, "Women don't get bored the same

way men do. They can sort of shut off their attention--but

they always know when men are bored. For instance, I knew

a girl whose marriages lasted just so long--until she heard

herself telling her husband a story she'd told him before.

Then she went to Reno. We can't have that--I'm sure to

Written across the top of the typescript in pencil, in Fitzgerald's
hand: "The trouble is of course that I forgot the real idea—
this is Nora, or the world, looking at *me*."

Day Off from Love

On the afternoon they decided to marry they walked through the wood over damp, matted pine needles, and rather hesitantly Mary told him her plan.

"But now I see you every day," Sam mourned.

"Only this last week," Mary corrected him. "This was because we had to find out whether we *could* be together all the time and not—not—"

"Not drive each other mad," he finished for her. "You wanted to see if you could take it."

"No," Mary objected, "Women don't get bored the same way men do. They can sort of shut off their attention—but they always know when men are bored. For instance, I knew a girl whose marriages lasted just *so* long—until she heard herself telling her husband a story she'd told him before. Then she went to Reno. We can't have that—I'm *sure* to repeat myself. And we'll *both* have to take it."

She repeated even now a gesture that he loved, a sort of hitch at her skirt as if to say, "Tighten up your belt, baby. Let's get going—to any pole." And Sam Baetjer wanted her to repeat on the same costume forever—the bright grey woolen dress with the scarlet zipper vest and lips to match.

Suddenly he guessed something. He was one of those men who seem eternally stolid, even unobserving—and then announce the score added up to the last digit.

"It's because of your first marriage," he said. "And I thought you never looked back."

"Only for warnings." Mary hesitated, "Pete and I were close like that—for three years—up to the day he died. I was him and he was me—and at the end it didn't work—I couldn't die with him." Again she hesitated, not sure of her ground. "I think a woman has to have some place to go inside herself—like a man's ambition."

So there was always to be a day off from love, a day in every week when they were to live separate geographical lives. And there was to be no talking over those days—no questions.

115

"Have you a little one hidden away?" Sam teased her. "A twin brother in the pen? Are you X9? Will I ever know?"

When they came to their destination, a party in one of those elaborate "cabins" that dot the Virginia foothills, Mary took off her scarlet vest and stood with her feet planted far apart before the great fire, telling the friends of her youth she was going to be married again. She wore a silver belt with stars cut out of it, so that the stars were there and not quite there—and watching them Sam knew that he had not quite found her yet. He wished for a moment that he were not so entirely successful nor Mary so desirable—wished that they were both a little broken and would want to cling together. All the evening he felt a little sad watching the intangible stars as they moved here and there about the big rooms.

Mary was twenty-four. She was a professor's daughter with the glowing exterior of a chorus girl—bronze hair and blue green eyes and a perpetual high flush that she was almost ashamed of. The contrast between her social and physical equipment had set her many problems in the little college town. She had married a professor whom there was no special reason for marrying and made a go of it—so much so that she had come near to dying with him, and only after two years had found the nights unhaunted and the skies blue. But now marrying the exceptional young Baetjer, who was reorganizing coal properties just over the West Virginia line, seemed as natural as breathing. The materials are all here, she knew, weighing things in her two handed way, and love is what you make of it.

* * *

The next Tuesday too she went to the mountain village, a county seat—a court house square with its cast iron Confederate soldier and a movie house, its population male and female in blue denim and the blue ridge rising as a back-drop on three sides. This time she felt she had rather exhausted its possibilities—the purely physical side of her disappearance act would be when Sam took his seat in Congress this fall. Once the little town had been a health center in a small way. There was a sanitarium on a hillside above and a little higher up the central building of what in 1929 was to have been a resort hotel. She asked about it and was told that all the beds had been stolen, the furniture disappeared little by little, and looking again at [the] white shell in its magnificent location she drove up there idly in the late afternoon.

"—anyhow in the opinion of a poor widow woman," she told the stranger up at Simpson's Folly.

"In theory," said the stranger, "But in theory this fellow Simpson could have made this the greatest resort hotel in the country."

"There was the depression," said Mary, looking around at the empty shell, high on its crag—a shell from which the mountaineers had long removed even the plumbing.

"You had your depression," ventured the stranger, "and look at you now, as full of belief and hope as if it was all a matter of trying. Why on your first day off—even before you're married you meet a man, or the remnants of one. Just suppose we fell in love and you met me up here every week. Then that day would grow more important than all the six days you spent with him. Then where's your plan?"

They sat with their legs hung over a cracking balustrade. A spring wind was sweeping up warm from the valley and Mary let her heels swing with it against the limestone.

"I've told you an awful lot," she said.

"You see—you're interested. Already I'm the man you told a lot to. That's a dangerous situation—to start out with a trust that people spend weeks working up to."

"I've been coming up here to think for ten years," she protested. "It's the wind I'm talking to."

"I suppose so," he admitted. "It's a hell of a good wind to sass—especially at night."

"Do you live up here?" she asked in surprise.

"No—I'm visiting," he answered hesitantly. "I'm paying a visit to a young man."

"I didn't know anyone lived here."

"No one does—the young man is—or rather was myself."

He broke off. "There's a storm coming."

Mary looked at him curiously. He was in his middle thirties and all of six feet four, a gaunt man with a slow way of talking. He wore high-laced hunting boots and a chamy windbreaker that matched his brown rather ruthless eyes. About his face was some of that cadaverous look that lingers after a long illness and he lit a cigarette with unsteady fingers.

Ten minutes later he said:

"Your car won't start and it's a four hour job. You can coast down to the garage at the foot of the hill and then I'll drive you into a town."

They were quiet on the way in. A day of deliberately absenting herself turned out to be a long time, and she felt a twinge of doubt about the whole plan. Even now as they drove along the principal street toward her father's house it was only six o'clock with an evening to dispose of.

But she toughened herself—the first day was the hardest. She even kept an eye on the sidewalks with the mischievous hope that Sam would see her. The stranger at least had a hint of mystery.

"Pull over to the curb," she said suddenly. Just ahead of them she had seen Sam's roadster slowing up. And as both cars stopped she perceived that Sam was not alone.

"Yonder is my love," she said to the stranger. "He seems to be having a day off too."

He looked obediently.

"The pretty girl with him is Linda Newbold," said Mary. "She is twenty and she made a great play for him a month ago."

"You're not disturbed?" the stranger asked curiously.

She shook her head.

"They left jealousy out of me. Probably gave me a big dose of conceit instead."

FSF (with his broken shoulder)
and his nurse at the Grove Park Inn.

"Cyclone in Silent Land" is one of his stories influenced by Scott's and Zelda's time in hospitals. It is the first of a series Fitzgerald planned about a student nurse who rejoices in the name of Benjamina Rosalyn—"Trouble to her friends"—and the young intern, Bill Craig, who loves her. Her beauty, to the beholders, jeopardizes her career though she is smart and professional: Trouble is essentially too attractive to be borne by the staff or the patients. The "silent land" in the title not only equates Trouble with a cyclone in the hushed world of a hospital, but also sounds a movie allusion that becomes stronger in the increasing action sequences, when little or nothing is said. The shift from silent movies to talkies is something to which Fitzgerald gave much thought, as the Pat Hobby stories have long shown.

Fitzgerald was proud of "Cyclone in Silent Land," telling Harold Ober on May 31, 1936, "When I finished that story I felt absolutely sure it was the best story I had written in a year." He very much wanted it to be published, and was looking forward to writing more stories about Trouble. But though in need of money, he was determined not to submit to any requests for revisions, and wanted it to be printed as he had written it. If the *Saturday Evening Post* had the temerity to turn it down "on such grounds as purely moral ones" or any other, he told Ober, Ober should alter their longtime arrangement of offering Fitzgerald's stories to the *Post* first. To say he felt strongly about this is understatement: "I'd rather put Zelda in a public insane asylum and live on *Esquire's* $200 a month."

On June 29, 1936, the *Post's* editor, George Lorimer, and fiction editor, Adelaide Neall, asked for revisions, with Neall saying, "Personally, this last piece encouraged me a great deal because it shows that Mr. Fitzgerald still can write the simple love story, free of the melodrama that he introduced into his recent manuscripts." Fitzgerald did not revise it, and the *Post* declined "Cyclone in Silent Land." He also held the line on its sequel, "Trouble," writing to Neall in October 1936, "I have thought that you underestimated *Trouble* as a story, and if you can make any possible constructive suggestion about it, please do so, but I like it as it stands now." The *Post* then belatedly accepted "Trouble," which was published in the March 6, 1937, issue. It was the last of Fitzgerald's stories in the *Post*, after nearly two decades of regular appearances there.

CYCLONE IN SILENT LAND

by

F. Scott Fitzgerald

"Why don't you just pull the socks off? Get an orderly to help you. Good Lord, that's what I'd do if a patient kept me up all night with idiotic calls."

"I've thought of that," Bill said. "I've tried to think of everything in my whole medical training. But this man is a big shot--"

"You're not supposed to pay any attention to that--"

"I don't mean just rich--I mean he has the air of being a big shot in his own profession like Dandy and Kelly in ours--"

"You're nervous," said the other interne. "How're you going to lecture to those girls in two hours?"

"I don't know."

"Oh, lie down and get some sleep. I've got to get over to the bacteriology lab and I want to get some breakfast first."

"Sleep!" Bill exclaimed. "I've tried it plenty times tonight. Soon as I get my eyes closed that ward rings."

"Well, do you want some breakfast?"

Bill was dressed--or rather hadn't been undressed all night. Harris had finished dressing and after adjusting his

Cyclone in Silent Land

"Why don't you just pull the socks off? Get an orderly to help you. Good Lord, that's what I'd do if a patient kept me up all night with idiotic calls."

"I've thought of that," Bill said. "I've tried to think of everything in my whole medical training. But this man is a big shot—"

"You're not supposed to pay any attention to that—"

"I don't mean just rich—I mean he has the air of being a big shot in his own profession like Dandy and Kelly in ours—"

"You're nervous," said the other interne. "How're you going to lecture to those girls in two hours?"

"I don't know."

"Oh, lie down and get some sleep. I've got to get over to the bacteriology lab and I want to get some breakfast first."

"Sleep!" Bill exclaimed. "I've tried it plenty times tonight. Soon as I get my eyes closed that ward rings."

"Well, do you want some breakfast?"

Bill was dressed—or rather hadn't been undressed all night. Harris had finished dressing and after adjusting his necktie suggested to Bill Craig:

"Change your whites. You're mussy."

Bill groaned.

"I've changed them five times in two days. You think I run a private laundry?"

Harris went to a bureau.

"Put on these—they ought to fit—I used yours plenty times last fall. Come on now. Slip into these—breakfast is on the schedule."

Bill pulled himself together and started living on his nervous system—enough to live on, for it was solid and he was a good physical specimen with a tradition of many doctors behind him; he struggled into the proffered whites.

"Let's go. But I think I ought to leave some word for this man on the way."

123

"Oh, forget it. Come on—we'll have breakfast. A man that won't take off his socks!"

But Bill was still fretted as they went out into the corridor.

"I don't feel quite comfortable. After all the poor guy hasn't got anybody to depend on except me."

"You're going sentimental."

"Maybe."

And now up the corridor came Trouble, Trouble so white, so lovely, that it didn't identify itself immediately as such. It was sheer trouble. It was the essence of trouble—trouble personified, challenging . . .

. . . trouble.

Starting to smile a hundred feet away it came along like a flying cloud—began to pass the internes, stopped, wheeled smart as the military, came up to both of them and figuratively pressed against them. All she said was:

"Good morning, Dr. Craig, morning Dr. Machen."

Then Trouble, knowing she'd done it, leaned back against the wall, conscious, oh completely conscious of having stamped herself vividly on their masculine clay.

It was a curious sort of American beauty, very difficult to show the charm of it because it was the blend of many races. It was not blonde, nor was it dark; it had a pride of its own; it was rather like the autumn page from the kitchen calendars of thirty years ago with blue instead of brown October eyes. It went under the registered name of Benjamina Rosalyn—Trouble to her friends.

What more did she look like? To the two internes she looked like a lovely muffin, like the cream going into the coffee in the breakfast room.

This all happened in a moment. Then they went on, Bill insisting after all on stopping at the desk and leaving a note as to where he could be found.

"You're going nuts about that old man," Harris warned him. "Why don't you concentrate on clipping his sympathetic nerves like we're going to do tomorrow? That's when he really will need help."

Miss Harte at the desk was saying:

"It's a call for you from Ward 4, Dr. Craig. Do you want to take it?"

Harris pulled him toward the dining room but Bill said:

"I'll take it."

"You've got to lecture in half an hour. You'll miss your breakfast."

"Never mind. It's from Room 1B, isn't it?"

"Yes, Dr. Craig."

"Gosh, I'd like to hear your lecture to those probationers," said Harris disgustedly. "But go on—boys will be boys."

Bill went into 1B on Ward 4. Mr. Polk Johnston, robust and fifty, sat up in bed.

"So you came," he said gruffly. "They said you probably wouldn't but you're the only person here I can trust—you and that little nurse they call Trouble."

"She's not a nurse—she's only a probationer."

"Well, she looks like a nurse to me. Say, what I called you here for is to know the name of that operation again."

"It's called sympathectomy. By the way, Mr. Johnston—let me take that sock off, will you?"

"No," the man roared. "I thought you were doctors, not chiropodists. I'll keep my sock on. If you think I'm crazy how did I make my money?"

"Nobody thinks you're crazy. Now Mr. Johnston, I've got to go along and lecture—I'll be back."

"How soon?"

"Say an hour."

"All right then. Send the little girl."

"She'll be at the lecture too." Bill escaped on the old man's groan.

The hospital was housed in three buildings connected by cloisters of plane trees and bushes. When Bill came outdoors on his way to the classroom he stopped for a moment, leaning against a protrudent branch. What was this feeling of intense irritation—maybe he was never meant to be a doctor.

"But I've got the physique for it," he thought. "I've got the courage—I hope I have. I've got the intelligence. Why can't I kill this nervous business?"

He went on, pushing a bush out of his way.

"I've got to face these girls as something. Pull yourself up, Bill, my boy. You were hand picked for this lecture job and they're going to be plenty other patients to run you ragged."

From where he was in the green cloister he could see the probationers flocking into class, twenty of them, and he took advantage of the fact to organize the few words that would inaugurate his lecture while they examined the rabbit. The rabbit was anesthetized, the heart exposed and ready to respond to adrenalin, to digitalis, to strychnine. The girls would take their seats and regard the phenomenon. They were nice girls, ignorant as a rule, but nice. He knew some doctors who didn't like trained nurses.

. . . Forty years ago, those doctors said, girls went into this because they had heard about Florence Nightingale and a life of service. Many still did go in for it in that spirit, others simply went in for it. The best hospitals tried to weed these out. It took three years to be a nurse—in one more year you could be a doctor. If a woman was serious why not take the whole thing? But then Bill thought:

"Poor kids. Half of them haven't any sort of education to start with, except what we give them . . ."

The flock of girls were in. With his notes and two books under his arm he followed.

"Sweet heaven!" he exclaimed, and decided to wait by the door till they quieted down. For a moment he looked over the parapet, over miles of morning, thinking again about himself. Then, at the moment when he started to go into the classroom, the green skirt of a probationer blew out the door frantically.

"Dr. Craig—" she panted.

"What's the excitement?"

"You ought to see what! It's about the rabbit."

"Now listen. Calm down. Now what?"

He couldn't tell whether the girl was laughing or crying. His exasperation came to the fore—figuratively he took her by the shoulders and shook her.

"What nonsense! What on earth?"

He marched her into the classroom before him. An echolalia of idiotic laughter filled his ears—and he pushed his way through to the center of it crying: "What's the matter?"

—and came upon Trouble. There she was in all her gorgeous beauty, standing beside the rabbit split for dissection, weeping wildly.

He couldn't believe his eyes that it was she—because in spite of being God's gift to men she had shown more promise than any other probationer.

—A girl suddenly fainted at his side and he pulled her up. Hysteria had swept the room and he saw that this girl had caused it by the sheer force of her personality—this girl who knocked him sidewise every time he saw her. All in a split second he decided not to shout, but he spoke through gritted teeth.

"You bunch of quitters," he said. "You bunch of quitters!"

He was losing control of himself and he knew it, but he went on.

"You're trying to *help* people—and you're scared of a dead rabbit. You—"

The girl, with all the beauty going out of her face, managed to throw her shoulders back and face him.

"I'm so sorry, doctor," she sobbed. "But I kept rabbits when I was a girl and here's this little bunny—split open—"

Then he said the word—a big word. It did not deny that they were females but it denied that they belonged to the race of *homo sapiens*, but rather a certain four-footed tribe. Even as he heard it resound about him, the door opened and the superintendent of nurses came in.

He looked at her—all the temper rilled suddenly out of him.

"Good morning, Mrs. Caldwell."

"Good morning, Doctor." He saw in her face that she had heard, that she was shocked and amazed.

"All you students go out of here," he said. "Wait on the terrace. Lecture's postponed for a few minutes."

There was a confused moment with the girls trying to apologize, and not knowing whom to apologize to. They realized that something epochal had happened, that they had been sworn at by a doctor, but they didn't know how to evaluate the act or estimate the consequence.

"Why, Dr. Craig!" Mrs. Caldwell said. She came up to him almost like Trouble in the corridor.

"Why, Doctor—have my ears mistaken me or did I hear you use that word to those girls—" she faltered on the pronouncement of it. Her very fooling about with it renewed his exasperation, and he hinged his career on his arrogant answer.

"You bet you heard it."

"And those young innocent girls—and you say that in front of them. I know where my duty lies!"

"Go and do it then."

"I certainly shall, Dr. Craig. And I prefer that the lecture be called off this morning."

Bill sat down in the deserted classroom. Perhaps he shouldn't have been a doctor, he thought again. He had no intention of apologizing or of trying to fix it up in any way. They would fire him. That was almost certain. He would go and say goodbye to Mr. Polk Johnston and Harris; he'd try to keep them from firing Trouble.

. . . That's where he stopped thinking, simply stood there looking out the window, his hand sometimes absently touching the rabbit. He was very glad his father was dead—his father had been a doctor.

II

Bill sat across the desk from the superintendent, half an hour later.

"Now, Doctor Craig—exactly what *did* happen?"

"I lost my temper and swore at them."

Dr. Haskell arose and took a few steps down the room, and then back to his chair. He was a fair man; Bill had always liked him.

"Go on fire me, sir," he said. "I know I deserve it."

"All right. I'm going to fire you. I'm glad you're going to take it that way. I knew your father—"

"Oh, please skip that. You're not going to penalize anybody else, are you?"

"Well naturally. Mrs. Caldwell inquired around and Miss Rosalyn's got to go. Not that that excuses you."

"She's as good now as any graduate nurse in the hospital."

"Yes," said Dr. Haskell dryly, "it seems too bad."

"And I want to tell you something about Johnston."

"Who's he? How does he come into this case? What department's he in? Is he an orderly?"

"No, he's a patient."

"Oh, you mean Mr. Polk Johnston, the hypertensive. Now you're making sense. What about him?"

"I'd like to tell you about him."

Dr. Haskell who had sat down got up again:

"We know about his socks that he won't take off." He said, "We know he's rich as Croesus, and his people control some American hospital. He and his brother are in Shanghai or Canton. Have you anything to add to that?"

"Just this: I know he's awful scared and he may try to stall off the thing. If he leaves here without an operation something tells me he's not long for this world—"

The door opening interrupted Bill. It was the private secretary.

"Dr. Haskell, it's Mrs. Caldwell, and she has that nurse with her. I can't seem to remember her name—the pretty one they call Trouble."

"I don't want to see them now. Anyhow I thought Mrs. Caldwell was taking care of that herself."

"Let them come in, sir, please," Bill begged suddenly.

"I don't see why I should."

"Please, sir," Bill repeated.

The secretary looked from one to the other—at the young desperate face, at Dr. Haskell deciding.

"Oh, let them in then."

"Thanks," Bill said.

Mrs. Caldwell and Trouble were both rather white; all the lovely color had left Trouble's face till it was pale as the white fur of the rabbit that had caused the scene this morning.

The older woman spoke.

"Now, Dr. Haskell—"

She was interrupted by Bill's voice:

"Now Mrs. Caldwell, do you think it's just to dismiss a girl for one small attack of nerves?"

Dr. Haskell turned to him and said: "Will you be quiet, sir?"

"Thank you, Dr. Haskell," said Mrs. Caldwell. "Lately, he's been the most difficult, the most difficult—"

"The most difficult what?"

"Well, I can't stand swearing. I was brought up on a farm in the Pennsylvania hills and we never learned those tough words. How am I expected to stand them—I—I—"

The younger nurse was at her side now: "Oh, Mrs. Caldwell—don't worry about it now."

Dr. Haskell had nodded at the door, and Bill catching the gesture, got up and closed it.

Mrs. Caldwell got control of herself. "This girl is just too pretty, that's all," she said.

"*What!*" Dr. Haskell demanded.

"You know it, everybody knows it. She's too pretty for this."

"Since when did that disqualify anyone?" Dr. Haskell said. "It seems to me I've seen hundreds of pretty nurses in my time."

"I should hope so," said Bill.

"I wasn't speaking to you, Dr. Craig. I was under the impression you'd resigned."

Then they all spoke at once:

"Excuse me," said Bill.

"I guess it was all my fault," said Trouble.

"No wonder they all call you 'Trouble'," said Mrs. Caldwell.

"I thought this was supposed to be a hospital!" thundered Dr. Haskell.

But Bill was not to be subdued. The sweet parting of the young girl's hair as she had bent over Mrs. Caldwell moved him intolerably, and he knew the long hours, the daily nursing, the hard duty that was the lot of the probationer as they learned their little beginnings of anatomy and chemistry. There was more excuse for her break than for his.

"I'll apologize to Miss Rosalyn for the language I used, if that'll help her case," he said. "She certainly didn't do enough to provoke what I said."

"But you didn't apologize to me," said Mrs. Caldwell.

"I will if it'll help her."

"And I thought at first you were very much of a gentleman," said Mrs. Caldwell.

"I thought maybe I was, but I guess I was wrong."

"That'll do, Dr. Craig," said the superintendent. "This has been very unfortunate. I bid you goodbye, sir, and wish you the best of luck in the future."

With a despairing look at Trouble Bill turned quickly and left the room.

And now it was Trouble's turn. And she knew very well that she was being punished just as much for her flirtations as for her attack of nerves this morning. Well, to these people medicine was an idol, and she had stuck chewing gum around the alabaster pedestal . . .

"We will refund your tuition," said Dr. Haskell gently.

She went back to her room and faced herself in the mirror. Throwing herself on her bed she wept for a moment; then she got up and packed her bag, the same bag she had once carried as a hoofer on the four-a-day.

"And here I am," she said, terribly sorry for herself, "just because I wanted to be something more than just good to look at."

There was an extra package to be made of left-overs and she had quivered the last string into place when an orderly knocked at the door.

"You're wanted at 1B on Ward 4."

"Yes I am. I'm leaving. I'm fired."

"Well, they told me to tell you."

"All right."

She closed the door. Then she realized suddenly that she still had on her nurse's uniform.

—All right, she thought, "I'll go down and tell that old Johnston I *will* marry him. He's thought of nothing else for a week."

On the way downstairs she passed a young nurse who grabbed at her arm as she passed.

"We're all so sorry, Miss Rosalyn."

She was touched, but the same sort of ill-humor that had possession of Dr. Craig this morning made her say:

"Call me Trouble, please."

"All right, 'Trouble' then, we're all sorry."

The ward was deserted. She could see no one at the desk but it didn't worry her. She didn't hesitate. She took a deep breath, made an instinctive motion at her sides as if brushing off something and went into the room.

The room was empty.

So was the bed. It had been stripped clean of sheets and blankets—the evidence of what had been done with them was bound about the bureau which had been laid on its side to hold the improvised rope trailing over the window-sill into the dark afternoon. Mr. Johnston had escaped.

She reacted simply and spontaneously.

—The man must have been crazy with fright, she thought. He'll kill himself trying to get through that gravel pit down there. In his condition!

She hadn't shinnied since she was a baby but once she was over the sill the knotted cords between sheet and sheet helped her, and when she fell on her face at the end she didn't feel her nose to see if it wobbled.

"My face never brought me any luck," she said to herself as she started across country. "I hope it's ruined."

For a moment she almost believed herself but she was woman enough to cross her fingers.

Bill Craig came into the room less than two minutes after Trouble had left it. He saw exactly what she had seen but his first instinct was to ring the patient's bell. When a nurse arrived he said:

"Do you know anything about this?"

"Why, Dr. Craig! He seemed all right this morning and Miss Rosalyn went in to say goodbye so I went for a quick coffee—"

"Miss Rosalyn was here?"

"Yes, sir."

"Well, notify the ward interne what's happened, will you?"

"Yes, Dr. Craig."

He waited till she was gone before climbing out the window.

It had been a red morning, and now it was a rapidly darkening afternoon as Bill turned into the station. The station lights were on and his borrowed whites seemed yellow in the light of half-burned out lamps. Unless a train had already carried the old man away he expected to see them both there: he understood Mr. Polk Johnston's flight from the operation and he was almost sure that Trouble had either fled with him or followed him. The station was the natural destination—he left it to the hospital staff to search their own vicinity—for himself he scarcely looked out the window of the cab he caught on the outskirts of the small city.

In a minute he spotted them across the dingy waiting room, and turning into the cafeteria watched them through the smoky glass. She was sitting very still on her corner of the bench, her lovely eyes cast down gazing at nothing. As always he seemed to see something new in her. Trouble has that awesome quality, Trouble and Beauty, of showing new facets without preparation. People who passed her, salesmen, casual travelers, stopped for the break of an instant, stared, and then went on . . .

Bill finished his coffee and stood up from the counter, thankful to Harris for the whites—when he had accepted them it was without any idea of what the day would offer. They were scarcely soiled, scarcely mussed. As he approached the pair on the bench he saw that Mr. Polk Johnston, on the contrary, showed signs of his recent experience. What had looked to Bill like a swarm of bees incomprehensibly gathered upon him presently developed as a great gathering of burrs. They clung around him, as unnecessary epaulets on his shoulders and shin-guards on his knees; a full cluster adhered to his waist line and service stripes of them trailed down his cuffs.

They were engrossed in conversation when he addressed them.

"Good afternoon, Mr. Johnston. Good afternoon, Miss Trouble."

Mr. Johnston looked at him with startled eyes. "And what are *you* doing here?" he demanded. "—did they send you after me?"

"No, I came of my own accord."

Johnston relaxed.

"What did you do to your nose?" he inquired.

"Well, you see, Mr. Johnston, that ladder you made wasn't strong enough for three people in succession and the joke was on me. One of the knots gave way half way down."

Trouble laughed.

"I could have made it better," said Johnston resentfully, "if I had the time."

Bill had a picture of the whole hospital swarming suddenly out the window and down Mr. Johnston's rope-ladder.

"How long have you been here?" he asked.

"About twenty minutes," said Trouble. She looked at her wrist watch. "It took me about an hour—I got a bus at the city limits."

"I hitch-hiked," said Mr. Johnston complacently. "I got here only five minutes after she did."

"I got a taxi," said Bill, "and came in a poor third. We ought to enter the Olympics like Bonthron and Venski and Cunningham."

"Hm!" said Mr. Johnston. He did not seem as friendly as upon previous occasions—in fact Bill got the sense that his presence was considered an intrusion.

"I'm not going to the Olympics," Mr. Johnston continued, "in fact my intention is to go to Tibet this summer. I understand they have a drug that relieves high blood-pressure without this crazy operation."

"That's a long way," said Bill.

"Oh, I'm not going alone. Miss Trouble has just consented to go with me—in the capacity of my wife."

"I see," said Bill, but he felt his face re-set in a curious uncomfortable way.

"I see you don't like the idea," said Johnston observantly. "Old man's darling and all that. Well, why didn't you ask her when you had the chance?"

And then suddenly Bill did ask her, not in so many words but by looking straight into her rather stricken blue eyes.

"Internes are not in a position to ask anyone to marry them."

Trouble hardened protectively.

"You to ask me, Dr. Craig! You that only this morning referred to us as—"

"Can't we skip that," said Bill. "We're out of the hospital now. Anyhow I guess I've intruded."

"You certainly have," said Trouble, trying desperately to make her eyes fall into line with her bitter voice. What was her choice—back to rock with her mother on the porch of a farmhouse through the best days of her life, or back with her sister making three night stands in movie houses from Bangor to Tallahassee?

So engrossed was she with her thought that only Bill's eyes, leaving hers suddenly, made her look at Mr. Johnston. He was dead white, the left side of his face was twitching in time to his right hand and arm which played an invisible drum. Bill grabbed his shoulders just in time to keep him from slumping to the floor.

"Stay with him!" he ordered abruptly. "I'll get coffee."

III

He sent it back at a run by the cafeteria waiter and phoned the police emergency department for an ambulance. When he came back a small crowd had gathered.

"Stand back!" he ordered without raising his voice. "This man is very sick indeed."

"What are you going to do?" Trouble demanded.

"Wait for the ambulance. Did he take all the coffee—pour it all into him, Trouble."

"I couldn't quite. I could feel his pulse in his shoulder. He just about hasn't got any."

"I didn't think he would." Again he motioned the crowd away from the bench, and beckoned the huskiest bystander.

"Give me a hand, will you? I'm going to try artificial respiration."

He straddled the man and went through the motions. Just when he was sure it was hopeless he caught the quiver of a reaction beginning; simultaneously Trouble said in his ear:

"The ambulance orderlies have come. What shall I do?"

"Have them stand by."

"Yes, Doctor."

"Need any help, sir?" one of them asked.

"No—just keep that crowd back."

Life was returning to Mr. Johnston—it came in a gasp, a lurch, then a sudden grasp on his faculties that made him realize his predicament, try unsuccessfully to sit up and almost with his first breath begin to gasp orders.

"Who are all these people? Take them away! Have them removed."

"You lie down." Bill smiled inwardly, as he climbed off the resuscitated torso, thinking: "What does he suppose they are, waiters?"

"Off we go," he said to the orderlies. "You brought in a stretcher of course."

"Yes, sir."

"Well, load him on. We go to the Battle Hospital."

He started to follow, somewhat exhausted by his exertion. He felt alone; then he saw what was the matter—Trouble was hanging back.

"Am I supposed to go?"

"Come on, you idiot. Of course you are. Hurry up. They've got him in."

"Do you think anybody there would ever want to see you and me again?"

"Come on now. Don't be stupid."

In the darkness of the ambulance Mr. Polk Johnston weakly demanded a cigar.

"I don't think they furnish them," said Bill.

"Then I want to go in some ambulance where they do. You ought to know—you're the only doctor any good out there."

"Well, I don't think I can supply you with—"

Dr. Craig never finished that sentence. He was tossed forward precipitately to land on the chair ahead in the approximate straddling position he had used on Mr. Johnston. He saw Trouble flying past him at the same jolt, heard her yelp as she took it on a shoulder against the unbreakable glass. Mr. Johnston was flung up and back like a doll. It was a full minute before Bill could reach around the darkness of the ambulance and get out to see what had happened—then he saw plenty.

They had been run into by a school bus which lay, burning, half on its side against a tall bank of the road, with the little girls screaming as they stumbled out the back. He made a lunge for one who was afire, bumped into Trouble who had chosen the same one and rolled over on to another, beating at the flames with his hands. The two orderlies being in front had guessed the situation earlier and were already at it.

"Is there anyone left inside?" Bill cried after the first wild moment.

Simultaneously he saw that there was one, and acting deliberately wrapped a handkerchief around his palm and smashed the glass. The ambulance driver put his thick gabardine coat over the sill and they dragged the little girl over it. Bill was burning himself and he rolled for a moment in a wet ditch. Half a dozen other cars had come up and they had help now. A quick roll call of the girls by one of them showed no one missing.

"Anyone who lives close go for some flour," Bill said. "You girls pile into the ambulance—all of you. One of you orderlies stand by the door and see that no clothes are still smoldering. Don't let anyone you're not sure of get into that ambulance."

"Yes, Doctor."

"Then go on, quick as you can. Emergency Ward."

"How about you, sir?"

"I'm all right. I'll get someone to take me."

He went back to the ditch and plastered his hands with wet mud— then he discovered Trouble beside him doing the same.

"Let's get a hitch right over," he said. "I think maybe they'll let us in now, don't you?"

"How about Mr. Johnston?"

"I hadn't thought about him. He's off to the hospital in the ambulance. I hope they're not sitting all over him."

"They're not. The orderlies lifted him out to make room. He's lying over across the road."

"Alive?"

"Very much so. They've tried twice to get him into that car."

"The old devil. I'll get that sock off him now or know the reason why."

He repeated this remark as he knelt to take Johnston's pulse.

"No, you won't," Johnston answered.

"Why won't I?"

"Because it's off. I felt sort of ashamed the way you people have to work, so I thought I'd do that for you."

Bill stooped to the exposed foot.

"Well, I'll be a son-of-a-gun. It's nothing but a supernumerary toe!"

"You think that's nothing! It's worried me all my life."

"We'll take it off tomorrow."

Bill stood up. He breathed.

"So that's all it was. Well, it'll cost you the expenses of all these little girls."

"No," insisted Mr. Johnston, obstinate as ever. "It'll cost me enough to build you a pediatric wing for your damn hospital—if they'll take you back. You and your girl."

Fitzgerald is still this side of Paradi[se]

Francis Scott Key Fitzgerald (post-War apostle of the younger generation) and Frances Scott, his contribution to our younger generation: he is at work on a series of medieval short stories, and there is talk of "Tender Is the Night" as a play

Scott and Scottie, 1937.

In late 1935 Fitzgerald began a series of stories about a girl in her early teens. Just the age of Scottie Fitzgerald at the time, Gwen, with her "bright blue eyes" and eager, curious ways, and her interest in boys, good northeastern colleges, and New York City, has much in common with the Scottie one sees in Fitzgerald's well-known letters to her.

He wrote to Harold Ober in mid-December,

This story ["Too Cute for Words"] is the fruit of my desire to write about children of Scotty's age. . . . I want it to be a series if the *Post* likes it. Now if they do please tell them that I'd like them to hold it for another one ["The Pearl and the Fur"] which should preceed [*sic*] it, like they did once in the <u>Basil</u> series. I am not going to wait for their answer to start a second one about Gwen but I am going to wait for a wire of encouragement or discouragement on the idea from you.

Although Fitzgerald was recovering from a terrible case of flu during which he spat up blood, he was in good spirits about his work: "I enjoyed writing this story which is the second time that's happened to me this year, + that's a good sign." He worked hard on the story and its revisions through the spring; Ober was enthusiastic about the Gwen idea, not least because he thought it could save Fitzgerald from a return to writing for the movies: "I think it is much wiser for you to work on this series than to try Hollywood so let's forget that."

The *Post* accepted Fitzgerald's first Gwen story, "Too Cute for Words," and published it on April 18, 1936, without waiting, as Fitzgerald had wished, for "The Pearl and the Fur," which was meant to precede it. Instead, they turned down "The Pearl and the Fur," asking for substantial changes. Discouraged, Fitzgerald worked on the screenplay of "Ballet Shoes" for a while instead, telling Ober, "I've spent the morning writing this letter because I am naturally disappointed about the *Post*'s not liking the Gwen story and must rest and go to work this afternoon to try to raise some money somehow though I don't know where to turn." Fitzgerald's own money struggles are reflected here in Gwen's family: her father has lost money in the Depression and, evidently, has to deny her many things.

Fitzgerald soon returned to "The Pearl and the Fur," but declined the suggestions for revisions supplied to him by Ober and Ober's assistant Constance Smith. Ober disliked the whole taxi ride south, and the desolate beauty of Fitzgerald's imagined Kingsbridge: "A good deal of the taxicab material seems to me improbable. . . . I have checked up on the subway station at Kingsbridge and 230th Street and it is as closely settled as any part of New York City. The subways leave every three or four minutes. If anyone were in a hurry to get from 230th Street to 59th Street one would never think of taking a taxicab and there are no subway terminals that are in unpopulated districts as you describe." Smith objected, "Why would anyone take a chinchilla coat to the West Indies in Spring?" When the *Post* rejected the story again, Fitzgerald refused to resubmit it there. Ober's files indicate that three versions of it were destroyed on May 14, 1936. The *Post* did publish one more story featuring Gwen, "Inside the House," on June 13. Six days earlier, "The Pearl and the Fur" had been sold to the *Pictorial Review* for $1,000, with the characters' names changed so it would no longer be a competing "Gwen story." It never appeared, and the *Pictorial Review*—at the beginning of the decade a popular women's magazine with a circulation of 2.5 million—failed in the spring of 1939, a casualty of the Depression.

THE PEARL AND THE FUR

by

F. Scott Fitzgerald

Gwen had been shopping all Saturday afternoon and at six she
came home heavy laden. Among other things she had purchased two
dozen little tin cylinders to attach to her hair at bedtime and let
dangle through the night; a set of grotesque artificial finger nails
which violated all disarmament treaties; a set of six inch pennons
of Navy, Princeton, Vassar and Yale; and a packet of travel booklets
describing voyages to Bermuda, Jamaica, Havana and South America.

Wearily--as weariness goes at fourteen--she cast it all on
the couch and phoned her friend Dizzy Campbell.

"Well, guess what?" she said.

"What?" Dizzy's voice was full of excitement. "Was it real?"

"It was not," said Gwen disgustedly, "I took it to the jewel
man at Kirk's and he said it was just a piece of shell that they
often have in oysters."

Dizzy sighed.

"Well, then we don't go for a trip this Easter."

"I'm so mad I can scarcely see. Daddy was sure it was a
pearl when he almost broke a tooth on it in the restaurant."

"After all we'd planned," Dizzy lamented.

"I was so sure that I went to the travel bureau first and got
a lot of books with the best pictures of people sitting around swimming pools on the deck and dancing with the cutest boys only seventy
dollars minimum--if Daddy would listen to reason."

They sighed audibly in full mutual comprehension.

The Pearl and the Fur

Gwen had been shopping all Saturday afternoon and at six she came home heavy laden. Among other things she had purchased two dozen little tin cylinders to attach to her hair at bedtime and let dangle through the night; a set of grotesque artificial finger nails which violated all disarmament treaties; a set of six inch pennons of Navy, Princeton, Vassar and Yale; and a packet of travel booklets describing voyages to Bermuda, Jamaica, Havana and South America.

Wearily—as weariness goes at fourteen—she cast it all on the couch and phoned her friend Dizzy Campbell.

"Well, guess what?" she said.

"What?" Dizzy's voice was full of excitement. "Was it real?"

"It was not," said Gwen disgustedly, "I took it to the jewel man at Kirk's and he said it was just a piece of shell that they often have in oysters."

Dizzy sighed.

"Well, then we don't go for a trip this Easter."

"I'm so mad I can scarcely see. Daddy was sure it was a pearl when he almost broke a tooth on it in the restaurant."

"After all we'd planned," Dizzy lamented.

"I was so sure that I went to the travel bureau first and got a lot of books with the best pictures of people sitting around swimming pools on the deck and dancing with the cutest boys only seventy dollars minimum—if Daddy would listen to reason."

They sighed audibly in full mutual comprehension.

"There is one thing, though," said Dizzy, "—though it isn't like the other. Mrs. Tulliver wants to take four or five girls from school to New York for a few days. Mother says I can go but I said I'd tell her later because I was waiting to hear about the pearl—Father said it probably wouldn't be any good if it was cooked anyhow. This would be better than nothing."

"I guess so," said Gwen doubtfully. "But you don't suppose she'd take us to the Rainbow Room and places like that, would she? Would it just be kind of museums and concerts?"

"She'd take us to the theatre and shopping."

Gwen's bright blue eyes began to come back to life.

"Well, I'll ask Daddy," she said, "He ought to do *that* anyhow after being wrong about the pearl."

II

Five young ladies of fourteen and fifteen rode to New York the following Monday. Mrs. Tulliver's original plan was to stop at an inn for women only, but upon their vehement protest that they wanted music with meals they put up at a "quiet" hotel in the fifties. They saw two plays and went to Rockefeller Center, bought summer clothes according to their allowances and had a touch of night life in the afternoon by going to a hotel famous for its tea dances and listening to a favorite orchestra play, though they had no partners of their own.

All of them had tried to provide against this contingency by pledging boys to "come up if you possibly can" and even writing frantic letters to long neglected swains met last summer that they would be in the great city on a certain date. Alas, though they leapt at the sound of the telephone it was invariably one of their rooms calling the other.

"Heard anything?"

"No. Had one letter—so sorry and all that sort of thing."

"I had a wire from a boy in New Mexico."

"Mine was from California. Isn't there ever anybody in New York?"

It was all pretty tame, Gwen thought, though they enjoyed themselves. The trouble was not so much the lack of boys as the impossibility of doing anything very gay and glamorous without boys. On the next to the last day Mrs. Tulliver called them together in her room.

"Now I'm not blind or deaf and I know you haven't had all the excitement you expected, though I didn't promise we'd paint the town red. Still I don't want you to feel you've been chaperoned to death so I have a little plan."

She paused and five glances were bent on her expectantly.

"My plan will give you a few hours of complete independence and it ought to be useful when school opens again."

The gleam went out of the ten young eyes, though they still gave formal attention.

"Now tomorrow morning I want each of you to go out by herself and make an investigation of some part of New York—find out all about it so you could write a composition if you had to—though I'm not going to ask you that in vacation. I'd say go in pairs but I know you'd find out much more if you went by yourselves. You're old enough for such an adventure. Now don't you think it sounds sort of fun?"

"I'll take Chinatown," Gwen volunteered.

"Oh, no, no!" said Mrs. Tulliver hurriedly, "I wasn't thinking of anything like that. I meant something more like the Aquarium for instance though I want each of you to invent some individual experience."

Gathered by themselves the clan debated the matter cynically. Dizzy complained: "If she'd let us go out at night, each to a different night club and bring back our reports in the morning then there'd be some sense to it. I don't know what to do—we've been up in the Empire State and we've seen the flower show and the Planetarium and the flea-circus. I think I'll just go over to the Ritz Hotel and inspect that. You always hear about things being 'Ritzy' and I'd like to see about it."

Gwen had a plan formulating in her head but she did not mention it. The idea of a trip was persistently in her mind, a trip with a set destination perhaps, but nevertheless a voyage, sharply different from the stationary life of school.

I'll get on a 5th Avenue bus, she thought, and go as far as that goes. And then I'll get on a street car or elevated and go as far as that goes.

At nine next morning the troup embarked on their separate destinies. It was a fine day with the buildings sparkling upward like pale dry ginger ale through the blue air. An officious woman sitting next to her on top of the bus tried to begin a conversation but Gwen quelled her with a steely regard and turned her eyes outward. The bus followed Riverside Drive along the Hudson and then came to a region of monotonous apartment rows, which embody the true depths of the city, darkly mysterious at night, drab in the afternoon and full of bright hope in the morning. Presently they had reached the end of the line. Gwen asked a question of the conductor and he indicated the mouth of a subway half a block down the street.

"But isn't there an elevated?" she demanded.

"The subway gets to be an elevated part of the time."

The northbound train for Kingsbridge was almost deserted. Kingsbridge—Gwen could see it already: great mansions with Norman keeps and Gothic towers. Southampton was probably somewhere around here and Newport, all such fashionable places, which she vaguely supposed resembled the outlying sections of her own city.

At Two hundred and thirtieth Street she followed the last two passengers out into Kingsbridge—and found herself on a bleak plain, scarred with a few isolated "developments," a drug store, a gas station and a quick lunch. Going up a little hill she looked back with some pride over the distance she had come. She was actually at the dead end of New York—even in the chrystaline air the skyscrapers of Manhattan Island were minute and far away. She wondered if Dizzy was really rowing a boat on Central Park Lake or if Clara had gone to enroll herself in a theatrical casting agency—this last having been Gwen's suggestion. They were somewhere within that great battlement of a city and she was without, as detached as in an aeroplane.

Gwen looked at her watch and discovered she had been traveling a long time—she could just get back in time for one o'clock lunch. Returning to the subway she saw the train by which she had come gathering momentum as it left the station. A negro cleaning the platform told her there would be another one in an hour.

—Here's where I miss the matinee, she mourned. And it was the last one.

"Do they have taxies out here?" she asked.

"They's a stand by the drug store, but ain't usually no cabs around."

She was in luck, though. A single taxi stood there and beside it was the driver, a very young man wearing an expression of some anxiety. When Gwen asked him if he was free this seemed to clear away, as if her words were an open-sesame to something and he said with obvious eagerness:

"I certainly am free. Walk right in—I mean step right in."

Shutting the door after her he got in front.

"Where do you want to go?"

She named her hotel. He produced a little red book, brand new, and thumbed through it.

"Madison and Fifty-fifth Street," he announced.

"I could have told you that," said Gwen.

"Yes—I suppose you could. I'm not very familiar with the city yet. Excuse me for being so dumb."

He sounded rather nice.

"Don't you live in New York?" she asked.

"I do now, but I'm from Vermont. What's that street again—Madison and—?"

"Madison and Fifty-fifth."

He started the motor and as quickly shut it off—turned around apologetically.

"I'm sorry, there'll be a short delay. This is what they call a dead-head—"

"Something wrong with the car?"

"No—nothing wrong with the car. In the taxi business they call this a dead-head and when you're at one you've got to call up the office and say you're leaving."

With that he was out of the car and into the quick lunch shop, whence presently she heard his voice saying something inexplicable over the phone. Presently he was back inquiring:

"You're not the miscall, are you?"

"The what?"

"The party that called and then took the subway instead. That's why I'm a dead-head."

Their eyes met and stared gravely. Gwen was the first to appreciate the situation.

"I still don't know what a dead-head is," Gwen protested, "But how could I have called a taxi and then taken the subway and still be here?"

"That's right," he admitted. "You see a dead-head is—"

"I know—it's a man that takes drugs."

"No, that's a hop-head," he corrected her. "A dead—"

"I think we ought to start," she suggested primly.

"Oh, that's right."

Obediently he climbed in the driver's seat again. But as they started off he was constrained to turn around once more.

"I might as well tell you frankly: This is the first time I've ever driven a cab. Oh, don't be scared," he added at her alarmed expression, "I didn't say a car, I said a cab. It just happens it's my first day—you've got to start somewhere."

Still perturbed Gwen demanded as they drove off.

"How old are you?"

"Seventeen—I mean eighteen—" He looked back at her quickly, dodging a milk wagon, "I'm sixteen, if you want to know. I've got a driver's license but the company only takes you at eighteen, so I said I was eighteen to get the job."

After a few miles they reached the first out-lying apartment houses, first an isolated sextet of green-gray brick, then two forlorn streets on an ambitious scale save that where they should have led into a public square and a fountain, they slipped coyly into a rubble field, as though they had suddenly forgotten. In one of these rural intervals he volunteered:

"You asked me what was a dead-head. Well, I've just got it straight myself. It's when you report that you're going somewhere without a passenger or else when they send you where there *might* be a passenger and you have to wait and see. I didn't know but what they might be kidding me this morning because I was a new driver, sending me out there. And on my first day I didn't want to be wasting time—"

"Yes," Gwen said.

She was not listening. For several minutes her eyes had focused straight before her, but not on this morning's dream of endless peregrination.

"—They seem to mean two things by it," the young driver continued, "They mean—"

Gwen reached down suddenly and drew it up over her knees. At first she had taken it for a robe; but it didn't look like a robe. And when she saw the jeweled ornament pinned at the shoulder and felt the indescribable softness of it, she knew she was holding a chinchilla cape worth several thousand dollars.

III

She hummed a bar from "Goody-Goody" to conceal the slight swish it made as she dropped it to the floor of the car again. Two ideas occurred to her. This nice young man might, for all she knew, be a crook who had forgotten he had left it in the car. He had told her it was his first trip as a driver.

—and second that it might not be real after all.

She settled back in the corner of the cab, pushing at the cloak with her feet to keep it out of sight, and picked up his voice again.

"—I'm probably talking too much, but I haven't talked to anyone in a week except one hard-boiled guy that trains the new drivers. Look at me, the completed product."

"You said something about college."

"Oh, I'll shut up." He was a little hurt—she could see it even from behind in the grim slant of his young cheek.

"I only said I wanted to go to Williams College and I had a teacher who thought I could so I passed three College Board examinations. But shucks, there's so many fellows trying to work their way through. I thought if I could make something out of this I might try it."

"Williams," she said vaguely.

"Yes, it's one of the best colleges."

He turned his head around rather defiantly. "My teacher went there."

"Stop here," Gwen said suddenly.

"Where? Why?"

"Here. Right in front of this church."

He put on his brakes forcibly as he continued.

"Williams College is—"

"I know what it is," said Gwen, made impatient with her secret. "I know some girls whose brothers go there. But you look at this."

"At what?"

She shook it at him.

"This!"

He got out and standing beside the cab regarded it wonderingly as she turned it here and there.

"It's a fur," he remarked at last.

"A *fur*? It's a chinchilla, I think. I didn't know at first whether to tell you. I thought you might be a gangster. But when you said you were going to Williams I thought I'd tell you."

"I didn't say I was going to Williams. I said I wanted—"

"Well what about this? What do you think about it?"

"It's no coonskin," he said appraisingly.

"I mean what is it doing here?" Gwen demanded. "Do you suppose somebody just threw it in?"

He considered.

"I never did look in back. I took over the cab from a fellow named Michaelson—and he said he'd been a dead-head at the Grand Central since three o'clock—"

"Oh, stop talking about dead-heads."

"I explained to you—"

"I've got to get back to my hotel and we've got to do something about this."

"Don't lose your temper!" he said.

"What?"

"I mean don't let's fight about nothing. Do you think it's really a valuable coat?"

He shook it out in the sunlight and looked at it.

"—maybe it is. Must have been left in the taxi last night. The thing is to go to the home office and see if there's any inquiry about it. Maybe there's a reward."

He threw the coat back into an ignominious heap at the bottom of the cab.

"Let's go there then," Gwen said, "Honestly, I've got to get back to my hotel. They're probably starting lunch by this time, and they'll think I've been murdered."

"Shall I drive you to your hotel? Let's see, it was—" He fumbled once more for the little red book.

"No, to your garage."

"I'll go to the main one. The dispatcher out at 110th Street is kind of disagreeable."

"What's your name?" asked Gwen as they drove off.

"I think it's Callahan or something."

"Don't you know your own name?"

"Oh, *my* name—my name's Ethan Allen Kennicott. See, it's on my card here with my picture."

They talked on the way down town. There was a sort of bitter amusement in him, as if life had flung him about so carelessly that he preferred to stand a little apart and ask "What's next." His family had been comfortably off in a small town way, until two years ago. In reciprocation of his confidence Gwen told him about how her father could no longer afford to do the things they had once done, and about the disappointment of the black pearl. She realized though that beside his difficulties, her own were trivial.

"Girls have to wait for a break," he said suddenly. "Men have to make their own breaks my teacher used to say."

"So do girls," Gwen said.

"Yes, they do," he scoffed. "Catch a girl doing something she isn't told to do—by somebody."

"That isn't true," said Gwen, loyal to her sex, "Girls start lots of things."

"When some man's behind them."

"No, all by themselves."

"Sure, they find a fur—if you call that starting something."

She withdrew disdainfully from the argument. When they reached the garage on Forty-sixth Street he parked outside and went in. Emerging five minutes later he announced:

"It's wanted all right. Who do you suppose it belongs to?"

"Who?"

"Mrs. Peddlar TenBroek."

"Whew!"

"It's probably worth a fortune—I heard the dispatcher saying the TenBroek family own the land the garage is on." He frowned. "Michaelson was in there too."

"Who's Michaelson?"

"He's the man who drove this car last night. The notice says where the coat was lost and it's got him thinking maybe he drove the party that lost it. He asked me if I found it and I told him no."

"Why did you tell him that?"

"Well, you found it, didn't you? Anyway he's a tough guy and he might make trouble. He might claim the reward."

"Well, *he* certainly didn't find it," said Gwen, "But I don't want any reward."

But while he was in a drugstore looking up Mrs. TenBroek's address she realized she wouldn't mind a reward one single bit.

"Anyway it'll be half yours if we get one," she said when he came out, "Maybe it would help you go to Williams College."

Ten minutes later they waited impressed at the door of a Fifth Avenue Chateau. A very old butler glided out between great white pillars and when he heard Gwen's story quavered:

"You may leave the fur with me."

"No, I want to see Mrs. TenBroek."

"You'd far better leave it with me," the butler wheezed—he put out his hand for the garment, whereupon Ethan Kennicott reached forward gently and separated his fingers from it.

"Where is Mrs. TenBroek?" Gwen demanded.

"She is not at home. I'm not permitted to give out any information to strangers."

Gwen considered. It was after two—in a few minutes Mrs. Tulliver and her charges would be watching the curtain rise on the first act of "Oh, Mr. Heaven." In a minute she made her decision.

"We'll sit right out here in the taxi till she gets home. She'll have to pay the taxi fare, though."

As they went down the steps there was a sudden commotion behind the butler—the hall seemed suddenly full of boys, and one of them put his head over the butler's shoulder and called to her in a decidedly English voice:

"I say—what have you got to sell?"

She turned back.

"Do you live here?" she asked.

"Most of the time. I say, is that the cape Alicia Rytina lost?"

"It belongs to Mrs. Peddlar TenBroek," Gwen said.

"That's right—but she lent it to Alicia Rytina, the opera singer. My mother had most of the Metropolitan here last night and Alicia Rytina thought she had tonsillitis—I don't mean my mother—I mean Rytina. And she left it in a taxi."

There were now three other boys beside him on the steps.

"Where is Mrs. TenBroek?" said Gwen.

"To tell you the truth she's on a boat."

"Oh."

"But it hasn't sailed yet—she likes to get on board four hours ahead of time and get used to the motion. In fact we're going down presently to see her off."

"I'd like to give her the cape personally," said Gwen.

"Good enough. It's the *Dacia*, Pier 31, North River. Can we drive you down?"

"Thanks, I've got a taxi."

The other three boys—they were aged about sixteen or seventeen—had begun to dance in unison on the steps. It was American dancing but it had an odd jerky English enthusiasm about it.

"These are the three mad Rhumba dancers of Eton," explained Peddlar TenBroek. "I brought them over for the spring vacation."

Still dancing they bowed together and Gwen laughed.

"Do you dance the rhumba?" TenBroek inquired.

"I used to," she said tolerantly.

The three dancers looked somewhat offended. Gwen went down the steps.

"Tell Mother we'll be there soon," said TenBroek.

As Ethan Kennicott drove off she said: "They were attractive, but I wonder what made them think they were doing a modern dance."

He was silent on the way to the pier. Even when they were held up by a long line of strawberry trucks he said nothing and she wondered if he was envying those other boys who had no worries at all.

She found out presently. When he had parked the car and they had started toward the pier entrance, he stopped suddenly.

"This is foolishness," he said in an odd strained voice.

"What is?"

"Returning this fur. She shouldn't have left it around." He talked faster and faster as if he did not quite want to hear his own words. "She has dozens of furs and this is probably insured anyhow. It ought to be finders keepers—it's really as much ours as the pearl your father found in the restaurant."

"Oh, no it isn't," she exclaimed, "Because Father had paid for the oysters."

"We could probably get thousands for it. I could find out where to take it—"

Shocked, she cut him off.

"I wouldn't think of such a thing—when we know exactly who owns it."

"Nobody knows we've got it except those boys, and you don't live in New York and they don't know your name—"

"Stop it!" Gwen cried. "I never heard anything so terrible in my life. You *know* you wouldn't do that. Come along right away—we'll ride up on this thing."

Taking his arm she drew him toward the moving belt that was carrying baggage up to the pier. She plopped down on it thinking he would sit beside her but at the last moment he shook himself free; and as she was borne slowly aloft surrounded by bags and golf clubs he stood looking after her—with the cape over his arm.

"Hey, what do you think you're doing?" a guard called to Gwen, "That's for baggage."

But Gwen's impassioned voice cut across his.

"Come right up here with that cape!"

Ethan shook his head slowly, and called back:

"You come down here—I want to talk to you first."

An English voice behind him said suddenly:

"What's all the trouble?"

Confused, Ethan turned around to confront Peddlar TenBroek and his three friends.

"The young lady went up on the moving belt," he said, flushing.

"So she did. Well, we will too."

The three English youths were in fact already on it, following in Gwen's wake to the audible fury of the guard.

"We'd better go up the stairs," said Peddlar throwing a curious look at Ethan. But when they joined the others above Gwen said nothing— only she averted her eyes from Ethan Kennicott.

The three Englishmen led the way clogging out the pier.

For a moment the wild activity about the gang-plank, hurrying stewards, the rumbling iron wheels of a hundred hand trucks, the swift smell of the harbour—momentarily drove the episode from Gwen's mind. On the boat they went along many corridors lined by stewardesses with correctly folded arms. A huge bouquet preceded them, a bouquet sheathed in night jasmine, made of rare iris, delphinium, heliotrope and larkspur, with St. Joseph lilies, fresh from New Orleans. They followed in its fragrant path. When it had been crowded through a door the steward guiding them said:

"Here is Mrs. TenBroek's salon."

A blond flower of a woman, chic by Gwen's most exacting standards, stood up to receive them and one of the English boys said:

"You can't get away from the mad rhumba dancers, Mrs. TenBroek— even by going to the West Indies."

The words thrilled Gwen; this was the trip of the bright catalogues—of tropical moons and flashing swimming pools and soft music on enchanted beaches.

Mrs. TenBroek saw the cape suddenly and exclaimed:

"Oh, so it's been found!" She took it and looked it over eagerly. "Tell me, where was it found?"

"It may be a little dusty," said Gwen, "It was out at 216th Street."

"But what was it doing out there? I lent it to Madame Rytina, the singer, and surely she doesn't live out there."

"It was in this driver's car," said Gwen. "We both found it."

"Well, you must sit down and tell me about it. I'm so relieved because it's such a nice little cape."

In a minute Gwen found herself telling what had taken her to 216th Street. When she had done Mrs. TenBroek said:

"And now you've missed your matinee—what a shame!" She looked at Gwen tentatively, not quite certain how to proceed. "I mentioned a reward in the afternoon paper—"

"Really this driver found it as much as I did," Gwen interrupted quickly.

They all looked at Ethan Kennicott and Peddlar TenBroek said suddenly.

"That's all very well—but I'd like to know what he was doing with the cloak down at the foot of the pier saying he wouldn't bring it up to you."

Ethan flushed.

"I didn't say that."

"You said something like that. Mother, she found the cape—he didn't really have anything to do with it."

"I never claimed I did," said Ethan.

"Well, what about it?" inquired Mrs. TenBroek, "Who did find it?"

She broke off as the bell rang and the door opened emitting a rancid breeze from another world. The arch type of all the taxi drivers of legend stood there—soiled, sinister and tough as pig-skin.

"Anybody here lose a cape?" he demanded in no uncertain voice.

"What's all this, steward?" asked Mrs. TenBroek sharply.

"He claims he found a cape, Madame."

"Not ezatly found it," Mr. Michaelson corrected him, "But I was driving the car when it was left in it. Then I turn the car over to this mug—" He indicated Ethan—"and he finds it and doesn't tell me about it. I thought there was something funny when he came to the garage this morning and the old guy at your house tipped me off."

Mrs. TenBroek looked impatiently from one driver to the other.

"I ought to get a split of that reward," Michaelson said, "After I dropped them parties last night I went to the Grand Central and slep three hours without movin the car, just as if I was taking care of it."

"But you didn't know it was there."

"Not *exatly*. This young guy comes along this morning and drives the car away before I can look in it. Here I been with the company nine years and this is the first day he was ever out and he finds it and don't say nothing. And me with a wife—"

"I've had enough of this," Mrs. TenBroek interrupted. "It's quite plain that the young lady found the cape, and neither of you have the faintest claim to any reward."

"What young lady?" demanded Mr. Michaelson. "Oh, her."

"If you looked in the afternoon papers," continued Mrs. TenBroek, "—you'd see I didn't mention any sum so I'll call it three dollars for each of you to pay for your time."

She opened her purse and took the elastic from a row of bills.

"Three dollars for a chinchilly coat! Well, if that ain't—"

"Be careful now," interrupted Peddlar TenBroek.

"I got this guy to thank for it," said Michaelson, "The rat never told me."

He took a sudden step toward Ethan Kennicott and hit him a smashing left on the jaw, knocking him back over a low trunk and up with a smack against the wall. Then snarling "Keep your small change, lady," he left the room.

"I say, he can't get away with that!" exclaimed Peddlar TenBroek, and started after him.

"Let him go!" his mother ordered. "I can't endure such scenes."

One of the English boys had helped Ethan to his feet; he leaned rockily against the wall, his hand over his eyes.

Fumbling in her purse Mrs. TenBroek found a bill.

"Give this one ten dollars and tell him he can go too."

Ethan stared at the bill and shook his head.

"Never mind," he said.

"Put it in his pocket," she insisted, "And make him go."

"Somebody ought to help him off," said Gwen, agonized, "He's hurt."

"I'll help him off," said the English boy. He asked one of the others to give him a hand.

As Gwen, shaken and confused, started to follow, Mrs. TenBroek stopped her.

"Do wait a minute till I get my breath? I want to talk to you."

"He shouldn't have hit him like that," Gwen said.

"It was terrible—you shouldn't ever get mixed up with such people." She turned to her son. "Order me a glass of sherry, Peddlar, and some tea for this young lady."

"No, thanks, I've got to go," Gwen said. "I have to telephone my chaperone at the hotel."

"You can phone from the ship. Go with her and find the phone, Peddlar."

Gwen hoped that her party had gone to the matinee as planned, but on the other hand Mrs. Tulliver might be still at the hotel worrying about her. After a few minutes she was startled to hear Dizzy's voice over the wire.

"Why aren't you at the play?" Gwen demanded.

"I was late—Mrs. Tulliver left two seats and a note for us and I was just going over."

"Well, tell her I'm all right."

"Where are you?"

"I'm on a boat going to the West Indies," said Gwen ambiguously.

"What?" Dizzy exclaimed. "Did you find a real pearl?"

"I mean the boat's going, but I'm not. I wish it would start and I'd get left aboard by accident. Why were you late?"

"I got locked up in the bird house."

"The what?"

"I went to the zoo and the keeper went out to lunch. Oh, it was the dumbest thing—I never want to see a bird again."

When Gwen went back to Mrs. TenBroek's suite, that lady was full of an idea.

"It's hard to offer a reward to someone like you," she said, "But I've thought of something. I'm just making this trip to pick up an old aunt of mine and bring her back to New York and I wonder if you'd like to go along and keep me company—I'm sure I could arrange it with your family by long distance."

The magnificent prospect rushed over Gwen like a champagne cocktail, but after a minute's reflection she shook her head.

"I don't think you could," she said. Adding frankly, "Daddy would know your name, of course, but he doesn't really know anything about you."

"I know quite a few people down there who might be willing to recommend me," said Mrs. TenBroek.

"I'm so much obliged, but I don't think I'd better."

"Very well, then." She had taken a fancy to Gwen and she was disappointed. "In any case I'm going to insist that you take two hundred dollars and buy yourself a nice evening dress, or whatever you want."

"Two hundred dollars," Gwen exclaimed, "That's ten evening dresses!"

"Is it? Well, use it as you like. Are you quite sure you'd rather have the money than the trip?"

Tight-lipped, Gwen said:

"Yes, I would, Mrs. TenBroek."

—It was too bad the child was mercenary. Mrs. TenBroek had felt that behind those bright blue eyes lay the sort of romance that had haunted her own youth—she was sure she would have chosen the West Indies.

She counted out four new fifty dollar bills.

On the decks the cymbals were crashed and voices were calling "All ashore that's going ashore." When the *Dacia* had slid out into the harbour to the flutter of handkerchiefs the five young people left the pier. In the street Peddlar TenBroek said:

"We thought maybe you could have dinner with us this evening. You said there were four of you, and there's four of us and we haven't a thing to do. We could have dinner and dance up in the Rainbow Room."

"That'd be wonderful," said Gwen, "But I don't know whether our chaperone, Mrs. Tulliver—"

"I'll talk to her myself," he said confidently.

"All right," she hesitated, "But would you take me somewhere else first? Or rather two places—I've got to go to the first place to see where the second place is."

"Just tell the chauffeur where you want to go."

Half an hour later Gwen knocked softly at a thin door and at a listless response, went in.

It was a barren room furnished only with table, chair, and iron bed. In the corner was a cardboard suitcase with books piled beside it; a street suit and a hat hung from a hook on the wall. Ethan Kennicott, the side of his face blue and swollen, sat at the table, staring straight ahead of him, through half closed eyes. When he saw her his head jerked up, and with a tense movement he got to his feet.

"What do you want?" he asked harshly.

"I just came for a minute. My father says nobody ever ought to go to bed angry no matter what's happened."

"Tell that to one of those smoothies," he said bitterly. "They can spend all their lives being polite. But it just happens that I lost my job."

"Oh, I'm so sorry."

"What did you expect? Sure, I suppose I deserved it too."

"I sort of think it's my fault."

He shook his head defiantly.

"It's my fault—and I don't care any more. I don't care if I get an education—I don't care about anything."

"You oughtn't to feel that way," she said, shocked. "You've got to get an education."

"Big chance." He gave an unsuccessful little laugh. "I tell you I don't want one. I'm not fit for one, but when you've been half starved for three months—and too proud to take relief and then you see a chance like that. You think I'm a thief, don't you—well, let me tell you I never did a thing like that before in my life. I never even thought a thing like that, any more than you did."

"I thought it," she lied.

"Yes, you did."

"Yes, I did—my family hasn't got much money any more and I thought if we sold the fur I could go on a trip or something."

He looked at her, incredulous.

"You did?"

"I didn't think it long," she said hastily. "But I did think it." A memory of the pearl that wasn't a pearl rose in her mind to help her out, "I thought finders keepers losers weepers too."

"But you didn't think like that very long."

"Neither did you."

As she gave him back his self respect moment by moment, his whole posture changed.

"Maybe I wouldn't have," he said meditatively, but with recurrent bitterness he shrugged his shoulders, "It's too late now though—the job's gone. And I don't know when I'll ever get another."

She had come up close to the table, her hand clasped tight around the four fifty dollar bills so that they had become a compact little lump.

"This ought to help," she said and tossed the wad quickly onto the table.

Then before he could move or say a word she ran childishly from the room, slammed the door and hurried downstairs to the waiting car.

It was very wonderful in the Rainbow Room. The floor floated in the sky while two orchestras tore the spectrum into many colors for Gwen's avid eyes. The archaic quality of the English youths' dancing was being dissipated under expert tutelage, and if the girls had felt that their trip had been wanting up to now, this evening atoned for everything. It was fun crying "Poop-poop!" at Dizzy and pretending to order birdseed for her; and it was fun for Gwen to know that Peddlar TenBroek was completely at her service and that she'd get letters from England all the rest of the spring. It was all fun—

"What are you thinking of?" Peddlar asked her.

"Thinking of?" She came back to reality. "Well, if you have to know, I was thinking about that young taxi driver. He really did want to go to Williams College. And now he has no job and I was just thinking he was probably sitting in his room feeling so blue."

"Let's call him up," said Peddlar promptly, "We'll tell him to come and join us. You say he's a good fellow."

Gwen considered.

"No, it wouldn't be best," she decided with a touch of wisdom beyond her years, "He's sure to have a hard time and this wouldn't help him. Let's skip it."

She was happy, and a little bit older. Like all the children growing up in her generation she accepted life as a sort of accident, a grab bag where you took what you could get and nothing was very certain. The pearl her father had found hadn't been a pearl but this night's pleasure came from the fact that she had stumbled upon the skins of two-score South American rodents.

Months later when Gwen could not have told what tunes the orchestra played, she would still remember the other pearl, the one she had strung upon her personal rosary—though of course she didn't think of it like that, but rather felt a sense of guilty triumph that she had put something over on life. She didn't tell Dizzy about that. She never told anyone at all. Girls never started anything, didn't they? The pearl and the fur they were accidents—but it was no accident when she gave him her voyage to the blessed isles, gave to him out of a pity that was so deep in her that she could never even tell Dizzy about it—never told anyone at all.

FSF, front row, second from left, 1918.

"Thumbs Up" and "Dentist Appointment" are variant versions (with very different endings) of a story cut and changed into "The End of Hate" and published in *Collier's* (June 22, 1940). Fitzgerald maintained, late in his life, that one day he wanted to write a Civil War novel. These stories, and the play he wrote as a teenager (*[The] Coward*), show his lifelong interest in the war.

All three stories stem directly from Edward Fitzgerald (1853–1931). His father has scarcely been acknowledged as an influence on Fitzgerald's life or work, but on June 26, 1940, Fitzgerald wrote to his cousin Ceci Taylor: "Did you see a very poor story of mine that was in Collier's a few weeks ago? It was interesting only in that it was founded on a family story—how William George Robertson was hung up by the thumbs at Glen Mary or was it Locust Grove? Aunt Elise would know." Robertson was Edward Fitzgerald's cousin and neighbor, and was indeed one of John Singleton Mosby's raiders during the Civil War. Edward himself was born at Glenmary Farm in Maryland, not far from the plantation at Locust Grove, also called the Magruder House, built between 1773 and 1781.

Sometime after January 1931, Fitzgerald wrote a few longhand sheets, with the title "The Death of My Father" on the first page. These were later torn in half, but taped back together. The short set of memories concludes:

> I ran away when I was seven on the fourth of July—I spent the day with a friend in a pear orchard + the police were informed that I was missing and on my return my father thrashed me according to the custom of the nineties—on the bottom and then, let me come out and watch the night fireworks from the balcony with my pants still down + my behind smarting + knowing in my heart that he was absolutely right. Afterwards, seeing in his face his regret that it had to happen I asked him to tell me a story. I knew what it would be—he had only a few, the Story of the Spy, the one about the Man Hung by his Thumbs, the one about Earlys March.
>
> Do you want to hear them. I'm so tired of them all that I can't make them interesting. But maybe they are because I used to ask father to repeat + repeat + repeat.

Fitzgerald dictated "Thumbs Up" in the late summer and autumn of 1936, while he was recovering from a broken shoulder. Harold Ober was enthusiastic after receiving the first version in August: "I like THUMBS UP very much indeed. I think it is one of the best stories you have written for a long time." When the story failed to sell, Ober suggested shortening it considerably, and told Fitzgerald that October, "The Civil War story is in many ways a good piece of work but it is not what editors expect from you." Ober elaborated on this in December, quoting one of the editors who had rejected the story as saying, "'I thought it was swell but all the femmes down here said it was horrid. The thumbs, I suppose, were too much for them.' I have talked to several editors and I think it is mostly because of the incident with the thumbs that this story has not sold."

Fitzgerald knew it had been a mistake to try to combine, through the figure of a dentist, his father's stories. However, he was not going to give up the grim story of what he had been told had actually happened to his father's cousin. In early 1937 he wrote to Ober from a hospital bed in Baltimore:

> I can do no more with <u>Thumbs Up</u>. I think I told you that its shifting around was due to my poor judgement in founding it arbitrarily on two unrelated events in father's family—the Thumbs Up and the Empresses Escape. I don't think I ever put more work on a story with less return. Its early diffuseness was due, of course, to my inability to measure the

length of dictated prose during the time my right arm was helpless—
that's why it strung out so long.

Despite his statement that he could "do no more" with the story, he
revised it in March, scrapping the "Empresses Escape" or spy portion
and giving the story another ending, set in St. Paul, and another title,
"Dentist Appointment." (Other alternatives he tried out included "No
Time for That," "Two Minutes Alone," "Midst War's Alarms," "When
This Cruel War," and "Of All Times.") *Collier's* bought the story in June
1937, but asked for more revisions. That August, Kenneth Littauer told
Ober and Fitzgerald the story "still leaves a great deal to be desired. For
reasons too numerous to mention we don't like the new ending. . . .
The best of this story has always been the part that takes place in the
farmhouse."

On October 8, now at work full-time in Hollywood on a screenplay
based on Erich Maria Remarque's post–World War I novel *Three Comrades*, Fitzgerald wrote to Ober:

> I am going to do something about ["Dentist Appointment" and "Off-
> side Play"] but have definitely postponed it until after THREE COM-
> RADES is in the bag—as I told you which is a matter of three weeks
> more. Then I will either take a week off or simply find time some way
> in the early morning. So tell Colliers not to fret about it. The longer I
> wait the more I am liable to get a fresh point of view. . . . Both of them
> come so near to being right that I am sure the actual writing won't be
> any trouble.

The fresh point of view changed the end of the story once more.
Fitzgerald set the conclusion in Washington, D.C., and titled this version "The End of Hate." *Collier's* did not commit to it financially for
two more years, finally agreeing on a price in June 1939. Ober wrote
to Fitzgerald on June 2: "I'm delighted to hear that you are going to do
some more stories as I think it is time that your name should be appearing again, and I don't think there is any reason for your coming down
to Two Thousand Dollars and I [don't] think any magazine will ask you
to." *Collier's* finally published the story, cut to the bone, in their June
22, 1940, issue, with a lavish lead illustration of a blonde Yankee belle
and wounded Confederate soldier by Mario Cooper. Fitzgerald wrote
one word on his clipping of the story: "File."

His father's old bedtime story stayed on his mind for the remainder of
his life. In early 1940, Fitzgerald tried, and failed, to sell MGM on a Civil

War movie based in part on the stories. He sent a screenplay scenario to producer Edwin H. Knopf that rewrote the "thumbs" story yet again with details from "The Night of Chancellorsville" (1935) thrown in:

> The girls are separated and their first task is to find each other. One of them meets a confederate private from Alabama who at first she dreads and dislikes. In a Union counter attack the Confederate private is captured. He is identified as a Mosby guerilla by a man who bears him a grudge and hung up by his thumbs. (This actually happened to a cousin of my father's in the Civil War and I have embodied the incident in another story called "When This Cruel War" which Collier's bought last spring but has not yet published.) The northern girl cuts down the Confederate soldier and helps him to escape. The girl has begun by being impatient of her sister's gayety. During their time behind the Confederate lines she has conscientiously continued her search for her brother's grave. Now, after helping her enemy escape, and at the moment of a love scene between them she finds that they are only a few yards from her brother's grave. Entwined with the story of the two girls I would like to carry along the semi-comic character of one of those tarts, using her somewhat as Dudley Nichols used the tart in *Stagecoach* . . .
>
> We can all see ourselves as waving swords or nursing the sick but it gets monotonous. A picture like this would have its great force from seeing ourselves as human beings who go on eating and loving and displaying our small vanities and follies in the midst of any catastrophe.

The movie pitch got no bites. This story, or rather this series of stories, many-told tales with different twists and endings, shows Fitzgerald working his way through the major fault lines of nineteenth-century American history, from the Civil War to the frontier range wars. Issues of race and ethnicity abound and complicate. The swirl of international relations and the questioning of both French empire and republicanism, with the sympathies of the former Confederate soldier pivoting him in a particular direction, are also worth noting.

THUMBS UP

by

F. Scott Fitzgerald

The buggy was progressing at a tired trot. Its two
occupants had driven since before dawn and were as tired as their
horses when they turned into the Rockville Pike toward Washington.
The girl was tawny and lovely. Despite the July heat she wore a
light blue dress of bombazine cloth and on this subject she
had listened politely to her brother's strictures during the
drive down. If she was to nurse in a Washington hospital she
must not present herself in gay regalia. Josie was sad about
this. It was the first really grown-up costume she had ever
owned. A lot of boys at home had observed the unholy glow of
her hair since she was twelve, but Josie belonged to a strict
family moved out to Ohio from Massachusetts. Nonetheless she
was approaching the war as if she were going to a party.

"When do we get there, brother?" She dug him lightly
with the handle of the buggy whip, "Is this still Maryland or
are we in the District of Columbia?"

Captain Doctor Pilgrim came alive.

"D. C. I guess--unless you've managed to turn us around.
Let's stop and get water at this farmhouse just ahead. And, Josie,
don't get enthusiastic with these people down here. Most of

Thumbs Up

The buggy was progressing at a tired trot. Its two occupants had driven since before dawn and were as tired as their horses when they turned into the Rockville Pike toward Washington. The girl was tawny and lovely. Despite the July heat she wore a light blue dress of bombazine cloth and on this subject she had listened politely to her brother's strictures during the drive down. If she was to nurse in a Washington hospital she must not present herself in gay regalia. Josie was sad about this. It was the first really grown-up costume she had ever owned. A lot of boys at home had observed the unholy glow of her hair since she was twelve, but Josie belonged to a strict family moved out to Ohio from Massachusetts. Nonetheless she was approaching the war as if she were going to a party.

"When do we get there, brother?" She dug him lightly with the handle of the buggy whip. "Is this still Maryland or are we in the District of Columbia?"

Captain Doctor Pilgrim came alive.

"D. C. I guess—unless you've managed to turn us around. Let's stop and get water at this farmhouse just ahead. And, Josie, don't get enthusiastic with these people down here. Most of them are secesh, and if you're nice to them they take advantage of it. Don't give them a chance to get haughty with you."

"I won't," she said, "I'll show them what we feel."

They were possibly the only people in the vicinity unaware that this part of Maryland was temporarily Confederate. To ease the pressure on the Southern army at Petersburg, and make a last despairing threat at the capital, General Early had marched his corps up the valley to the city limits of Washington. After throwing a few shells into the suburbs he had turned his weary columns about for the march back into Virginia. The last infantry had scarcely passed, leaving a faint dust along the road, and the girl had been rather puzzled by the series of armed tramps, who had been limping by them in the last ten minutes, and there was something in the determined direction of the two men riding toward her which made her ask with a certain alarm, "What are these men, brother, secesh?"

165

To Josie or indeed to anyone who had not been to the front, it might have been difficult to guess the profession of these men—even more so to guess what cause they served. Tib Dulany, who had once contributed occasional verse to the *Lynchburg Courier*, wore a hat that had once been white, a butternut coat, blue pants that had once belonged to a Union trooper, and as his only designating badge, a cartridge belt stamped C.S.A. All that the two riders had in common were their fine new carbines taken last week from Pleasanton's cavalry.

They came up beside the buggy in a whirl of dust and Tib said:

"Hi there, Yank!"

Remembering her brother's caution about being haughty Josie reined in her horses.

"We want to get some water," she said to the handsomest young man. "We—" she stopped short seeing that Captain Doctor Pilgrim's elbow was poked backward, his hand at his holster, but immobile; Josie saw why—the second rider was holding his carbine three feet from his heart.

Slowly, almost painfully, Captain Pilgrim raised his hands.

"What is this—a raid?" he asked.

Josie felt an arm reaching about her and shrunk forward; Tib was taking her brother's revolver from its holster.

"What is this?" Dr. Pilgrim demanded, "Are you guerrillas?"

"Who are *you*?" Tib and Wash inquired in unison. Without waiting for an answer Tib said to Josie, "Young lady, walk your team up a little way and turn in yonder at the farmhouse. You can get a drink of water up there."

He realized suddenly that she was lovely, that she was frightened and brave, and he added: "Nobody's goin to hurt you. We just aimin to detain you a little."

"Will you tell me who you are?" Captain Pilgrim demanded, "Do you know what you're doing?"

"Calm down!" Tib told him. "You're inside Lee's lines now."

"Lee's lines!" Captain Pilgrim cried. "You think every time you Mosby murderers come out of your hills and cut a telegraph—"

The team, barely started, jolted to a stop—Wash had grabbed the reins, and he turned black eyes upon the northerner.

"Say one thing more about Major Mosby and I'll drag you out of that buggy and clean your little old face with dandelions."

"There's a lady here, Wash," Tib said, "and the officer simply isn't informed of the news. He's a prisoner of the Army of Northern Virginia."

Captain Pilgrim looked at them incredulously as Wash released the reins and they drove in silence to the farmhouse. Only as the foliage parted and gave a sudden vista of two dozen horses attended by grey-clad orderlies, did he awake to a premonition that something was wrong—that his news was indeed several days behind.

"What's happened?" he asked Wash. "Is Lee's army *here*?"

"You didn't know that?" Tib said. "Why, right now we got Abe Lincoln in the kitchen washing dishes—and General Grant's upstairs making the beds."

"Ah-h-h!" grunted Captain Pilgrim.

"Say, Wash, I sure would like to be in Washington tonight when Jeff Davis walks in. That Yankee rebellion didn't last long."

—And Josie, she believed the whole thing. Her world was crashing around: The Boys in Blue and the Union forever and Mine eyes have seen the Glory of the Coming of the Lord. Her eyes were full of hot tears of grief.

"You can't take my brother prisoner. Why, he's not really just an officer because he's a doctor. He was wounded at Cold Harbor—"

"Doctor, eh? Don't know anything about teeth, does he?"

"Oh yes—that's his specialty."

They reached the porch and the scouts dismounted.

"So you're a tooth doctor?" Tib said. "Well, that's just what we been seeking all over Maryland, my Maryland for the last hour. If you'll be so kind as to come in here you can probably pull a tooth of one of the real Napoleons, a cousin of the Emperor, Napoleon III."

Captain Pilgrim cautioned Josie:

"They're joking but don't say anything."

"Joking?—we're sure not joking. He's attached to General Early's staff and he's been bawling in here for the last hour but the medical men went on with the ambulances and nobody on the staff can pull teeth."

A staff officer came out on the porch and gave a nervous ear to a crackling of rifles in the distance; then bent an eye upon the buggy.

"Lieutenant, we found a tooth specialist," Tib said. "Providence sent him right into our lines and if Napoleon is still—"

"Good heavens!" the officer exclaimed. "Bring him in. We didn't know whether to take him or leave him."

Suddenly Josie had her first real picture of the Confederacy staged for her on the vine-covered veranda. There was a sudden egress: first a grizzled man in a fine grey riding coat, followed by two younger men cramming papers into a canvas sack. Then came a miscellany of officers, one on a single crutch, one stripped to an undershirt and with the gold star of a general pinned to a bandage on his shoulder, one laughing as a man laughs who has just told some joke himself but the general air was not of cheerfulness—and Josie saw in their tired eyes the reflection of some disappointment.

Then they made a single gesture as one man; perceiving her, they wheeled toward her and their dozen right hands rose to their dozen hats, topping them slightly, and they bowed faintly in her direction.

Josie bowed back stiffly, trying to bring some expression into her face—of hauteur, scorn, reproach—but she was unable to do aught but respond to their courtesy.

. . . In a moment the staff had swung into their saddles; the aide who had first come out of the farmhouse paused at General Early's stirrup.

"Good enough," the General said.

He looked for a moment at the city that he could not conquer, at the arbitrary swamp that another Virginian had conceived. "No further change in orders," he said. "Tell Mosby that I want couriers every hour up to Charlestown. One battery of horse artillery to put up a big noise while the engineers blow up the bridge over Montgomery Creek—you understand, Major Charlesworth."

"Yes, sir."

"I guess that's all, then." He turned. "Oh, yes." His sun-strained eyes focussed on the buggy. "I understand you're a doctor. Prince Napoleon is in there—He's been with us as an observer. Pull out his tooth or whatever he needs. These two troopers will stay with you. Do well by him now—they'll let you go without parole when you've finished with him."

Then all was drowned out in the clop and crunch of mounted men moving down a lane. The little group was left standing by the porch as the last sally of the Army of Northern Virginia faded swiftly into the distance.

"We got a dentist here for Prince Napoleon," said Tib to the French aide-de-camp.

"That's very well," the aide exclaimed, leading the way into the front room of the farmhouse. "He is in the most great agony."

"The doctor is a Yankee," Tib continued. "One of us will have to stay while he's operating."

The stout invalid across the room, a gross miniature of his world-shaking uncle, tore his hand from his groaning mouth and sat upright in an armchair.

"Operating!" he cried. "Mon Dieu! Is he going to operate?"

"This is the doctor," Tib said. "His name is—"

"Pilgrim," the doctor supplied coldly. "My sister—where will she be?"

"I'll put her in the parlor, Doctor. Wash, you stay here."

"I'll need hot water," said Dr. Pilgrim, "and my instrument case from the buggy."

Prince Napoleon groaned again.

"What you do? Cut my head off my neck? How do you know what to do about this before you see even? Ah, cette vie barbare!"

Tib consoled him gently.

"This doctor specializes in teeth, Prince Napoleon. He won't hurt you."

"I am a trained surgeon," said Dr. Pilgrim stiffly. "Now, sir, will you take off that hat?"

The Prince removed the wide white Cordoba which topped a miscellaneous costume of grey tail coat, French uniform breeches and dragoon boots.

"Can we trust this medicin if he is a Yankee? How can I know he will not cut to kill? Does he know I am a Frenchman citizen?"

"Prince, if he doesn't do well by you we got some apple trees outside and plenty rope."

Tib went to summon a servant; then he looked into the parlor where Miss Josie sat frightened on the edge of a horsehair sofa.

"What are you going to do to my brother?"

Very sorry for her pretty, stricken young face, Tib said, "We ain't fixin to hurt him. I'm more worried what he's about to do to the Prince."

An anguished howl arose from the library.

"You hear that?" Tib said. "Your brother's the one going to do the damage."

"Are you going to send us to that Libby Prison?"

"Don't you get excited now, young lady. This time we don't want any prisoners. You're going to be held here till your brother fixes up the Prince. Then, as soon as our cavalry pickets come past, you and your brother can continue your journey."

Josie relaxed.

"I thought all the fighting was down in Virginia."

"It is. That's where we're heading—this is the third time I rode north into Maryland with the army and I reckon it's the third time I'm heading back with it."

"What did my brother mean when he said you were a gorilla?"

She looked at him for the first time with a certain human interest.

"I reckon because I didn't shave since yesterday." He laughed. "Anyway he didn't mean 'gorilla' he meant 'guerrilla.' When it's a Yankee on detached service they call him a scout but when it's one of us they call us spies and string us up."

"Any soldier not in uniform is a spy," Josie said.

"Me not in uniform? Look at my buckle. Half of Stuart's cavalry wouldn't be considered in uniform if they had to have the uniforms they started with. I tell you, Miss Pilgrim, I was a smart-looking trooper when I rode out of Lynchburg four years ago."

He described to her how the young volunteers had been dressed that day; Josie listened, thinking it was not unlike the scene when the first young volunteers had got on the train at Chillicothe.

"—with a big red ribbon from Mother's trunk for a sash. One of the girls read a poem I wrote in front of the troop."

"Oh say the poem," Josie exclaimed, "I would so enjoy to hear it."

Tib considered. "Reckon I've forgot it. All I remember is 'Lynchburg, thy guardsmen bid thy hills farewell.'"

"I love it."

Josie repeated slowly, "'Lynchburg, thy guardsmen bid thy hills farewell,'" and forgetting the errand on which Lynchburg's guardsmen were bent she added, "I certainly wish you remembered the rest of it."

Came a scream from across the hall and a medley of French expletives. The distraught face of the aide-de-camp appeared at the door.

"He has pulled out not just the tooth but the stomatic—He has killed him, he has done him to the death!"

A face pushed over his shoulder.

"Say, Tib—the Yank got the tooth."

"Did he?" said Tib, but absently. His tendency to metaphor had suddenly reasserted itself and he was thinking, "All inside of half an hour one Yank got a tooth and his sister got a heart."

II

A minute later Wash dashed back into the living room.

"Say, Tib, we oughtn't to stay here. A patrol just went by mighty fast shootin back from the saddle. Ain't we fixin to leave? This here Doctor knows we're Mosby's men."

"You leave without *us*?" the aide demanded suspiciously.

"We sure do," said Tib. "The Prince can observe the war from the Yankee side for a while. Miss Pilgrim, I don't want to take advantage of a prisoner but I must say that I never knew a Yankee girl could be so pretty."

"I never heard anything so ridiculous," she answered. But she was pleased at the compliment stretched across the Mason-Dixon line.

Peering hastily into the library Tib found the Prince so far recovered as to be sitting upright, panting and gasping.

"You are an artiste," he exclaimed to Dr. Pilgrim. "You see I live! After all the terror I still live. In Paris I am told that if they take from you the tooth you have hemorrhage and die. You should come to Paris and I will tell the Emperor of you—of that new instrument you use."

"It's just a kind of forceps," said Dr. Pilgrim gruffly.

Wash called from the door.

"Come on, Tib!"

Tib spoke to the Prince.

"Well, au revoir, sir."

There was firing very near now. The two scouts had scarcely unhitched their horses when Wash exclaimed: "Hell fire!" and pointed down the drive. Half a dozen Federal troopers had come into view behind the foliage of the far gate. Wash swung his carbine one handed to his right shoulder and with his free arm reached for a cartridge in his pouch.

"I'll take the two on the left," he said.

Standing concealed by their horses they waited.

"Maybe we could run for it," Tib suggested.

"I looked the place over. It's got seven rail fences."

"Don't fire till they get nearer."

Leisurely the file of cavalry trotted up the drive. Even after four years on detached service up and down the valley, Tib hated to shoot from ambush, but he concentrated on the business and the front sight of his carbine came into line with the center of the Yankee corporal's tunic.

"Got your mark, Wash?"

"Think so."

"When they break we'll ride through 'em."

But the ill luck of Southern arms that day took shape before they could loose a shot. A heavy body flung against Tib and pinioned him. A voice shouted beside his ear.

"Men, they're rebels here!"

Even as Tib turned, wrestling desperately with Dr. Pilgrim, the Northern patrol stopped, drew pistols. Wash was bobbing desperately from side to side to get a shot at Pilgrim, but the Doctor maneuvered Tib's body in between.

In a split second it was over. Wash loosed a single shot but the Federals were around them before he was in his saddle. Furious, the two young men faced their captors. Dr. Pilgrim spoke sharply to the Federal corporal:

"These are Mosby's men."

Those years were bitter on the border. The Federals slew Wash when he made another attempt to get away—grabbing at the revolver in the corporal's hand. Tib, still struggling, was trussed up at the porch rail.

"There's a good tree," one of the Federals said, "and there's a rope on the swing."

The corporal glanced from Dr. Pilgrim to Tib.

"Are you one of Mosby's men?"

"I'm with the Seventh Virginia Cavalry."

"Didn't ask you that. Are you one of Mosby's men?"

"None of your business."

"All right, boys, get the rope."

Dr. Pilgrim's austere presence asserted itself again.

"I don't think you should hang him but certainly this type of irregular has got to be discouraged."

"We hang them up by their thumbs, sometimes," suggested the corporal.

"Then do that," said Dr. Pilgrim. "He spoke of hanging me."

. . . By six that evening the road outside was busy again. Two brigades of Sheridan's finest were on Early's trail, pursuing and harassing him down the valley. Mail and fresh vegetables were moving toward the capital and the raid was over, except for a few stragglers who lay exhausted along the Rockville Pike.

In the farmhouse it was quiet. Prince Napoleon was waiting for an ambulance from Washington. There was no sound there—except from Tib, who, as his skin slipped off his thumbs, gradually down the knuckles, said fragments of his own political verses aloud to himself. When he could think of no more verses he ruminated on what was happening to him.

"Thumbs are like a glove—they turn inside out. When the nails turn over I'll yell out loud . . ."

He kept singing a new song that he had sung just before they had marched out of Lynchburg:

> *We'll follow the feather of Mosby tonight;*
> *We'll steal from the Yankees our horse-flesh and leather.*
> *We'll follow the feather, Mosby's white feather.*
> *'Twas once made a sign of a sin and a shame;*
> *The plume was of white but he gave it a name*
> *As different from shame as the dark is from light*
> *So we'll follow the feather of Mosby tonight.*

Josie had waited till it was full dark and she could hear the sentry snoring on the porch. She knew where the step-ladder was because she had heard them dump it down after they had strung up Tib. When she had half sawed through the rope she went back to her room for pillows and moved the table under him and laid the pillows on it.

Josie did not need any precedents for what she was doing. When he fell with a grunting gasp, murmuring "—serve your country and nothing to be ashamed of," Josie poured half a bottle of sherry wine over his hands. Then, sick suddenly herself, she ran back to her room.

III

As always with victorious causes, the war was over in the North by sixty-seven. Josie was grown at nineteen and proud at helping along her brother's career with her tact atoning for his arrogance. Her lovely face shone for the young men on Government pay when she danced at the balls with President Johnson's profile at the end of the room melancholy against the massed flowers from the Shenandoah.

"What is a guerrilla—exactly?" she asked a military man one time. "You're holding me quite tight enough thank you."

But she didn't marry any of them. Her eyes had seen the coming of the glory of the Lord and then she had seen the glory of the Lord hung up by the thumbs.

Just home from market she called to the maid:

"I'll answer, Candy."

But on the way to the door her hoop slipped from its seam and tripped her and she only called through:

"Who is it?"

"I want to see Dr. Pilgrim."

Josie hesitated. Her brother was asleep.

"I'm afraid he can't see you now," she said.

But as she turned away from the door the bell rang again, harsh and imperative. This time Candy had lumbered up from the kitchen.

"Tell him the Doctor can't see anybody this morning."

She went into the drawing room and rested a moment. Candy interrupted her.

"Miss Josie—that's a right funny man out there. Look to me he fixin to do some mischief to y'all. He got kind of black gloves on him that wobble when he talk."

"What did he say?" asked Josie in alarm.

"He only say he want to see your brother."

Josie went out into the hall again. It was a small quadrangle, lit by a semicircular window that shed a blue and olive glow. Candy had left the door faintly ajar and Josie peered out cautiously from the safe semi-darkness. She saw half a hat and half a coat.

"What do you want?"

"I've got to see Dr. Pilgrim."

She had a peremptory "No" ready when another visitor came into view on the door-step, and she hesitated, feeling unjustified in sending away two callers without consulting her brother. Reassured by this second presence she threw open the door. In a second she wished she hadn't because the two figures standing there brought back in a sudden rush of memory another July day three years before. The man just arrived was the young French aide-de-camp who had been with Prince Napoleon; the other, the one in whose tone Candy had scented undefined danger Josie had last seen in a crumpled mass of agony on a farmhouse table. The Frenchman was the first to speak.

"You probably do not recollect me, Miss Pilgrim. My name is Silvé. I am now military attache at the French embassy here and we have met on that day that your brother rendered such service to Prince Napoleon in the war."

Josie steadied herself against the door-frame, with an effort restraining the impulse to cry out, "Yes, but what is the Southerner doing here?"

Tib had not spoken, but Josie's mind was working so fast that words could not have made plainer to her the nature of his errand, though her appearance and the simultaneous arrival of the other visitor had confused him. The light in his eyes was of a purpose long conceived, long planned; for two years he had so haunted Josie's dreams that she had reconstructed in her imagination his awful return to consciousness that night, his escape before sunrise and the desperate agony that must have accompanied his search for shelter that morning—after her months in the soldiers' hospital Josie could envisage the amputation of his torn thumbs.

The Frenchman spoke again: "It is only because the Paquebot Rochambeau leaves on the day after tomorrow that I dare present myself at such an hour. Miss Pilgrim, the Prince has not forgotten the great service that your brother rendered him. This morning even cables of the most serious nature have been postponed so that I should come to see your brother. At this moment there is a toothache in Europe of such international significance—" For the first time in a cautious glance he became fully cognizant of Tib's presence, but there was no mutual recognition. "If I could talk to your brother for a moment?"

A voice spoke suddenly over Josie's shoulder:

"I am Dr. Pilgrim. Who wants to speak to me?"

Instinctively Josie blocked the space of sunlight between Tib Dulany, ex-sergeant of Stuart's cavalry, and her brother.

"I'm sorry, gentlemen," said Dr. Pilgrim, "but I can't see you now." To Josie he said, "This is the morning that I've promised to devote to Candy's tooth—that's why I got up so confounded early." He pressed past her and faced the two men. "We have a faithful negro servant whom I have long intended to supply with a tooth and I am afraid that I can have no other appointments for this morning. My sister will take your addresses and arrange any consultations."

Josie saw he was in one of his icy humors. On his way downstairs he had called Candy from the kitchen; she was bustling behind him with a basket on her arm.

Josie, the only one of the five who grasped the entirety of the situation, sparred for time.

"Very well. If you gentlemen will give me your addresses—"

"I only ask for a moment of the Doctor's time," said Captain Silvé.

"I will give you just that moment," said the Doctor impatiently. "This poor colored woman needs me more than anyone and I have never thought to put white before black with those who need my services."

For the next few minutes while Captain Silvé explained himself and Dr. Pilgrim unbent to the extent of walking with him to the edge of the veranda, Josie was alone with Tib—alone with him in spirit. She could not untie those old cords which she had once cut through—but for that little time she could hold him with her bright beauty.

"My brother doesn't know who you are," she said quickly. "What do you want here?"

Again she read through to the dark hours and brooding years that lay behind his eyes.

Tib looked aside.

"I only came to get an appointment."

Dr. Pilgrim turned about. "My time is limited as I said. Josie, you may tell any further callers that I will be available after four o'clock."

Nodding briefly to Tib he started down the steps still listening with a distant air to Silvé's plea. All of a sudden the five of them were in motion down the sunny street, Josie, without a bonnet, walking beside Tib, and Candy bringing up the rear.

"—but it's a court appointment," Silvé pled earnestly. "You will be assistant to the great Doctor Evans, patronized by everyone in Paris. It is what the English would call a 'command,' you comprehend, Doctor."

Dr. Pilgrim stopped and the procession stopped behind him.

"I am an American first and I shall depend entirely upon my own judgment as to whether or not to accept an offer so suddenly—if at all."

Captain Silvé flung up his hands in despair. "Surgeon to the French Empire! High fees, probably the *Legion d'honneur*, a fine equipage to drive in the Bois de Boulogne—yet you would consider staying here in this mud hole?"

Dr. Pilgrim had begun to walk again.

"It is not a mud hole to me," he said. "You have seen that building on our left?"

"Certainly. It is the Capitol."

"It was from those steps that our martyred president delivered the second inaugural."

A voice behind Josie breathed humbly:

"I don't know whether you all is goin where you is goin on account of me but I feels as if I's jest trailin along."

Candy's urging made Josie realize that she herself was simply an element in a parade, and she called to her brother in her most positive voice, "Where are we going, Ernest?"

"We're going to the jeweler's of course," Dr. Pilgrim answered, "I can't make a gold tooth out of nothing, and I told you I used the last piece of gold leaf yesterday afternoon."

If the young Southerner would only speak Josie might have been able to resolve the situation but he only reflected her uncertainty as to the next step.

At the next corner she turned upon him with an almost intimate anger:

"Will you kindly excuse us, sir? You may call another time when my brother is able to see you."

"I think I shall accompany your brother," said Tib grimly.

"Oh please," she whispered, "is this some more of that awful war?"

"I hope there will be no violence in your presence," said Tib.

Setting the pace Dr. Pilgrim threw a glance over his shoulder.

"Walking is more healthful if one makes better time." And he continued his discourse upon the Capitol up to the portal of Viner's Jewelry Store on Pennsylvania Avenue.

At this point his two early callers became conscious that they were upon an errand in which they had no concern, and momentarily fell back while Dr. Pilgrim, Josie, and Candy went in.

"I cannot understand it," said Captain Silvé. "No pleasure except duty would hold me in Washington. Two or three buildings, some beautiful girls like Miss Pilgrim and nothing more."

He reached for the door-knob at the same moment as Tib and withdrew his own hand with a start. His thumb had pressed through another thumb, soft and tangible within its black kid covering.

"Have I hurt you?" he exclaimed.

"What? Oh I see." What Tib saw was that the thumb of his stuffed glove had been crushed flat by the accidental encounter. Instinctively his other hand bent to reshape it while he held the door open with his elbow. "You didn't hurt me—that was an accident I was in. I haven't any thumbs."

Captain Silvé, brought up in the proudest traditions of Saint Cyr, would request no information when none had been offered. But he looked curiously at Tib as they went into the store. Then, being French, he became fascinated by the bargain that was being transacted within.

Mr. Viner had produced from his stock a velvet covered board on which reposed several dozen gold pieces, each of them representing some badge of office, distinction or occasion, or obscure foreign coinage. Some were topped by multi-color ribbons. Over them bent Candy, muttering to herself that she was "jest steadyin" while Dr. Pilgrim weighed one of the pieces in his hand.

"This is the best gold," he said.

Candy was enjoying the most important moment of her life and in spite of her respect for the Doctor there was to be no trifling about it.

"Doctor, you told me I could pick my own tooth." She looked up at the jeweler. "You got any real gilt?"

Dr. Pilgrim sighed. He might have had a dozen clients this morning. "Candy, I explained to you that gilt wasn't anything like gold. I can't make you a tooth out of gilt because it wouldn't chew."

"All I know is where I wuked gilt was thought more high of than gold. I know what I'm talkin about, Dr. Pilgrim, when I sent away for my first wedding ring it melted down on me half an hour before the ceremony and I been washin gilt frames for years and I never took but a little off em."

After a nervous glance at Tib Josie addressed herself to helping her brother straighten out Candy's conceptions of the precious metals.

"Candy, you couldn't make a tooth out of a piece of orange peel, could you?"

"No ma'am, but it seems to me I've seen lots of gilt in Dr. Pilgrim's office, just like what used to fall off the portraits."

"That was gold leaf," said Dr. Pilgrim. "There just isn't any in Washington. We just have to melt up this scrap and make you a tooth. If you want to pick out your own incisor you got to do it quick. Now here you have *For a United Ireland* and *The Friends of the Freedman*—" He spoke sharply to the jeweler, "This thing isn't gold at all; it's a bottle top or else I never filled a tooth."

Mr. Viner pocketed it anxiously. "It must have got on there by mistake."

Dr. Pilgrim gave him a reproving glance and turned to Candy.

"The morning is passing, Candy. It's going to take me some time to pound out this instrument. Make your choice. Here you've got *United Veterans of the Mexican War, Thirty-five years service with J.P. Wertheimer.*"

"I never did work for no Wertheimers."

"Well now, here's the last one of all, Candy, and if you don't like this one I'm just going to pick out one myself. This says, *The Legion of Honor, Private George Aiken, for Valor Extraordinary, killed at Gettysburg, July 2, 1863.*"

Tib spoke suddenly to Dr. Pilgrim: "And you would make a nigger's tooth out of that."

Captain Pilgrim turned on him stiffly. "Sir, I don't know who you are or why you are with us but nigger is a word that is not used in our household."

Josie saw the line of Tib's revolver paralleling the edge of the show counter. Her glance ran along it to her brother's breast pocket like a carbine that had been pointed at the same target three years before.

"Hands up, Pilgrim," said Tib.

The Doctor's hands weighing two pieces of metal rose higher.

"Who are you anyhow?" Dr. Pilgrim demanded. "What is this confounded nonsense?"

"Open your hand wide. All right, like that."

The barrel of the gun had lifted to forty-five degrees, following the Doctor's hands.

"Higher, Doctor. Do you mind turning your palm over so that the coin is in my line of fire? I am going to shoot that out of your hand—higher still."

"You are a mad man."

"Once you ordered me strung up by the thumbs. I came to kill you but I reckon I'll just shoot those medals out of your hands."

"Get away, sister," said Dr. Pilgrim, "this man is crazy."

Tib waited; he didn't know for what. He tried to think back to the awful nights; he tried to fortify himself in a forceful jerk of memory of the day he had first run a plow over an acre with his mutilated hands.

"Stand away," he said menacingly.

Josie made a movement to throw herself between them but Captain Silvé pulled her back.

"He's crazy," he said.

Mr. Viner had disappeared from the stationary picture and made a quick duck behind the counter. Captain Silvé suddenly realized where he had seen Tib's face before.

"Wait a minute," he said. "You realize Miss Pilgrim is here?"

"Yes," Tib said.

"Do you realize that Miss Pilgrim cut you down that night? At first I did not recognize you but I was in the farmhouse that night with Prince Napoleon and I know that next morning she was almost put under arrest."

Suddenly in Tib's moment of shock and surprise two people were in front of Dr. Pilgrim. Josie was in front of her brother and Candy in front of Josie.

"It would have been better if she had left you hanging there," said Dr. Pilgrim. "Get away, sister."

"I didn't know about that," said Tib in a strained voice and he added, feeling the intention with which he had lived for three years being torn from him:

"I guess I can't do it then."

"I shouldn't think so," said Candy indignantly, "seeing you'd have to shoot through all us three."

Tib backed toward the door.

"I didn't know that, Miss Pilgrim," Tib said. "You can't shoot through an angel."

He was gone and the five people were alone in a sudden silence. Mr. Viner came up cautiously from behind the counter at almost the moment that Dr. Pilgrim's hands came slowly down.

"Shall I pursue him," Mr. Viner inquired, "shall I—"

"No," said Dr. Pilgrim. He laid the medal of the Legion of Honor on the counter and said briskly to Mr. Viner, "This is by far the best piece of metal."

IV

Even in France Josie sometimes saw the black gloves coming around corners. Her brother went to work helping the great Dr. Evans arrange the china smiles of royalty and before Prince Napoleon's disgrace they were firmly entrenched as units of the American colony.

When she returned from a trip to the States in sixty-nine a rough crossing put her on her back until the last day. When she made her way on deck in Havre harbor the sudden quiet made her giddy as the motion had, and she scarcely noticed the man who steadied her and held her elbow as the boat slid gently through quiet shallows. When, a moment later, they recognized each other she could not think of any of the cool or distant things that she should have said to him. They talked about the disasters attending French arms on the border and were anxious for the news that they would get after their three weeks isolation at sea.

When they had found a first-class compartment on the train to Paris she asked:

"Are you touring?"

"I'm a war correspondent," said Tib, "I'm going to the front representing the *Richmond Times-Dispatch*, the *Danville News* and the *Lynchburg Courier*."

"Well if you are in Paris—" Josie stopped herself. She had been at the point of inviting him to call but she finished, "—you'll find the consul very helpful."

Tib had been conscious for some minutes of four men loitering outside the open door of the compartment, but he was unprepared for what happened. Even as the train whistled, signaling its departure, the four men came in and in a second two of them were escorting him into the next car "for a little questioning, Monsieur." Behind him as they crossed the vestibule he heard Josie's voice protesting with equal surprise and indignation.

"What is this?" he demanded.

"Are you bound for Alsace?"

"What business is that of yours?"

"This is the one, that's sure," said the man who was pinioning him from behind. "They will find it in the woman's hat."

In the car behind Josie was having her troubles.

"There's nothing in my hat. It's a hat I bought in America."

"Unfortunately," said one of her captors, "it has a French label."

"Naturally, it's a French hat."

"And naturally you are not Madame Shirmer," the man said ironically, "and your friend is not Signor Mario Villizio in the pay of the Prussian government."

A man in uniform entered the situation.

"You are idiots," he said. "They have been caught four cars up forward."

"But these are easily the ones. You could see it on their faces."

"Let us examine her hat immediately. The train is being separated. These last four cars are to wait for the British mail boat."

In three minutes they had handed back to her a mass of feathers, rosettes, ribbons in the bowl of what had once been a Paris hat.

"Our pardon, Madame. You would like to join your companion?"

"Yes," said Josie, "or no; I don't care. I want to get on the first train."

"Then you must hurry, Madame."

There had been the bump of an engine and the sound of uncoupling ahead. It was at the moment when she reached the vestibule that the sections began to pull apart.

"Ah, alas, Madame, your husband has gone ahead."

"He is not my husband," said Josie.

"Your friend then," he said. "After all the other section is coming back."

But the other section was merely hesitating. Tib meanwhile had shown his credentials and being released hurried back to rejoin Josie. They stood on the two platforms surrounded by shrugging Frenchmen who regretted that they had been the cause of separating what were probably two lovers. But before anything could be done about it the first section had made up its mind and started off in earnest.

"Are you all right?" Tib cried to her.

"I'm fine," she said, "but they have ruined my hat."

The first section chugged into the distance. She stood on the rear vestibule with the French captain of police.

"The country is lovely around here," he said consolingly.

"Yes," she agreed shortly.

"And when one is in love things are always more lovely," he pursued gallantly. "Do not worry, you can rejoin your friend in Paris."

"You might at least leave me alone now," said Josie.

He bowed. "I can appreciate that too, Mademoiselle."

The trains had moved so far apart now that she could see nothing but a small blot in the distance and her chance of seeing him again was as small as that. She stood desolately looking at the torn rosettes in the soup dish of felt. All her experiences with Tib had been like that.

V

Dr. Pilgrim, *Grand Maitre de l'Ordre de l'Hygiene Publique*, assistant to the great Dr. Evans, dental surgeon to the court and to various Bourbons, Cecils, Churchills, Vanderbilts, Hapsburgs, Chambruns and

Astors, had just received a gift of flowers. It had been sent him by a gardener at the Tuileries whom he had treated for nothing—but they did not touch him. He did his charity work faithfully but coldly and he was much more interested in the new chair that he and Dr. Evans had just invented. He was glad the war was over even though the French had lost. Practice would be better now. He heard the doorbell ring once and again. The third time he went out into the hall to see why it wasn't answered—and ran into Josie rushing excitedly up the stairs.

"Why isn't the door attended to?" he inquired but she interrupted him.

"Oh bother the doorbell. Let me tell you who just came in and is waiting downstairs."

"I don't care," said Dr. Pilgrim. "The doorbell must be answered."

As a matter of fact it was being answered at just that moment. The young man waiting there was rather surprised by the words of the woman who let him in.

"You are from Dr. Evans?"

"No, ma'am. I represent the *Richmond Times-Dispatch*, the *Danville News* and the *Lynchburg Courier*."

"How did you know I was here?" she asked.

"I don't understand," said Tib.

"Oh," said the lady nervously. "Well, I guess you might as well come in."

As they came under the gas light of the waiting room she said:

"Are you in pain?"

"No," he said.

She seemed somewhat agitated and as if she felt she must apologize for it.

"I haven't waited in a doctor's office since I was very young. It makes me feel rather strange."

"Are you in pain?" he asked her in turn.

The woman nodded.

"Yes," she said, "I am in pain—the pain of insult and degradation."

Tib looked at her curiously.

"I can understand that feeling," he said.

"You are an American," the woman remarked. "My father was an American citizen, though he was born in Scotland."

"I am not an American," denied Tib. "I am a Virginian. Those two things will never mean the same again in my lifetime."

The woman sighed.

"Alas, I am from nowhere. I have been trying very hard for thirty years to be a Frenchwoman but now I know that I am of no race."

Tib nodded. "That's like me—I am a citizen of nowhere, part of a lost cause, broken and beaten with it."

The door opened and Josie Pilgrim came into the room and walked swiftly up to the woman.

"Your Majesty, Doctor Evans' horses will be here in five minutes."

"I have not minded waiting," said the Empress. "I have been talking with this young American."

Josie cast a surprised glance at Tib, bowed, and said to the Empress, "Do you want to come up to my room?"

"I should not like to move. I am sitting on my jewel case."

Tib had seen the crowd streaming past the Tuileries half an hour before, and had wondered fleetingly about the Empress and the court, whether the fair Spaniard of tortuous destiny would be made into a new Marie Antoinette. Now he looked at the faded lady in the black hat and knew without question that this was the Empress.

"Can I be of any service?" he asked.

"No thank you," said Josie hastily. "My brother and Dr. Evans are taking care of everything."

"But he *can* be of service. With three Americans I shall be even safer than with two. If he rides with us I shall esteem it a great favor."

"I am mounted," said Tib.

"All the better," said the Empress. "You will be our escort."

. . . Ten minutes later the little party assembled at the stables. From the streets they could hear many voices, snatches of Beranger songs, imprecations against the Emperor, the Empress, and the court, and a continual scuffle of steps upon cobble-stones, moving toward fire and catastrophe. Dr. Evans, tense and determined, stood between the Empress and the red glare of the torches from the street, as if to shut out all he could of menace and hatred abroad.

"So you're riding with us," he said to Tib. "Remember, we have agreed to pretend that this is an insane woman whom we are taking to Trouville."

"I insane!" exclaimed the Empress, "I begin to think I am. Let this young Virginian ride inside with us and we can talk about being exiles. The good Dr. Pilgrim will be glad to take his horse and play postilion for the evening. Is that not so, Dr. Pilgrim?"

Dr. Pilgrim glared at Tib.

"Yes, your Majesty."

"Are we ready?" asked Dr. Evans.

The cortege was starting out through the wild avenues that led to the Porte Maillot. They were shouted at several times but no attempt was made to stop the carriage; out in the suburbs chalk white windows looked down indifferently at them in sleeping roads; toward midnight Josie's eyes closed drowsily and Tib could at last watch her just as he wanted to watch her, while the last of the French Sovereigns drove out of the Ile-de-France.

In the Inn des Mariniers at Trouville a consultation was held as to the next step. A yacht rode at anchor in the harbor and they ascertained that it flew the Union Jack and belonged to Sir John Burgoyne. The Empress was persuaded to lie down under Dr. Evans' care and Tib and Dr. Pilgrim started along the water-front making discreet inquiries for the use of a dinghy. They had no reason to think that their departure from Paris had been traced. Only a single episode just now, a curious look that a waiter had thrown at the Empress, worried them. But when they had secured the boat and Josie appeared panting beside them both men had a moment of apprehension.

"What is it?"

"Dr. Evans wants you back at the inn to talk to that waiter. The man is hanging around the hall outside the Empress's room and when I spoke to him he just laughed and pretended he couldn't understand my French."

"I'll go back," said Tib.

"No, it's better for me to go," said Dr. Pilgrim. "I've only once been in a rowboat and I should not care to attempt it alone."

He started briskly back and then noticing that Josie was not with him turned and saw her getting into the dinghy with Tib.

"It's all right," she called, "I've rowed a lot and two of us are better than one."

Dr. Pilgrim continued on to the inn.

It was a gorgeous morning and the glittering harbor made Josie forget the gloomy events of the night before and the anxious errand on which they were bent. Then they crossed a dark line of water across the harbor and suddenly were in rough water and a wind from the outside sea. The little dinghy progressed more slowly. The handles of the oars were large and suddenly noticing that Tib's thumbless hands were clumsy in the rougher water she said:

"I'm going to take this pair of oars and help so we can make quicker time."

"No," he insisted, "I'd rather you wouldn't."

But she had already taken her place on the stern thwart and was slipping the oars into the locks.

"All right," he said, "You have to set the stroke."

In a moment she was sitting back in his arms with one of the oars floating away to sea.

"Oh I'm so sorry," she gasped, "I really can row."

"It's all right with me," he said.

"I want to try again," Josie insisted. "Your hands the way they are—" She stopped herself.

"My hands are all right," said Tib. "I think I can take care of us both."

"I know you can," said Josie impulsively. She sat humbly in the stern until they came alongside the shining yacht and a dignified, formidable British sailor spoke to them from the polished rail.

"Who is it wishes to see Sir John Burgoyne?" he inquired.

"He wouldn't know me," said Tib.

"I am sorry, sir, but Sir John is having his kippers and can't be disturbed until later in the forenoon."

"It's all right," said Josie, "I'm his niece."

The sailor looked at her suspiciously. At this point Sir John Burgoyne appeared upon the deck.

"This lady says she's your niece, sir," said the sailor.

The old captain came to the rail.

"Now I don't happen to have a niece," he remarked.

Josie spoke quickly to him in French. "The Empress Eugenie is in Trouville. She is trying to get to England."

In a few minutes they had convinced him of the truth of their story; he left his kippered herring and toast to cool and discussed plans with them. After it was decided that the Empress had best not come aboard until twilight he beckoned to his boatswain.

"Pipe all hands on deck."

Following the whistle two dozen men formed themselves into attendant statues on three sides of a square, and after a gruff "All present, sir" there was no sound on board.

"I don't want any of you men to go ashore today. The Empress of the French people is coming on board this evening. I count on every one of you to give no indication or signal as to why you were kept on board. Dismiss."

. . . It was dark when oars again disturbed the water beside the yacht and Dr. Evans assisted the Empress up the accommodation ladder.

"You have no waiting women with you?" Sir John asked. "I suppose this young American lady will be along."

"I'll go gladly," said Josie.

"And Dr. Evans will come also?"

"If the Empress likes I will be glad to. Dr. Pilgrim will take care of my affairs in Paris."

"I am afraid there is slight accommodation on board," he said politely to Tib.

"I must go back," Tib said, but the others could not help noticing the slight expression of regret in his and Josie's faces.

"When will you be back in Paris?" Tib said to her quickly. "I expect to be there for several months representing the *Richmond Times-Dispatch*, the *Danville News* and the *Lynchburg Courier*."

"I'll be back soon if you keep the peace," said Josie.

When they left the quays there had been a restive curious crowd gathering.

"We are putting to sea immediately though I look for a rough crossing," Sir John said.

The Empress Eugenie, distraught and grief-stricken, was distributing louis d'or to the sailors.

"And these two young Americans must have a souvenir also."

She took two matched bracelets from her wrists, handing one to Tib and one to Dr. Pilgrim.

"You two men have looked at each other sometimes as though you had some quarrel. In memory of your great help to me and for the sake of the pretty Josie will you not forget it all forever? I should like to feel that I had done some good during these days when you have been so good to me."

"Our quarrel is over so far as I'm concerned," said Tib.

The two younger men started back toward shore in the dinghy and the hands that waved to them from the yacht as they gradually lost sight of it in the growing dark were like a symbol that the cruelty of a distant time was receding with every stroke of the oars into a dimmer and dimmer past.

FSF as a Confederate officer in his play [*The*] *Coward*, 1913.

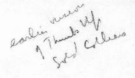

DENTIST APPOINTMENT

by

F. Scott Fitzgerald

The buggy progressed at a tired trot and its two occupants, up since dawn, were as weary as their horses when they turned down the pike toward Washington. The girl was tawny and lovely-- despite July she wore a light blue dress of bombazine cloth and because of this she had listened politely to her brother's strictures during the drive down: nurses in Washington hospitals did not dress like women of the world. Josie was saddened for it was the first really grown-up costume she had ever owned. She came of strict stock, but many youths at home had observed the charming glow of her person since she turned twelve and she had prepared for this trip as if she were going to a party.

"Is it still Maryland, brother?" She dug him with the handle of the buggy whip, and Captain Doctor Pilgrim came alive.

"Why--we're approaching the District of Columbia--unless you've turned us around. We'll stop and get water at this farmhouse just ahead. And, Josie, don't be too sweet with these people down here - They're almost all secesh, and if you're nice to them they take advantage of it and get haughty.

The Pilgrims were possibly the only people in the vicinity

Dentist Appointment

The buggy progressed at a tired trot and its two occupants, up since dawn, were as weary as their horses when they turned down the pike toward Washington. The girl was tawny and lovely—despite July she wore a light blue dress of bombazine cloth and because of this she had listened politely to her brother's strictures during the drive down: nurses in Washington hospitals did not dress like women of the world. Josie was saddened for it was the first really grown-up costume she had ever owned. She came of strict stock, but many youths at home had observed the charming glow of her person since she turned twelve and she had prepared for this trip as if she were going to a party.

"Is it still Maryland, brother?" She dug him with the handle of the buggy whip, and Captain Doctor Pilgrim came alive.

"Why—we're approaching the District of Columbia—unless you've turned us around. We'll stop and get water at this farmhouse just ahead. And, Josie, don't be too sweet with these people down here—They're almost all secesh, and if you're nice to them they take advantage of it and get haughty."

The Pilgrims were possibly the only people in the vicinity who did not know that this part of Maryland was suddenly in Confederate hands. To ease the pressure on Lee's army at Petersburg, General Early had marched his corps up the Shenandoah Valley to make a last desperate threat at the Capitol. After throwing a few shells into the suburbs, he learned of Federal rein for cements and turned his weary columns about for the march back into Virginia. His last infantry had scarcely slogged along this very pike, leaving a stubborn dust, and Josie was rather puzzled by a number of what seemed to be armed tramps who limped past them. Also there was something about the two men galloping toward the carriage that made her ask with a certain alarm, "What are those men, brother? Secesh?"

To Josie, or anyone who had not been to the front, it would have been difficult to place these men as soldiers—soldiers—Tib Dulany, who had once contributed occasional verse to the *Lynchburg Courier*, wore a hat

189

that had been white, a butternut coat, blue pants that had been issued to a Union trooper, and a cartridge belt stamped C.S.A. All that the two riders had in common were their fine new carbines captured last week from Pleasanton's cavalry. They came up beside the buggy in a whirl of dust and Tib saluted the doctor.

"Hi there, Yank!"

"We want to get some water," said Josie haughtily to the handsomest young man. Then suddenly she saw that Captain Doctor Pilgrim's hand was at his holster, but immobile—the second rider was holding a carbine three feet from his heart.

Almost painfully, Captain Pilgrim raised his arms.

"What is this—a raid?" he demanded.

Josie felt a hand reaching about her and shrank forward; Tib was taking her brother's revolver.

"What is this?" repeated Dr. Pilgrim. "Are you guerrillas?"

"Who are *you*?" the riders demanded. Without waiting for an answer Tib said, "Young lady, turn in yonder at the farmhouse. You can get water there."

He realized suddenly that she was lovely, that she was frightened and brave, and he added: "Nobody's going to hurt you. We just aiming to detain you a little."

"Will you tell me who you are?" Captain Pilgrim demanded.

"Cultivate calm!" Tib advised him. "You're inside Lee's lines now."

"Lee's lines!" Captain Pilgrim cried. "You think every time you Mosby murderers come out of your hills and cut a telegraph—"

The team, barely started, jolted to a stop—the second trooper had grabbed the reins, and turned black eyes upon the northerner.

"One word more about Mosby and I'll clean your little old face with dandelions."

"The officer isn't informed of the news, Wash," said Tib. "He doesn't know he's a prisoner of the Army of Northern Virginia."

Captain Pilgrim looked at them incredulously; Wash released the reins and they drove to the farmhouse. Only as the foliage parted and he saw two dozen horses attended by grey-clad orderlies, did he realize that his information was indeed several days behind.

"Is Lee's army *here*?"

"You didn't know? Why, right now Abe Lincoln's in the kitchen washing dishes—and General Grant's upstairs making the beds."

"Ah-h-h!" grunted Captain Pilgrim.

"Say, Wash, I sure would like to be in Washington tonight when Jeff Davis rides in. That Yankee rebellion didn't last long, did it?"

Josie suddenly believed it and her world was crashing around her. The Boys in Blue, the Union forever—Mine eyes have seen the Glory of the Coming of the Lord. Her eyes filled with hot tears.

"You can't take my brother prisoner—he's not really an officer, he's a doctor. He was wounded at Cold Harbor—"

"Doctor, eh? Don't know anything about teeth, does he?" asked Tib, dismounting at the porch.

"Oh yes—that's his specialty."

"So you're a tooth doctor? That's what we been looking for all over Maryland-My-Maryland. If you'll be so kind as to come in here you can pull a tooth of a real Bonaparte, a cousin of Emperor Napoleon III. No joke—he's attached to General Early's staff. He's been bawling his head off for an hour but the medical men went on with the ambulances."

An officer came out on the porch, gave a nervous ear to a crackling of rifles in the distance, and bent an eye upon the buggy.

"We found a tooth specialist, Lieutenant," said Tib. "Providence sent him into our lines and if Napoleon is still—"

"Thank God!" the officer exclaimed. "Bring him in. We didn't know whether to take the Prince along or leave him."

Suddenly a glimpse of the Confederacy was staged for Josie on the vine-covered veranda. There was a sudden egress: a spidery man in a shabby riding coat with faded stars, followed by two younger men cramming papers into a canvas sack. Then a miscellany of officers, one on a single crutch, one stripped to an undershirt with the gold star of a general pinned to a bandage on his shoulder. The general air was of nervous gaiety but Josie saw the reflection of disappointment in their tired eyes. Perceiving her, they made a single gesture: their dozen right hands rose to their dozen hats and they bowed in her direction.

Josie bowed back stiffly, trying unsuccessfully to bring hauteur and pious reproach into her face. In a moment they swung into their saddles. General Early looked for a moment at the city that he could not conquer, a city that another Virginian had conceived arbitrarily out of a swamp eighty years before.

"No change in orders," he said to the aide at his stirrup. "Tell Mosby that I want couriers every half hour up to Harper's Ferry."

"Yes, sir."

The aide spoke to him in a low voice and his sun-strained eyes focused on Dr. Pilgrim in the buggy.

"I understand you're a dentist," he said. "Prince Napoleon has been with us as an observer. Pull out his tooth or whatever he needs. These two troopers will stay with you. Do well by him and they'll let you go without parole when you've finished."

There was the clop and crunch of mounted men moving down a lane, and in a minute the last sally of the Army of Northern Virginia faded swiftly into the distance.

"We got a dentist here for Prince Napoleon," said Tib to a French aide-de-camp who came out of the farmhouse.

"That's excellent news." He led the way inside. "The Prince is in such agony."

"The doctor is a Yankee," Tib continued. "One of us will have to stay while he's operating."

The stout invalid across the room, a gross miniature of his world-shaking uncle, tore his hand from a groaning mouth and sat upright in an armchair.

"Operating!" he cried. "My God! Is he going to operate?"

Dr. Pilgrim looked suspiciously at Tib.

"My sister—where will she be?"

"I've put her into the parlor, Doctor. Wash, you stay here."

"I'll need hot water," said Dr. Pilgrim, "and my instrument case from the buggy."

Prince Napoleon groaned again.

"Will you cut my head off of my neck? Ah, cette vie barbare!"

Tib consoled him politely.

"This doctor is a demon for teeth, Prince Napoleon."

"I am a trained surgeon," said Dr. Pilgrim stiffly. "Now, sir, will you take off that hat?"

The Prince removed the wide white Cordoba which topped a miscellaneous costume of red tail-coat, French uniform breeches and dragoon boots.

"Can we trust this medicin if he is a Yankee? How can I know he will not cut to kill? Does he know I am a French citizen?"

"Prince, if he doesn't do well by you we got some apple trees outside and plenty rope."

Tib went into the parlor where Miss Josie sat on the edge of a horse-hair sofa.

"What are you going to do to my brother?"

Sorry for her lovely, anxious face, Tib said: "I'm more worried what he's about to do to the Prince."

An anguished howl arose from the library.

"You hear that?" Tib said. "The Prince is the one to worry about."

"Are you going to send us to that Libby Prison?"

"Most certainly not, Madame. You're going to be here till your brother fixes up the Prince; then as soon as our cavalry pickets come past you can continue your journey."

Josie relaxed.

"I thought all the fighting was down in Virginia."

"It is. That's where we're heading, I reckon—this is the third time I've ridden into Maryland with the army and it's the third time I'm heading back with it."

She looked at him for the first time with a certain human interest.

"What did my brother mean when he said you were a gorilla?"

"I reckon because I didn't shave since yesterday." He laughed. "It's 'guerrilla,' not 'gorilla.' When it's a Yankee on detached service they call him a scout but when it's one of us they call us spies and string us up."

"Any soldier not in uniform is a spy, isn't he?"

"I'm in uniform—look at my buckle. Believe it or not, Miss Pilgrim, I was a smart-looking trooper when I rode out of Lynchburg four years ago."

He told her how he had been dressed that day and Josie listened, thinking it was not unlike when the first young volunteers had got on the train at Chillicothe, Ohio.

"—with a big red ribbon of my mother's for a sash. One of the girls got out in front of the troop and read a poem I wrote."

"Say the poem," Josie exclaimed, "I would so enjoy hearing it."

Tib considered. "Reckon I've forgot it. All I remember is 'Lynchburg, thy guardsmen bid thy hills farewell.'"

"I love it." Forgetting the errand on which Lynchburg's guardsmen were bent she added, "I certainly wish you remembered the rest of it."

Came a scream from across the hall and a medley of French. The distraught face of the aide-de-camp appeared at the door.

"He has pulled out not just the tooth but the estomac—He has done him to the death!"

A face pushed over his shoulder.

"Say, Tib—the Yank got the tooth."

"Did he?" said Tib absently. As Wash withdrew he turned back to Josie.

"I certainly would like to write a few lines to express my admiration of you."

"This is so sudden," she said lightly.

She might have spoken for herself too—nothing is much more sudden than first sight.

II

A minute later Wash looked back in.

"Say, Tib, we oughtn't to stay here. A patrol just skinned by shootin back from the saddle. Ain't we fixin to leave? This here Doctor knows we're Mosby's men."

"Will you leave without us?" the aide demanded suspiciously.

"We sure will," said Tib. "The Prince can observe the war from the Yankee angle for a while. Miss Pilgrim, I bid you a sad, I may say, a most unwilling goodbye."

Peering hastily into the library Tib found the Prince so far recovered as to be sitting upright, panting and gasping.

"You are an artiste," he was assuring Dr. Pilgrim. "After all the terror I still live! In Paris sometimes if they take the tooth from you you have hemorrhage and die."

Wash called from the door.

"Come on, Tib!"

There were shots very near now. The two scouts had scarcely unhitched their horses when Wash exclaimed: "Hell fire!" and pointed down the drive where half a dozen Federal troopers had come into view behind the foliage of the far gate. Wash swung his carbine one-handed to his right shoulder and reached for a cartridge in his pouch.

"I'll take the two on the left," he said.

Standing concealed by their horses they waited.

"Maybe we could run for it," Tib suggested.

"The place has got seven-rail fences."

"Don't fire till they get nearer."

Leisurely the file of cavalry trotted up the drive. Even after four years on detached service, Tib hated to shoot from ambush, but he concentrated on the business and the front sight of his carbine came into line with the center of the Yankee corporal's tunic.

"Got your mark, Wash?"

"Think so."

"When they break we'll ride through 'em."

But the ill luck of Southern arms that day was with them before they could loose a shot. A heavy body flung against Tib and pinioned him. A voice shouted beside his ear.

"Men, they're rebels here!"

Even as Tib turned, wrestling desperately with Dr. Pilgrim, the Northern patrol stopped, drew pistols. Wash was bobbing desperately from side to side to get a shot at Pilgrim, but the Doctor maneuvered Tib's body in between.

In a few seconds it was over. Wash loosed a single shot but the Federals were around them before he was in his saddle. Furious, the two young men faced their captors. Dr. Pilgrim spoke sharply to the Federal corporal:

"These are Mosby's men."

Those years were bitter on the border. The Federals slew Wash when he made an attempt to get away by grabbing at the corporal's revolver. Tib, still struggling, was trussed up at the porch rail.

"There's a good tree," one of the Federals said, "and there's a rope on the swing."

The corporal glanced at Dr. Pilgrim.

"You say he's one of Mosby's men?"

"I'm in the Seventh Virginia Cavalry," said Tib.

"Are you one of Mosby's men?"

"None of your business."

"All right, boys, get the rope."

Dr. Pilgrim's austere presence asserted itself again.

"I don't think you should hang him but certainly this type of irregular has got to be discouraged."

"We hang them up by their thumbs, sometimes," suggested the corporal.

"Then do that," said Dr. Pilgrim. "He spoke of hanging me."

. . . By six that evening the road outside was busy again. Two brigades of Sheridan's finest were on Early's trail, harassing him down the valley. Mail and fresh vegetables were moving toward the capital again and the raid was over, except for a few stragglers who lay exhausted along the Rockville Pike.

In the farmhouse it was quiet. Prince Napoleon was waiting for an ambulance from Washington. There was no sound there—except from Tib, who, as his skin slipped off his thumbs, repeated aloud to himself fragments of his own political verses. When he could think of no more verses he tried singing a song that they had sung much that year:

> We'll follow the feather of Mosby tonight;
> And lift from the Yankees our horse-flesh and leather.
> We'll follow the feather, Mosby's grey feather . . .

When it was full dark and the sentry was dozing on the porch someone came who knew where the step-ladder was, because she had heard them dump it down after stringing up Tib. When she had half sawed through the rope she went back to her room for pillows and moved the table under him and laid the pillows on it.

She did not need any precedents for what she was doing. When Tib fell with a grunting gasp, murmuring "Nothing to be ashamed of," she poured half a bottle of sherry wine over his hands. Then, suddenly sick herself, she ran back to her room.

III

After a war there are some for whom it is over and many unreconciled. Dr. Pilgrim, irritated by the government's failure to bring the south to its knees, left Washington and set out for Minnesota by rail and river. He and Josie arrived at St. Paul in the autumn of 1866.

"We are out of the area of infection," he said. "Why, back in Washington rebels already walk the streets unmolested. But slavery has never polluted this air."

The rude town was like a great fish just hauled out of the Mississippi and still leaping and squirming on the bank. Around the wharves spread a card-house city of twelve thousand people, complete with churches, stores, stables and saloons. Walking the littered streets, the newcomers stepped aside for stages and prairie wagons, bull teams and foraging chickens—but there were also some tall hats and much tall talk, for the railroad was coming through. The general note was of heady confidence and high excitement.

"You must get some cowhide boots," Josie remarked, but Dr. Pilgrim was engrossed in his thought.

"There will be southerners out here," Dr. Pilgrim ruminated. "Josie, there's something I haven't told you because it may alarm you. When we were in Chicago I saw that man of Mosby's—the one we captured."

Drums beat in her head—drums of remembered pain. Her eyes had seen the glory of the coming of the Lord, and then seen the glory of the Lord hung up by the thumbs . . .

"I had an idea he recognized me too," Dr. Pilgrim continued. "I may have been wrong."

"You ought to be glad he's alive," said Josie in an odd voice.

"Glad? Frankly, that wasn't my thought. A Mosby guerrilla would be capable of vindictiveness and revenge—when such a man comes west he means to seek out desperadoes like himself, the kind who rob the mail and hold up trains."

"That's absurd," she protested, "you're the one who's vindictive. You don't know anything about his private character. As a matter of fact—" She hesitated. "I thought he had a rather fine inner nature."

Such a statement was equivalent to giddy approval and Dr. Pilgrim looked at her with resentment. He did not altogether approve of Josie—in Washington she had had three proposals within the year, actually six but, rather than be classed as a flirt, she did not count the ones she stopped unfinished. But almost from the moment her brother mentioned Tib Dulany she looked rather breathlessly for him among the swarms of new arrivals in front of the hotel.

Tib came to St. Paul with no knowledge of this. He had not recognized Dr. Pilgrim in Chicago, nor were his thoughts either vindictive or desperate. He was going to join some former comrades in arms further west, and Josie came into his range of vision as a pretty stranger having breakfast at the hotel lunch counter. Then suddenly he recognized her or rather he recognized a memory and an emotion deep in himself, for momentarily he could not say her name.

And Josie, in the instant that she saw him, looked at his hands, at where his thumbs should be but were not, and the smoky room went round about her.

"I'm sorry I startled you," he said. "You know me, don't you?"

"Yes."

"My name is Dulany. In Maryland—"

"I know."

There was an embarrassed pause. With an effort she asked:

"Did you just arrive?"

"Yes. I didn't expect to see you—I don't know what to say. I've often thought—"

. . . Josie's brother was out seeking an office—at any moment he might walk in the door. Instinctively Josie threw reserve aside.

"My brother is here with me," she said. "He saw you in Chicago. He thinks you may have some idea of—revenge."

"He's wrong," Tib said, "I can honestly say that at no time have I had such an idea."

"The war isn't over for my brother. And when I saw—your poor hands—"

"That's past," he said. "I'd like to talk to you as if it had never happened."

"He wouldn't like it," she said, and then added, "but I would. If he knew you were at this hotel—"

"I can go to another."

There was a sudden interruption. Tib was hailed by three young men across the room who started over toward him.

"I want to see you," he whispered hurriedly. "Couldn't you meet me this afternoon in front of the post office?"

"Tonight is better. Seven o'clock."

Josie paid her bill and went out, followed by the eyes of the new arrivals, a dark young man with undefeated southern eyes burning under a panama and two red-headed twins.

"It didn't take you long, Tib," said the former, Mr. Ben Cary, late of Stuart's staff. "We've been here three days and we haven't found anything like that."

"Let's get out of here," said Tib, "I have reasons."

Seated in another restaurant, they demanded, "What's it all about, Tib? Is there a husband in the wind?"

"Not a husband," said Tib. "There's a Yankee brother—he's a dentist."

The three men exchanged a glance.

"A dentist. Boy, you interest us strangely. Why are you running away from a dentist?"

"Some trouble during the war. Suppose you tell me why you're in St. Paul. I was starting out to meet you in Leesburg tomorrow."

"We're here on business, Tib—or rather it's a matter of life and death. We're having Indian trouble up there. About two thousand Sioux are camped on our door-step threatening to tear our fences down."

"You've come to get help?"

"Fat chance. Do you reckon the government would back a rebel colony against a privileged Indian. No, we're on our own. We think we can persuade the chief that we're his friends, if we can do him a big favor. Tell us more about the dentist."

"Forget the dentist," said Tib impatiently. "He just arrived here. I don't like him and that's the whole story."

"Just arrived here," repeated Cary meditatively, "that's very interesting. They have three here already and we've been to see them all and they're the most cowardly white men that ever breathed—" He broke off and demanded, "What's this man's name?"

"Pilgrim," said Tib, "but I won't introduce you."

Another glance passed between them and they were suddenly uncommunicative. Tomorrow they would all start for Leesburg—Tib was relieved that it was not tonight. But his relief would have been brief had he heard their conversation when he left them.

"If this dentist has just arrived he's still traveling, so to speak—a little bit further won't hurt him."

"We won't consult him. We'll have the consultation out where the patient is."

"Old Tib would enjoy it—right in the Mosby line. But then again he might object. It's been a long time since I saw a girl like that."

IV

Dr. Pilgrim began the installation of his office that evening—Josie gave an excuse to remain at the hotel to sew. She slipped out at seven to the post office where Tib waited with a rented rig, and they drove up on the bluff above the river. The town twinkled below them, a mirage of a metropolis against the darkening prairie.

"That represents the future," he said. "It doesn't seem much to leave Virginia for—but I'm not sorry."

"I'm not either," Josie said. "When we got here yesterday I felt a little sad and lost. But today it's different."

"The trouble is that now I don't want to go any further," he said. "Do you know what made me change?"

Josie didn't want him to tell her yet.

"It must have been the little signs of the east," she said. "Somebody's planted some lilac trees and I saw a big grand piano going through the street."

"There'll be no pianos where I'm going, but then there hasn't been much music in Virginia for the last few years." He hesitated. "Sometime I'd like you to see Virginia—the valley in spring."

"'Lynchburg thy guardsmen bid thy hills farewell'," she quoted.

"You remember that?" He smiled. "But I didn't want to stay there. My father and two brothers were killed and when Mother died this spring it was all gone. And then life seemed to start all over again when I saw your pretty face in the hotel."

This time she didn't change the subject.

"I remembered waking up that morning two years ago and crawling off through the woods trying to think whether a girl cut me down or whether it was part of the nightmare. Afterwards I liked to believe it was you."

"It was me." She shivered. "We really ought to start back. I must be there when my brother comes in."

"Give me a minute to think about it," he begged, "it's a very beautiful thought. Of course I would have fallen in love with you anyhow."

"You hardly know me. I'm just the only girl you've met here—" She was really talking to herself, and not very convincingly. Then after a minute neither of them were talking at all. In such a little time, that place, that hour, the shadow cast by the horse and buggy under the stars had suddenly become the center of the world.

After a while she drew away and Tib unwillingly flapped the rein on the horse's back. They should have made plans now but they were under a spell more pervasive than the breath of northern autumn in the night. They would meet tomorrow somehow—the same place, the same time. They were so sure that they would meet—

Dr. Pilgrim had not returned and Josie, all wide awake, walked up the street to his office, a frame building with rooms for professional men. She stepped into a scene of confusion. A group gathered around the colored scrubwoman trying to find out exactly what had happened. One thing was certain—before Dr. Pilgrim had so much as hung out his shingle he had been violently spirited away.

"They wasn't Indians," cried the negress, "they was white people dressed up like Indians. They said they chief was sick. Whenever I told them they wasn't Indians they begun whoopin and carryin on, sayin they was goin to scalp me sure enough. But two of them had red hair and they talk like they come from Virginia."

The life went out of Josie—and terror took its place. No vindictiveness, no revenge—and this was what his friends had done while he gallantly occupied her attention. An eye for an eye—no better than men had been a thousand years ago.

Traces of the guilty parties appeared. A number of citizens had noticed the "Indians" when they entered the building, and assumed it was horse-play. Later that night a wagon, accompanied by riders who answered the negress's description, had driven out of town on the run.

Josie remembered the name Leesburg, a trading post, two days journey west of St. Paul. She had letters of introduction not yet presented and next day some sympathetic merchants helped her get the ear of the commandant at Fort Snelling. At noon, accompanied by a detail of six troopers, she started for Leesburg on the Fargo stage.

V

Dr. Pilgrim had once before been kidnapped for professional reasons, so the experience did not even have the charm of novelty. To be carried off by imitation Indians somewhat paralyzed his faculties at first, but when he learned the reason for the abduction he expressed this opinion fluently:

"For the sake of a savage!" he raged. "Why, Indians don't know what dentistry is: they have their medicine men—or nature takes care of them."

They sat in a wooden blockhouse, one of the half dozen edifices of Leesburg. A caucus of citizens, all hailing from below the Mason-Dixon line, listened with interest to the conversation.

"Nature didn't take care of Chief Red Weed," said Ben Cary, "so you'll have to. You see before he had the toothache he didn't mind the fences—now he's calling in his braves from over the Dakota line. Like to ride out to their village and take a look?"

"I don't want to see hide or hair of any Indians!"

"It isn't his hide—it's his teeth."

"Confound his teeth! They can rot away for all I care."

"Now, Doctor, that seems kind of inhuman. The chief is a savage, like you say, but the government says he's a noble savage. If he was a darky wouldn't you go for that tooth?"

"That's different."

"Not so different. This Indian is mighty dark, isn't he boys? Especially when you get him in his wigwam. While you're operating you can just pretend he's a nigger—then you won't mind it a bit."

The tone of bitterness only stiffened the doctor's resolution.

"It's the insult to my profession. Would you kidnap a surgeon to sew up an injured wildcat?"

"Red Weed isn't so wild. He may even take you into his tribe. You'd be the only redskin dentist in the world."

"The honor does not appeal to me."

Cary tried another tack.

"In a way, you've got us, Doctor—we can't force you. But we believe that if you fix up one sick Indian you can save women and children from what happened here in '62."

"That's a matter for the army—they handled the rebellion."

He was on thin ice now but there was no answer except a long silence.

"Boys, we'll let the doctor think it over." Cary turned to the Indian interpreter, "Say to Red Weed that the white medicine man won't come to the village today because he must purify himself on his arrival."

An hour after this interview Tib Dulany accompanied by a guide rode into Leesburg on lathered ponies; he had read the morning paper in St. Paul and set out long before the stage. He was wildly angry when he dismounted and faced Ben Cary.

"You damned fools! They'll send troops from St. Paul."

"It was an emergency, Tib—we acted the best way we knew how." He explained the situation but Tib was unsympathetic.

"If anybody shanghaied me I'd rather be shot than do what they wanted."

"Didn't you do a little body-snatching for Mosby in your day?"

"There's no comparison. What do you reckon that girl thinks of me now?"

"That's a pity, Tib, but—"

Gradually as he talked of the imminent danger the image of Josie temporarily receded from Tib's mind.

"Pilgrim's a stubborn man," he said. "Does he know I'm one of you?"

"I thought you wouldn't want that mentioned."

"Well, it seems I'm in it now. Maybe I can do something. Tell him there's another patient wants to see him—that and nothing more."

Dr. Pilgrim had braced himself resolutely against persuasion—and when Tib came to the door a tirade was on his tongue. But the words were not spoken—his jaw dropped and he stared as his visitor said quietly:

"I've come to see you about my thumbs."

Then Dr. Pilgrim's eyes fell upon what a pair of gloves had hidden in Chicago.

"An odd sight," said Tib. "I found it an inconvenience at first. But then discovered I could think about it two ways, as a battle wound, or as something else."

The doctor tried to summon up that moral superiority so essential to his self-respect.

"In other days," continued Tib, "It would have been quite simple. These Indians out here would understand. They have a torture that isn't very different—put thongs through a man's chest and hang him up till he collapses." He broke off. "Dr. Pilgrim, up to now I've tried to consider my thumbs as a war wound, but out here closer to nature I begin to think I was wrong. Perhaps I ought to collect my bill."

"What are you going to do to me?"

"That depends. You did a cruel thing. And you don't seem to feel any regret about it."

"It was perhaps an extreme measure," admitted the doctor uneasily. "To that extent I am sorry."

"That's a lot from you, but it isn't enough. All I asked of you that day in Maryland was to pull that Frenchman's tooth. That wasn't so terrible, was it?"

"No, it wasn't. I tell you I do regret the incident."

Tib got to his feet.

"I believe you. And to prove it you'll come along with me and pull another tooth. Then we'll call the account square."

The doctor was trapped, but in his moment of relief he could find no words of protest. Irascibly he picked up his bag and a few minutes later a little party started for the Indian village through the twilight.

At the outpost they were delayed while a message went to Red Weed; word came to pass them through. Arrived at the chief's wigwam Dr. Pilgrim, accompanied by an interpreter, stepped inside.

Five minutes later a triumphant yell arose from the squaws and children who lined the street—the Fargo stage, surrounded by braves in war paint, drove up with four disarmed soldiers and half a dozen civilians inside.

VI

Instinctively Tib ran to the side of the stage but at Josie's expression his throat choked up and no words came. He turned to the cavalry corporal.

"Dr. Pilgrim is safe. At this moment he's in the chief's wigwam working on him. If we sit tight we'll all get out of this."

"What's it all mean?"

Ben Cary answered him:

"It means things are about to break here but your Colonel wouldn't listen to us because we're Virginians."

"I'm in this now," Tib said to Josie, "but I didn't know anything about it that night."

From the wigwam issued a stream of groans followed by a wailing cry and the warriors crowded in around the tepee.

"He'd better be good," said Cary grimly.

Ten minutes passed. The complaining moans rose and fell. The face of the interpreter appeared in a flap of the tent and he said something rapidly in Sioux, translating it for the benefit of the whites.

"Him got two teeth."

And then to Tib's wonder Josie's voice called to him out of the dusk.

"It's all right, isn't it?" she said.

"We don't know yet."

"I mean everything's all right. It doesn't even seem strange to be here."

"You believe me then?"

"I believe you, Tib—but it doesn't seem to matter now."

Her eyes with that bright yet veiled expression, described as starry, looked past the wailing Indians, the anxious whites, the ominous black triangle of the tepee, at some vision of her own against the sky.

"Whenever we're together," she said, "one place is as good as any other. See—they know it, they're looking at us. We're not strangers here—they won't harm us. They know we're at home."

Hand in hand Tib and Josie waited and a cool wind blew the curls around her forehead. From time to time the light moved inside the wigwam and they could distinguish the doctor's voice and the guttural of the interpreter. One by one the Indians had squatted on the ground and a soldier was taking a food hamper from the wagon. The village was quiet and there was suddenly a flag of stars in the bright sky. Josie was the only person there who knew that there was nothing to worry about now, because she and Tib owned everything around them now further than their eyes could see. She felt very safe and warm with her hand on his shoulder while Dr. Pilgrim kept his appointment across the still darkness.

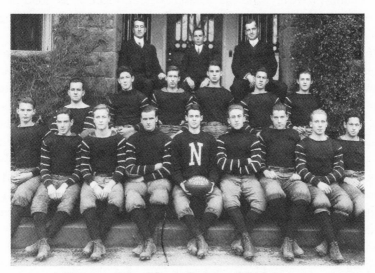

Newman School football photo: FSF front row,
third from the left.

Fitzgerald started "Offside Play" in North Carolina in March 1937,
telling Harold Ober, "Anyhow I've begun the football story but God
knows where the next two weeks rent come from. . . . What in hell shall
I do? I want to write the football story unworried + uninterrupted."
He sent Ober a draft in April under the title "Athletic Interview," asking for money in advance. It is something of a throwback—perhaps a
reminder of better and happier times, as its writer sat broke in a hotel
in the Smoky Mountains, creating for himself the company of blue-
eyed, blonde Kiki, watching a game at the Yale Bowl. However, it also
contains cheating, lying, sex, and corruptions of various kinds against
its glittery Ivy League backdrop. It is an example of Fitzgerald trying to
turn out what he himself called "identical product"—the sort of story
people still associated with him—but managing to make his pretty characters gritty and even dirty instead. He also envisaged this as a story to
be sold for a screenplay, calling it "a football story for the coast."

Ober liked it, telling him "you are back in your stride." Fitzgerald
agreed: "I feel the stuff coming back as my health improves." However, the *Saturday Evening Post* declined the story, now titled "Athletic
Interval," because it was too long. Ober reported, "They say it lacks the
warmth of your best work and it hasn't the 'incandescent' quality your
readers expect. This gives me a pain. The story may not be your very

best—no author can be his very best all the time; but it is so much better than 9/10 of the stories they buy that their criticism is absurd." Ober did suggest, however, "perhaps you can do something to Kiki or Considine that will make them more likable."

Fitzgerald left these two central characters as they were. However, he worried over naming actual colleges, making the school Van Kamp had attended a fictional one, and considered changing Yale to Princeton, his own alma mater. He worked on the story in June 1937, but then put it aside when he arrived in Los Angeles with his new MGM contract and immediately set to work on screenplays. In October 1937, he was still thinking about the story, now called "Offside Play," and about "Dentist Appointment," writing to Ober: "In regard to the stories, I am going to do something about them but have definitely postponed it until after THREE COMRADES is in the bag—as I told you which is a matter of three weeks more. Then I will either take a week off or simply find time some way in the early morning. So tell Colliers not to fret about it. The longer I wait the more I am liable to get a fresh point of view. . . . Both of them come so near to being right that I am sure the actual writing won't be any trouble." Ober's card files note that he never sent them another draft, and that the office ultimately returned all their copies of the versions of the story to Fitzgerald.

OFFSIDE PLAY

by

F. Scott Fitzgerald

The sun shone bright on Kiki, a brisk November sun, blue in
the drifting cigarettes of the crowd. It rendered her full justice
as a lovely person radiantly happy, but she assured herself such
a state of things couldn't last.

"-- because at present I'm one of those dreadful people who
have everything."

She exaggerated, of course -- other heads grew the same golden
thatch to brighten northern winters, other eyes had been steeped in
the same blue smoke of enchantment and at the; and hers was by no means the
only rakish mouth in the Yale Bowl. Also there were doubtlessly
other hearts around that had stopped being like hotels. But here
at the beginning picture Kiki as the happiest girl on earth.

The moment endured, glittered, then slipped into eternity --
As the man beside her, the infinitely desired, the infinitely admirable
Considine, said something which disturbed her balance on the
pinnacle.

"I want to talk to you very seriously after the game," was
what he said. But he did not press her hand or look at her as he
said it -- he simply gazed straight ahead at the teams on the field,
yet not staring at something, only staring away.

"What is it?" she demanded. "Tell me now."

Written in Fitzgerald's hand at the top: "Change to Princeton."

Offside Play

The sun shone bright on Kiki, a brisk November sun, blue in the drifting cigarettes of the crowd. It rendered her full justice as a lovely person radiantly happy, but she assured herself such a state of things couldn't last.

"—because at present I'm one of those dreadful people who have everything."

She exaggerated, of course—other heads grew the same golden thatch to brighten northern winters, other eyes had been steeped in the same blue smoke of enchantment. [and hers was by no means the only rakish mouth in the Yale Bowl. Also there were doubtlessly other hearts around that had stopped being like hotels. But here at the beginning picture Kiki as the happiest girl on earth.]

And as the moment endured, glittered, then slipped into eternity—the man beside her, the infinitely desired, the infinitely admirable Considine, said something which disturbed her balance on the pinnacle.

"I want to talk to you very seriously after the game," was what he said. But he did not press her hand or look at her as he said it—he simply gazed straight ahead at the teams on the field, yet not staring at something, only staring away.

"What is it?" she demanded. "Tell me now."

"Not now." A scrimmage came to earth and his eyes dropped to the program. "Number 16 again—that little guard Van Kamp. Weighs a hundred and fifty-nine and he's stopping every line play by himself."

"Is he on our side?" she asked absently.

"No, he's on the Yale team, and he ought not to be," he said indignantly. "They bought him, by Heavens! They purchased him body and soul."

"That's too bad," she said politely. "Why didn't Harvard make an offer for just the body?"

"We don't do things like that, but these people haven't any conscience. Here they go—look! See him jump over that play—heads up, never gets buried."

Kiki was not paying much attention—she had guessed that there was trouble on the sunny air. But if things were wrong there was nothing she wouldn't do to right them. Alex Considine "had everything," he had been the Man of Promise at Cambridge the year before—also she adored him.

Between the halves big drums beat and the sun went out and people pushed past them, shouting from row to row.

"I've never seen a lineman dominate a game like this Van Kamp," said Considine. "If he had on a crimson jersey he'd be beautiful."

In the third quarter the paragon blocked a punt and recovered it himself—within a few plays his team scored, and the rest of the game was a breathless flight of long passes through a stratosphere of frantic sound. Suddenly it was over; Kiki and Alex moved with the hushed defeated half of the crowd out of the stadium, met friends for a hurried half hour and rushed to the train. They should be alone now, but they found only a single place and Considine sat half on the arm, half in the crowded aisle.

"I've got to know what's on your mind," she said.

"Wait till we get to New York."

"Oh, what is it?" she demanded, "you've got to tell me—is it about us?"

"Well—yes."

"What about us—aren't we all right? Aren't we on the crest? I simply won't wait two hours to find out." Lightly she added, "I know what it is—you're throwing me over and you don't want to do it in public."

"Please, Kiki."

"Well, then let me ask you questions. First question—do you love me? No, I won't ask that—I'm a little afraid to. I'll tell you something instead—I love you, no matter if it's something awful you're going to tell me."

She saw him sigh without a sound.

"Then it is awful," she said. "Then maybe it is what I thought—" She broke off; there was no gaiety left in the suspense. Close to tears she had to change the subject.

"See the man across the aisle," she whispered, "the people behind me say it's Van Kamp, the Yale player."

He glanced around.

"I don't think so—he wouldn't be going to New York so soon. Still it looks like him."

"It must be, with those awful scratches—if it wasn't for that he'd be beautiful."

"That's because he plays heads up."

"He's beautiful anyhow—really one of the handsomest men I've ever seen. You might introduce me."

"I don't know him. Anyhow, he doesn't understand any words—just signals."

It was the first light remark he had made all afternoon and she had a flash of hope but immediately the gravity came back reinforced into his face, as though he had laughed at a funeral.

"Maybe he's a great mathematician and thinks in numbers," she rambled on unhappily. "Maybe Einstein teaches him—but he's at Princeton."

"I'll bet he had a full time tutor to get him through."

"I had one myself when young. You can't convince me that man's stupid."

He looked at her quizzically.

"You like all kinds, don't you?"

She gave up trying to talk and borrowing his program turned to the players' statistics.

Left Guard   Eubert G. Van Kamp   Newton H.S.   5'11"   159   Age 21

He was Considine's age but only a sophomore in college. At twenty-one men had written masterpieces, commanded armies.

—at eighteen girls had killed themselves for unrequited love—or gotten over it or pretended that it had never been love in the first place.

At the next station people debarked and Considine could at last drop into the seat beside her.

"Now can you talk?" she said.

"Yes, and it's going to be very frank. Kiki, I'm fonder of you than of any girl I know. Last summer when we—"

"Did you see him play last summer?"

"See who play?"

"That man Van Kamp. I mean if you saw him play last summer why didn't you just offer him more money than they did?"

He looked her unsmilingly.

"Seriously, this is something that has to be faced—"

"Oh, shut up."

"What do you mean, Kiki?"

"Go and face it yourself. I've known what you were going to say for two hours."

"I—"

"—and I'm very particular about the way I'm thrown over. Here's your ring—put it in your archeological collection—put it in your pocket. The man over the way is looking at us—this is a picture that tells a story."

"Kiki, I—"

"Shut up—up—up—up!"

"All right," he said grimly.

"Write me a letter instead and I'll give it to my husband. I may marry Van Kamp. As a matter of fact I'm glad you spoke, or didn't speak, just when you did—or didn't. I'm stepping out with a new number tonight, and I want to feel free. And here's the station—"

The second they were on their feet she left him, threading her way up the aisle swiftly, desperately, running against people, finally with a passionate intention of eluding him at any cost, catching at the arm of a swiftly moving passenger who seemed to have the right of way, and being borne with his momentum out the door and on to the station quay.

"I'm sorry," she panted, "I beg—"

It was Van Kamp. Confused she ran along beside him, returning his smile.

"Really you played the most gorgeous game," she panted, "and there's someone after me, the most frightening person. Will you walk with me to a taxi? I really haven't been drinking but he's broken my heart and all that and the symptoms are much the same effect."

They hurried up the runway into the hushed marbled tomb of the Grand Central.

"Can't you win him back?" His question was half serious but Kiki disregarded it.

"Your poor face!" she exclaimed. "Really you were wonderful. I was with a Harvard man and he was simply overwhelmed. No, I'm not going to try to win him back. I thought at first I would, but at the last minute I decided not to."

They reached the taxi stand. He was going uptown—could he take her?

"Oh, please do!"

In the cab they looked at each other by the exciting first lights that twinkled in the window. Van Kamp was blue of eye, made of wrought iron and painted ash gold. He was shy and in that sense awkward but he had most certainly never made a clumsy movement in his life.

And seeing this, Kiki, who had been plunged into a sudden vacuum, made herself over suddenly into his kind of girl. She was alone with him with no plan except such plans as they would make together. He had a date but after a few minutes there seemed to be no hurry about it—she was calling him Rip before they ordered dinner.

"I almost went to Harvard," he told her. "For a while I thought I'd play pro football, but I decided to get an education."

"How much do they pay you?"

"Pay me? They don't pay me anything."

"I thought that was the idea."

"I wish it was. Some boys I know get a hundred a month at a college out West. All I got was a loan. And of course I eat at training table, but I have to work too—I've got half a dozen jobs around the campus."

"That isn't right," she said, "they ought to pay you; you draw people to the games to watch you. You have something valuable to sell, just like—like—"

"Just like brains. Go on, say it. Sometimes I wonder why I went to college."

"Anyhow they should pay you for staying there."

"Would you mind telling them that?"

Every few minutes Kiki thought of Alex Considine with a start, wondering if he were sorry now, wondering what it was that made him not love her, something she had done or some way she was, or if there was another girl. But each time she looked very hard at Eubert G. ("Rip") Van Kamp, weight 159, height 5'11", and thought that no one had ever been so beautiful.

They went dancing and when the orchestra played "Gone" or "Lost" she felt empty and frightened inside, for last month she had danced to those pieces with Considine. But when they played "Goody-Goody," it was all right because dancing with Van Kamp was very odd and fine in quite another way. Then in the taxi she kissed him, completely, almost with abandon, as much as he wanted her to. She played the whole game until within a few hours he had become that strange dreamy figure of one whom we have been very close to and who is neither a stranger nor quite a friend.

II

At four o'clock next day he called at Kiki's house, shy at its splendor.

"What do you suppose I've been doing all day," she said. "Reading the papers—the sporting section. Have you seen this?

David was a lineman. And there was not one Goliath but seven. That's what
they are saying at New Haven today after one of the hardest fought games

in the sixty years of the Yale-Harvard series. A one hundred and fifty-nine pound guard stole the spotlight from the fleet backs—

"It can't be me," he said lightly, "I weighed a hundred and fifty-seven. And let's not play that. I came to see you—I spent all morning explaining to someone where I was last night."

—He must have many girls, she thought. Aloud she said:

"I'm interested in what we talked about at dinner. It's ridiculous that they don't pay you money for what you can do."

"The bowl would be full whether I was there or not—they've managed to carry on without me for sixty years."

"Full for the big games, yes—but not for every game. I'll bet you'll make them thousands of dollars extra."

"Oh no, I'm just one man out of eleven."

"The papers say you were the whole team."

"Oh no—it just looks that way because after the first plays I can usually tell where they're going."

Then suddenly, to Kiki's eyes, Rip's corporeal person began to grow dim, literally to fade away to the end of a long perspective. And she was alone there with Considine who had just walked into the room.

For a moment she was numb, and so controlled by her most intimate instincts that if he had come up to her she would have risen and walked like a stunned fighter into his arms. But the indirect consequences of yesterday decided the matter—he was overwrought and desperate and even more unfit than Kiki to cope with the situation. Not perceiving himself the wild relief that sprang into her eyes he talked words, words that were like bricks, building up a wall between them.

". . . I've got to see you for a minute . . . everything was such a mess . . . before I leave for Greece . . . explain why I was so absurd . . ."

—And as he stood there, blind and fumbling, the expression faded from Kiki's eyes and hurt and humiliation surged back over her. When he did look at her she was as steely and formidable as her voice.

"This is Mr. Van Kamp . . . I'm sorry but I can't see you now—There's nothing I want to discuss, Alex. You'll have to excuse me."

Incredulously he looked at Van Kamp, realizing his presence for the first time. Then, perceiving too late that this was not a matter for words, but rather a struggle against what had been said, he went toward her—and just as quickly she retreated, as if revolted by his proximity. Even Rip bristled slightly and Alex stopped, his half raised arms falling to his side.

"I'll write you," he whispered. "This is such an awful mistake."

"It might have been," she said. "Please go away."

He was gone—and for a minute, in the awful reverberating thunder of his absence, she looked toward the door thinking that he had come back, that he couldn't stop loving her, that she might have forgotten everything in his arms. A great shiver went over her—then she turned to Rip and answered a question he had just asked.

"Yes, that was the man."

"He looks awful sorry."

"Let's not talk about him. I don't know him any more. Come here, Rip."

"Here?"

"Don't put your arms around me. Just sit where I can look at you." She was like a stifling person come to a window for air. Thinking with grim pleasure how intensely Alex would have disapproved, she said:

"Rip, in Hollywood there are dozens of people your age without half your good looks, making fortunes."

"You think I ought to go in the movies?"

"No, you ought to stay in college. But you ought to get a great deal of money for this thing you can do better than anyone else—and save it up for the time when other people can do things better than you."

"You think I'll end up as a night watchman or something?" He frowned. "I'm not so stupid—I've thought of that. It's kind of sad, isn't it?"

"It's kind of sad, Rip."

"But of course you can't be sure of anything. There must be a place in the world for people like me."

"There is, I'm sure of that—but you ought to start now to build it. I'm going to help you. Don't worry—I won't fall in love with you."

"Oh, you won't?"

"Certainly not—I've been thrown over once and I haven't faintly recovered—if I ever do." She moved away from him gently. "Please stop. Don't you understand that was last night, it wasn't even me—you don't even know me, Rip, and maybe you never will."

III

That winter there were many men for Kiki, but her heart was empty and she paid them off in deflated currency. As if asleep she walked through a February inspection of the colleges, but at New Haven she opened her eyes long enough to search for Rip Van Kamp through the swirling crowd, and not finding him sent him a message to his room. Next day they strolled through a light blinding snow, and his face, statuesque against the winter sky, brought a sudden renewal of delight.

"Where were you last night?" she demanded.

"I haven't got a white tie and tails."

"How ridiculous!" she exclaimed impatiently. "But I've got my plans for you—gross material ones. I think I've found you an angel. Wait till you hear."

Sitting in his study before a wood fire she told him.

"It's a man named Gittings, class of 1903, a friend of the family. Well, last month he was staying with us and one day I found him writing something very mysterious that he tucked away when I came in. I had to find out what it was and I did. It was a list of names—Ketcham, Kelley, Kilpatrick, and so forth—and he finally confessed it was a football team made up of old Yale players whose names began with K. He told me that whenever he had a little time to kill he chose a letter of the alphabet and picked a team. I knew right away that we had our man."

"But even if he got down to the letter V," said Rip, "I can't see how—"

"Don't be dumb—football's his passion, don't you see? He's a little crazy on the subject."

"He must be."

"—And he ought to be willing to pay for his fun—I mean pay you."

"I certainly appreciate your interest."

"You don't—you think I'm pretty fresh, but you don't know all yet: I've started the ball rolling. I've planted the seed in his mind. I told him you'd been offered a lot of money to go to college out West—"

He jumped to his feet.

"Be calm, Rip. Though I must say Mr. Gittings wasn't. He stormed around yelling that it was criminal. Finally he asked who the offer was from—but I thought I'd better stop there. Are you angry?"

"Why no—but would you mind telling me why you're doing all this?"

"I don't know, Rip—maybe it's a sort of revenge."

They walked over the old campus through the early twilight and she stopped where a bracket lamp made a yellow square on the blue snow.

"You've got to use intelligent self-interest." She said, as if to herself, "For one thing it'll help you get the girl you want, when you decide you want a girl."

"I've never known a girl like you," he said, "After I left you last fall I couldn't stop thinking about you, even when you told me it didn't mean a thing."

"Did I say that?"

She looked very lovely and he told her about her cheeks.

"So pretty. Very white."

"So are yours."

They took a step together out of the light and their faces touched in the frosty darkness.

"Somebody's waiting for me at the Taft, Rip," she said. "Come to our house in New York next Saturday afternoon. Mr. Gittings will be there."

IV

In spite of his alphabetical football teams, Mr. Cedric Gittings was not soft-minded. He was one of the many Americans whose mother had liked Little Lord Fauntleroy and the sportive ideas that obsessed him at fifty were a simple and natural reaction. Every autumn the eleven young men who ran out on the football field of a crisp Saturday represented something very lovely to him that he had not found in life.

He was glad to meet Rip—honored and impressed.

"That was a beautiful game," he said. "It seems I grabbed the feathers from a lady's hat and threw them into the air. I think I went after the feathers because when you made that touchdown I felt light as a bird. When we lose it makes me physically sick. Tell me, young man, what's this about your leaving college?"

Kiki spoke up:

"Rip doesn't want to leave—it would almost break his heart—but he hasn't any money. And anyhow, Yale won't have much of a team next year."

"Why, of course they will," exclaimed Mr. Gittings.

Kiki looked hard at Rip who said obediently,

"There's not much in the line."

"There's *you*, man—you're a line in yourself. I can see you coming out and leading that interference—"

"But if the team doesn't win," Kiki interrupted, "the professionals won't be after Rip. I think he ought to accept the offer of this western college."

"What college?" demanded Gittings fiercely.

Rip looked at Kiki and managed to say:

"I'm not at liberty to tell."

"This buying up players is an outrage. I'd rather see us lose every game than think the team was bought and paid for."

"Rip's got to think of the future," said Kiki mildly. "You hear of so many players getting to be night watchmen or bouncers and even landing in jail."

"In jail! I've never heard of any good football players going to jail. Why, you're remembered forever. If I was a judge and some football star came up before me I'd say 'this must be a mistake'—any man with such beautiful muscular coordination ought to have the benefit of the doubt."

"If I ever sink that low," Rip said, "I hope the judge will agree with you."

"Of course he will. Judges are human just like anyone else."

Kiki felt that the conversation was becoming somewhat gloomy.

"Rip only wants to go where alumni are more liberal so he can earn a living."

"What do they offer you out West?" asked Mr. Gittings.

"An awful lot," Kiki said promptly.

"Well, you'd be a fool to accept, young man."

"I'd hate to leave college," said Rip. "Still, anything's better than jail."

Gittings groaned.

"There you go on jail again. I'll keep you out of jail. I'll leave a fund in case you go wrong."

"Now that's sensible," applauded Kiki. "A fund is something he could depend on."

"I'll get him a chance with some good firm as soon as he's out of college."

"The fund idea seems better to me."

"It seems to me you're pretty mercenary about this, young lady." He sighed. "When would he have to go?"

"Right away, I suppose. He has to enter now in order to be eligible next fall. They're very particular."

"Particular!" cried Mr. Gittings disgustedly. "Particular! Just tell me this: How much do they offer?"

At the moment it was a great disadvantage to him that he had never before bribed an athlete. He had no idea what they were paid, and the whole matter seemed so lawless and obnoxious that the question of how much was of relatively little importance. Kiki finally closed the deal at five thousand dollars.

V

And now Kiki went away for six months and things happened to her of which there is no room to tell here. There are idealists who would take it amiss that she suffered with the moonlight in Honolulu and on the Italian Lakes and almost married a man who does not even come into this story. He had a certain break in his voice or he dressed with humor—and then he did something or failed to do something and after that had no more connection with the dawn, wind or the evening stars. Late in October she called it off and hurried back to America.

Arriving Kiki looked around tentatively, what she expected to find she didn't know—certainly not Considine who was on an archaeological expedition in Crete. But there was a lost feeling and she was glad to find a wire from Rip Van Kamp. He wanted to see her urgently and suggested she come up to the Dartmouth game. She went feeling that she was going to find something she had left there—the first youth and illusion lost in the Bowl a year ago.

If any college player was ever worth five thousand Rip was worth it that season. It was a poor team, light backs behind a raw line, and this brought Rip's play into high relief. He had a style of his own which no coach had ever tried to change—it was like nothing so much as a legal form of holding and many an official laid for him in vain. His charge was quick and rather high with knees and hips in it and elbows loose, so that he seemed at the crucial moment to be wrapped around the defensive man, yet with such a small area of actual contact that he was free even as the play passed. And when a man outweighed thirty to sixty pounds gave such an exhibition Saturday after Saturday even Mr. Gittings could ask no more.

Tingling with expectation, Kiki met him after the game.

"When I watch you play I'm just the adoring high school girl," she said.

"I wish you were."

"So do I. At least I could lead the cheers. At present I can't be any help at all. I wish you had some real problems."

"I have," he said, frowning. "I'm in a terrible mess. That's why I wired you."

"Why, Rip—what's the matter?"

They were at the Sachem Tea House with many men and girls oddly quiet after the game. First glancing around, Rip took out a newspaper clipping and handed it to her.

"Read it and I'll explain," he said. "It isn't about me."

CAMPUS JEWEL THIEF RETURNS LOOT
YALE DEAN GETS ANONYMOUS PACKAGE

Frightened by an aroused campus swarming with Philo Vances and Hercule Poirots, the thief who has been operating in the

Yale dormitories yesterday sent about three hundred dollars worth of his booty to Dean Marsh through the mail. It was in the form of watches, pins, wallets and miscellaneous jewelry. From the thief's knowledge of the students' lecture hours, etc. he is believed to be an undergraduate.

"So what?" asked Kiki.

"I told you about my brother Harry being a sophomore. He had some hard luck—broke his knee in freshman football and he can't play any more. So he turned thief. I can't understand it. A man in his class spotted him and came to me and I took every cent I had to buy the stuff back. Now I need more."

"Out of the five thousand? Oh, Rip—I thought I was to take care of that and you weren't to touch it till after college."

"I can't help it. Harry's my brother. He's not going to jail."

"But you've sent the things back."

"I haven't told you everything. The man who knows about it is a low skunk, and he has to be squared."

They seemed to have descended suddenly into another world. Kiki had thought of Rip as detached from any past, the masterpiece of an anonymous sculptor. Now the shadow of the brother fell across his shoulders.

"Wouldn't it settle it if your brother leaves college? He oughtn't to be here anyhow if he's—" She balked at the word.

"It wouldn't satisfy this man. Of course I could break his neck—"

"You can't get mixed up in it, Rip." She sighed with distress. "How much does he want?"

"He mentioned a thousand dollars."

"Oh Rip! I almost wish you'd broken his neck."

"I will if you think it's best."

"No—we'll have to pay him. But you've got to send your brother away before he gets into more trouble."

"If he leaves college it'll look funny." He frowned. "I can't stand to send him away. I never told you but he and I were brought up in an orphanage and I've always looked out for him."

Now she knew all about him—she had never liked him better than at this moment.

"But sooner or later he'll get you in a worse jam just when you've got this start and I've made plans to get more money for you—Rip, you've got to send him away."

"Anyhow, you see I've got problems," he said.

"We'll deal with them," she said brightening.

After supper, walking along the shady darkness of Hillhouse Avenue she turned to him suddenly:

"Rip, I'm so very fond of you."

"Fond of me? What does that mean? The people in the Bowl are fond of me."

She heard herself lying to him.

"I've thought about you all summer—so much."

He put his arm around her and drew her close. The moon was up rosy gold with a haze around it and bells were pounding through the Indian summer darkness. Thus she had stood with the love of her girl-hood, with Alex Considine, a year ago, with another man on a starry deck last summer. She was happy and confused—when you were not in love one attractive man seemed much the same as another. Yet she felt very close to Rip—what he had said about his brother reminded her of all that was missing in his life and for a moment she felt that she could supply it—it would not be hard to fall in love with him. She was plagued with her bright unused beauty.

"You couldn't love me," he said suddenly. "It'll be somebody with a head on his shoulders."

But she was full of new thoughts about him when they said goodbye in the station and she took her seat in the parlor car. As the train started, the seat in front of her swung about and she faced Alex Considine.

Her first reaction was that he was not the man she had seen ten months before, but rather the very stranger whom she once met—the stranger with kind keen eyes and a face alive with the appreciation and understanding that had first attracted her. Then she remembered and gave him a smile that began charmingly so as to be all the more chilling when it suddenly stopped.

"You look fine, Kiki," he said quietly.

"Did you expect me to be withered away?"

"I've thought about you a great deal this summer."

It was what she had said to Rip—she supposed it was equally exaggerated.

"I was going to phone you tomorrow," he said, "Then I saw you after the game."

"There's a vacant seat up the car," she suggested. "Would you mind moving up there?"

"I'd rather not. The expedition is going back to Crete in December and I think it would be fine if you'd come along—just to prevent any talk we could get married."

"Perhaps I'd better move," she said. "This seat is over the wheels."

"You wouldn't want me to apologize," he said. "That would be merely revolting."

"Just why did you throw me over?" she asked. "I don't give a darn about you now but I'd like to know."

"I wanted a little time alone out in the world. Some day I'll explain, but now all I can think of is that I've lost ten months of you."

Her heart made an odd reminiscent tour of her chest.

"Did you like the game?" she asked. "For a Harvard man you show great interest in Yale."

"I was doing a little scouting. I played football as a sophomore."

"I didn't know you then."

"You didn't miss anything. I wasn't any Van Kamp."

She laughed.

"I think it was from you I first heard the name. You told me Yale bought him."

"They did—but I'm not sure it'll do them much good."

Instantly alert she demanded, "What do you mean?"

"I shouldn't have said that. We don't know anything for certain yet."

Kiki's imagination raced over the possibilities. Had Mr. Gittings in his cups boasted of his bargain? Did it have something to do with Rip's brother?

"It may come to nothing," he said, "and it doesn't sound well from me, because I suppose I ought to consider him a rival."

"That's all right, I've learned not to expect much from you, Alex."

She got up suddenly and went to the other seat but he followed and bending over her said: "I can't blame you, Kiki—but I'm very concerned with your happiness."

"Have I got to go into the day coach?"

"I'll go up there myself."

She hated him and for a moment she wished Rip was there, coolly and gracefully "breaking his neck." But after all this was no football field and Rip wouldn't show to advantage. Poor Rip—who had done nothing except risen in the world on the leverage of his magnificent body.

From the station she tried without success to get him on the phone—finally reached him next morning at training table. In masked words she told him what Considine had said. There was a long pause at the other end—then his voice with a desperate note:

"I can always leave college."

"Rip, don't talk like that. But I want you to be careful. Have you ever told anyone about Gittings?"

"No."

"Then don't admit anything. And Rip—remember that whatever happens I'm with you."

"Thank you, Kiki."

"I mean it—whatever happens. I wouldn't mind if everyone knew it."

Flushed and exalted she hung up the receiver. Her protective instincts were marshaled on his side and it was beginning to feel real. She was proud and pleased when he performed brilliantly against Princeton. There, three days later, she opened to the football news to find a shocking headline.

INELIGIBILITY RUMOR DENIED AT YALE
MAJOR STAR BELIEVED INVOLVED

New Haven, Connecticut: The Chairman of the Yale Athletic Association today denied the rumor that a certain varsity star would not play against Harvard Saturday.

"The same line-up that faced Princeton will start Saturday's game," he said. "We have had no official protests against the eligibility of any players."

The rumor stemmed from Cambridge and has been traced to the Harvard Club in New York. The material at New Haven has been under par this year—only twelve "iron men" were used against Princeton—and the loss of any one of several key players might considerably affect . . . .

Kiki's heart stood still. Again she ran over all possible avenues of leakage. Mr. Gittings had denied any indiscretion, but the check, drawn on a New York bank, might have passed through the hands of some Harvard man who recognized the name. Yet it would be difficult to produce evidence. Beyond that, Kiki was sure that Rip had been careful—had shied away from an offer to play baseball for a hotel last summer.

In a sudden panic she looked up Alex Considine's number—startled at the familiar digits. He was in Cambridge but expected back today and off and on all day she called him without leaving her name—just missed him at six to find that he would be at the Harvard Club for dinner. Slipping into a dinner dress she drove down to 44th Street and asked a suspicious doorman to take him a note. He came out surprised, without his hat, and seated in a grill nearby she came to the point:

"I saw the paper this morning. It's Rip Van Kamp they mean, isn't it?"

"I can't tell you, Kiki."

"You did tell me on the train. I want to know what you've got against him."

Alex hesitated.

"I can say this—if we had absolute proof against him we'd have acted by this time."

"Then you haven't got proof?"

"At this moment I personally don't know any proof."

From his phrasing she guessed at the truth.

"You're waiting for some proof right now."

"Are you in love with this man, Kiki?"

"Yes."

"Somehow I can't believe it."

"Can't you? Well, if you do anything to bar him out I'll marry him tomorrow night—if he wants me."

He nodded.

"That I can believe—you're a stubborn girl, Kiki, and you're one of the best. But I don't think you're in love with Van Kamp."

Suddenly she was crying angrily because she knew it was true. She was only getting started at being in love. It would be all right, it would come soon, it would atone for everything. But just now until it came she was so vulnerable. She could not avoid comparing Rip, boyish and unoriented, oblivious to so much, to Alex Considine, a grown man, confident and perceptive, with a will of his own making and his own mistakes.

"You'll see," she said chokingly, "You've always had everything and he's come up from nothing, and so you try to drag him down. It's so cruel, so mean."

"Kiki, I didn't start this. The information—" He broke off. "You sound as if you knew something—"

"Oh, no," she said quickly, "But even if there is something I'll stick by him."

She got up and left him with the untouched cocktails. Utterly confused she stopped at a telegraph office to send Rip a message of tenderness and cheer.

VI

Rip had given her four tickets and she went up to Cambridge with friends, arriving at the stadium in a thin grisly snow. Remembering last year, the floaty joy and the sunshine, she was sad—even though the morning papers had relieved her worst apprehensions. Neither Athletic Association had given out any statement and the official line-up included Rip's name. She opened a program.

Left Guard   Van Kamp   5'11"   159   22   Newton High

The short history of a life—the boy from an orphanage with his brain in his nervous system. He was out there now in mid-field facing a crimson player in a white helmet, while a half dollar flipped up and fell in the snow. Yale strung out across the turf behind the ball—the leather boomed and Rip led the race down the field, skirting one blocker, sliding around another to make the first tackle of the game.

"He ought to be an end," said a man behind her. "He could be anything."

"But who can play guard like that—watch any halfback and you're just watching the ball, watch Rip Van Kamp and you're watching the game."

The snow fell thicker—when a man slid twice his own length in the muddy mush it made a sentence for paper or radio, giving the game a wild haphazard quality, making it into an obstacle race and a winter sport. The tricks and laterals that were breath-taking anyhow assumed a miraculous flickering aspect in the chalky haze.

She watched Rip sitting on his haunches while the other team huddled. Quick as the play started he was on his feet, borne backward momentarily on a shoulder, then free and over at the other side of the line, running smack upright into the play. That was why the crowd could see him, because he went in like that, it was why his face was ribbed with scabs all through the season.

The half ended with Yale leading, 10–3. It was growing colder, the people next to Kiki were taking measure to keep warm and their voices rose—the girl beside Kiki said to her companion:

"I don't know him but that's his brother Harry with the black hat two rows down."

Kiki looked. Harry was one of those blue faced men who shave futilely twice a day and who have contributed their affliction to our conception of the ungodly. He had no redeeming points—his eyes were set far apart as if pushed out by the spreading and flattening of his nose— yet Kiki felt disloyal as she saw a certain undeniable resemblance.

With the opening of the second half Harvard came to life—within ten minutes roars of triumph tolled across the field from the crimson side and the faces around Kiki were frowning and foreboding. She peered at

Rip through field-glasses; as ever he was cool, white and impassive—as the game went into the fourth quarter with the score tied, there was a time when he was the only man on that weary team who seemed alive. That was when he knocked down a dazed Yale man who was trying to run out an intercepted pass from behind his own goal.

Ten minutes to play. Yale, taking the ball on its own twenty, came out of the huddle with both tackles on the right side of the line. Suddenly the left end was in motion running toward the side-line, but two seconds before the ball was snapped cutting back toward his own goal while a halfback stepped up into the line on the right. This made the guard eligible for a pass and Rip caught the soggy ball almost in the clear for a forty yard gain and a first down.

The Yale stand came alive with hope, but almost immediately time was called and there was a puzzled murmur from the crowd. Three men with the air of a delegation had appeared at the Yale bench and the coaches were on their feet talking to them while the substitutes, shrouded in blankets, gathered around the argument. A moment later one substitute threw off his blanket and dashed out of the group, warming up; then seized his headguard, ran out and reported to the referee. The murmur grew when he spoke to Rip Van Kamp and the voices around Kiki were asking:

"What is it?"

"Taking Van Kamp out?"

"They're crazy. He isn't hurt."

"Can you beat it? With the score tied!"

Kiki saw Rip tear off his headgear and run to the sidelines. Still ignorant of what had happened the crowd rose in a wild thundering cheer, which died away in wonder as he exchanged words with the coach, turned and ran toward the showers. The murmur broke out again—this time the guesses bordered on the truth.

"Was he put out? Did he foul somebody?"

"They didn't pull him out because they wanted to."

"It must be Van Kamp that the newspapers—"

It was all through the crowd in a minute—the connection was made by everyone at once and the confirmation drifted up from the seats closest to the field. Rip Van Kamp had been taken out on a protest by the Harvard Athletic Association.

Kiki shrank down in her seat covering her face as if she were the next victim of a mob. It had happened—here at the very end they had taken it all away from Rip, sent him off like a disgraced schoolboy. In a second she was on her feet pushing past her friends, running up the aisle and down the dark entrance and then along under the stand in the direction he had taken.

"Where's the dressing room?" she cried. A vacuous drunk looked at her blankly and there was a roar overhead as the game resumed its course. She ran from gate to gate along the snowy cinder walk until a guard directed her, adding:

"You haven't a chance of getting in there. They don't even let old players in."

"When do they come out?"

He told her and she went to an iron grill and waited. After a long time she heard the game end with the perfunctory disappointed cheering of a tie score and saw the first dribble of the crowd come down the runways, then the great waves of it, surging past her as if it were rolling, careless and insensible, over her and over Rip. . . .

Time passed. There were only streams, then trickles and finally individuals like drops. A truck marked *Harvard Crimson* drove up in a rush and a boy jumped out with a bundle of papers.

"Final game score! Harvard protests Van Kamp! Yale Guard played in West!"

Kiki bought a paper and held it with trembling fingers. The thing was in hasty large type just under the score.

> *Van Kamp was removed from the game on Harvard's claim that he played with Almara College in Oklahoma in 1934. Identification was made by his co-ed wife. . . .*

That was all, but Kiki could have read nothing more. After she had said aloud in a fierce voice "That's a lie," she knew suddenly and without question that it was true.

VII

Much later she wondered how Alex Considine knew where to look, for it was he who found her sitting against a cement pillar with the paper in her lap, staring at nothing.

"I have a car," he said, "We can walk to it if you'll let me help you."

"I'm all right. I just sat down to think things over."

"I've been looking for you, Kiki. Just at the end I hoped it wasn't going to happen. At first the girl wouldn't talk until—"

"Don't tell me," Kiki said quickly. "What will they do to Rip?"

"I imagine he'll have to leave college. He must have known the rules."

"Oh, poor Rip—poor Rip."

Suddenly she told him about the money from Mr. Gittings, everything.

"And I wish it had been more," she said passionately. "He deserved it. I didn't want him to die like Ted Coy with nothing left but his gold football."

"He was a great player—they can't take that away from him and he'll probably play professionally."

"Oh, but it's all spoiled now—and he was so beautiful."

They drove into Boston through the twilight.

"It's a long trip to New York," he said. "Why don't we go out in the country to some friends of mine. I know you don't want to be engaged to me again but supposing we just get married? I can vouch for the weather on the Nile."

When she was silent he said:

"You're thinking of Van Kamp."

"Yes. I wish there was something I could do. If I could only think that he wasn't alone."

"You love him?"

"No. I was lying to you that night. But I keep thinking of how they'll turn on him—when he's given them so many grand afternoons."

He pulled up the car suddenly.

"Shall I take you to him—I know where the team's staying."

Kiki hesitated.

"I haven't got anything for him now. It was all wrong—the directions were different. I'll go with you, Alex."

"I'm glad."

The car sped on through the city, turning the right corners, stopping at the right signs, and then into the country, always gathering speed—out on the right road at last.

FSF with gloves and a glare.

"The Women in the House," later cut severely and revised into "Temperature," is a medical story centered on a patient with heart trouble—which Fitzgerald was himself at the time he wrote it. But it is also about famous stars, dope, drinking, dazzle, and the Hollywood he knew. As he told Kenneth Littauer, when trying to sell it directly to *Collier's* himself in the summer of 1939, "It is absolutely true to Hollywood as I see it."

Fitzgerald finished the fifty-eight-page story in June 1939. He sent it to Harold Ober, and Ober responded by advising that he should cut six thousand words, chiefly those that dealt with drinking and drug use: "I think the closet scene and a lot about the nurses could be cut. Also the part of the story where Monsen is intoxicated." Fitzgerald wrote back that about five thousand words were as much as could be "pried out of the story (by this old hand). . . . I know it's a difficult length, but unfortunately that's the way the story was." Fitzgerald also said—showing how glad he was to be once again writing stories—"One's pencil gets garrulous after that snail's pace movie writing."

Both the *Saturday Evening Post* and Ober still felt it was too long, and after arguing about this in some of their last exchanges, Fitzgerald reluctantly cut the story further to forty-four pages and then thirty-four. His desire to keep "The Women in the House" as a long story, possibly published in two parts, and Ober's insistence that it be cut helped trigger the unfortunate break between Fitzgerald and Ober that began at this time.

When sending the story himself to Littauer, Fitzgerald wrote frankly about it, and with both humor and deep self-knowledge as a writer:

> Asking you to read it I want to get two things clear. First, that it isn't particularly likely that I'll write a great many more stories about young love. I was tagged with that by my first writings up to 1925. Since then I have written stories about young love. They have been done with increasing difficulty and increasing insincerity. I would either be a miracle man or a hack if I could go on turning out an identical product for three decades.
>
> I know that is what's expected of me, but in that direction the well is pretty dry and I think I am much wiser in not trying to strain for it but rather to open up a new well, a new vein. You see, I not only announced the birth of my young illusions in <u>This Side of Paradise</u> but pretty much the death of them in some of my last <u>Post</u> stories like <u>Babylon Revisited</u> [February 1931].

Fitzgerald viewed "The Women in the House" as a "sort of turn" for his writing—opening up "a new well, a new vein." He'd made a start, but was not yet happy with it, and particularly not with a version diminished to someone else's specifications.

The story, in any of its versions, feels like a cross between a short story and a screenplay, unwilling to give up being either, and too uncomfortable to be both. Two movie stars are in supporting roles: Carlos Davis, a "Dakota small town boy" who "had been born with a small gift of mimicry and an extraordinary personal beauty"; and Elsie Halliday, a cypher of a Golden Age silver-screen goddess. The hero is a dashing explorer-scientist with some kinship to Richard Halliburton, as well as to F. Scott Fitzgerald. Fitzgerald uses movie-speak for segues often: "And at this point, as they say in picture making, the Camera Goes into the House, and we go with it." The plot is a mix of Fitzgerald fiction standbys, including mistaken identity (in this case, the patient who is really ill, and the one who isn't) and love lost with love anew ensuing—all stirred with a large serving of 1930s Hollywood screwball comedy. Present also are a maid and her African-American boyfriend, not exactly standard Fitzgerald fare.

One of the shorter cut-down versions of this story was published as "Temperature" in *Strand Magazine* in July 2015. On the finished typescript of that version of the story, Fitzgerald has written across the top of the first page, in his traditional No. 2 pencil: "File Under False Starts."

First page, early manuscript draft in first person.

THE WOMEN IN THE HOUSE
by
F. SCOTT FITZGERALD

This is one of those stories that ought to begin by
calling the hero "X" or "H----B----" -- because there were
so many people drawn into it that at least one of them will
read this and claim to have been a leading character. And
as for that current dodge "No reference to any living character is intended" -- there's no use even _trying_ that.

Instead we come right out and state that the man in the
case was Emmet Monsen, because that is (or almost is) his
real name. Three months ago you could consult the pictorials and news magazines and discover that he was just returning from the Omigis on the S.S. Fumataki Nagursha and landing
at the port of Los Angeles with notable information on
tropical tides and fungi. He was in the pictorials because
he was notably photogenic, being thirty-one, slender and
darkly handsome, with the sort of expression that made
photographers say:

"Mr. Monsen--could you manage to smile _once_ more?"

---but I am going to take the modern privilege of starting a story twice, and begin again--at a medical laboratory
in downtown Los Angeles forty-eight hours after Emmet Monsen
left the dock.

The Women in the House
(Temperature)

This is one of those stories that ought to begin by calling the hero "X" or "H—B—"—because there were so many people drawn into it that at least one of them will read this and claim to have been a leading character. And as for that current dodge "No reference to any living character is intended"—there's no use even *trying* that.

Instead we come right out and state that the man in the case was Emmet Monsen, because that is (or almost is) his real name. Three months ago you could consult the pictorials and news magazines and discover that he was just returning from the Omigis on the *S.S. Fumataki Nagursha* and landing at the port of Los Angeles with notable information on tropical tides and fungi. He was in the pictorials because he was notably photogenic, being thirty-one, slender and darkly handsome, with the sort of expression that made photographers say:

"Mr. Monsen—could you manage to smile *once* more?"

—but I am going to take the modern privilege of starting a story twice, and begin again—at a medical laboratory in downtown Los Angeles forty-eight hours after Emmet Monsen left the dock.

A girl, a pretty girl (but not the leading girl) was talking to a young man whose business was developing electro-cardiograph or heart charts—automatic recordings of that organ which has never been famed as an instrument of precision.

"Eddie hasn't phoned today," she said.

"Excuse these tears," he answered. "It's my old sinus. And here're the heart charts for your candid camera album."

"Thanks—but don't you think when a girl is going to be married in a month, or at least before Christmas, he could phone her every morning."

"Listen—if he loses that job at Wadford Dunn Sons, you won't be able to afford a *Mexican* marriage."

The laboratory girl carefully wrote the name "Wadford Dunn Sons" at the top of the first heart chart, swore in a short but vicious California idiom, erased, and substituted the name of the patient.

"Maybe you better think about your job here," added the laboratory man. "Those cardiographs are supposed to go out by—"

Telephones interrupted him—but they by no means bore a message from Eddie; it was two doctors, both very angry at once. The young lady was galvanized into frantic activity which landed her a few minutes later in a 1931 model, bound for one of those suburbs which make Los Angeles the most far-flung city in the world.

Her first destination was exciting for it was the country estate of young Carlos Davis, whom, so far, she had seen only in flicker form and once in Technicolor. Not that there was anything the matter with Carlos Davis' heart—it worked the other way—but she was delivering the cardiograph to the tenant of a smaller house on his estate, originally built for his mother—and if Davis happened not to be at the studio she might glimpse him in passing.

She didn't, and for the present—after she delivered the cardiograph at the proper door—she passes out of the story.

And at this point, as they say in picture making, the Camera Goes into the House, and we go with it.

The tenant was Emmet Monsen. At the moment he sat in an easy chair looking out into the sunny May-time garden, while Doctor Henry Cardiff opened the big envelope with his huge hands to examine the chart and the report that went with it.

"I stayed out there one year too long," said Emmet, "and like a fool I drank water! Man I worked with had the idea—he hadn't touched water in twenty years, only whiskey. He was a little dried up—skin like parchment—but no more than the average Englishman."

The maid flashed darkly in the dining-room doorway and Emmet called to her.

"Marguerite? Have I got that name right?"

"Margerilla, Mist Monsen."

"Margerilla, if Miss Elsa Halliday calls up, I'm at home to her. But to nobody else—not a soul. Remember that name—Miss Elsa Halliday."

"Yes suh, I won't be like to forget *that*. I seen her in the *mov*ing picture. Frank and I—"

"All right, Margerilla," he interrupted politely. "Just remember I'm not home to anyone else."

Dr. Cardiff, having finished his reading, arose in half a dozen gigantic sections and paced up and down meditatively, his chin alternately resting on his necktie or following his gaze toward the chandelier, as if he thought his eight years of training were lurking there like guardian angels, ready to fly down to his assistance. When Margerilla had gone he sat down in his chair, interlocking his hands in a way that to Emmet vaguely suggested the meeting of two spans of The Grand Coulee.

"So what?" Emmet asked. "Maybe it's a growth? I swallowed a piece of fungi once—I thought it was a shrimp. Maybe it's attached itself to me. You know—like women. I mean like women are supposed to do."

"These," said Dr. Cardiff in a kind voice—too kind, Emmet thought, "are not radio plates. This is the cardiograph. When I made you lie down yesterday and attached the wires to you?"

"Oh, yes," said Emmet, "and forgot to slit my trousers—and get a last minute confession."

"Huh-huh," uttered the doctor, a laugh so mechanical that Emmet half rose from his chair, suggesting:

"Let's open some windows."

—but instantly the doctor's great bulk loomed over him and forced him gently down.

"Mr. Monsen, I want you to sit *ab*solutely in place. Later we'll arrange a means of transportation."

He gave a quick glance about, as if expecting a subway entrance, or at least a small personal derrick, to be in a corner of the room. Emmet watched him—many thoughts crowding swiftly across his mind. Much too young for the world war he had been brought up on tales of it, and most of his thirty-one years had been spent along the fringe of danger. He was one of those Americans who seem left over from the days when there was a frontier, and he had chosen to walk, ride or fly along that thin hair line which separates the unexplored and menacing from the safe, warm world. Or is there such a world—

Emmet Monsen sat immobile waiting for the doctor to speak, but the expression in his handsome eyes was alert and wide-awake.

"I knew on the boat I was running a fever—that's why I'm laying up in California, but if this chart proves something serious I want to know about that too. Don't worry—I'm not going to go to pieces."

Dr. Cardiff decided to tell all.

"Your heart is apparently enlarged to a—to a—"

He hesitated.

"To a dangerous degree?" Emmet said.

"But not to a *fatal* degree," answered Dr. Cardiff hastily.

"Obviously," said Emmet, "since I can still hear my own voice. Come on Doctor, what is it? Is the heart quitting?"

"Oh, now!" protested Cardiff. "That's no way to look at it. I've seen cases where I wouldn't have given the man two hours—"

"Damn it, please get to the point," Emmet exclaimed. "And I'm going to smoke"—as he saw the doctor's eye follow his reaching hand. "I'm sorry, Doctor, but what's the prognosis? I'm no child—I've taken people through typhoid and dysentery myself. What's my chance—ten per-cent? One per-cent? When and under what conditions am I leaving this very beautiful scenery?"

"It depends, Mr. Monsen, to a great extent on yourself."

"All right. I'll do anything you say. Not much exercise I suppose, no highballs, stick around the house till we see what nature—"

The colored maid was in the doorway.

"Mist Monsen, that there Miss Halliday's on the phone and it sure did thrill me down to my marrow—"

Emmet was up before the doctor could hoist himself from his chair and on his way to the phone in the butler's pantry.

"Well, you *did* get a minute off," he said.

"I've thought of you all morning, Emmet, and I'm coming out this afternoon. What did the doctor say?"

"He says I'm fine—little run down, wants me to take it easy a few days. What time are you coming out?"

A pause.

"Can I speak to the doctor?" Elsa asked.

"Sure you can. *What?* What do you want to speak to the doctor about?"

He said "Excuse me" as he realized that someone had brushed by him from behind and gone on into the living room; he caught a glimpse of a white starched uniform as he continued into the telephone:

"Sure you can. But he isn't here now. Elsa, do you know that except for those few minutes at the dock I haven't seen you for two years?"

"Two years is a long time, Emmet."

"Don't say it quite that way," he objected. "Anyhow come as soon as you can."

As he hung up the phone he realized that once more he was not alone in the pantry. There was the face of Margerilla and at her shoul-der quite a different face that he stared at absently and abstractedly for a moment, as if it had no more reality than a magazine cover. It belonged to a girl wearing a powder-blue dress. Her face was roundish and her eyes were round—after all, not so astonishing—but the expres-sion with which she regarded him was so full of a sort of beautiful atten-tion, a fascinated and amused surprise that he wanted to say something back to it. It did not quite ask, "Can it be *you?*" like some girls' faces do;

rather it asked: "Are you having fun out of all this nonsense?" Or else it said, "We seem to be pardners for this dance," adding: "—and this is the dance I've been waiting for all my life."

To these questions or statements hinted at in the girl's smile, Emmet made a response which he later decided was not brilliant.

"What can I do for you?" he enquired.

"It's the other way, Mr. Monsen." She had a somewhat breathless voice. "What can I do for *you*? I was sent here by Rusty's Secretarial Bureau."

It is well known that we seldom take out our annoyances upon the objects that inspire them; Emmet repeated the words: "Secretarial Bureau!" in a tone which made the place into a day nursery for gun molls, an immediate field of investigation for Messrs. Dewey and Hoover.

"I'm Miss Trainor and I'm answering the call you made this morning. I have a reference from Mr. Rachoff, the musician. I worked for him till he went to Europe last week—"

She held a letter toward him—but Emmet was still in a mood.

"Never heard of him," he announced pontifically, then corrected himself, "Yes, I have. But I never believe in references. Anybody can fake references."

He looked at her closely, even accusingly, but her smile had come back—and seemed to agree with him that all references were nonsense and she'd thought so for years—only she was glad to hear it said at last.

It seemed quite a while to have been in the pantry; Emmet got up.

"That downstairs room will be your typing office. Margerilla will show you."

He nodded and returned to the living room, where he was increasingly conscious that the doctor was waiting.

But not alone. He was in grave and secret conference with the figure in white who had brushed by Emmet in the pantry. So intense was their confluence that even Emmet did not interrupt it—it flowed on in a sort of sustained mumble for some time after Emmet settled in his chair.

"Sorry I was so long. People kept coming in. They told me it would be quiet out here—this Davis even had guards and all to keep his admirers away."

"This is Miss Hapgood, your day nurse," said Dr. Cardiff.

An unconfident bell-shaped lady smiled and then appraised Emmet with the expression of a fur-trader looking at a marten pelt.

"I've told her everything—" continued the doctor.

The nurse confirmed this by holding up a pad covered with writing.

"—and I've asked her to call me several times during the day—four, wasn't it?"

"Four, Doctor."

"So you can be sure you're being well looked after. Huh-huh."

The nurse echoed his laugh. Emmet wondered if he had missed a joke.

The doctor then "ran along"—a process which consisted of picking up his bag several times, setting it down, writing a last minute prescription, sending the nurse on a goose-chase for his stethoscope—and eventually blocking out the living room door with his bulky figure. But by this time, Emmet who had no stop-watch, had concluded that "running along" was merely a figure of sick room speech. In any case, he was distracted by the sight of Miss Hapgood flat on the floor where she had tripped over the threshold. Before he could rise she was by his side, firmly clinging to his right wrist.

"Mr. Moppet, I suppose we ought to begin by getting acquainted."

Emmet was about to begin by supplying his real name when she added:

"One thing I think you ought to know is I happen to be very clumsy. Know what I mean?"

Having travelled widely Emmet had been asked questions in languages he did not understand and often been able to answer by signs—but this time he was stumped. "I'm sorry" did not seem to have the right ring, nor did "What a pity!" In fact he was about to blurt cruelly "Isn't there something you can do about it?" when the nurse answered the question by releasing his wrist, rising suddenly and in the same gesture toppling over a brass topped table bearing a twelve piece silver tea-service which Emmet had conceived as being placed a long way across the room.

Then, as if the sound of many gongs being struck were a cue in a motion picture, he saw the young face of Carlos Davis in the doorway and beside him the Trainor girl. Carlos Davis was a Dakota small town boy, with none of the affectations ascribed to him—it was no fault of his that he had been born with a small gift of mimicry and an extraordinary personal beauty.

Emmet stood up—trying not to crush a small cream pot under his foot.

"Hello there, Mr. Davis."

"Greetings!" said Davis, adding reassuringly, "And don't think I'm the 'looking-in' kind of landlord. It happened I ran into the Doc and I wanted to ask if there's anything I can do."

"Well—that's very kind of you."

Davis' eyes swept fractionally aside to where Miss Hapgood was having some vague traffic with the silverware—which could not accurately be described as "picking it up," for the gong sound continued at intervals throughout the conversation.

"I just want you to know I'm at your service, and that I'll leave my private phone number with your—your—" His eyes completed the Trainor girl with visible appreciation—"your secretary. It's not in the book, but she's got it." He paused. "I mean she's got the *number*. Then I'll go along—one of these broadcasts! Cripes!"

He did a short melancholy head-shake, bade farewell in a wave-salute, vaguely reminiscent of Queen Elizabeth arriving in Canada, and departed with what developed, as he reached the hall, into a series of long athletes' leaps.

Emmet sat down and spoke to Miss Trainor.

"I don't see your lips moving," he said, "and there goes the maiden's prayer."

"I tried to keep him out," she answered coolly. "It was physically impossible. Is there anything special you want from me at this moment?"

"Sure. Sit down and I'll give you an idea of what the job will be."

She reminded him of a girl for whom he had suffered deeply at the age of seven—except that instead of pigtails she wore her russet, yellow-streaked hair at shoulder length, and that her smile with its very special queries and promises was like nothing he had ever encountered.

"I've written a sort of scientific book. It's in the kitchen—the delivery man left the box from the publishers there. It's being published tomorrow and nobody's going to read it." He looked at her suddenly. "Do you get all flustered about ocean changes and the genesis of tidal waves?"

The girl looked at him, as if considering.

"Why not?"

"I mean: would you buy a book about that?"

"Well—" A pause "—under certain circumstances I would."

"Diplomat, eh?"

"Frankly I *wouldn't* if I thought I had a chance for an autographed copy."

"Diplomat," he grunted. "I should have said 'Ambassador.' Anyhow this book will go into the geographic sections of libraries and gather termites till somebody new comes along with the same quirk I had. Meanwhile I've got a hunch for an adventure book—might interest boys. Fun to have somebody actually read what you wrote. I've taken thousands of notes—will you see if there's a brief case in the hall."

"Mr. Mop—" began his nurse in a tone of disapproval but Emmet said:

"Just a minute, Miss Hapgood." When the Trainor girl returned with the brief case he continued: "The stuff checked with a red crayon ought to be typed up so I can take a look at it. It'll be clear enough. Now the question of hours. I don't think the doctor'll let me work very much— say five or six hours a day."

She nodded.

"So you can meet your admirers in time for dinner," he continued.

She did not smile and Emmet felt as if he had been a little fresh, and wondered if she were engaged or married.

"Are you from somewhere near Boston?" he asked quickly.

"Why—yes. I guess I still talk like it."

"I was born in New Hampshire."

They looked at each other, both suddenly at ease, their minds far away across the republic.

Perhaps Miss Hapgood misinterpreted their expressions, or else remembered that this was a crucial case, for she asserted her presence with a sudden up-tilt of a bridge-lamp.

"Mr. Moppet—I have these instructions and we want to begin the treatment before *anything*."

She threw a glance at the door and the Trainor girl, realizing that she stood for "*anything*," picked up the brief case and withdrew.

"First we'll get to bed," said Miss Hapgood.

In spite of the wording of this sentence Emmet's thoughts could have been printed in the *Youth's Companion* as he arose and followed her toward the stairs.

"I'm not going to try to help you Mr. Mom—Mister—because of this clumsiness, but the doctor would like you to walk up slowly, clasping the bannister rail like this."

Emmet once on the stairs did not look around but he was conscious of a sudden screech of wood followed by a short deprecatory laugh.

"They build these things so jerry in California, don't they," she tittered. "Not like in the East."

"Are you from the East?" he asked from the top of the stairs.

"Oh yes. Born and raised in Idaho."

He sat down on the side of the bed and untied a shoe, annoyed that his sickness didn't make him feel sicker.

"All diseases ought to be sudden," he said aloud, "like the Bubonic Plague."

"I've never taken Bubonic Plague cases," said Miss Hapgood smugly.

Emmet looked up.

"Never taken—"

He decided to go on with his shoes but now she was on her knees, converting his laces expertly into a cat's cradle. The same knack applied in a moment to the removal of his coat brought to mind an improvised straitjacket he had once seen on a berserk dockhand.

"I can take care of the trousers myself," he suggested—whereupon Miss Hapgood stepped lithely around to the other side of the bed, dislodging a brass fire-screen, which spread itself in three great gasps on the floor.

"Quite all right," he said quickly. "Pajamas are in my suitcase—I'm not quite unpacked."

After a search Miss Hapgood handed him a full dress shirt and a pair of corduroy slacks—luckily Emmet caught the glint of the studs before the shirt was entirely on. When he was finally in bed with two pills down him and a thermometer in his mouth Miss Hapgood spoke from the mirror—where she stood drawing his comb through her neatly matted hair.

"You have nice things," she suggested. "I've worked in homes lately where I wouldn't spit on the things they had. But I asked Dr. Cardiff to find me a case with a real gentleman—because I'm a lady."

She walked to the window and cast an eye over the early harvest of the San Fernando Valley.

"Do you think Carlos Davis is going to marry Marya Thomas? Don't try to answer till I take the thermometer out."

But it was already out and Emmet was sitting up.

"That reminds me—I didn't intend to go to bed until after Miss Halliday paid her call."

"I gave you two sleeping pills, Mr. Mom."

He swung his legs out of bed.

"Couldn't you give me an emetic or something? I could get rid of the pills. Some salt and water."

"Bring on a convulsion?" Miss Hapgood exclaimed. "In a *heart* case?"

"Then order some hot coffee—and dig out that silk dressing gown. Next thing I'll forget my name."

He did not mean this as a reproach, nor was Miss Hapgood offended for she merely shook her head, sat down and did piano scales with one hand.

"Well, I'll sleep now," Emmet decided desperately. "Miss Halliday probably won't be here for a couple of hours. You'll wake me up, won't you."

"You can't sleep in that position."

"I always go to sleep on my elbow."

She collapsed him with the most adroit movement she had made during their acquaintance.

II

When he awoke it was dark outside, and in the room save for a small lamp shaded by a towel. Miss Hapgood was not in evidence but his eyes accommodated themselves to the fact that another woman in white sat in an overstuffed chair across the room—a woman from the same gigantic tribe as Dr. Cardiff. As he looked at his wrist watch to find it was half past ten the lady started awake and gave him the information that she was his night nurse, Mrs. Ewing.

"Have there been any visitors?" he asked.

"Miss Halliday. She said she'd try to drop in tomorrow. I told her you couldn't possibly be disturbed."

He mourned silently as Mrs. Ewing rose and ballooned into the hall; he was conscious of a conversation outside his door.

"Who is it?" he inquired. A breathless voice with a glow in it answered: "It's your secretary, Mr. Monsen."

"What are you doing here at this hour?"

The two women—one monstrous, one simply a woman, reduced almost to frailty beside the other, blocked out the doorway. A failing yellow bulb in the hall still revealed Miss Trainor's smile—repentant now, almost mischievous, but as if she was quite sure that he wouldn't be too severe about it.

"Frankly, Mr. Monsen," said Mrs. Ewing frankly, "—frankly I didn't know what sort of man you'd prove to be when you awoke. And when I found the maid was out frankly I asked this—this—" She glanced at Miss Trainor as if for some final confirmation, "—this secretary, to stay until you woke up."

Emmet's eyes were not quite accommodated to the dim light, either in the bedroom or the hall but he could have sworn that at some point the Trainor girl winked at him.

"Well, perhaps you'll let her go now," he suggested.

"Good night, Mrs. Ewing," said the Trainor girl. "I hope you have a good night, Mr. Monsen."

As her steps had faded on the stairs Emmet asked:

"What sort of person did you expect to find when I woke up?"

"I didn't know."

"Didn't you talk to Dr. Cardiff?"

"No. I had only the nurse's chart to go on—and some of it I couldn't read, but I've done a good deal of work with alcoholics and junk addicts."

Emmet was as wide awake as he had ever been in his life but this last expression conveyed nothing to him except a suggestion of some stories of Booth Tarkington about an antique dealer.

"Dope fiends, to you laymen," said Mrs. Ewing casually.

They regarded each other and Emmet swiftly recreated her past—and a wave of sympathy went out from him toward the helpless drunkards and drug victims that she must have crushed into the ineffectuality of swatted mosquitoes.

Then he wanted to laugh but he remembered that Dr. Cardiff had told him he must not laugh very deeply or do anything to agitate his diaphragm, so he took it out in a remark:

"I have my opium cooked right in with my milk toast. And the liquor—well, what I'm sore about is that I didn't go at it a year ago, when we had to put tablets in our drinking water. But if you can't read the chart please call Dr. Cardiff."

He added politely:

"You see Miss Trainor has work to do in the daytime. You wouldn't want to have to help her with her typing, would you?"

Mrs. Ewing changed the subject firmly.

"Shall we have a bath?"

"I took a bath today. Am I running much fever for the day—I think Miss Hapgood wrote it down."

"You'll have to ask Dr. Cardiff those questions, Mr. Monsen."

There was nothing much he could do about this but, concluding that his mood of irritation was his own fault, he decided it was *his* turn to change the subject.

"Mrs. Ewing, there's some stuff I got in Melbourne that usually takes down these fevers," he said. "I forgot to tell Dr. Cardiff. It's made out of some sub-tropical herb. You'll find it in that medical kit that Margerilla put in the closet across the hall."

"She went off for the evening, Mr. Monsen. I'll give you some medicine." "No—you can find the kit—brown leather—the stuff's in green capsules."

"I couldn't very well give a medication without the Doctor's permission."

"Find the stuff, call him up and read him the formula that's pasted on the bottle. Or I'll talk to him."

She swelled near him and their eyes met. Then, with ponderous doubt, she launched herself across the hall and presently he heard her in the impromptu medicine cabinet, clicking open a case. A minute later she called:

"It isn't here. There's quinine, and some typhoid serum and some first aid things, but no green capsules."

"Bring it in here."

"I've got my electric torch, Mr. Monsen, and I've taken everything out of the bag."

He was out of the bed and starting for the trunk room, impatiently grabbing at a quilt in passing as he discovered that he was damp with perspiration.

"Mr. *Mon*sen! I told you."

"I'm sure the stuff's here. One of those side pockets."

There was a gentle click behind them—the significance of which neither of them realized as Emmet groped into the bag.

"Please turn that torch here—" He realized in mid-sentence what had happened: the door had swung gently closed in some casual draft. Moreover, in the full inquisitive light of the torch it was apparent that there was no bolt or handle on the inside corresponding to the lock without. Simultaneously as if from the shock the battery of the nurse's torch expired without a sound.

III

Emmet's mind, travelling faster than Mrs. Ewing's, was the first to realize that they were in a situation. His second thought was quite selfishly of himself: it was cold in the closet and he drew the quilt around him Arab fashion, conscious of the nurse's heavy breathing, thinking of men in trapped submarines, and of how long the oxygen would last when consumed and expired by that pocket-cruiser of a chest.

"Cruiser" was an apt thought for within a minute Mrs. Ewing was in such active motion as to convince him that the closet was not as large as he had imagined. Whether she suspected that this was part of a plot, or whether she was already fighting for air, he could not determine in the darkness—so he merely dodged about for a minute in his dampening burnouse, trying to keep from being crushed against the wall. Until relief came with her sudden explosive announcement:

"There's a window!"

There indeed was a window and only the blackness of the night outside had kept them from perceiving it before. The question was whether it led to a roof or opened on a sheer drop—presently the forward section of Mrs. Ewing was outside the window, trying to determine which against a sightless sky. Then she made an exultant discovery.

"I can see now," she said. "There's a roof below this and I can reach it."

The spirit of the girl scouts sprung into fire somewhere in her geography, and before Emmet could even caution her she was entirely out the window and he heard a tin roof give a discouraged creak. The aperture let in a cool breeze and as Emmet crouched down on the floor Mrs. Ewing's voice blew back into the trunk room.

"I can't see anything."

"The doctor will be here in the morning," Emmet said hopefully; deciding hastily that humor was out of place, he added:

"Call for help. No—don't call 'Help'! Call 'Trouble at Mr. Monsen's' or something like that. And say: 'no burglars'—otherwise somebody's liable to come over with a shotgun and spray you."

"Trouble at Mr. Monsen's," she thundered obediently, "—no burglars!"

She continued without response. In the interval Emmet imagined them castaway there for a week, living off the green capsules and then the iodine from the medical kit.

Between shivers he realized that Mrs. Ewing was in conversation he could only half hear with someone below. In a moment she reported:

"It's a man in a white coat."

He listened.

"How'ya baby." The voice was outside and far below.

Then the nurse:

"The kitchen door may be unlocked. If it isn't, you come up here and I'll give you directions."

"Got couple drings for us, baby?"

"This is serious," Mrs. Ewing said indignantly. "I am a Registered Nurse—locked in a medicine closet."

"Any *my* kind of medicine in that closet?"

At this point Emmet missed a few sentences but presently Mrs. Ewing looked back into the closet.

"He *seemed* to understand," she said. "But he was *aw*fully drunk. He's going to try the kitchen door."

Once more a character passes out of this history. Neither of them laid eyes upon this stray personage again. But ages later, perhaps twenty minutes later, Emmet spoke up.

"Come in and shut the window," he said. "It's getting colder."

"I prefer to sit out here."

"Shut the window then."

A pause.

"I'd come in, Mr. Monsen, but you understand I hardly know you."

"I understand. I hardly know you either."

She hesitated a moment longer—then she came to a decision and climbed back in, half shutting the window after her.

"We'll just have to wait," he said drowsily. "I took some aspirin."

There was another gap in time for which Emmet could not accurately account though he felt sure that Mrs. Ewing, crouching delicately across from him, did not close her eyes. Then he was awakened by the sound of her fists beating on the doors, her voice calling "Margerilla! Margerilla!"

"What!" he demanded.

"It's Margerilla," she cried. "I heard her car!"

"Solution," muttered Emmet, but the tone of Mrs. Ewing's cries had not served to reassure Margerilla below—it was some time before the key turned in the lock.

Margerilla atoned for her dilatory attitude by a burst of coy laughter.

"Why, you *two!*" she exclaimed. "Whatever you doin' in *there?*"

Emmet stood up, drawing his burnouse around him. He called in vain on the chivalry of his youthful reading, but nothing occurred to him.

"We got locked in the medicine closet," said Mrs. Ewing majestically.

"Yes," said Emmet haughtily, "we did."

Like Caesar in his toga covered with many wounds, he could only follow the nurse past the giggling Margerilla, and collapse into bed behind the door of the sick room.

He woke up into a world that even as he opened his eyes seemed vaguely threatening. It was still May; the gardens of the Davis estate had erupted almost overnight into a wild rash of roses, which threw a tangle of sweet contagion up over his porch and across the window screen; but he felt a sharp reaction from the humorous desperation that had carried him through the day before. Had he been told the absolute truth about his condition? And would Elsa Halliday come today—and be the same girl whom he had parted with two years before? Would he himself seem different with fever burning in him, its secret in his heart?

When he was indiscreet enough to open his eyes it was to see Miss Hapgood, back "on duty" and rushing toward him, with a thermometer held stilletto-like in a wavering hand.

Something would have to be done about her he knew—as she arrested her rush and shook down the thermometer—shook it in fact all the way to the floor where it rolled in sections beneath the dresser.

Wearily he rang twice—a signal arranged for the secretary the day before. As she appeared he hunched up on his pillow—then he followed her infectious glance toward the window. "Lot of them, aren't there?"

"I'd just let them grow right into this room," the Trainor girl suggested. "And Miss Halliday sent flowers this morning."

"Did she?" He grew eager. "What kind?"

"Roses." After a moment she added, "American Beauties."

"Get them, will you, Miss Hapgood?" Then to Miss Trainor: "What are these on the porch?"

"Talismans—with a few Cecile Brunners." As the door closed behind Miss Hapgood, she volunteered: "I'll drive down to the drug store and get another thermometer. I see there's been an accident."

"Thanks. The most important thing is to see that I'm awake when, and *if*, Miss Halliday comes. Apparently I'm getting sick man's psychology in a rush—I feel as if there's a conspiracy between the doctor and nurses to keep me sort of frozen—like that woman in the magazine."

She opened the screen window, pinched off a rose and tossed it to the pillow beside him.

"There's something you can trust," she said; then briskly: "You have mail downstairs. Some men like to start a day with the mail—but Mr. Rachoff always liked to get through his planned work before he even read the newspaper."

Emmet conceiving a faint hostility toward Mr. Rachoff, weighed the possibilities.

"Well, any phone call from Miss Halliday comes first, and I wish you could find out when she's coming without appearing too anxious. About the work—I felt like it yesterday—now I don't feel like anything till I know what this doctor's planned. Give me that nurse's pad, will you."

"I'll ring for Miss Hapgood."

"Oh no."

He was half out of bed when Miss Trainor yielded suddenly. In possession of the chart Emmet settled down and read steadily for several minutes; then he was out of bed in earnest, reaching for his dressing gown with one hand and ringing three times for the nurse. There were words too—words that he merely *hoped* Miss Trainor didn't understand, impeded as they were by the increasing bronchitis contracted in the medicine closet.

"Get me Dr. Cardiff on the phone! And then *read* it—read it yourself! Lie on my right side three hours—then I ask the nurse to turn me gently to the left! This isn't a routine! These are instructions for an undertaker, only he forgot the embalming fluid!"

Some of the blame that later fell on the Trainor girl must fairly be partitioned to her, for it was from the moment that she handed Emmet the chart that the complexion of the case changed. Later she confessed that she could have seized it and darted from the room but in Emmet's state of mind this suggested a chase, perhaps the greater of the two evils.

Emmet descended to the living room, sat in his armchair and brooded. He asked the Trainor girl to sit in the room because something about her made him rather ashamed to speak crossly or harshly. Her eyes with their other-world astigmatism, their suggestion of looking slantwise upon a richer and more amusing universe must never be corrected back into the dull vision of the truth at which he stared at present. Emmet did not want her to see the things he did. When Dr. Cardiff arrived he felt comparatively calm.

"Let me have the first go," he suggested, "because what you say will be the final authoritative word and all that."

Dr. Cardiff nodded, with obvious patience.

"I looked at that chart," said Emmet, "and Doctor—I can't live like that for four months."

"I've heard that before," said Dr. Cardiff scathingly. "I've heard dozens of these so called 'high pressure' men say: 'If you think I'm going to stay in this —— bed you must be crazy!' And a few days later when they get scared they're meek as—"

"But that business of staring at the ceiling all day—and the bedpan and the mush diet—you'd have a nut on your hands!"

"Mr. Monsen, since you insisted on reading the chart you should have read it *all*. There is provision for the nurse reading to you—and there's half an hour in the morning when you can have your mail read, sign checks and all that. Personally I think you're lucky to be sick out here in this beautiful country—"

"So do I," Emmet interrupted, "I'm not refusing to lead a completely vegetable life—I'm saying you'll *have* to modify it. I can't do it—I ran away from home when I was twelve and beat my way to Texas—"

The doctor arose.

"You're not twelve now. You're a grown man. Now, sir—"

He slipped off Emmet's dressing gown and said, as he adjusted a blood-pressure apparatus:

"You should be in bed this minute!"

The machine sighed down—Dr. Cardiff looked at the gauge and unwound the flap; then Miss Hapgood was at her patient's side and Emmet felt a gouge in his arm.

Dr. Cardiff turned to Miss Hapgood. "We'll get Mr. Monsen upstairs."

"I'm quite able to get upstairs . . ."

Miss Trainor, who happened to be in the hall, saw him go—assisted on either side. She was a grave, slow-thinking girl, despite the very special delights that showed in her face, and she seldom yielded to intuition. But she could not dismiss a persistent doubt as to whether Dr. Cardiff had his fingers on the pulse of this business.

She felt it even more strongly the next day at one o'clock as she sat at her typewriter looking out a window and across a rose bed into the kitchen. Mr. Monsen was at the stove in person, accompanied by the increasingly faint Miss Hapgood.

It seemed that Margerilla had not yet appeared though it was long past one o'clock. She had telephoned from some vague locality about eleven and Miss Trainor had received the vague impression of a grandmother with a broken leg. Margerilla had promised to arrive later but the patient was in an increasingly impatient and nervous mood.

Miss Trainor listened:

"Mr. Monsen, you can't cook with a temperature of 103°."

"Why not? Think of the Huns. They used raw steak for their saddles all day—that broke down the fibre of the meat—just like a modern kitchen range."

"Mr. *Mon*sen!"

Miss Trainor heard him chopping savagely at some meat and bent resolutely to her transcription. He had seemed such a pleasant, attractive man.

"You're too weak," said Miss Hapgood forlornly.

"You think so? Well, there's a bottle of fine brandy in the pantry there. Do you think it makes me any stronger to take those sedatives, that keep you in a daze for twenty-four hours?"

The patent percolator cracked and the chopping sound ceased.

"I don't want anything to eat anyhow," Emmet declared. "And please don't apologize. We'll send Miss Trainor for sandwiches. All I really want to do is stew that medical chart in castor oil and feed it to Dr. Cardiff."

The Trainor girl wished she had better news for him than what he had received over the telephone half an hour before—that Elsa Halliday was not able to come out that day—would probably manage it tomorrow. She heard him wander into the living room—then she was suddenly distracted by the sound of a car driving to the back door.

Five minutes later, followed by Miss Hapgood, she hurried into the living room.

"What's the matter?" he asked, looking up drowsily from his chair.

"It's Margerilla," chattered Miss Hapgood. "You know she did come at last, but she smells so *fun*ny. Well—"

He interrupted, demanding of Miss Trainor, "What is it?"

"The maid's drinking," she said. "We suspected it yesterday. She just turned up—she has a big fellow with her down there and he's drunk too—he's asleep across her bed—"

"When I asked her if she could get luncheon for us," wailed Miss Hapgood, "—all she said was 'I ain't even hungry'!"

Miss Trainor resumed:

"I can call the police—or else get some gardeners from Mr. Davis, but I didn't like to do anything without telling you. The man's too big for Miss Hapgood and me to handle."

Emmet got up. The situation was rather stimulating in the oppressive calm, but realizing that he was in no shape for trouble, he whipped himself into imposing indignation. With a menacing tread he entered the kitchen and approached the scene.

Margerilla, eyes unfocused, mouth ajar, teetered uncannily in front of the stove, doing something undetermined with a sauce pan. In the doorway of her bedroom, adjoining the kitchen, stood a huge, well-built negro. He lowered a flask cheerfully and grinned at Emmet.

"Morning, sir. Took liberty of coming along, Mr. Monsen. I valeted a lot of picture people and I thought—"

"Why, Mr. Monsen," cried Margerilla happily. "You know I told 'at nurse I wouldn'ta come back at all less he brought me. I knew you such a nice man *you* wouldn't care, and you got plenty women look after *you*."

Emmet walked past her and up to the negro.

"That your car in the court?"

"Sure is. Have a drink, Mr. Monsen?"

"Turn the car around, pointing *out*. Then go into Margerilla's room and help her get her things."

"Mr. Monsen, you wouldn't fire Margerilla for a little thing like that. An' if you did, then how about *me* taking care of you—"

"Get out!"

The expression on the man's face changed; he recapped his bottle and looked Emmet over.

"I don't know Margerilla ought to be workin' in a house like this. One of them composers got fresh with me one time and I—"

As Emmet took a step forward the man's face changed. He broke into a silly laugh, turned and went out the door. Encouraged, Emmet steered Margerilla by both arms into her bedroom.

"You be out of here in five minutes," he said. "Pack quick."

She started to collapse but he opened a bureau drawer and propped her on it. Returning through the kitchen he saw that Miss Trainor was leaning against the door to the butler's pantry—and too late she tried to conceal the brown gleam of a revolver inside the folds of her dress. Then he understood the change of expression in the negro's face and felt somewhat less formidable.

"Whose revolver?" he asked.

"Yours."

"Thanks. Will you please make out a check for Margerilla?"

From Margerilla's room came sobs and protestations to her boy friend, who was assisting her. Emmet sat down in a kitchen chair before the self starter had commenced to hum and was resting his head on his hand, trying to think things out again when he heard Miss Halliday's name pronounced in the pantry. He was tense again as the Trainor girl brought him the message.

"That was Miss Halliday's secretary. Miss Halliday's on her way out—be here any minute."

"Where's the nurse?" he exclaimed, jumping up.

"Making out her chart. Can I help?"

"Hold Miss Halliday downstairs," he shouted back from the stairs.

In his bedroom he induced Miss Hapgood to sponge him briefly with a wet towel, and by attaching himself to her like a pilot fish to a shark, collected some clothes to wear.

This was possibly the great moment of his life. It had been Elsa Halliday's face on a screen in Ceylon that told him he was a fool to leave her—Elsa's face meeting him on the dock three days ago that made him sure. And now he must face her only to stall, conceal, evade because he did not know himself what was in store for him.

—I've done harder things, he thought grimly.

"We haven't had a temperature for hours," said Miss Hapgood—and as though to prolong that situation she cracked the thermometer in her hand. The tiny glass snap acted as a signal: Emmet and all his immaculate clothes were instantaneously drenched with sweat.

"Try to match everything I've got on," he ordered frantically. "She'll *be* here any minute."

Miss Hapgood was still looking hopefully at the two pieces of thermometer when Miss Trainor knocked. At her announcement that the guest was below Emmet pressed her into service to collect another outfit, and redressed gingerly in the bathroom. Then he walked downstairs.

Elsa Halliday was a brunette with a high warm flush that seemed to photograph, and long sleepy eyes full of hush and promise. With the exception of Priscilla Lane she had made the steadiest rise in pictures of the past two years. Emmet did not kiss her, only stood beside her chair, took her hand and looked at her—then retreated to a chair opposite, momentarily thinking less of her than of his ability to control the damp he felt on brow and chest.

"How are you?" Elsa asked.

"Much better. Let's not even talk about it—or think about it. I'll be up and around in no time."

"That's not what Dr. Cardiff said."

At this his undershirt was suddenly wet.

"Did that ass talk about me?"

"He didn't say much. He told me you ought to take care of yourself."

Emmet was equally angry with them both, but he managed to tack away from the subject.

"You've done some grand work lately, Elsa. I know that—though I'm a couple of pictures behind. I've seen you in movie houses where only a few people could read the dubbed titles—less than a silent picture to them; but I've watched their eyes and their lips move with yours—and seen you hold them."

She stared into an imperceptible distance.

"That's the romantic part," she said. "How much real *good* you can do to people you will never meet."

"Yes," he answered.

—Of course Elsa must learn not to make remarks like that, Emmet thought, as he recalled the plots of *Port Said Woman* and *Party Girl*.

"The gift of vividness," he said after a minute. "Vividness in beauty— like those painters who discovered motion where there was no motion— though perspective came at the same time and overshadowed—"

He realized he was over her head and came down quickly:

"At the time when you and I were very close to each other your beauty used to scare me."

"When I talked about marriage," Elsa supplied, coming awake.

He nodded frankly.

"I used to feel like an art dealer, or like those bankers who try to be seen with opera singers—as if they'd bought the voice like a phonograph record."

"You did a lot for my voice," Elsa said. "I still have the phonograph and all the records and I may sing in my next picture. And the Juan Gris and Picasso prints—I still tell people they're real—though I've developed a lot of taste now and I get inside information about which paintings are going to be worth anything. I remember when you told me a painting *could* be a better investment than a bracelet—"

She broke off suddenly.

"Look, Emmet—that isn't why I came out here—to talk about all those old things. My director's sick but we may be shooting again tomorrow and I wanted to see you while I could. You know—catch up? Really talk about everything—let down my back hair—you know?"

This time it was Emmet who was scarcely listening. His shirt was now drenched and, wondering when there would be dark evidence on his shirt collar, he buttoned up his light coat. Then he was listening sharply.

"Two years is two years, Emmet, and we might as well get to the point. I know you *did* help me and I certainly did lean on you for advice—but two years—"

"Are you married?" he asked suddenly.

"No. I am not."

Emmet relaxed.

"That's all I wanted to know. I'm not a child. You've probably been in love with half the leading men in Hollywood since I've been gone."

"That's what I *haven't* done," she answered, almost tartly. "It shows how little you know about me, really. It shows how far people can drift apart."

Emmet's world was rocking as he answered.

"That could mean either there's been nobody. Or else that there's somebody in particular."

"Very *much* in particular," her voice became less brisk. "Heaven knows it's awful telling you this, when you're sick and maybe going—I mean, it's an awful hard position for a girl. But I've been so busy these last three days. In the industry you're just an ottoman, you know—you've got no more control of your time than if you were a shop girl type or something—"

"Going to marry this man?" Emmet interrupted.

"Yes," she said defiantly. "But I don't know how soon—and don't ask me his name, because your doctor said—because you might be delirious sometime—and these columnists would drive a girl crazy."

"This isn't something you decided within the last week?"

"Oh, I decided a year ago," she assured him, almost impatiently. "Several times we planned to go to Nevada. You have to wait four days here—and every time—"

"Is he a solid man—will you tell me that?"

"Solid is his middle name," said Elsa. "Catch me tying myself to some shyster or drunk. Next January I move into the big money myself."

Emmet stood up—he could time the moment when it would arrive at the lining of his coat.

"Excuse me," he said, getting up.

In the pantry he steadied himself at the sink. Then he tapped on the secretary's door.

"Get rid of Miss Halliday!" he said, catching a glimpse of his face—white, hard and haggard in a mirror. "Tell her I'm sick—anything—get her out of the house."

Hating compassion from anyone, he hated the face of the Trainor girl as she rose from her desk.

"Do it quickly! It's part of your job!"

"I understand, Mr. Monsen."

"I don't ask so much," he continued unnecessarily. "But I want it well done."

He went on out, feeling for the pantry sink, then for the swinging door, the back of a kitchen chair. A contemptuous line ran through his head in savage rhythm: "I never think much of a man who reaches for a glass of whiskey every time anything goes wrong."

He turned to the closet where there stood the brandy bottle.

IV

A rash youth taking down his first few gulps of spirits is moved not to homicide or wife beating, but to a blatant commotion, expressed in every fibre of heart and soul. An Englishman climbs, an Irishman fights, a Frenchman dances, an American "commotes" (the word is not in the dictionary).

So it happened to the abstemious Emmet—he commoted. It was in the bag from the instant that the cognac tumbled into contact with his burning fever—and it had gathered momentum while he sat on the side of his bed and let Miss Hapgood try to extricate him from his soaking clothes. He suddenly vanished—and almost as suddenly reappeared from the clothes-closet, clad in a sort of sarong surmounted by an opera hat.

"I am a Cannibal King," he said. "I am going down into the kitchen and eat Margerilla."

"Margerilla's gone, Mr. Monsen."

"Then I am going to eat Carlos Davis."

In a moment he was on the telephone in the hall, talking to Mr. Davis' butler. If Mr. Davis was home would he please come right over?

Hanging up the receiver Emmet leaped nimbly aside to avoid a jab of Miss Hapgood's syringe.

"No, you don't!" he advised her. "I'm going to act now, in full control of all faculties. Need all my strength."

To test this last quality he suddenly bent down and plucked out a spoke of the bannister railing.

The ease of the operation fascinated him. He leaned over and plucked out another—and then another. It was like one of those unpleasant nightmares where one detaches one's own teeth with uneasy awe.

The course of the operation led him downstairs. He kept in his hand one single spoke with which he intended to render Mr. Davis unconscious as he entered the door—in preparation to preparing and eating him.

However he made a single miscalculation. When in the vicinity of the kitchen he remembered the brandy bottle and had some short swift traffic with it—almost immediately he found, or lost, himself upon a sack of potatoes under the kitchen sink, his bludgeon beside him, his black silk crown awry.

Fortunately he was not conscious of the quick events of the next few minutes—of how Miss Trainor looked into the twilit garden and saw Carlos Davis making a short cut across it with the intention of entering his tenant's house through the rear door—nor of how Miss Trainor stepped outside the kitchen screen to intercept him, closing the door behind her.

"Hello there! Cheerio! Good morning, and all that. Monsen wanted to see me, and I always say visit the sick and all that."

"Mr. Davis, just after Mr.—Mom—" in her anxiety she parroted Miss Hapgood, "—called you, his brother phoned from New York. Mr. Mom wants to know if he can get in touch with you later—or tomorrow."

As the Trainor girl prayed that there would not be a sound from beneath the kitchen sink she heard the slow bounce of a potato across the kitchen floor.

"Cripes yes!" said Davis heartily. "Script's held up two more days. My writer's on a bat! That rat!"

He whistled—and then looked admiringly at Miss Trainor—a reversal of the usual process.

"Like to see the swimming pool sometime? I mean you don't work always. I mean—"

"I'd love it," Miss Trainor said—then covered up a species of groan from inside with the remarkable statement: "There's his buzzer now."

A puzzled look crossed Davis' face—faded. She sighed with relief.

"Well, cheerio and keep your chin up and all that sort of thing," he advised her.

When he was ten feet off she stepped back into the kitchen. Emmet Monsen was no longer there but there was not any doubt as to where he was, for she heard the sound of spokes leaving the bannister, of window glass splintering—and then his voice:

"No! *You* going to drink it. I know what it is—it's chloral hydrate—it's a 'Mickey Finn.' Why, I can smell it!"

Miss Hapgood stood on the stairs and smiled ineffectually as she held out the glass.

"Drink it!" Emmet commanded, not even pausing in his wrecking task, which consisted in throwing the extracted spokes through a broken window into the garden. "When that Cardiff comes I want to have you all passed out in rows before he drinks his! My God! Can't a man die in peace!"

Miss Trainor turned on the hall light against the darkening day—and Emmet Monsen looked ungratefully at her.

"And *you* with your smile, as if it was all so pretty. California!" The name of the state was accompanied by a long-drawn splintering of the top stair rail.

"I'm from New England, Mr. Monsen."

"Never mind! Write yourself a check anyhow. And write Miss Hapgood a check—on her chart."

Miss Hapgood rose to the occasion. Perhaps a vision, like Joan of Arc's, had come to her, a ghostly whisper from Florence Nightingale:

"Mr. Monsen—if I *do* drink this, will you go to bed?"

Hopefully she raised the glass of chloral.

"Yes!" agreed Emmet.

But as she lifted it to her mouth the Trainor girl darted up the stairs, tilted her arm and spilt the liquid.

"Somebody's got to watch!" she protested.

The hall below seemed suddenly crowded with people. There was Dr. Cardiff, massive in himself; there was Mrs. Ewing coming on her shift; there was a gardener from the Davis estate with a letter in his hand.

"Get out of here," Emmet shouted. "That includes Dr. Hippocrates."

His arms were full of broken wood as he backed up a few steps and braced himself against what remained of the toothless bannister.

"I'm going to have him disbarred at the next port. Write him a check, Miss Hapgood. You're off the case. I'm treating myself. Go on! Write checks! Get away!"

Dr. Cardiff made a step up the stairs and Emmet weighed a chunk, snarling happily. "Right at those spectacles. No curve—just a fast one. I hope you've got insurance on the sockets!"

While the doctor hesitated Emmet proved his aim by clipping off the light of the upper hall with a minor fragment.

Then the gardener, a man of seventy, started slowly up the stairs, holding out an envelope toward Emmet. Emmet's hand tightened on the big chunk but the fearless old face reminded him of his own father.

"From Mr. Davis," the gardener said, expressionless. He put the envelope through the gap in the balcony and started down.

"All of you get out!" Emmet cried, "while you're still whole. Before I—"

The world was spinning around him in cyclorama—

—and then suddenly he knew that the hall was empty. There was no sound in the house. For a few minutes he stood there, all his energies bent upon an attempt to focus. With a last resurgence of tension he crutched himself down the stairs—and listened. He heard a door shut far away—motors starting.

Leaning over so that he touched his hands to the steps he crept back up; at the head of the stairs his fingers touched an envelope. He lay on his back on the floor and ripped it open:

My Dear Mr. Monsen:
I had no idea of your condition. I saw the spokes come out the window—one of them hit me. I must ask you to vacate by nine o'clock tomorrow.

> *Sincerely*
> *Carlos Davis*

Emmet sat up, and accidentally his legs flung out over space through the gaps where the spokes had been. The house was absolutely quiet now. There was an echo as he experimentally dropped a last spoke down into the stair well. Presently, he told himself, he would get in bed. It was so nice and quiet. There were no people in the house. He had won.

V

When Emmet awoke there seemed to be no light save in the lower hall, but he had the half-waking memory of a sound far away in the dark house. He lay silent, seeing from the circlet moon in a window that it was late—somewhere between midnight and two.

The faint sound came again, with a suggestion of caution in its pitch, and Emmet sat up carefully. He tiptoed into his bedroom, put on his dressing gown and felt for his revolver in the drawer of his bureau. Snapping out the chamber he found to his annoyance that it was unloaded; and his hand came into contact with no bullets in the drawer. The chances were that anyone trying to break in was some discouraged tramp, but he put the empty gun in the pocket of his gown as he tiptoed down the stairs.

In the door of the dark living room he listened again—then he waited again outside the kitchen and the secretary's office—hearing the sound once more, as if from somewhere behind him.

He took the revolver in his hand and crept to the door of the living room—

A voice spoke suddenly from a corner.

"It's Miss Trainor, Mr. Monsen."

"What?"

"Trainor. The light switch is beside your hand."

Blinking at the glare he saw her curled in the big armchair, as if she herself had just awakened.

"You can't get on relief at night," she said. "So I just stayed."

"I heard something," Emmet said. "And if you're asleep it couldn't have been you. Know anything about the bullets for my revolver?"

"Mrs. Ewing took them out, that first night."

"You mean that gun was empty when you brought it in the kitchen?" Miss Trainor nodded.

"Sh!" he warned her suddenly, and flipped out the light. After a moment he whispered:

"There's somebody here. Do you know where she put those bullets?"

"No, I don't. And I went through the house myself a little while ago."

Unconvinced, Emmet prowled back toward the kitchen. Either his nerves were still in collapse or there were intermittent creaks that might be footsteps. Again he whispered to Miss Trainor, primed with suspicion:

"It isn't those medical masqueraders? That doctor or those nurses. Tell me frankly."

No answer—and for a moment he thought he had hit upon it—then he realized that Miss Trainor was no longer near him. A moment later, as she approached softly from the drawing room, he repeated his question.

"They've left, Mr. Monsen." She hesitated. "There *has* been a carpenter here but he's gone; he's coming back at six-thirty with new spokes for the bannister, and a new window frame."

Emmet forgot the suspected prowler as he asked in astonishment:

"Why?"

"Well," she seemed embarrassed. "I had nothing to do—so I gathered up the spokes."

"Mr. Davis wrote me that one of them hit him," he interrupted. "He told me to get out."

She paused, then her voice brightened.

"Well, it didn't stick in him, because the spokes were all out there in the garden—and if they're back in place he'll have a hard time suing you."

"How did you get a carpenter at this time of night?"

"My father," she said. "He used to be [a] shipwright."

"Damn nice of you." He added suddenly, "Sh!"

They listened—but when Emmet looked at her she shook her head negatively; her smile was sad; she wanted to agree with him that there had been a noise, but conscientiously she couldn't.

"It's this house," he decided suddenly. "The place is thoroughly haunted. I'm going out and walk a few minutes. I think if I could smell a field growing—"

He was in the hall putting a light overcoat over his dressing gown when Miss Trainor suggested:

"Do you mind if I walk along with you?"

Suspicion came back into Emmet's voice.

"You won't give me any orders?"

Ashamed of himself, he changed his tone:

"I don't mind."

Passing in front of the garage Emmet once more thought he heard a peculiar sound—but when it was not repeated he struck out with the Trainor girl across a dirt road—and off Carlos Davis' property.

It was a down-hill path and presently, with no particular fatigue, he sat down on one of the mounds of new-mown hay that dotted the field.

"You settle for the next pile," Emmet suggested considerately. "After all, you still have a reputation—which is one up on me."

Presently she spoke from a rustle ten feet away:

"There may be animal life here, but this is something I always wanted to do."

"Me too—what's the technique? Do you pull the hay over you? Or do you burrow down into it? You don't suppose I'd find Miss Hapgood!"

No answer. He stared at the waning moon for awhile, then murmured drowsily, "It all smells good."

—This wouldn't be a bad place to end, he thought drowsily. Even Elsa didn't seem especially to matter. But for a long time there had been no sound from the other pile, and curiosity made him ask: "Dreaming about New England?"

"Not dreaming at all—I had coffee with father. I'm wide awake."

"I feel saner myself minute by minute."

"You were never very bad."

Emmet sat up, feeling almost insulted as he wiped the glossy bristles from his ears.

"What do you mean! Why I was *menacing*! I was told to vacate!"

The Trainor girl was on her feet and near him.

"We must face the truth," she said, "There's a heavy dew and this hay is dampish. I'm leaving you."

"What do you mean? It's the finest hay."

No answer.

"Leaving me!" he exclaimed. "I thought you asked to come along."

Her voice reached him from thirty yards off.

"The hay's damp—and you told me not to give you any advice."

"You might at least *wait* a second."

He sighed—he stood up, and started after her. The path was up-hill now and when he caught up with her they stopped every few minutes. After the third time they had established somehow the convention that each time they stopped they would wink at each other.

"We'll have trouble explaining this to the burglar," he said, as they approached the house. "Maybe we better brush each other off."

"Virtue is its own reward."

But she slapped the particles conscientiously from his coat—and she did the same for herself as he looked back at the moon, and at the silver-spotted field below them. Then they stepped into the kitchen and she flipped on the light. Her smile seemed brighter than anything outside or in, brighter than anything Emmet had ever known.

VI

We shift the Camera Angle: Shooting toward Carlos Davis getting up in an exclusive bedroom set. It is eight-thirty in the morning but he awakes upset by the events of the night before.

Carlos Davis had scarcely begun his morning exercises when his Philippino came in.

"Doctor take care of Mr. Monsen—he want to talk to you on phone. Ver important."

Carlos Davis removed the encyclopedia from his abdomen while

Manuel plugged in the phone. A few grave sentences between himself and Dr. Cardiff established the facts of Emmet Monsen's conduct of the night before.

Then the doctor's voice sank almost to a whisper.

"Did it ever occur to you, Mr. Davis, that there may be another factor in this eclusion—this coronary thrombosis?"

"Is that what you call it? I thought it was just delirium tremens. Cripes! When they bean you with *bannister* spokes—"

"That's *about* the idea, Mr. Davis." The doctor spoke slowly. "But we know there was only that one bottle of brandy in the house—and he drank less than half of it . . ."

There was a pause over the telephone.

"Let me put it another way: when a doctor leaves the case at the mere whim of a patient—"

"Whim!" protested Davis. "If that's his idea of a whim!"

"When patient has only a twenty-five per-cent chance for life the doctor naturally wants to know *all* the facts—so he can inform the next doctor."

Carlos Davis was thoroughly mystified as Dr. Cardiff continued: "What do you know about Monsen, Mr. Davis?"

"Nothing—except he's a sort of—well-known man—and all that sort of—"

"I mean about his private life. Has it ever occurred to you that there are articles which can be concealed in a smaller space than alcohol?"

Davis found this hard thinking for this hour of the morning—a difficult script.

"You mean like stillettos—and dynamite?" he suggested, and then:

"Why don't you come out this afternoon and talk to me?"

Davis dressed in a state of some agitation, deciding in the middle of breakfast to collect a posse of gardeners, and see if his tenant had cleared out. He was within his legal rights. It was past nine—the hour he had set. However, he wanted, above all things, to avoid a scandal, and as he was not a timorous young man he left his followers outside and went in alone by the kitchen door.

The house was silent. He peered into the secretary's office, approached the living room—where he stopped short in the doorway. There, stretched on the sofa, apparently alive, but lost in the softest sleep, lay Miss Trainor. He stared at her momentarily, frowned, uttered a sigh, was half tempted to wake her and ask the address, but, with Macbeth's reverence for sleep, forced himself to turn away. He mounted the stairs.

In the big bedroom he found Emmet Monsen, also in a peaceful reverie. A little puzzled he began to retrace his steps, when suddenly he remembered the spoke that had flown from the window—and stood transfixed, staring at the bannisters: the spokes were *there*. Lightly he bounded up and down several times, then, with a slight feeling of nausea, he tried his eyes on several other objects—retreating finally to the kitchen.

Here he recovered his aplomb—certainly a half empty bottle of brandy stood in plain sight on a closet shelf—and with his relief a portion of Dr. Cardiff's conversation came back to him—this time with meaning.

"—articles that can be concealed in a smaller space than alcohol."

Carlos Davis dashed outside and in front of the garage took deep breaths of the pure California air.

Cripes! That was it—Dope! Emmet Monsen was a Secret Dope Fiend! Dope—the subject was somehow confused in his mind with the movies of Boris Karloff but it seemed to explain everything—only a dope fiend would have had the diabolical cleverness to wrench out bannister spokes, and then replace them without a flaw before morning!

And the girl asleep on the sofa—he groaned—she had probably led a pretty decent life before this Monsen, full of Tropical devices, had tricked her into a first whiff of the opium pipe a few days before . . .

He walked with the head gardener toward his house. Since he was not apt at phrases he quoted the doctor.

"There are articles that can be hidden in a smaller space than alcohol," he said darkly.

The gardener got it—glanced back wonderingly.

"My golly! One of them hopheads!"

"*And* American womanhood!" Davis added cryptically.

The gardener did not make a connection—but his mind jumped to another: "Mr. Davis, I should of spoke to you—maybe you know, down around the old stable—"

Davis was hardly listening—he was headed toward the telephone and Dr. Cardiff.

"—them weeds growing there is hemp, and it ought to be cut down and burned—"

"All right—all right."

"—because I read how them G-Men are cutting it down—because guys sell it to school children, and I had to chase some fellas out of there one day—"

Davis stopped.

"What are you talking about?"

"That marijuana, Mr. Davis. The peddlars make them reefers out of it and it drives them school children crazy. And if it got in the papers that marijuana was on *your* estate—"

Carlos Davis stood in place and uttered a long mournful cry.

VII

The Trainor girl, lately subject to Carlos Davis' commiseration, awoke about noon feeling that there were people in the room and that they were staring at her. She stood up, with those indispensable dabs at the hair that, though symbolic in their result, give a woman a sense of being "fixed up."

The party that had entered consisted of Dr. Cardiff, and two husky younger men with a firm, alert manner—and, hovering tentatively in the background, that celebrated shadow known as Carlos Davis.

Dr. Cardiff said Good Morning somewhat grimly, and continued a conversation with the two young men.

"The County Hospital has given you your instructions; I am simply here at the request of Mr. Davis. You know the ingenuity of these people—and how *small* a syringe can be."

The young men nodded. One of them said: "We understand, doctor. We look under mattresses and down the drains, and inside of books and powder-boxes."

"Behind their ears," supplemented the other young man. "Sometimes they keep it there."

"And be pleased to examine those bannister spokes," proposed Dr. Cardiff. "Monsen may have been trying to get at it." He brooded momentarily. "I wish we had one of those broken spokes."

Carlos Davis spoke up nervously.

"I don't want any violence. Don't start looking behind his ears till you get him in custody."

A new voice sounded strange from the doorway.

"What's this about my ears?"

Emmet, fatigued from the effort of shaving, found his way to a chair and looked at the doctor for an explanation, but he found none, nor on any other face till he met the eyes of the Trainor girl—who winked solemnly. This time, behind the wink, he divined a warning.

Other signals were going on. The two young men exchanged cryptic glances, whereupon one departed the room while the other drew a chair close to Emmet, and sat down.

"My name is Pettigrew, Mr. Monsen."

"How-do," said Emmet shortly—and then, "Sit down, Davis—you must be tired. I saw you from my window an hour ago—reaping that weed patch behind your stable. And you were pitching in!"

Dr. Cardiff may have detected the sudden sweat upon the young actor's forehead, for he gave him that headshake that all over the world means: Don't pay any attention.

Pettigrew reached out and patted Emmet's knee gently.

"Mr. Monsen, I understand you've been sick, and sick people aren't always responsible for taking the right medicine. Ain't that true, Doctor?" He looked at Dr. Cardiff, who gave him encouragement. "Now I'm a deputized commissioner from the county police—and I'm also a male nurse—"

At this point the doorbell rang, and since all the other people in the room seemed concentrated upon the chair where Emmet sat, the Trainor girl went into the hall.

Upon the steps stood a pretty girl in a state of agitation, holding a package in her hands; she stared uncertainly at Miss Trainor.

"Are you the lady here?" she asked.

"I'm Mr. Monsen's secretary."

The new arrival gave a gasp of relief.

"If you're a working girl you'll understand. I'm from the Johanes Laboratories—and there was a mix-up, a hurry call and I—and they sent the wrong cardiograph here." For a moment she tried to bluff it out—fell before the infinite forgiveness of the smile. "You know? The wrong heart chart?"

Miss Trainor nodded—she was so intent upon what was going on inside the house that she was giving the girl only half her attention.

"It was almost very serious. The man that got Mr. *Monsen's* chart thought he was so well that he was just going to take up polo again— and *his* chart that Mr. *Monsen* got—"

She ran out of breath—but by this time the Trainor girl's smile had brightened—by what can only be measured in ohms. She took over.

"Does this package have Mr. Monsen's correct chart?"

"Yes."

"All right—I'll take care of this. You needn't worry. Dr. Cardiff isn't on this case anymore."

After the girl had gratefully departed Miss Trainor stood there unwrapping the envelope. The cardiograph meant little to her—but she was so presumptuous as to read the explanatory letter that went with it before she went back into the living room.

The situation there was physically unchanged but—enlivened. The second young man had returned from his search of the house and stood over Emmet, weighing half a dozen capsules in his hand. Emmet was not amused. His expression was one she had never seen before—it was like the calm he had described in his book, before the up-rush of some immense monsoon.

"Those are pills that Dr. Cardiff gave me," he said slowly. Then he turned to the other man and sank his voice to a confidential note:

"If you want to know who's been giving me this stuff—" He turned toward Davis. "There's a certain plant that grows wild in various sections—"

He broke off at a new interruption—this time a weary voice from the doorway.

"Hello, Charlie."

Pettigrew looked up with recognition at a third young man who stood there.

"Hello, Jim!" he exclaimed. "What you doing here?"

"Here on call," he said. He indicated Miss Trainor with a touch of reproach: "The lady got me out here last evening—but I guess she forgot about me. I've been asleep in the back seat of a car."

Miss Trainor spoke up, addressing Carlos Davis.

"This man's a nurse too," she said. "I had him come here after Mr. Monsen dismissed the others."

"She made me keep out of the way," Jim complained. "She had me dodging around from room to room—then they went out for a walk! I didn't get to sleep till seven!"

"Find any junk?" demanded Pettigrew eagerly.

"Find any junk? Say, that's what I slept in—a 1932—"

"That's my car," objected Miss Trainor. "And a very good one."

It was perhaps this last remark which prompted her to step forward and hand the revised cardiograph to Dr. Cardiff—with a few of those brisk words—the kind that are sometimes described as "well-chosen."

There were still roses around the door a week later—Angele Pernets and Cherokees and Cecile Brunners in the yard, and Talismans and Black Boys climbing over the porch in a multi-colored rash and peering around the corner of screens. They seemed to have a curious herbal effect not usually attributed to roses, for Emmet did not even use the last of the green capsules to cure up his malaria.

On the contrary, he dictated—and, as that word has come to have a harsh sound, let it be amended to say that there were long times when no words at all were necessary—where the two of them merely communicated. And though the roses were quitting for the year pretty soon, it seemed likely it would go on between these two forever.

—end—

FSF passport, 1924.

In April 1939, Zelda and Scott went on vacation to Cuba. It was horrible for them both; he drank to excess and had to be hospitalized in New York, and Zelda then had to return to Highlands Hospital alone. It would be the last time the Fitzgeralds ever saw each other. "Salute to Lucy and Elsie" is born of that time. Fitzgerald began writing it almost as soon as he returned, still sick, to California from New York.

Fitzgerald submitted "Salute to Lucy and Elsie" directly to Arnold Gingrich, the editor of *Esquire*, in the midsummer of 1939. Gingrich liked it, and sent it on to his reader Alfred Smart, with the notation "Al—What's your feeling about this modern-day version of 'Fathers + Sons' as a story for Esquire?" On August 15, Smart replied negatively. "Evans letter to George is pretty hot, and the Catholic angle would have to be washed and laundered." Gingrich wrote to Fitzgerald the next day, a detailed letter explaining the many things he liked about the story, but not addressing the heat of Wardman Evans's letter to George, nor "the Catholic angle." He praised the story, saying "The whole development seems right as rain to me," but objected to one marriage. "I realize that the objection I am raising goes to the very guts of the story and isn't a small matter of incidentals," Gingrich went on, almost apologetically, but still asked for the change: "can something else happen, instead of the second marriage?" Fitzgerald changed nothing.

Two additional pages of an alternate typescript version of the story show that at one time the focus of the story was not on fathers and sons at all, but on fathers and daughters. The man from whose point of view this version unfolded was Chauncy Garnett, a Philadelphia architect, a friend of the families of both Lucy and her young husband, Llewellen. Lucy has run away to Connecticut to marry him, and things have gone very wrong thereafter, once the traditionally "right thing" has been done. These two pages were saved with a note from Gingrich explaining what they are, and returned to Fitzgerald's estate after his death.

SALUTE TO LUCY AND ELSIE

by

F. SCOTT FITZGERALD

Each time George Lawson Dubarry came down to visit his father in Cuba the same thing happened. George's mail arrived in Cuba before he did, and his father whose name was Lawson Dubarry, without the George slit open the first letter and read "Dear George" (or sometimes "George darling") before he realized that it was not for him. Always then he literally shut his eyes as he slipped it back in the envelope--and when later he gave the letter to his son, wore a guilty expression as he explained how it happened.

What Lawson afterwards referred to as "The Letter" arrived in his offices at the Pan-American Refining Company on a hot day in July. Perhaps it was the sweat on his glasses perhaps it was the letter's ambiguous beginning: "Greetings Old Boy" which made Lawson read the first few pages before recognizing the advance guard of his son's correspondence.

After that he had to go right through to the end.

George was eighteen, a sophomore at New Haven, whence Lawson himself had graduated. George's mother was dead and Lawson had worked hard and clumsily at the mother-and-father role until George managed to flop into Yale, in the manner of

Salute to Lucy and Elsie

Each time George Lawson Dubarry came down to visit his father in Cuba the same thing happened. George's mail arrived in Cuba before he did, and his father whose name was Lawson Dubarry, without the George, slit open the first letter and read "Dear George" (or sometimes "George darling") before he realized that it was not for him. Always then he literally shut his eyes as he slipped it back in the envelope—and when later he gave the letter to his son, wore a guilty expression as he explained how it happened.

What Lawson afterwards referred to as "The Letter" arrived in his offices at the Pan-American Refining Company on a hot day in July. Perhaps it was the sweat on his glasses, perhaps it was the letter's ambiguous beginning: "Greetings Old Boy" which made Lawson read the first few pages before recognizing the advance guard of his son's correspondence.

After that he had to go right through to the end.

George was eighteen, a sophomore at New Haven, whence Lawson himself had graduated. George's mother was dead and Lawson had worked hard and clumsily at the mother-and-father role until George managed to flop into Yale, in the manner of an exhausted gamefish flopping into a boat causing Lawson to hope that the worst was over.

The letter, postmarked Paris, was from George's roommate, Wardman Evans; after one reading Lawson went to the door and said to his secretary: "No phones for an hour."

Returning to his desk he read the letter a second time. Omitting the young man's scathing comments on foreign ways and places, his attention focused on the following:

> *June 30, 1939*
>
> *. . . Well, she gave in on the boat and I don't mind telling you I was scared about being the first. Scared for just a minute, because I thought she might lose her head and we were two days from Cherbourg. But the worst of it was she suddenly took it all so seriously*

269

*and I had an awful time shaking her off in Paris. She's seventeen
and in college and if it hadn't been me it would have been somebody
else. . . . How did it go with Elsie? Did you G. the L. or is she still
pulling that one about being a Catholic and doesn't believe in Birth
Control. Get 'em young is my theory and at least you won't run into
anything like I did last April . . . if you hear that we're going to get the
suite in Harkness send me a night cable. And when you write tell me
about Sweet Sixteen. We can compare some juicy notes if she went
through with it. (I meant to tell you that the doctor said before I left
God's Country that I'm O.K., but after a week in this crazy burg—
well, I'm more worried about myself than I am about Lucy.)*

Ever yours
Wardman (Roomie)

Lawson Dubarry had taken reservations at the Valedero Beach Club
where they would do a lot of fishing while he "caught up with his son."
But as he tapped the letter on the table he said to himself, "Catch up
with what?" and he could have sworn that no hour had elapsed before
his secretary opened the click latch and assured him it had.

"Could you bring me in a typewriter—I want to pound out a letter
myself."

"Can you type, Mr. Dubarry?"

"I think I can."

"Remember—" she said, "—if it's to your son he'll be on the Miami
clipper tomorrow. It'll cross him."

She saw from his expression that this was out of order and covered
up with an inquiry about the beach club reservation.

"Hold everything," Lawson said, "Or no, go ahead just as if—"

He stopped himself. He felt very much alone. There was no man
with whom he cared to discuss this—most certainly not with George.
He remembered with distaste a scoutmaster of his youth who had
talked about the dangers of "secret sin"—also of a robust friend who
had deliberately taken his boy to a "house" at seventeen. But Lawson
was of his day, and reticent and George *knew* it—and there would
be at best an orgy of embarrassment for them both. He had another
plan.

On the typewriter, slowly and painstakingly he wrote a letter to Wardman Evans.

He began by explaining how he had happened to open the letter—
then he descended swiftly into blackmail:

If you will remember its details you will understand that I can't pass it on to my son, and that I don't think it best for you two to room together next year. This implies no criticism of you, nor any suggestion that you have been a bad influence. Perhaps it's the reverse. But preoccupations such as you describe cannot but hurt both of you in your work.

I count on you as the elder to immediately notify the Yale registrar and my son of the change of plan about the room, inventing any excuse you want.

No doubt you will prefer such an extremely intimate and revealing letter returned—so at the same time that you send me a copy of your letter to the registrar send me also an address where you would like it mailed.

Yours—not without sympathy but thoroughly disturbed and entirely determined—

Lawson Dubarry

Lawson put on proper stamps for it to reach Wardman Evans in Paris—he should have an answer in three weeks.

There was a question as to whether Wardman would show fight. Lawson remembered him as a handsome, metallic boy with a wide-eyed frankness and thin Park Avenue manners.

Lawson had never met his father and casual seduction might be their family tradition, reaching back two generations to the emigrant ship, or twenty to the Crusades.

As he waited for the plane at the customs dock he kept thinking that there was nothing in the letter which convicted George and "Sweet Sixteen"—he winced at even thinking the girl's name. George might merely have toyed with designs in scarlet. Lawson's role was certainly to exercise patience and self-control, while he "won George's confidence" and encouraged him to unpack his ethical standards—if any. By the time Wardman's answer arrived he hoped that he and not Wardman would be George's best friend . . .

"*Father!* You look fine!"

Relief stole over Lawson. This healthy, generous, jovial specimen simply couldn't think in the manner of that letter. Lawson strutted with him from the dock.

"I wanted to work *with* you this summer," George said. "You shouldn't have planned all this vacation."

"It's my vacation too."

"But I want to sweat, like you have to. Let's save swimming and fishing for week ends. I've got a couple of house parties I'm going to in September."

At the end of the first week George dropped the name *Wardman Evans* while they were at luncheon at El Patio. It seemed to fall like a live grenade in Lawson's plate.

"He and I have the same sense of humor," George said. "That's one reason I like rooming with him. He's limited but when I get thoughtful I hang around with other guys."

"He impressed me as—rather ordinary," said Lawson evenly.

"Ordinary!" objected George. "He's dead sure of any Senior Society he wants!"

Lawson's thought: "that wouldn't prove anything" was left unsaid.

There was mail for George in Wardman's handwriting from here and there in Europe—mail which Lawson passed on to his son without a quaver. And there were girl's letters in many handwritings which Lawson read in his imagination; they were all signed by Elsie, all saying: "George—help me! What have we done?"

But in the mornings Lawson could be modern enough to think: "This isn't 1890. And it takes two to make a seduction."

Somewhat along this line George first displayed his ethical equipment.

"I'm steering clear of Philadelphia when I go back. My God! when a girl has a yen for a man she'll go to *any* lengths."

"Will she?"

"Absolutely. The old mouse trap play."

"Why don't they go after men in a position to marry?"

"That's later. I'm talking about sex, which I hope doesn't shock you. It still goes on you know."

—Lay low, Lawson whispered to himself—remembering only that George must be separated from Wardman, and that if George was brutally predatory he must be slowed up this side of disaster to himself and "Sweet Sixteen." So the weeks passed—with George making him both young and old. Then letters came.

Lawson's envelope, posted from London, contained a carbon of a letter to the Registrar. It informed him that he, Wardman Evans, would not be rooming with George Dubarry next term, but the reason it gave was: "—since I am resigning from the University and have so informed the Dean."

At the bottom was an addenda in pen and ink.

I hope this will please you. I am not enclosing a copy of my letter to George because a man does not have to take orders from anyone except his own father or employer but I assure you (in case you plan to "accidentally" open it) that it does not mention your letter in any way, shape or form.

Yours truly
G. Wardman Evans.

There was a letter for George in the same handwriting but George was on a two day business trip to Pinar del Rio and Lawson could only spend a bad week-end reading over Wardman's letter to George and his own letter to Wardman, wondering if he could have forced the young man to such an extreme. He consoled himself with the thought that since Wardman's interests were obviously not at New Haven, he would be no loss to the student body.

George, coming into the office on Monday, pocketed the letter addressed to him and talked of Pinar del Rio and his desire to abandon the house-parties and work in Cuba until college opened. But later that afternoon, when they met at Lawson's club, George was in a state of profound gloom.

"That fool Wardman! It isn't just the trouble of getting another room-mate though it won't be quite the same—but he's such a fool."

"What's he done?"

"Quit college," said George aghast. "Of all the insane things."

Lawson was silent, his nerves tingling.

"Why did he quit? Or is it a secret."

"Oh, you can't keep *that* a secret!"

"Well then—can I know—what has he done?"

"He seems to have married a little trollop named Lucy Bickmaster."

Lawson called a passing waiter and ordered a double whiskey. George took a beer. There was silence as George took out the letter and studied it.

"Why did he marry her?" Lawson asked.

"That's the mystery."

"Maybe he—had to."

"Don't make me laugh. I've known Lucy three years." Then he added quickly, "but don't get any ideas in your head, father—I never had designs on her. I simply know her character and my guess is he must have been tight."

"Aren't you jumping at conclusions about the girl," said Lawson coldly, "lacking evidence to the contrary can't you presume that a girl of seventeen—"

He stopped himself at George's puzzled look.

"How do you know she's a girl of seventeen?"

"I think you told me."

"I don't remember mentioning her."

Taking down his drink Lawson ordered another.

"He mentions you in the letter," George said.

Lawson's heart jumped.

"He sends his regards and he hopes you'll be a good influence on me."

"Let's forget it all," said Lawson. "I'm sorry because *you're* sorry, but he was a fool, as you say—giving up his education for a girl."

"He was trapped."

"Maybe."

They stood up.

"I don't know the girl," said Lawson, "speaking impersonally I only hoped she isn't trapped too."

He was tempted to snatch one more drink on the way out but that would have violated his rules. Then due to the slight frustration involved he made another slip.

"Maybe Wardman isn't such a prize physical package himself."

Stepping out of the club into the blinding sunlight Lawson felt triumphant and talkative; he was glad for the sake of discretion that George and he weren't spending the evening together.

. . . Later he stopped for a nightcap at a bar where young girls waited on the customers. On departing he tipped his hat in the Latin manner.

"Multa gratia, Lucia," he said jovially—and then to the other barmaid, "Adios Elsie."

He tipped his hat again and bowed and as he walked out left the two girls staring, unaware that he had bowed across two generations into an American past.

The feeling of triumph persisted into the next morning when he entered his office late and full of new hopes for his son and himself. George was not yet in but on the desk was an envelope in his handwriting marked "Personal." Lawson opened and read it. Then, as upon another occasion, he rang for his secretary and said "Please—no phones." Then he read it a second time:

—I guessed from your last remark that there was something pho-
ney going on. I worried about it all night and this morning when I

came in early your secretary handed me a letter which she said must have got into your files by mistake. Attached to it was your answer and I'm not even pretending that it was an "accident" that I read that too.

By the time you get this I will be on the clipper. The cashier advanced the wages due me. In saying goodbye I want to state I have tried to be a good son and act like a gentleman as far as I understand what the word means.

Not till weeks later, when he saw a newspaper item about George's marriage ("the ceremony was performed in Elkton, Maryland—Miss Elsie Johnson, the bride, is sixteen years old"), did Lawson realize that, in the welter of good intentions, that doubtful quantity, Elsie, had been saved—but the sacrifice was his son's.

He was never quite able to realize how he could have acted otherwise, but at certain times thereafter he would remark upon modern young women and their ways. His kindest comment was that they were the only hunters desperate enough to bait a trap with crushed and broken portions of themselves. And he would qualify even this with: "—it's not their own courage—it's the courage of nature."

There were other things that he caught himself saying which cannot be set down. Wardman Evans, among others, might have been honestly shocked to hear them.

FSF in uniform, 1918.

Sometime in 1939 or 1940, when he was most of the time freelancing and working on the screenplays of other writers, Fitzgerald came up with this "original" of his own. A typescript copy survives in the Fitzgerald Papers at Princeton.

"Love Is a Pain" is in some ways a return to the time and themes of *This Side of Paradise*, in that it is a mash-up of Princeton days and a world at war. Fitzgerald was long out of college, though, as he wrote it, and instead of the "war to end wars" he had missed fighting in as a young man, a more truly world war was beginning. That his mind should have returned to his own last days at Princeton is unsurprising, given that his time there ended on a campus that had by 1917 become an officer training camp.

The war and the foreign country the secret agent in this scenario serves are not specified. Thematically, "Love Is a Pain" is reminiscent of both Ernest Hemingway's strange Spanish Civil War play *The Fifth Column* (1937) and Hollywood's allegedly "light-hearted" war movies of 1938–1940 that refused to name Germany or Hitler as the enemy while making melodramatic love plots their focus (think of Clark Gable and Hedy Lamarr in *Comrade X* [1940], or *South of the Border* [1939], in which Gene Autry tries to save Mexico from "foreign spies" and falls in love with a beautiful local girl during a fiesta). "Love Is a Pain" is something Alfred Hitchcock might have filmed, were the college element stripped away. The dialogue around the game of cards is intriguing, and, as is often the case with Fitzgerald's film scenarios, "Love Is a Pain" makes one wish he had developed it into a short story instead.

"LOVE IS A PAIN"

An Original
by
F. SCOTT FITZGERALD

A very pretty girl of eighteen, Ann Dawes, arrives back from Europe, one of the last travellers to get out of the war zone. Two young men meet her at the dock. They have trouble locating her because she is not on the passenger list. This is because her wealthy grandfather detests the glamor girl idea. Let her get her name in the paper three times before she's twenty and she'll get nothing from him.

Did she get near the front?

No. But she talked to a few who had, and she certainly was glad to be back.

It is as they leave the customs house to drive to her grandfather's estate near Princeton that we realize she is being followed. She has not escaped from the war zone. She only **thinks** she has.

Tom, one of the young men, is observant and he notices the man. He remarks about it, but Ann merely laughs and his friend Dick accuses him of seeing things. Tom admits he must have been mistaken.

But after they leave Ann at her grandfather's, Dick too sees the shadower and they give chase, overtake him and capture him. But their prisoner, an extremely attractive man, shows a card which declares him to be a member of the American Secret Service and assures them that he has followed Ann Dawes for a good reason he cannot divulge.

Love Is a Pain

A very pretty girl of eighteen, Ann Dawes, arrives back from Europe, one of the last travellers to get out of the war zone. Two young men meet her at the dock. They have trouble locating her because she is not on the passenger list. This is because her wealthy grandfather detests the glamor girl idea. Let her get her name in the paper three times before she's twenty and she'll get nothing from him.

Did she get near the front?

No. But she talked to a few who had, and she certainly was glad to be back.

It is as they leave the customs house to drive to her grandfather's estate near Princeton that we realize she is being followed. She has not escaped from the war zone. She only *thinks* she has.

Tom, one of the young men, is observant and he notices the man. He remarks about it, but Ann merely laughs and his friend Dick accuses him of seeing things. Tom admits he must have been mistaken.

But after they leave Ann at her grandfather's, Dick too sees the shadower and they give chase, overtake him and capture him. But their prisoner, an extremely attractive man, shows a card which declares him to be a member of the American Secret Service and assures them that he has followed Ann Dawes for a good reason he cannot divulge.

The two young men are shocked. They release him.

Next morning they drive over to Ann's house and try to make her admit that she has been up to some mischief. First Ann takes it as a joke, then grows angry at their priggish and super-patriotic point of view. She sends them away, goes up to her room. The quarrel has left her full of nervous energy and a sense of injustice. She starts something she was too lazy to do the day before—unpack her trunk. At the very bottom she finds an unfamiliar leather satchel in which is a forty-five pound, 156 mm. artillery shell.

Her first reaction is fright; her second is to throw some clothes on top of it and close the trunk. Her third is to connect it up with the man who

279

has evidently been following her. If he is a secret service man the police already suspect her and she might get some very unfortunate publicity.

She is confused and hesitant. At this point I want to stress the fact that this part should be played by a young girl—perhaps a Brenda Joyce—a girl on the edge of maturity to whom parties are all important. A fully matured girl of, say, 19, would not hesitate about going to the police.

Ann decides to go to her grandfather and asks him, without telling him the truth, what *he* would do in a parallel case. Her grandfather, suspecting nothing, tells her that of course she should be on the side of the law—whereupon Ann tries to phone the police. But the line is dead.

She goes downstairs and out—on the front porch she meets an electrician who tells her he has come to fix the phone. We recognize, though she doesn't, the man who shadowed her the day before.

It is obvious that his mission has something to do with the shell— probably to get possession of it. But he had rather hoped to meet any member of the family except Ann. So they both stall. He asks to see the phone in her room, though of course he has cut the wires outside. Ann, fearing that he might not be honest, might open the trunk, goes upstairs with him and sits on the trunk as he works.

They fall into conversation. He is obviously well educated and tells her that he was trained as an engineer and that he has been forced to turn electrician very recently. We notice a faint foreign inflection, per- haps French, in his voice.

There is an immediate sympathy and attraction between them, but they are each absorbed in problems. Ann anxious to clear up the matter of the shell; the electrician anxious to be alone in the room. He asks for a hammer hoping she'll go for it—but Ann rings for the maid. He asks her for water; mistrustfully, she gets it from the bathroom. But finally he catches her off guard and when her back is turned throws some flaming waste out the window to land on a straw pile. Then he pretends to dis- cover the fire. The ruse works. Ann runs downstairs whereupon he opens the trunk quickly and starts to lift out the satchel containing the shell.

Downstairs we see that the fire has been noticed almost instantly from the kitchen and been put out at once by the servants. So Ann rushes back upstairs in time to hear the lid of the trunk falling. Cutting into the room we see that the electrician hearing her approach, has for a moment given up his intention of taking the shell. Connecting him now with the govern- ment she tells him frankly about the shell, and that she doesn't know how or where it got in the trunk. The electrician accepts the identification of himself as an American agent, telling her he will take the shell away.

She must forget the whole transaction. He is about to vanish from her life. But Ann has begun to feel romantic about this "G man" and doesn't want this to happen. She asks him where he is taking the shell. When he says to Washington, Ann asks if she can ride with him as far as Princeton. The secret agent agrees.

Ann elects to pass him off on her grandfather—to whom obviously he cannot be either an electrician or a G man—as an air-minded friend just come from a flying field. The grandfather accepts the electrician's costume as that of an aviator. Ann says she is going to Princeton to visit a friend.

Before they start out a letter from Dick is delivered in which he withdraws his invitation to the Princeton Prom. He still loves her and always will but everyone's duty is to America now and he doesn't want to have anything to do with her till she "comes clean." The letter, of course, is a veiled threat that if she comes to Princeton at all he will expose that she is in trouble with the police.

This fits in with Ann's plan. In Princeton she will let Tom and Dick see who she is with—thus clearing up the matter then and there. She doesn't give a damn about the prom now but she does care about her mystery man. She doesn't tell him this plan but when they get to Princeton gets him to stop his open car in front of the dormitory where the two boys live. She accosts a passing boy who obligingly yells up at the windows of Dick's room. When Dick and Tom come down she pulls her *coup* surprising both the boys and the secret agent by saying that he will clear her name. He does so—but only in the most general terms. There is no mention of the shell.

Dick, in his jubilation, insists that she stay the night in Princeton, will take no refusal. To clinch matters he reaches into the back of the car and starts to lift the satchel containing the shell.

"What have you got here?" he exclaims, "Lead!"

"That's mine," says the secret agent. "Leave it alone."

At this point a language professor passing along the walk sees the secret agent and calls him in a foreign language. His tone indicates his surprise at the agent's presence in this country.

This instantly suggests to Ann, Dick and Tom that the man is *not* an American citizen, and could not be a member of the American police. The secret agent impassively answers, "You must be mistaken," throws the car into first and starts away—carrying Ann with him.

On the outskirts of Princeton they turn into a road just at the moment that a man is about to put up a sign *Detour, Highway under repair. Detour.* They get on the road *before* the sign is put up. Then, a few miles out in the country, a tire blows out.

Up to this kidnapping, Ann has been all *for* the secret agent who seems the most attractive man that she ever met. Now, of course, she turns passionately against him. He is undoubtedly a spy and he is, in point of fact, kidnapping her.

He promises he will put her out of the car when they have driven further into the country, but not so near Princeton. She pretends to accept this but when he gets out to fix the tire she turns the key in the ignition and throws the car into gear. The secret agent detects her just in time, climbs in over the back seat and halts the car. When he gets out this time he takes the key with him, and also the shell as an extra precaution. This is done on his part with an air of perfect good humor.

Once again Ann waits—until just as he is pushing the jack under the rear axle. At this point he takes off his coat and throws it over the back of the open car—and Ann has seen him put the key in the pocket of the coat. Stealthily she draws the coat over and slips out the key.

This time she manages to get away. However, about fifty feet down the road she stops, keeping the motor running. She is afraid that if she leaves him there with the shell he will in some way disappear.

The secret agent puts the shell behind some trees at the side of the road and with charming blandishment, tries to come near Ann. But each time he tries she drives a little ahead. He gives this up. His situation is that if he strikes cross country with the shell she cannot follow him, but she *can* and will return to Princeton for help, even with the flat tire. Ann, for her part prays for another car to come along. She doesn't know what we know—that the road has been closed on both sides of them for repairs. *No one* will be along.

So time, which Ann thought was for her proves to be against her. Night falls. There is a patter of rain. Ann tries to raise the car top and can't do it alone. The secret agent takes advantage of this effort to sneak up on her—just as the clouds burst in earnest. She throws the key off into the underbrush, watching where it lands, but he doesn't notice this gesture. The storm is too bad to fix the tire but he gets the top up and they sit under that faint protection until we FADE OUT:

Next morning Tom and Dick at Princeton discuss the events of the day before. They know only that Ann has gone off, willingly or unwillingly, with a self-declared G man—whom a foreign professor claimed as a countryman of his. The professor's words were that he looked enough like Captain So-and-so, to be his own brother. But the professor also admitted that he *might* be mistaken, which accounts for the boys' confusion and delay. They decide to phone her grandfather's house and see if she's there, but a servant tells them that she has gone visiting a certain girl in Princeton. This, they know, is not true. Dick who is in love with her wants to tell the police. Tom remembers that Ann wants no newspaper publicity and thinks they ought to search for her themselves. Disturbed, they borrow a car and set out in the direction of Washington, knight-errants, with scarcely a clue to go on. The first thing they come to is the sign—*Detour—Road Under Repair*. They argue with a policeman but he will not let them through.

Meanwhile our principals are awake and hungry. The secret agent has an "iron ration" in the car which they share. They wash—on the honor system—at a nearby stream—then he firmly insists she return to the car and he starts to fix the tire at last in the bright sunshine. Only now does he notice the key is missing. He asks her for it and she laughs. She has control of the situation unless he makes physical threats and it is carefully planted that he is a gentleman. Once more he tries guile. Getting out he disconnects the starter without telling her and then he starts back down the road for the jack, left there the night before. But he keeps an eye on her and sure enough, when he has gone a little way, Ann gets out and looks hurriedly in the shrubbery for the key. The secret agent comes running. He now knows where she has thrown it and presently he finds it. He is again top dog.

It seems as if they have known each other a long time and there has been a good deal of humor in the running fight about the key.

As they start along the road at last Ann at least tries to get some light on the mystery. How did the shell get in her trunk? It happened abroad, of course, but she had to pass through so many countries coming back that she doesn't know in which one it occurred, nor does she know why it was sent here. He will tell nothing.

"The customs officer might have found it at the dock," she says, "if there hadn't been such a jam of refugees."

Off guard he answers: "That was our only risk."

This makes it plain to her that he is a spy, for a G man could have arranged with the customs house to possess the shell then and there. Her mood which has been gay all morning turns to anger. She has become a passionate patriot—though her mind had been full of nothing but dances just twenty-four hours ago.

Meanwhile, Dick and Tom reach the point where the detour ends and curves back into the main road. Here also they find a sign "*Road Under Repair*" and the foreman of a labor gang tells them that no one has taken the main road since 5 o'clock the preceding day when a bridge collapsed. They know, therefore, that Ann and her abductor are somewhere back along that road. But no amount of persuasion will convince the foreman to let their car in to the closed strip. He has his orders. So they abandon their car and get in his truck crowded with workmen bound for the damaged bridge. Added to other worries about Ann, is their anxiety that the car might have crashed at the bridge.

At the moment Ann and the secret agent are so absorbed by their quarrel. He has now admitted to her that he is not an American—he is a patriot of his own country, trying to do his duty.

"If you feel that way I don't think it's quite safe to release you. You'll just have to come along with me."

"Where?"

"Not very far now."

"I hate you."

"Why bother?" he asks. "We'll never meet again. If I'm caught, I'll go to prison. If not, my mission on this side is over. In the little while longer that we'll be together why bring hatred into it? Your country isn't at war with mine."

"What about that shell?" she asks.

"I can tell you nothing. It might endanger the lives of others."

"A lot of respect for human life you have to go around with that for your briefcase."

She indicates the article in the back seat.

"We don't always have the final word—"

He breaks off with the sudden realization that the shell is not in the car but back on the roadside. She realizes it too and breaks out with laughter. He turns to look at her and at this point the car goes over the bridge.

They are not hurt but are all wet again. They swim to the far bank, which is nearest and start to dry out. Ann suddenly notices a house that is half concealed by a grove of trees. She thinks of a trick to get there and to a possible telephone. She sees that the direct way to the house is covered by an expanse of sharp gravel. He has taken off his shoes to pour the water out of them. She still has her shoes on. Grabbing up his shoes she flees in the direction of the house. He starts after her on the gravel, but of course, the pain is terrific. He gives up and goes the long way around. She will reach the house comfortably in advance of him.

Inside the house a sinister figure is looking out the window—a very little woman in the uniform of a trained nurse. As I said, she is sinister and mysterious, but not particularly villainous looking. We do not make up our mind about her for the present. It is rather the haunted, barricaded character of the house which gives us this sense of menace. The nurse opens the door and Ann runs in.

At this point the truck loaded with workmen arrives at the bridge, and Dick and Tom, seeing the wrecked car, look about wildly. They spot the house.

The secret agent is on the porch of the house, but seeing that Dick and Tom are coming toward it, he slips over the side of the porch and for a short time disappears from the story.

Inside the house Ann has just stammered out a resumé of her situation. The nurse assures her that the man won't be able to break into the house, that every door and window is shuttered and they go upstairs to telephone. But Ann sees no telephone—instead the woman turns on her with a gun and demands her watch and rings. She gags her and handcuffs her to a ring in the wall. There is knocking downstairs but the nurse says "If you open your mouth I'll blow your head off."

Downstairs the two young men are trying to arouse the house. Not succeeding they conclude it is empty but decide to break in with the faint hope that there may be a telephone. Now they know disaster has come to Ann and the agent.

They manage to pry off a shutter and are confronted by the nurse. She tells them she has seen nobody, that she heard the auto crash but nothing more. They ask her why she, a trained nurse, did not do anything about it. She says it was none of her business and this makes them suspicious. They determine to have a look around the house whereupon the nurse confronts them with a revolver and locks them up in a closet.

The nurse now makes quick preparation for departure, keeping an eye on the workmen on the bridge. She packs a little bag, then carefully opens her window and whistles a bird call.

Out in the woods the secret agent, who is sitting calmly under a tree smoking, hears the whistle. He answers it and goes to the house. It is apparent that this is the rendezvous where he was taking Ann and the shell. The nurse tells him she has taken the rings for a blind but he cannot leave Ann like that. He takes the rings to the room where Ann is and says he will phone the police news of her whereabouts when he is safely away. His regret and shame are sincere. He even leaves the key to the handcuffs, but out of her reach.

With the nurse he starts out the door silently, lest the two young men hear the departure and raise a rumpus. The workmen at the bridge head have left their truck and gone to work on the bridge. The agent and the nurse approach the truck cautiously, get in and drive it across the field over a shallow ford to the other bank. They speed back along the closed road obviously to recover the shell.

In the house, Ann has slipped the gag and having heard what occurred downstairs she yells that they're gone. Dick and Tom break out, set her free. She tells them of the shell. They hurry to the labor gang at the bridge head. The foreman is waiting for another truck to go in pursuit. It arrives and Tom and Dick get in too.

Back at the section of the road where the shell was left. An old fashioned Norman Rockwell hobo is coming along. He wipes his brow and sits down beside the road for a rest. In fact, sits directly upon the shell which is so laid in the grass that it might be a log. He takes a packet of cards out of his pocket and starts to lay out the first row of a solitaire game. To make things brighter he reaches into another pocket and takes out a half pint of gin, gazes sadly at the two ounces residing therein. He empties it and as he lowers the bottle down from his mouth it hits the shell and breaks.

He eagerly opens the case, but when he sees the shell for the first time he is on his feet in a hurry, staring at it. He scratches his head and looks up at the sky. He shakes his head. How it got there, God alone knows. Suddenly he starts to run away from it, then his panic dies and obviously realizing that it must have some salvage value he goes back to it. He touches it gingerly, puts his ear down and listens to it; there is no tick inside. Gingerly he puts it back in its case, picks it up by the handles and lifts it with care. Then he hears the sound of a motor in the distance, steps with the case behind a tree.

The truck, with the secret agent and the nurse comes to a stop. "It's right about here," he says.

He hunts along the edge of the road, the tramp watching from behind the tree. Softly, the tramp sets down the shell behind the tree, moves away from it and into sight on the road, asking the secret agent if he is looking for anything. The secret agent describes the package at length. The tramp denies having seen it.

"The thing is gone," says the agent to the nurse.

But now the tramp makes the foolish mistake of saying, "I did see a car pick something up here, half an hour ago."

The secret agent and the nurse are walking back to the truck in despair when the impact of this hits them both at once. The secret agent says: "He couldn't have seen anybody pick it up. This road has been closed since last night. He's telling a lie."

They start back towards the tramp. He tries to bluff it out. The nurse faces him with her gun and they try to get the truth out of him. As they are about to succeed they hear a motor—which is that of the truck in pursuit. He tells her to drive the truck off for it will betray them. He socks the tramp and drags him back into the shrubbery where he sees the shell. But the nurse is gone.

The pursuing truck stops. Ann jumps out and looks where the shell stood the night before. But the foreman thinks of course it's been picked up and suddenly he sees the first truck come into sight at a point where the road climbs a hill. Not even waiting for Ann to get in the truck again, he starts after it.

Ann stands in the road. At this moment the shell which is on a slight knoll begins to roll in the direction of the unconscious tramp. It bumps him and he gives a groan.

Ann starts at the sound. The secret agent steps into the road and putting his fingers to his lips as if he had just yawned. He says, "You're a minute too late."

Cut to the pursuing truck and show that Tom and Dick, unwilling to leave Ann stranded on the road, are slipping off to go back to her. They have, however, already been carried half a mile.

The secret agent's situation seems hopeless. He is without means of transportation or hope of any, unless the "nurse" should elude her pursuers and come back for him. Not to mention the fact that he is in love with this girl and anxious to justify himself in her eyes. Besides, there is the tramp bound behind the trees who at any moment may become articulate. And in the thicket lies the shell—the shell which he has gone to all this risk to obtain.

Ann once more has the upper hand—and resenting the hand-cuff business, is inclined to use it.

"Now what?" she says.

"Well, we can always play cards."

He refers to the tramp's solitaire game which is still spread out along the edge of the road. He goes to it, sits down in the grass, gathers up the cards. She looks at him rather skeptically, wondering what he is up to now, this man who fascinates her, whom she could love if she did not have to constantly hate. She joins him reluctantly, sits down against a tree.

"What'll we play?" he asks, sorting the cards quickly in some fashion of his own. "Not bridge. We've had enough bridge."

He lays down first an ace. "One person alone—that's difficult. But there are so many things we have to do alone. Two. That's better—"

Ann interrupts: "Not always."

"But usually. Two hearts are better than one." The card lying before him is a two of hearts.

"I haven't got a heart," Ann says.

"Oh, yes you have. I saw it three times." He lays down a three of spades. "Once when I was an electrician, once when we were in the rain and once when the bridge wasn't there."

He lays down a four. Ann touches the card with her finger and says, "That was be*fore* I knew you for what you are."

"Can't think of anything for five," he says, laying down the card. "But except for this wretched war I don't think you and I would be at sixes and sevens."

After the six and seven, he puts down an eight and Ann says, "I can't remember when we last 'ate'—stop me, will you please?"

He covers the eight with a nine and speaks more gravely:

"Nine lives. That's what I need for this job." He looks quickly through the pack and she says, "You can't find a ten, so the game is about up, my friend."

He has found the ten somewhere in the pack and he slips it on top of the pile. She lifts her hand like a person shooting:

"I'm ready for the next one—come eleven!" and snaps her fingers.

"You're wrong for once," he says, laying down a Jack, "Jaques—that's my name or it was once. Really my name."

"Jaques," she says, testing the monosyllable.

"Silly name, isn't it, for such a serious business." He puts the queen on top of the pack, looks at it and then slowly lifts his eyes to hers.

"That's exactly how I feel about it," Jaques says, very slowly, gravely and sincerely. He puts down one more card and adds, "—if I were King."

They are sitting cross-legged, facing each other. At this point when they are each drawn forward toward each other—Dick and Tom have arrived unobserved and crept up softly. They spring, pinion Jaques' arms behind his back, with their neckties. It looks as if the game is up at last.

The tramp who is lying very still in the grass, is awake. He is looking through the bushes, amazed at the scene.

Dick and Tom look at Ann expecting applause. Instead she says almost with annoyance:

"Saving the country again."

At this point a sound truck comes along the road. Out springs a newspaper man with a microphone in his hand.

"Have you got anything to say?" he demands. "The program is 'People Met on the Road.' What're your names?"

He shoves the microphone at Ann. Into it she says:

"My name is Glamor O'Hara. I believe in everybody minding their own business."

In disgust the reporter says: "You people don't take this seriously." He rushes back to the truck shouting into the mike, "Never mind, friends. Those were some folks rehearsing a play. They wouldn't talk, friends. So now I'll tell you more about that *clean* feeling—"

But the stranded quartet are at his heels, the two young men grasping the secret agent by the elbows, Ann following unwillingly.

"We've got a prisoner," Dick says, "wanted by the police. He'll talk if you take us to Princeton."

They pile into the truck. Ann next to the driver, the prisoner beside her. Tom and Dick on one running board and the reporter on another. As the truck turns around and starts back toward Princeton, the reporter thrusts the microphone toward the secret agent, but Ann grabs it.

"He won't talk, either," she says.

"That's about right," says Jaques.

"The prisoner won't talk," says the reporter, "—but anyhow I think you'd rather have me tell you how to keep your clothes fresh and clean."

The outskirts of Princeton we discover that the sound truck is now being *followed* closely by the stolen truck driven by the nurse. Suddenly she drives ahead of the sound truck, stops suddenly, causing the sound truck to come to a swift and precarious halt, throwing the two young men off the running board and allowing Jaques to escape. During this play-by-play, the reporter's voice has never ceased—whether we were showing the action of the escape or getting the reactions of Ann who in her heart is tremendously glad.

"The prisoner has escaped, folks," says the reporter. "I don't know any details. It all looks very suspicious to me, friends, very suspicious to me."

On these words and upon an expression of regret in Ann's face that her great adventure is over, we dissolve to the part of the road where we left the tramp. He is holding the shell and trying to thumb a ride. A nice-looking coupe slows up, and the tramp gets in with his precious burden. As they start off he asks the good samaritan, "How far are you going?"

And the good samaritan says, "All the way to Washington. I'm a manufacturer. I've got business at the War Department."

The tramp thinks of the shell reposing at his feet and rises to the occasion: "So have I," he says and we fade out.

Fade in on a prom in the Princeton Gymnasium two months later. We follow Ann dancing, continually being cut in on by a squirearchy of boys. Her face is a little graver, more preoccupied than we have ever seen it. She is obviously not the high-spirited, careless girl we first met. Her expression suggests that she is looking for someone. As her partners are tapped on the shoulder for the cut-in, she turns eagerly to greet each newcomer. "Can it be him?" her eyes seem to say. But it never is and she adjusts herself graciously and politely to each disappointment.

Somewhere in the story Jaques has learned that she is going to this Prom.

And now suddenly he is there in a tail coat, sure of himself, unworried, undisguised, picking her out of the crowd with a look of expectation. As she sees him, she is frightened for him as well as for herself.

"May I, please?"

They talk, with an air of mingled fear, delight, repulsion and attraction.

"You've got your nerve," she says.

"No, this time I am within the law. I'm at our Washington Embassy, as attaché."

"If Dick and Tom see you—"

"I have diplomatic immunity."

At this she stops dancing.

"I hate you," she says. "I can't dance with you. What are you? Won't you tell me? What was it all about?"

"Dance with me and I'll tell you," he says.

She hesitates, wavers, then perhaps irresistible curiosity is the deciding factor.

"Tell me," she demands, breathless as they start dancing again.

During this dance she is constantly interrupting the secret agent by turning to the boys who try to cut in and saying, "Not now, thanks." Each time with a bright smile which changes to gravity as she turns back to face Jaques.

"In one country you visited," he said, "they had developed a shell that we wanted to know about. A collaborator of mine bribed a workman and got hold of the sample shell—on the very day war was declared. The question was how to get it to my country for examination and analysis. An American like you had the best chance of getting out of the country without a baggage examination—and your trunk was in the hall of a hotel marked 'not needed on the voyage.' He wired me in code. I won't tell you how we got it by customs because it might put ideas in the heads of your countrymen."

She bristles at his last words and he continues hastily.

"Excuse me, I mean *our* countrymen. When the war is over I'll live here, and you and I will belong to one country forever."

"It's not as easy as that. What became of the shell?"

"You've got me."

She smiles suddenly.

"Have I?" she asks as their arms tighten around each other.

Dissolve to the portal of the War Department in Washington where the tramp now in uniform is proudly standing guard.

FSF and dog in the Colosseum.

A work in progress, "The Couple" begins as a typescript, but the concluding pages of it are a manuscript in Fitzgerald's hand. It brings us as close to his writing process as is possible.

"The Couple" has been dated as early as 1920 and as late as 1931 by Fitzgerald scholars. The earlier side of this range is most likely. In the manuscript portion and on the penciled corrections to the typescript, Fitzgerald's handwriting still has the looping exaggeration characteristic of the early to middle 1920s. Moreover, the typed portion is on letter-sized paper watermarked "Hammermill Bond." This inexpensive Pennsylvania-made paper was a bestseller in the east, and easily available in the New York area, where the Fitzgeralds were living from April 1920 to May 1921. The manuscript end of the story, however, is on legal-sized Goldsmith's Bond paper. Goldsmith Book and Stationery Company, based in Wichita since the 1880s, was one of the largest stationers, and publishers, in the Midwest. Much later they would have stores on the East Coast, too, specializing in home décor—but Fitzgerald most likely bought this paper in St. Paul, where he and Zelda lived from August 1921 until October 1922.

So, too, Fitzgerald was fond of featuring people of his age, and fictionalizing events in his own recent past; every one of his novels follows this pattern. Here, the couple are in their middle to late twenties. They have been married for a while, and fighting for a while. Along with the watermarks, this points to the early 1920s as a composition date, when Fitzgerald, still young but not that young, and already mature, began looking to difficult themes of divorce and despair.

```
                 T H E   C O U P L E
                         by
                 F. Scott Fitzgerald


        The culmination of the tragedy took place on the great wide
    comfortable sofa which was almost the oldest possession of
    their married life.
        "All right," said young Pawling, very serious and sad, "let
    it go at that.  We can't agree and so we'd better separate.  We've
    tried it for a year and we've just played the devil with each oth-
    er's lives."
        Carrol nodded.
        "You mean you've played the devil with my life," she amend-
    ed.
        "No, I don't.  But let it go at that.  Let it go anyway.
    I'm not going to argue any more.  You don't love me and the only
    thing I don't understand is why you didn't find it out before we
    were married.  Now -- "  Pawling hesitated.  "When shall we
    actually -- actually --"
        The night air of early May was cool in the room and Carrol
    crossed over gracefully and stood before the open fire.
        "I'd like to stay here until Mother gets back from Europe,"
    she said, "that'll be two weeks and I can be packing up.  Of course
    I can go tomorrow if you like but I've no place special to go."
        "Don't think of going," said Pawling hastily.  "Stay right
    here.  I'll get out myself, first thing in the morning."
        "No.  If that's the way you feel I'll do the getting  I
    just thought if it didn't annoy you to have me here --"
```

The Couple

The culmination of the tragedy took place on the great wide comfortable sofa which was almost the oldest possession of their married life.

"All right," said young Pawling, very serious and sad, "let it go at that. We can't agree and so we'd better separate. We've tried it for a year and we've just played the devil with each other's lives."

Carrol nodded.

"You mean you've played the devil with my life," she amended.

"No, I don't. But let it go at that. Let it go anyway. I'm not going to argue any more. You don't love me and the only thing I don't understand is why you didn't find it out before we were married. Now—" Pawling hesitated. "When shall we actually—actually—"

The night air of early May was cool in the room and Carrol crossed over gracefully and stood before the open fire.

"I'd like to stay here until Mother gets back from Europe," she said. "That'll be two weeks and I can be packing up. Of course I can go tomorrow if you like but I've no place special to go."

"Don't think of going," said Pawling hastily. "Stay right here. I'll get out myself, first thing in the morning."

"No. If that's the way you feel I'll do the getting out. I just thought if it didn't annoy you to have me here—"

"Annoy me! Not a bit. Why—" He bit his lip. The whole reason for the separation was just that. Everything he did annoyed her terribly. He had given up the struggle to try to please her, several weeks ago.

"Of course you can stay here," he continued formally. "I'll move my junk out of the big room tonight."

"It's just for two weeks, you see."

"Why, I'll be de—" Again he broke off. He had been about to say delighted but he realized that it was not the right phrase. Nevertheless it would have been somewhere near the truth—his mind clutched at the thought of her staying here, if only for a fortnight. The separation was necessary, of course—but this brief interval when it was settled and yet not consummated would make the parting less harsh and violent at the end.

293

"Another thing," said his wife. "Two things. First, I've invited some people for dinner tomorrow night—"

"All right."

"—and second about the servants. Esther and Hilda are leaving in the morning and we'll have to have somebody until—until Mother comes home. So I got a couple in town today."

"Two. Naturally."

"No, I mean a couple. It's different. It's a man and his wife. She cooks and he acts as butler and helps her with the housework. This couple look very good—he's English and she's Irish. I wouldn't have taken them at all if I'd been sure we were separating—but since they're coming—"

Her voice faded off and her eyes focussed on a spot in the center of the carpet.

"Of course," muttered Pawling, looking at the same spot. He scarcely realized that she had stopped speaking and that there was silence in the room. He was thinking that in a few minutes he must go upstairs and, not in anger but only with what dignity was left to him, take his things out of the big front room—his brush and comb, the little box with his studs and cuff-buttons, the miscellaneous papers in his desk. Then his marriage would be over. Something would happen during the night when they each lay in their separate rooms, which would destroy forever the slim, mysterious hold they had had on each other, the intangible and half-vanished marriage of their hearts that had kept them from splitting up long before. In the morning they would each open their eyes upon a different world, conscious of having been apart and able to be apart forever.

Pawling got to his feet.

"I think I'll go up now," he said coolly.

"All right. I'll lock the door."

Half an hour later he turned out the light in the guest room and slipped into bed. Outside, the May night, cool and clear, brought back the memory of another Spring, a memory scratched and smeared in the recent months but in itself still a lovely and idyllic thing. He wondered if love ever came again with that intensity, with that gay magic of first love or if that was squandered now [and irrevocable] forever.

By and by he heard Carrol moving about below. The lights snapped and her footsteps fell on the stair. She walked very slowly as if she were tired and when she reached the top she rested for a minute just at the threshold of his room. Then she went into the big front chamber and closed the door after her and a heavy silence seemed to come in the window with the night air and settle through the house.

II

In the morning Pawling drove down to the station for the new servants, picking them out immediately from the crowd which disembarked from the ten o'clock train.

"Reynolds?"

The man, a middle-aged Briton with a long neck and a bland Cockney face, nodded profusely.

"Yes, sir—Reynolds."

He turned to a large lady of Irish extraction who stood immediately behind him.

"This is my wife, sir. Her name is Katy."

It seemed that there was a trunk. Reynolds went to inquire about it while Pawling and the large lady engaged in conversation upon the station platform—that is, Pawling remarked that it was a short trip out, and Katy nodded her head up and down in genial vibration.

"Been in this country long?" asked Pawling as they drove away from the station.

Reynolds nodded.

"Not very long," Katy disagreed. "Maybe two months."

"Work in New York?"

"No, we worked in Philadelphia—oh, for some very fine gentlemen there. Maybe you know them—Mr. Marbleton and Mr. Shafter?"

No, Pawling did not know them. He nodded understandingly, though, as if he knew how nice they must be.

Arrived at the house Pawling showed them the kitchen and hinted delicately that their rooms were just above. Then he left them to their own devices and strolled out on the front porch.

It was his vacation, this three weeks, the first in a year. It was convenient, of course, that his vacation should come now when the catastrophe of a divorce had overtaken him, yet he wished, in a way, that he had work to do. The melancholy of the affair would be accentuated by his inactivity—he could only sit through the soft May weather watching the days drift by that marked the ending of the unrepeatable adventure. He was glad of course that the last word had been said. Carrol's arrogance, her coldness, her growing dislike for him, had been beyond endurance. He was short-tempered himself and many times in the last month their disputes had hovered on the verge of physical violence.

"Lou."

He looked up to see her outside the porch screen in the bright sunshine.

"Hello," he said, rising to let her in, "your couple came all right. They're in the kitchen."

"Thanks," she said coolly, stepping up on the porch, her arms full of flowers. "I'll go right back and see them."

She was wearing, he noticed, a stiff starched dress of palest blue that she had not worn since the summer before. He looked at her closely to find signs of sleeplessness around her eyes, as he knew there were around his own, but she was as fresh and pink as the flowers in her arms.

"I've cut them for dinner," she said. "Aren't they lovely?"

"Very."

Without looking at him she went into the house.

[They had luncheon at one and as he sat down he told himself that this must be his last luncheon with her. He must find some way of passing the days in town. He had no taste for a series of meals eaten in silence with downcast eyes.]

Luncheon was scrappy and unappetizing. It would be, of course— the new couple had not had time to get used to the kitchen. But he wondered whether Reynolds' footsteps around the table were not unnaturally loud.

"They're new," said Carrol. "Everything's mixed up back there. It'll be different tonight."

The dessert arrived, sliced peaches—in a sauce dish.

"This is all right for now, Reynolds," said Carrol, "but for tonight of course I want the dessert served from a bowl."

"What, Madam?"

"I say I want the dessert served from a bowl—you know, the blancmange I told you about."

Reynolds nodded comprehendingly. He hesitated.

"Oh, and do you want me to cut the grass this afternoon?"

Carrol looked up in surprise.

"Why, yes—if you will. That is, perhaps you'd better wait till tomorrow."

"What?"

"I say perhaps you'd better wait till tomorrow," said Carrol in a slightly louder voice. "You'll be pretty busy this afternoon, you know."

Reynolds nodded and clumped into the pantry.

"He must be used to cutting the grass," said Carrol. "That must be one of the duties couples have." And she added in a low voice, "He seems to be a little deaf. I guess that's why he's so noisy when he walks."

Their guests that night were three, the Harold Gays from Portchester, whom they knew only slightly, and Roderick Barker, an old beau of Carrol's from New York.

Pawling found himself wondering if Barker, now when Carrol was free, would renew the courtship that his own had interrupted. He hoped not—not Barker at any rate; the idea of Carrol going places with Barker, of flirting with Barker, kissing Barker, appalled him—with an effort he drove the consideration from his mind.

"How's Twine?" asked Barker.

Twine was a minute poodle with scanty wool and the eyes of one far gone in drink who was alternately dear and repugnant to Carrol's heart.

"Twine's great," she answered, "He almost bit the new butler today. Oh, I forgot to tell you we have a butler now—aren't we grand."

"Well, this is absolutely the last word," exclaimed Barker enthusiastically.

"He's only part of a couple," confessed Carrol, "but he's straight from England, and you'll have to admit that's something."

In a minute the gentleman referred to appeared in the doorway and announced in a loud singsong voice:

"Dinner is ready!"

All eyes turned toward him. The tone of the interruption was somewhat startling and everyone rose precipitately as if they had been summarily ordered from one room into the other. Carrol made a mental note to speak to him about his voice tomorrow.

"I'm going to send him out and have it lowered," she remarked with an insincere facetiousness as they strolled in.

"Charming," murmured Barker, smiling.

A dozen times during dinner remarks were made, careless, casual things that made Pawling aware that everything was changed. Someone's divorce was discussed in detail, what "she" had said and how cruel "he" had been, a recital which included the details as to who the parties to the divorce "were going with now."

"They say you two set an extraordinary example in Rye," said Mrs. Gay genially, "You're the only known couple who never quarrel in public under any conditions."

"That's the most dangerous kind," remarked Barker, "It means they quarrel at home. It's a vice like secret drinking. If married people don't quarrel in public it's because they can't get the full flavor of brutality out of it unless they're alone."

Pawling and Carrol were both red as fire—the other three seemed to guess that something inept had been said and the subject shifted uneasily to golf.

The roast had been served according to Carrol's instructions, already carved in the kitchen, and as dinner progressed, she rang the bell for the second serving. Dreading Reynolds' resounding "What?" she caught his eye and nodded at her own plate. He nodded back and before she realized what he was doing he snatched it up and disappeared into the pantry. There was a faint, almost imperceptible lull in the conversation— one of those moments that might mean anything or nothing. Carrol saw Mrs. Gay's eyes fall curiously upon her empty place.

Then the pantry door burst open and Reynolds stamped eagerly in. He was bringing back her plate. He had heaped it with roast and vegetables and he set it down with a sort of flourish before her as if to say:

"There. Look what I did for you."

There was no hoping that this would pass unnoticed. Carrol was pink with embarrassment and her ears were privy to a short, repressed snicker to which each of the three men contributed a part.

"Serve everything again, Reynolds," she said impatiently.

"What?" He craned his long neck; his mouth was ajar in polite inquiry.

"Serve everything again."

Her one thought now was to get through dinner with as little emphasis as possible upon the service.

"Please find us a house in Portchester," she said quickly to Mrs. Gay. "We're going to live there next summer."

She met her husband's eyes over the table and the inexpediency of her remark appalled her but she rambled nervously on—"At least perhaps we are and perhaps we'll go to Europe and perhaps we'll be dead."

Luckily or unluckily Reynolds was excited now at his former blunder and determined at this point to make up for it by seeing that everyone had enough to eat.

"What?" he remarked to Mrs. Gay. "No asparagus?"

The irrepressible and, to Carrol, faintly ghastly laughter which ensued fell inaudibly upon his ears.

The man was apparently deaf as a post. Clump! Clump! Clump! went his footsteps, around the table and in and out of the pantry, interrupting the conversation, giving the impression, somehow, that pans were clanking and hammering was going on and china was continually crashing on the floor.

After luncheon Carrol had explained to him in detail about the dessert. He must take a dessert plate, she said, and on it place a doily and a finger bowl. The person served would himself remove the doily and the finger bowl.

All this had become very confused in Reynolds' mind. He knew how the plate and doily and finger bowl should look upon the table and he had a confused impression that something was going to be removed. How or why he did not know. But he was a resourceful man.

Just when the conversation had regained a certain animation he entered with the blancmange, advanced upon Carrol and after a moment's hesitation reached down and snatched away her finger-bowl. Then before she realized his intention he had spooned a large "order" of blancmange onto the linen doily. Without tarrying he stamped around to Barker and repeated the performance. Mrs. Gay with great presence of mind managed to remove the doily from her plate—the others gazed down in awe upon the vision of a wet linen dessert.

"If anyone wants any more," said Reynolds to his mistress in a confidential shout, "there's a lot of this in the kitchen."

III

The time was so short, twelve days now, that they decided next morning not to let the couple go. Once the dinner guests had departed it seemed to Pawling a vastly unimportant matter in comparison with the imminence of their separation. Not that he had ceased to desire the separation—far from it—he was more reconciled to it than he had been when it was agreed upon, but set in the cool tranquillity which succeeded the passionate quarrels of the last three months it seemed a grave and consequent matter.

Pawling went up to town early and spent the day at the Yale Club, feeling out of place among the younger men there, feeling older even than his classmates and already a little smirched in the light of his coming divorce. He looked forward in a way to his freedom. He could read and travel more, he would be away from the pressure of Carrol's high-strung, nervous temperament—but he could never be a bachelor again in quite the same way. It would be almost indecent of him to consider himself absolutely free.

When evening came he saw no reason why he should go back to the country. He could sleep at the Club and spend another day in town. But as the time drew near for the last afternoon train he knew he would go. The notion of Carrol alone in the house with two strange servants made him uneasy.

His presentiment was justified. As he let himself in he saw her sitting on the sofa with Twine in her lap, staring straight in front of her with angry eyes.

"You'll have to let these people go," she said immediately. "They're awful. We couldn't possibly stand them for two weeks."

"Why? What have they done now?"

"Well, in the first place they gave me an awful lunch and when I went in the kitchen and started to complain, that woman gave me an awful look as if she was going to bang me over the head with the saucepan. I was sort of afraid to say anything. The man's even worse."

"I'll speak to them."

"Something else too—they whipped Twine."

"Whipped Twine?" he asked incredulously. "What for?"

"Nothing. They said he bit the man—'Mr. Reynolds,' his wife calls him—but if he did they must have started it because Twine never bites anybody. Anyways I caught them beating him."

"What did you do?"

"I was afraid to do anything. That woman kept muttering around so and Reynolds was stamping up and down in the kitchen as if he'd been attacked by a grizzly bear. I picked up Twine and walked right in here and I've been in here ever since."

"Hm!" ejaculated Pawling. "I'll fire them right after dinner."

Dinner was uneatable. Carrol sat with her elbows on the table and her face in her hands and shook her head curtly whenever a dish was offered her. When dinner was over Pawling pushed open the pantry door.

"Reynolds!" he called.

"Yes, sir."

As if he had been waiting for the call Reynolds burst out of the kitchen with aggressive alacrity.

"Reynolds, I'm afraid we don't suit each other and we'd better not try it any longer."

Reynolds looked at him blankly. Obviously he had not heard a word.

"I said," repeated Pawling, "that perhaps we don't suit each other and we better not try this any longer."

Reynolds nodded.

"Oh, you suit us all right," he announced, craning his long neck and looking down fatuously at Pawling.

"But you don't suit us," went on Pawling impatiently, "And I think we'd better—"

"What's the matter with me?" demanded Reynolds. "Has the madam been complaining of me?"

"We'll leave the madam out of this."

"Why don't we suit you?"

"Because we want an experienced butler. We're paying you a big salary and we want someone who's trained."

"They can't even make the beds," said Carrol. She had come into the dining room and was standing at his elbow. "I looked at mine this afternoon and it was just pulled back, nothing but wrinkles—I had to make it all over again."

Reynolds had been glaring at them with an outraged expression in his pale eyes.

"I've never failed to give satisfaction before," he burst out. "When we were with those two gentlemen in Philadelphia they—they couldn't do enough for us."

His tone implied that the two gentlemen in Philadelphia had bathed them in tender emotion.

"I'm John Bull himself, I am," he went on, defiantly, "and if I've done wrong I want to know. Why doesn't your lady there tell me when I do wrong instead of raising all this trouble?"

"Because this isn't a training school," shouted Pawling. "You're supposed to be an efficient butler when you come here. You told my wife you were."

Reynolds took refuge behind his previous statement.

"I've never had any complaints before."

"The food's no good," shouted Carrol.

"What?" He looked at her incredulously. "Why, my wife and I ran a restaurant in England for ten years."

"Look here, I don't want to argue about this," cried Pawling. "Your way of serving and cooking may be all right but it isn't our way and that's all there is to it. So good night."

They came back to the living room.

"Why didn't you tell them to get out tomorrow?" demanded Carrol.

"I didn't have the heart. This is evidently their second job in America and it'll take a couple of hours to get it through his noodle that he's fired."

Carrol took a moving picture magazine from the table and went upstairs.

A few minutes later, clumping violently, Reynolds came into the living room.

"Well," asked Pawling, "what can I do for you?"

"I'd like to ask you for a recommendation."

At this surprising demand Pawling sat up on the sofa.

"A recommendation! Why, you've only been here three days."

"Yes," Reynolds agreed, "but we came all the way from Philadelphia."

"What's that got to do with it?"

Oblivious to this question Reynolds continued.

"You see we've only got one recommendation and it's awfully hard to get a position unless you've got two."

"Well," said Pawling hesitantly, "I suppose I can write you out something."

He went to the desk in the corner.

"What did you do before you were a butler?" he shouted.

"Oh, we kept a restaurant and then I was a postman in Devonshire."

Pawling began writing.

"Listen," he said in a moment. "I'll read it to you."

TO WHOM IT MAY CONCERN:

   THIS IS TO CERTIFY THAT JAMES REYNOLDS AND HIS WIFE HAVE BEEN IN MY EMPLOY AND HAVE SHOWN THEMSELVES TO BE WILLING AND HONEST. HE HAS BEEN A LETTER CARRIER AND HAS ALSO HAD EXPERIENCE AS A RESTAURANT MAN AND A BUTLER.

"How does that suit you? I'm afraid I can't say anything more."

Reynolds read over the letter, folded it slowly.

"And so you want to give me my month's notice," he remarked.

"Month's notice!" cried Pawling. "I want you to get out Saturday."

Reynolds' head shot forward like a duck's.

"Saturday?"

"Of course. We don't give any month's notice here."

Reynolds considered with deep melancholy.

"Very good," he said reluctantly. "You pay me my month's wages and we'll get out."

"Look here, man, I'm not going to pay you a month's wages! I'll give you two weeks' wages; why, you've only been here three days!"

"I can't agree to that."

Pawling reached up and plucked the letter of recommendation from Reynolds' hand.

"I'm not going to give you this," he said, "if you argue any more."

He felt a sort of pity toward the man and his incompetent helplessness but when, in the morning, the argument was resumed he lost patience. It seemed that Katy was very much hurt and disappointed indeed.

Pawling had his coat on and was starting for New York.

"See here," he said, "you can't argue me into changing my mind. If you've got anything to say you'd better take it up with Mrs. Pawling."

Paying no attention to Reynolds' importunate "Wait a minute," Pawling put his hat on and hurried out the door.

He was glad when the week was over. After breakfast on Saturday he opened the pantry door and called Reynolds into the dining room.

"I want to pay you your money whenever you're ready."

"What?"

"Your money."

Reynolds waved his hand airily.

"Oh, you can wait till the day we go."

"The day you go!" exclaimed Pawling. "This is the day you go. This is Saturday."

"We're going Wednesday," announced Reynolds placidly. "Mrs. Pawling said we could stay till Wednesday."

The pantry door had opened half a foot and from the aperture two angry black eyes were regarding Pawling over Reynolds' shoulder.

"That's what she said," spoke up Katy menacingly. "I talked to her myself."

When Carrol came downstairs Pawling approached her incredulously. "Did you tell them they could stay till Wednesday?"

She hesitated.

"Yes, I did."

"Why?"

"That woman—that Katy—" she said unevenly. "She came upstairs the other day after you went to town, and made me."

"*Made* you? How could she—"

"Well, she did. She came upstairs muttering and saying that I'd got her here with the promise of a job and then gone to you behind their back. She was all excited and talking loud and Reynolds was stamping up and down the hall like the British army so I got afraid and told them they could stay till Wednesday. Besides I was sorry for them—she said they had no place to go."

"Hm."

"It's only for a few days," she added. "I got a Marconi from Mother yesterday. She gets here Thursday on the *Mauretania*."

That afternoon, fatigued with the sleeplessness of three nights, Pawling lay down on the porch settee and dropped off into a hot doze. The hours slipped away, scarred with fretful dreams. At five he awoke suddenly to find Carrol standing over him sobbing out something in a terrified voice.

"What's the matter," he muttered, starting up.

"It's Twine," she cried. "They've killed him. I knew they would. He's been missing since this morning and I just saw a revolver on the kitchen table."

IV

Pawling jumped to his feet.

"What? Are you sure?"

"Positive. I heard the shot half an hour ago and a sort of yelp. Oh, to kill a poor helpless little dog—"

"Wait right here," said Pawling. "I'll find out about this."

"He'll shoot you," cried Carrol. "If I were you I wouldn't go in there without your pistol. They're raving crazy maniacs, that's what I think."

He found Katy alone in the kitchen, involved in a mass of dough which covered her large, muscular arms to the elbow.

"Where's Reynolds?" he asked abruptly.

"Mr. Reynolds is out."

"Where is he?"

She shrugged her shoulders heavily.

"Hasn't he got a right to go out and walk once in a while?"

This was a checkmate. Pawling's eyes roved quickly around the kitchen.

"Have you seen the dog?" he demanded in a more casual voice.

"The dog," Katy's eyes followed his around the room. "Yes, I've seen the dog. He's in and out here all the time. But I don't see him now. I don't like dogs," she added ominously.

"My wife wants to know where the dog is."

Katy pounded the dough up and down angrily.

"I didn't go into service in order to watch over a dog," she answered. "It's bad enough to have the smelly beast in the kitchen."

"It isn't smelly."

"It's smelly," said Katy definitely.

Again the conversation seemed to have reached an impasse. He tried a new tack.

"My wife tells me she saw a revolver in the kitchen."

Katy nodded unconcernedly.

"It belongs to Mr. Reynolds. He was cleaning it. He shot a burglar over in Philadelphia."

At this point the kitchen door opened and Reynolds came in. From his hand dangled a leather thong which Pawling instantly recognized as Twine's lead rope.

"Where have you been?" he demanded.

"Did what?" asked Reynolds.

"I say, *where have you been*?"

"I've been walking," said Reynolds calmly, tossing the lead onto the kitchen table.

"What are you doing with that?" Pawling pointed to the table.

"That? Oh, that's for the dog. I was going to take the thing for a walk."

"Did you?"

"I wasn't able to find it."

"Hm." Pawling wondered what this meant. If he had killed Twine in the yard he would scarcely have used the lead.

"What were you doing with a revolver?"

Reynolds' neck elongated with indignation.

"I'll carry a revolver any time I want to, and what do you think of that?"

"I think you're an idiot!" answered Pawling hotly.

Reynolds stepped forward suddenly and laid his hand on Pawling's shoulder.

"Look here, Pawling—" he began but got no further. Pawling stepped back angrily and the hand dropped.

"Watch out!" cried Pawling. "You're a servant here."

"I'm a servant," answered Reynolds haughtily, "but I'm John—"

"I don't care," interrupted Pawling. "At present you're taking my money as a servant and you keep your hands to yourself. You're going out of this house in the morning."

"I may be a servant," bleated Reynolds, "but I'm John Bull himself."

Pawling was torn between anger at the man's stupidity and amusement at his identification of himself with the British Empire.

"I've worked better places than this," went on Reynolds. "Why, those two gentlemen in Philadelphia, Mr. Marbleton and Mr. Shafter—"

"They couldn't do enough for us," shouted his wife.

Pawling rushed wildly from the kitchen. Outdoors he spent an hour combing the neighborhood for a newly made grave, peering into tall grass and even exploring into back yards. He was barked at by numerous police dogs but he was unable to find any trace of Twine. If the poodle had been done away with the murder had evidently been committed near home.

He searched his own yard next and every cranny of the garage, finally descending into the cellar and looking behind boxes and under the coal and into the cold furnace. It was no use. Twine had effectually disappeared.

They had dinner at the golf club, very coldly and formally and when they got home Carrol went upstairs to begin her packing. He knew miserably that in her heart she blamed him for the loss of her dog too—as though it were some last revenge he was taking on her for leaving him.

In his dreams that night he saw Reynolds set down Twine—Twine cooked *à la maître de Hotel*—before Carrol's mother on the *Mauretania*.

"I'm John Bull himself," said Reynolds as he covered the steaming dog with thick gravy.

"Good," answered Carrol's mother. "I'm going back to take my daughter away."

"Fine," said Reynolds, "I'll introduce your daughter to those two gentlemen in Philadelphia."

Pawling awoke, his body jerking nervously upright. The knob of his door had turned slightly; the door pushed slowly open.

"Who's there?" he said sharply.

"Lou." It was Carrol's voice in a frightened whisper. "There's someone downstairs."

Pawling got out of bed and slipping quickly into his dressing gown joined her in the hall.

"I think it's Reynolds," she whispered. "Whoever it is he's trying to walk softly."

"Hello," he muttered, looking down the stairs, "he's got the light on."

"Hadn't you better shout down at him?"

He shook his head.

Pistol in hand he descended the steps softly, traversed the short hall and put his head around the corner of the living room.

Reynolds, luxuriously attired in a flowered dressing gown, was kneeling before the desk, his fingers moving cautiously along the carving on the side as if trying to locate a secret spring. The desk drawers were open and the floor was littered with the paper they had contained.

He was not alone. Katy, also in a negligee was moving about the room, looking into jars and cigar boxes, behind books and along the mantelpieces with eager penetrating eyes. From time to time they exchanged a look and both shook their heads in unison, as if so far their search had yielded nothing of value.

Pawling stepped briskly into the room.

"Hands up!" he commanded, levelling the revolver at Reynolds.

The man was so startled that letting go his hold upon the desk he fell to a sitting position on the floor whence he regarded the pistol with mute alarm. With a little cry Katy raised her hands toward the ceiling.

"What's the idea?" asked Pawling.

Reynolds looked dumbly at his wife.

"We're poor people," she cried in a scared voice.

"You're dishonest people," snapped Pawling. "What's more, you're going to jail."

"Oh, no," Katy burst into tears, "Don't say that. We have such a hard time, sir, such a hard time. Mr. Reynolds' deafness is so bad that there isn't much we can do to get a living. We never done any harm."

"Just having some innocent fun, heh?"

"We had to do it!" cried Katy, "We're in America and we've got to live, so we made up our minds it was the only thing to do. I persuaded him into it, honestly I did, sir. This is the only thing of this kind we've ever done before."

Reynolds' mouth moved convulsively.

"You had it and we wanted it, that's all," he said.

"There's no harm done," repeated Katy tearfully. "It wasn't any good to you. We didn't think you'd mind."

"Not mind!" exclaimed Pawling. "Not mind your trying to burglarize my house!"

"Oh, good heavens," sobbed Katy, "if you'd only given it to us this wouldn't have happened."

"Why should I give you my money?"

"Money?" Reynolds and Katy exchanged a look.

"We don't want your money," said Reynolds with dignity, "except what you owe us."

"Then what the devil are you looking for?"

"I'm looking for my letter of recommendation."

"Your letter—"

"The one you almost gave me. I consider it by rights my property."

Pawling lowered his gun slowly.

"Do you mean to say that's what you came here for at this time of night?"

"Yes, sir," admitted Katy.

Reynolds got up stiffly from the floor.

"I'm John Bull himself," he said irrelevantly.

"Well, you go and be John Bull in your own bedroom. I ought to have you both arrested."

"It's just trouble ever since we came here," wept Katy. "I'm sure Mr. Reynolds and I aren't responsible. It's Mrs. Pawling that makes all the trouble. She just lies around all day and keeps a-crying and carrying on as if something was breaking her heart—"

"What?"

Pawling was so astonished that the gun missed his pocket and tumbled to the floor.

"And how does she think I can get the wrinkles out of the sheets," went on Katy, "when she tosses around all night long until it's a wonder she doesn't wear them out entirely?"

"My God!" cried Pawling. "Are you telling me the truth?"

"The truth? Why should I lie—"

"Make yourself at home," he broke out wildly. "Cigars on the table! Stay here all night!" Turning he rushed ecstatically from the living room and up the stairs two at a time.

"Carrol," he called, "Oh, Carrol!"

She was waiting on the top landing and she came down two steps to meet him. They melted together in the great square of silver which came in the open window, fresh from the full moon.

V

At ten o'clock next morning Mr. Reynolds, swathed in a brilliant blue ulster and drawing on suede gloves, appeared in the living room with Mrs. Reynolds by his side. When they came in they both bent a somewhat supercilious glance upon the plain morning clothes which the Pawlings had seen fit to put on.

"We are now leaving," announced Reynolds. "We have a taxi for the ten-thirty train. It's a very wet day."

Pawling went to his desk and after some rummaging around among last night's disarranged papers discovered his check book.

"And as man to man," added Reynolds, sniffing a little, "I want to ask you if you will kindly give us our recommendation."

When Pawling had written the check he reached in his coat pocket and pulling out a paper examined it with a frown.

"I forgot to sign it," he said suddenly.

He bent over it with the pen; then folding it around the check he handed it to Reynolds.

Nodding and smiling pleasantly Katy opened the door.

"Goodbye," said Pawling. "I wish you luck."

"Goodbye," called Carrol cheerfully.

"Goodbye, sir. Goodbye, Madam." Reynolds paused with his hand on the open door. "I just want to say this one thing. My only hope for you both that if you find yourself in a strange country you'll never be turned out into the cold on a day like this."

His effect was somewhat spoiled by the fact that the sun chose this very moment to appear. Nevertheless Reynolds turned up his coat collar dramatically, and pushing his wife before him walked out into what he evidently imagined to be a raging storm.

"Why, they're gone," said Pawling, shutting the door and turning around. "They're gone—and we're alone in the house."

She held out her arms and he went over and knelt down beside her.

"One thing," she said after a long while, "What did you do to that letter of recommendation? I saw you write something on it besides your name."

"I just changed one word." He began to laugh, a little at first and then hilariously until it became infectious and she laughed too. "I gave them a check for two hundred dollars," he said, "but I'm afraid they'll never be able to use that letter of recommendation."

"What did you change?" she demanded. "Tell me quick!"

"Why, there was a line in it that says he was a letter-carrier. I changed the word 'letter' to the word 'typhoid'."

"A typhoid carrier?" she repeated, puzzled.

Then she understood and suddenly they both began to laugh again, happily and irrepressibly—laughter that floated upstairs and into the bedrooms and baths and curled around through the dining room into the pantry and back again to where they sat. The whole house was full of sunshine now, and as the fresh breeze blew the garden odors in at the window life seemed to begin all over again as life has a way of doing.

At twelve o'clock noon, a small baldish poodle dog, with the eyes of one far gone in drink, might have been seen rounding a corner and approaching the Pawling house. Reaching the kitchen door he apparently realized where he was for he visibly started and made a hasty retreat. Traversing a wide, suspicious circle he approached the front door, where he announced his presence with a discreet cough.

["Hey," he barked, "I'm home."]

It was some time before he was able to obtain any attention. He had been noticing the drift of things and he feared for a moment that the place was deserted. But he was wrong: one couple, the couple he dreaded, had gone away, but there was still another couple in the house.

Uncollected
Stories

———•———

Postcard from Scott and Zelda's
trip to North Africa.

Fitzgerald wrote the brief piece "Ballet Shoes" ("Ballet Slippers") as a
movie treatment for Olga Spessivtseva and her manager, Arnold Braun,
after meeting him while on vacation in North Africa in early 1930. Spessivtseva was internationally famous from the early 1910s for dancing
Giselle. The plot is a story of immigration to America (from Russia), boot-
legging, and ballet, and is very roughly developed. Zelda Fitzgerald's own
passion for ballet, to the extent that it brought Fitzgerald to Spessivtseva
and the subject matter, the setting of New York City, and the fact that
these Russians are probably refugees from the Bolshevik Revolution are
compelling aspects of this story. The way in which Fitzgerald addresses
their status as immigrants, and assimilation through art and theater, is
contemporary and progressive.

No film was ever made of this synopsis. In 1937, Spessivtseva—who
had researched the role of Giselle by visiting asylums to see how young
women there moved and behaved—had a breakdown onstage in Australia, and was hospitalized for much of the rest of her life.

Fitzgerald wrote Harold Ober a long letter on February 6, 1936, discussing the synopsis in detail:

> The man Braun is a plain, simple man with a true instinct toward the arts. He is of complete financial integrity and we were awfully nice to him once during a journey through North Africa and I think he is honestly fond of both Zelda and me. I start with this because I don't want to mess up this chance with any of the inadvertencies and lack of foresight that lost me the sale of <u>Tender Is the Night</u> and ruined the Gracie Allen venture [*Gracie at Sea*]. You are now in touch with Hollywood in a way that you were not several years ago. This is obviously a job that I can do expertly—but it is also obviously a job that a whole lot of other people can do fairly well. Now it seems to me that the point can be sold that I am equipped to do this treatment which is the whole gist of this letter.
>
> [Braun] has gone out [there] to Hollywood and they will put some hack on the thing and in two minutes will have a poor imitation of Lily Pons deserting the stage for a poor country boy or a poor country girl named Lily Pons astounding the world in ten minutes. A hack will do exactly that with it, thinking first what the previous stories dealing with ballet and theatre have been about, and he will try to write a reasonable imitation about it. As you know Zelda and I have been through hell about the whole subject and you'll know, too, that I should be able to deliver something entirely authentic in the matter full of invention and feeling.
>
> It seems odd having to sell you such a suggestion when once you would have taken it at my own valuation, but after these three years of reverses it seems necessary to assure you that I have the stuff to do this job and not let this opportunity slide away with the rumor that "Scott is drinking" or "Scott is through."

Ober and his Hollywood contact, the agent Harold Norling "Swanie" Swanson (1899–1991), decided not to send the scenario for consideration. Ober's card file notes state simply, "Swanson does not want to offer."

"Ballet Shoes" ("Ballet Slippers") was published in the *Fitzgerald/Hemingway Annual* in 1976.

BALLET SHOES

or

BALLET SLIPPERS

by

F. Scott Fitzgerald

Ballet Shoes
(Ballet Slippers)

In 1923 a Russian family (semi-theatrical) arrives at Ellis Island and is interminably detained. Young daughter, 18, has been in Imperial Ballet. She dances for other passengers in steerage to accordion music. She has no idea of New York, and to attract man in small launch, who may get her in before her parents, she throws an old ballet shoe at him.

He is an adventurous young rum runner coming in from the fleet—and says that if she'll slip over the side he'll run her to New York.

They get there, but next day they can't get back. So she loses her family. He accompanies her to debarkation docks without success, and sadly she concludes they've been deported back to Europe.

The rum runner accompanies her to theatrical agencies interpreting the ways of New York to her. No go. On one pilgrimage she saves a little waif from traffic and in doing so breaks her ankle. She goes to emergency hospital and rum runner takes care of little girl. But she finds out she can never dance again. The ankle doesn't last.

Meanwhile the father *has* been admitted to U.S. but has changed his name from Krypioski to Kress, on advice received in first sequence on boat and Ellis Island by comic figure, not mentioned further in this sketch but running through picture as father's friend. He is a man who thinks he knows all about U.S. but never finds out anything. Father prowls streets looking for his daughter, thinking she has gone loose, stopping other girls. He speaks some English and becomes in course of time a theatrical booking agent.

On emerging from hospital heroine has decided to make little girl a great dancer as she can never be. She paints barn-like studio herself and starts ballet class with help of rum runner. He has inherited a small shoe factory and gone respectable. But she doesn't marry him, her only deep passion being for the ballet and the little girl's future, a substitute for her own.

Six years pass while the little girl grows up. The school struggles on.

The great Pavlova comes to New York but she and the little girl can't afford seats. The heroine has also changed her name on her beau's advice. Frequently she has talked to her father on the phone, he asking her to supply a dozen dancers for such and such a ballet and having no idea that "Madame Serene" is his own daughter.

The time for the little girl's debut has arrived. By sacrificing everything they have the money for it. The little girl sits in their apartment at 125th Street and sends her last pair of shoes to the cobbler because the ex–rum runner is to bring her some from his own little factory. She does not know that with his arms full of shoe boxes (including some ballet shoes he has made) he has been stopped at 48th Street by a detective who wants him as witness for some misdemeanor, committed six years before in his rum running days.

The time has grown short—the young protégé finds that a pair of worn ballet shoes are the only shoes in the apartment. Putting them on she starts for the theatre with one nickel for subway. She loses it in a grating and has to walk from 125th Street to the theatrical section. She reaches there exhausted and crying, and, to the Russian girl's horror, with her feet in awful shape.

They try it however. The curtain goes up on her number and the Russian woman (the heroine) dances in the wings in time with the young girl, to keep her morale up. The number goes over.

There is a sudden interruption to the second number. The hero, intent on delivering the shoes, has broken away from the detective, but has been followed.

Now meanwhile, in the audience, the father has been impressed with young girl and gone behind scenes to engage her. He comes in on the row and in the course of it finds that his daughter is the teacher. It is implied that he can bring pressure to bear to exonerate the young man from what were only false charges.

The show is over, the stage is cleared. The Russian girl dances alone on the stage before her father who sits at the piano and plays for her. The hero and the young girl watch from the wings. The music of St. Saens, *The Swan* rises to a crescendo and there are tears in the father's eyes—

—as the picture ends.

A portrait of the author as a young man.

"Thank You for the Light" is the very short story of a traveling saleswoman pausing, at the end of a long day, and hoping to relax with a cigarette. That Mrs. Hanson is not only a saleswoman but a widow, and has for many years traveled through the Midwest as a successful businessperson, selling ladies' undergarments, might alone have been sufficient reasons for the *New Yorker* to reject the story in the summer of 1936. That it is intensely Catholic and concludes with a miracle further ensured its refusal.

The *New Yorker* initially turned down the story because it was "so curious and so unlike the kind of thing we associate with [Fitzgerald] and really too fantastic." These are the very reasons it was popular, and engendered so much critical comment, when it finally did appear in their pages seventy-six years later, on August 6, 2012.

THANK YOU FOR THE LIGHT

by

F. Scott Fitzgerald

Mrs. Hanson was a pretty somewhat faded woman of
forty who sold corsets and girdles, travelling out of Chicago.
For many years her territory had swung around through Toledo,
Lima, Springfield, Columbus, Indianapolis and Fort Wayne and
her transfer to the Iowa, Kansas, Missouri district was a promotion, for her firm was more strongly entrenched west of the
Ohio.

Eastward, however, she had known her clientele
chattily and was often offered a drink or a cigarette in the
buyer's office after business was concluded. But she soon found
that in her new district things were different. Not only was
she never asked if she would smoke but several times her own
inquiry as to whether anyone would mind was answered half
apologetically with:

"It's not that I mind, but it has a bad influence on
the employees."

"Oh, of course, I understand."

Smoking meant a lot to her sometimes. She worked
very hard and it had some ability to rest and relax her psychologically. She was a widow and she had no close relatives to write

Thank You for the Light

Mrs. Hanson was a pretty somewhat faded woman of forty who sold corsets and girdles, travelling out of Chicago. For many years her territory had swung around through Toledo, Lima, Springfield, Columbus, Indianapolis, and Fort Wayne and her transfer to the Iowa, Kansas, Missouri district was a promotion, for her firm was more strongly entrenched west of the Ohio.

Eastward, however, she had known her clientele chattily and was often offered a drink or a cigarette in the buyer's office after business was concluded. But she soon found that in her new district things were different. Not only was she never asked if she would smoke but several times her own inquiry as to whether anyone would mind was answered half apologetically with:

"It's not that *I* mind, but it has a bad influence on the employees."

"Oh, of course, I understand."

Smoking meant a lot to her sometimes. She worked very hard and it had some ability to rest and relax her psychologically. She was a widow and she had no close relatives to write to in the evenings, while more than one moving picture a week hurt her eyes, so that smoking had come to be an important punctuation mark in the long sentence of a day on the road.

The last week of her first trip on the new circuit found her in Kansas City. It was mid-August and she felt somewhat lonely among all the new contacts of the past fortnight, and she was delighted to find at the outer desk of one firm a woman she had known in Chicago. She sat down before having herself announced and in the course of the conversation found out a little about the man she was going to interview.

"Will he mind if I smoke?"

"What? My God, yes!" said her friend. "He's given money to support the law against it."

"Oh. Well, I'm grateful for the advice—more than grateful."

"You better watch it everywhere around here," her friend said. "Especially with the men over fifty. The ones that weren't in the war. A man

321

once told me that nobody who was in the war would ever object to any-one smoking."

But at her very next stop Mrs. Hanson ran into the exception. He seemed such a pleasant young man but his eyes fixed with so much fascination on the cigarette that she tapped on her thumb-nail that she put it away. She was rewarded when he asked her to lunch and during the hour she obtained a considerable order.

Afterwards he insisted on driving her to her next appointment, though she had intended to spot a hotel in the vicinity and take a few puffs in the wash room.

It was one of those days full of waiting, everyone was busy, was late, and it seemed that when they did appear they were the sort of hatchet faced men who did not like other people's self indulgence, or they were women willingly or unwillingly committed to the ideas of these men.

She hadn't smoked since breakfast and she suddenly realized that was why she felt a vague dissatisfaction at the end of each call, no matter how successful it had been in a business way. Aloud she would say, "We think we cover a different field. It's all rubber and canvas, of course, but we do manage to put them together in a different way. A thirty per cent increase in national advertising in one year tells its own story."

And to herself she was thinking: "If I could just get three puffs I could sell old-fashioned whale-bone."

She had one more store to visit now but her engagement was not for half an hour. That was just time to go to her hotel but as there was no taxi in sight she walked along the street, thinking: "Perhaps I ought to give up cigarettes. I'm getting to be a drug fiend."

Before her she saw the Catholic cathedral. It seemed very tall—suddenly she had an inspiration: if so much incense had gone up in the spires to God a little smoke in the vestibule would make little differ-ence. How could the Good Lord care if a tired woman took a few puffs in the vestibule?

Nevertheless, though she was not a Catholic, the thought offended her. It didn't seem so important whether she had her cigarette, because it might offend a lot of other people too.

Still—He wouldn't mind, she thought persistently. In His days they hadn't even discovered tobacco . . .

She went into the church; the vestibule was dark and she felt for a match in the bag she carried but there wasn't any.

"I'll go and get a light from one of their candles," she thought.

The darkness of the nave was broken only by a splash of light in a corner. She walked up the aisle toward the white blur, and found that it was not made by candles and in any case it was going out soon—an old man was on the point of eliminating a last oil lamp.

"These are votive offerings," he said. "We put them out at night. They float in the oil and we think it means more to the people that give them to save them for next day, than it would to keep them burning all night."

"I see."

He struck out the last one. There was no light left in the cathedral now, save an electric chandelier high overhead and the ever-burning lamp in front of the sacrament.

"Good night," the sexton said.

"Good night."

"I guess you came here to pray."

"Yes I did."

He went out into the sacristy. Mrs. Hanson knelt down and prayed.

It had been a long time since she had prayed. She scarcely knew what to pray for, so she prayed for her employer, and for the clients in Des Moines and Kansas City. When she had finished praying she knelt up. She was not used to prayer. The image of the Madonna gazed down upon her from a niche, six feet above her head.

Vaguely she regarded it. Then she got up from her knees and sank back wearily in the corner of the pew. In her imagination the Virgin came down, like in the play "The Miracle," and took her place and sold corsets and girdles for her and was tired just as she was. Then for a few minutes Mrs. Hanson must have slept . . .

. . . She awoke at the realization that something had changed; and only gradually she perceived that there was a familiar scent that was not incense in the air and that her fingers smarted. Then she realized that the cigarette she held in her hand was alight—was burning.

Still too drowsy to think, she took a puff to keep the flame alive. Then she looked up again at the Madonna's vague niche in the half-darkness.

"Thank you for the light," she said.

That didn't seem quite enough, so she got down on her knees, the smoke twisting up from the cigarette, between her fingers.

"Thank you very much for the light," she said again.

FSF, Nice, 1924.

Acknowledgments

The Trustees of the Estate of F. Scott Fitzgerald invited me to edit this collection. To Eleanor Lanahan, Blake Hazard, and Chris Byrne, my especial thanks. Lanahan shared her knowledge, photographs, and so much more to make her grandfather and his writings closer to me, and to us all. Harold Ober Associates remain the careful stewards of Fitzgerald's literary estate, as Harold Ober was for Fitzgerald's lifetime as a professional writer. Phyllis Westberg, Craig Tenney, and Karen Gormandy carry on Ober's tradition with intelligence and grace. The Department of Rare Books and Special Collections at the Princeton University Library houses the papers of F. Scott and Zelda Fitzgerald; Linda Bogue, Sandra Bossert, Brianna Cregle, AnnaLee Pauls, Chloe Pfendler, Gabriel Swift, and Squirrel Walsh were liberal with help during my months there. Thanks to Elizabeth Sudduth and Michael Weisenburg of the Irvin Department of Rare Books and Special Collections at the University of South Carolina, and to the staff of the Beinecke Library at Yale.

I first met the Scribner team who brought this book into being in Princeton, on Fitzgerald's birthday, as we looked at the manuscript of *The Great Gatsby* together. From that auspicious start, it was a pleasure at every twist and turn to work with Kara Watson, Janetta Dancer, Katie Rizzo, and Rosie Mahorter.

To Don C. Skemer, James L. W. West III, and James L. Pethica, scholars and gentlemen: without your expertise, generosity, and friendship, this book and I would both be far the poorer. Many fêtes, kind sirs.

Thanks to Bernett Belgraier, who cast a cold eye over dotted i's and crossed t's. For advice, friendship, information of one sort or another, and kindnesses that have enriched my work on this volume, I am also indebted to A. Scott Berg, Margaret Rogers Bowers, Jackson R. Bryer, James Campbell, Elinor Case-Pethica, Sarah Churchwell, Margaret Daniel, Scott Donaldson, Robin Dufour, Neil Gower, Katherine Graham, Patricia Hill Meyer, Scott Jordan Harris, Peter Hellemaa, Lorraine Koffman, Bryant Mangum, Margaret McPherson, Thomas Patrick Roche Jr.,

Jeff Rosen, Cecilia Ross, Kim Ruehl, Mike Scott, Charles Scribner III, and Elaine Showalter; and to the F. Scott Fitzgerald Society, Princeton Alumni Association, Princeton Triangle Club, Princeton Class of 2017, and University Cottage Club.

i.m. Thomas F. Bergin '46, Garrick P. Grobler '86, and A. Walton Litz '51.

AMD
New York City 2017

Explanatory Notes

3 *female apaches*: The word "apaches," taken from the Native American tribe but pronounced "a-PASH," is a term applied to knife-wielding Parisian girls, reportedly an informal gang, of the early 1900s. "Les Apaches de Belleville" in turn gave their name to a rather violent Jazz Age dance, in which the partners cuff each other around and melt into a concluding waltz.

3 *Samuel Butler*: Samuel Butler (1835–1902), author of the anti-Victorian autobiographical novel *The Way of All Flesh* (1903); Theodore Dreiser (1871–1945), journalist and author of the naturalistic novels *Sister Carrie* (1900) and *An American Tragedy* (1925); James Branch Cabell (1879–1958), novelist best known for *Jurgen* (1919) and the subsequent prosecution of Cabell and his publisher for obscenity. Fitzgerald regularly broke the "i before e" rule—Meyer Wolfshiem, in *The Great Gatsby*, is an example—and spelled Dreiser's name incorrectly; most likely he would have been diagnosed as dyslexic today. Fitzgerald wrote fan letters to Cabell, and received responses that he pasted into the scrapbooks he compiled for most of his adult life.

3 *psychic research*: Since 1885, when the American Society for Psychical Research was founded, scientists, psychologists, dream researchers, clairvoyants, and physicists had published books pondering issues from telepathy to life after death. Not coincidentally, 1913 was the last year of peacetime before World War I broke out—Fitzgerald here makes the booming interest in psychic research, and particularly communication with the dead, an outgrowth of a world shattered by war.

4 *April 15th*: Not a tax deadline in the 1920s. However, Scribner tended to publish Fitzgerald's own books in late March and early April.

4 *Dundreary whiskers*: Long, particularly bushy sideburns. They take their name from the comic character Lord Dundreary in Tom Taylor's play *Our American Cousin* (1858). The play was best known for Lord Dundreary and his silliness until it became, on April 14, 1865, the play President Abraham Lincoln was watching at Ford's Theatre in Washington, D.C., when he was assassinated.

4 *Mohammed (or was it Moses?)*: In *Essays* (1625), Francis Bacon stated the proposition "If the hill will not come to Mahomet, Mahomet will go to the hill." Moses went to Mount Sinai—there was never a question of Mount Sinai coming to him—to receive God's commandments; see Exodus 19:34.

6 *"Basil Kings"*: William Benjamin Basil King (1859–1928), an Anglican rector from Prince Edward Island, Canada, began to write successful novels with a spiritual bent after 1900. *The Abolishing of Death* (1919) is based on his own communications with the dead, particularly in the period following the Armistice of November 11, 1918. In 1923, the *Harvard Crimson* described King as "one of the outstanding figures in American literature." Fitzgerald surely satirizes King in the figure of Dr. Harden.

7 *drug-store . . . cocktail*: The Eighteenth Amendment to the U.S. Constitution barred the "manufacture, sale, or transportation of intoxicating liquors within, the importation thereof into, or the exportation thereof from the United States" after

January 1920. However, the Volstead Act, which implemented and enforced the amendment, was full of loopholes. Cider and wines could be homemade, in small amounts. And doctors could legally write prescriptions for distilled spirits, chiefly whiskey and brandy, that were filled at drugstores—hence the "drug-store cocktail." When, in Chapter 6 of *The Great Gatsby*, Daisy Buchanan tells her husband that Gatsby "owned some drug-stores, a lot of drug-stores. He built them up himself[,]" she confirms that Gatsby is, among other things, a bootlegger.

8   *"printer's devil"*: An apprentice who did the menial tasks in an old-style print shop, including carrying type.

9   Philadelphia Press: The *Philadelphia Press* ceased publication on October 1, 1920.

10   *"Thalia"*: Of the Nine Muses, she is the Muse of comedy and of short pastoral poetry. From the Greek for the verb *to bloom*; *blooming*.

10   *"crocked off"*: What Dr. Harden has written is a crock of shit; or, in the polite translation, nonsense. Also encompassed here is the English sense of a crock, or old crock, as something broken down and useless. However, these are very old usages, and the point here is that Thalia is using modern slang. A RIT dye advertisement of 1923 promises to restore blouses where the color has "crocked off," which seems relevant. In 1924, though, the expression was used in a short story— serialized in an Ohio newspaper—to mean someone has died.

10   "prom": Thought of today as high school dances at year's end, proms were large college parties that went on for days of events during the course of the academic year. The centerpiece was a formal dance; each class had their own prom, with that of the senior class being the most socially sought-after invitation. In Fitzgerald's day as an undergraduate at Princeton, the campus paper, the *Daily Princetonian*, was full of advertisements for the best places to order one's prom invitations and dance cards, the lineups for musical entertainment, and lavish columns on the events. Thornton Wilder, in 1928 a graduate student and resident advisor studying French literature at Princeton, complained to Fitzgerald that February, "I'm dog-tired just now: the House is always restless during the Winter-term and espec. just before the 3-day Prom."

10   *105th Infantry*: An infantry regiment from New York State. It suffered heavy losses at Ypres and the Somme.

12   *Sing Sing*: A maximum-security prison built on the Hudson River in Ossining, New York, and opened in 1826.

12   *Red Queen's in* Alice in Wonderland: Lewis Carroll's Red Queen actually appears in *Through the Looking-Glass, and What Alice Found There* (1871). She is cold and severe, with a remarkable sense of logic that she and her counterpart, the White Queen (both drawn from chess pieces), try to apply to Alice.

13   *"ten thousand a year"*: The average annual wage in the United States in 1920 was just over one thousand dollars.

15   "Toledo Blade" . . . "Akron World": A checklist of Ohio's city and town newspapers.

16   *sell five hundred thousand copies*: In 1920 and 1921, Fitzgerald's debut novel, *This Side of Paradise*, sold just under fifty thousand copies and, based upon this, was deemed a great success.

"NIGHTMARE" ("FANTASY IN BLACK")

19   *pleasant section of New Hampshire*: Fitzgerald seems here to have made an imaginative combination of the sanitarium at Glencliff, New Hampshire, and the State Hospital in Concord. Patients with tuberculosis came to "The San" in Glencliff, in the southwestern White Mountains, from 1909 until the early 1970s, when it became a home for the elderly. The State Hospital, initially the New Hampshire Asylum for

the Insane, opened in 1842; it encompassed in the 1930s just such a cluster of varied buildings, for different purposes, as Fitzgerald describes in this story.

19 *Suppé's* Light Cavalry: The overture to this operetta by Austrian composer Franz von Suppé (1819–1895), with its constant horns and light, elegant strings, has been popular since its 1866 premiere.

19 *"Mrs. Miller . . . curls"*: An allusion to Alexander Pope's mock-heroic poem *The Rape of the Lock* (1712). In it, the beautiful Belinda loses one of her long curls to a lout of a lord and his sly scissors while her head is bent over an afternoon game of cards.

20 *"New York, New Haven and Hartford"*: The New York, New Haven and Hartford Railroad was a major commuter rail line between New York's Grand Central Terminal and points northeast.

22 *"market crash in twenty-nine . . . ticker-tape"*: The Wall Street crash culminating in "Black Tuesday," on October 28, 1929, was the New York manifestation of a worldwide economic collapse brought on by speculation in stocks. Billions were lost as prices for stock tumbled, and the "ticker tape" paper strips, transmitting stock prices via a stock ticker, told of the catastrophe in print. The suicides of bankers and business executives broken by the crash, like J. J. Riordan of the County Trust Company and Robert M. Searle of Rochester Gas and Electric Company, were front-page news in national newspapers, though the urban-legend tales of legions of stockbrokers jumping from Wall Street windows on that Halloween are baseless.

22 *"South America . . . railroad securities"*: As with the 1929 crash, Fitzgerald has chosen triggering events for each of the Woods brothers' breakdowns. Walter, in charge of the Foreign Bond Department, is institutionalized after the "revolutions in South America"—during the late 1920s and early 1930s, there were uprisings in Mexico, Brazil, Peru, El Salvador, Nicaragua, and other Latin American countries. John, who speculates in railroad securities, breaks down in autumn of the year in which railroad securities were worth barely more than a tenth of their pre-crash value, and almost twenty railroad lines had gone bankrupt.

23 *"Rockefeller Institute"*: The Rockefeller Institute for Medical Research, now Rockefeller University, describes itself as the "first institution in the United States devoted solely to using biomedical research to understand the underlying causes of disease." Founded in 1901 by John D. Rockefeller, Sr. (1839–1937), America's first billionaire, thanks to Standard Oil of Ohio, the university continues to benefit from the family's active involvement, particularly that of Rockefeller's 101-year-old grandson David.

23 *"manic-depressive psychosis"*: Today, manic depression is termed bipolar disorder. Zelda's brother Anthony Sayre, who committed suicide by jumping from a hospital window to his death in the summer of 1933, was given a diagnosis of manic depression, according to Fitzgerald. On May 4, 1934, Fitzgerald wrote to Zelda's doctor at Craig House in Beacon, New York: "I have just fully realized that her brother was not a schizophrenic but a manic depressive, that in fact the hospital in which he died simply characterized his condition as 'depressed,' though he had touches of suicidal and homocidal [*sic*] mania. If at any time it comes naturally to disassociate in my wife's mind her own tendency to schizophrenia from her brother's case I think it would be invaluable if you could do so. That is to say, there is a new defeatism in her arising from the fact that she believes the whole case to be familial and the whole family doomed."

29 *"faded summer lu-uve"*: "Faded Summer Love" was a 1931 fox-trot with lyrics and music by Phil Baxter. It was a hit for Ruth Etting, Bing Crosby, and Rudy Vallée in the 1930s.

31 *"ergotherapy"*: Treating a disease through physical functions and efforts; literally, work-treatment. By the 1920s this part of hospitalization and recovery was also called occupational therapy. Psychiatrist Adolph Meyer (1866–1950) of Johns

Hopkins Hospital in Baltimore, Maryland, was one of ergotherapy's chief proponents. Meyer applied what he called "ergasiology" in the Henry Phipps Psychiatric Clinic at Hopkins, where Zelda Fitzgerald was his patient in 1932 and again, briefly, in early 1934.

33 *helpless shell*: "I am sorry too that there should be nothing to greet you but an empty shell." Letter from Zelda to Scott, June 1935.

36 *"hydro-therapatical"*: Hydrotherapy, using hot or cold water, was commonly used in mental institutions in the early twentieth century. Cold water was used on patients diagnosed as manic depressive or psychotic, and unable to control motor activities. Warm baths were for patients who were overly excited and agitated, or assaultive. These baths were meant to have water flowing continuously over the patient to prevent the water from being fouled as a person was restrained in them, sometimes for days; and hydrotherapy baths were meant to be strictly monitored to prevent drowning.

37 *hypnosis*: In his keynote *Textbook of Insanity*, translated into English in 1905, Richard von Krafft-Ebing (1840–1902) noted the success of the treatment of neuroses by hypnosis, and speculated that it could be applied to "mental treatment in cases of insanity."

38 *Elixer Shop*: In the nineteenth and early twentieth centuries, barbers often occupied space in apothecary shops or drugstores, offering haircuts along with the shop's miracle elixirs (many alcohol-based, and curing little or nothing).

"WHAT TO DO ABOUT IT"

41 *Philadelphia turnpike*: Begun in 1792 and one of the oldest major east–west routes on the East Coast. The turnpike here is running past the pricey Philadelphia suburbs of the "Main Line" (think of the Katharine Hepburn and Cary Grant characters in and the setting of *The Philadelphia Story*, 1940).

41 *1927 tire-lock*: In 1927, the Ford Model T went out of production and was succeeded by the Model A. Other cars were of course widely available in America then, but a young doctor without much money would have been constrained to the most affordable. Whatever the car, it is seven years old and has had hard wear. The tire-lock held the spare tire in place quite firmly, to prevent easy theft.

42 *Italian painters . . . corner angels*: Used in *The Love of The Last Tycoon*: "Just a girl, with the skin of one of Raphael's corner angels and a style that made you look back twice to see if it were something she had on."

43 *"Chicago Opera . . . Louise"*: Grace Moore (1898–1947) was discovered by George M. Cohan and made her Broadway debut in 1920 in Jerome Kern's *Hitchy-Koo*. "The Tennessee Nightingale" was a popular musical star, but was performing onstage at the Metropolitan Opera by the end of the 1920s. She had also made a splash in Hollywood, starring as Jenny Lind in the Irving Thalberg production *A Lady's Morals* (1930). Her most celebrated performances were in the title role of the poor seamstress who ends up with her beloved Julien and is crowned Queen of Montmartre, in Gustave Charpentier's *Louise* (1900). Moore sang the role in the late 1930s with the Chicago Opera Company, in Chicago and on tour, and Charpentier directed her in a film version. She was an acquaintance of the Fitzgeralds' on the Riviera in the 1920s.

45 *"EX-WHITE-SLAVER . . . Who Still is one"*: One of many lines in his stories and novels taken from Fitzgerald's so-called notebooks. From his notes, made on everything from notebook pages to shards to paper doilies that went under drinks as coasters, Fitzgerald took phrases, paragraphs, dialogue, and ideas for later writings. See *The Notebooks of F. Scott Fitzgerald*, entry 419.

45 Fountains of Tivoli: The hundreds of Renaissance fountains at the Villa d'Este in Tivoli were in major disrepair for centuries, but had been partially restored and reopened during the 1920s.

45 *The Robin*: Fitzgerald uses euphemism upon euphemism here for the boy's gesture. "The Robin" is a way of saying "the bird," by then long in use.

46 *Diamond Dick*: Richard Wade was a flashy, Robin Hood–style Western hero, a character written by many hands, who first appeared in *Street and Smith's New York Weekly* in 1878. "Dashing Diamond Dick" starred in a weekly series, and was also a dime-novel hero, until 1911.

47 *"Charlie Chaplin"*: Known for his comedies in the 1920s—when Bill Hardy was young—Charlie Chaplin (1889–1977) was by the time of this story's setting regarded as something of a Hollywood has-been. Though still a controlling partner of United Artists, he was viewed as a silent-movie man and had taken an extended break from films beginning in 1931.

47 *"Garbo"*: Greta Gustafsson (1905–1990) was a Swedish-born dramatic actress and already more of an icon than a mere movie star by the middle 1930s. Garbo was not known as a comedienne until *Ninotchka* (1939), one of her last films.

47 *"Dietrich"*: Like Greta Garbo, Marlene Dietrich (1901–1992) was an exotic international star, a femme fatale and dramatic actress, whose career had stalled in the mid-1930s. *Destry Rides Again* (1939), the Western-comedy with Fitzgerald's fellow Princeton graduate and Hollywood friend Jimmy Stewart, made Dietrich a star again.

47 *"Constance Bennett"*: Finally, the boy names a comic actress, but no wonder Dr. Hardy raises an eyebrow. Constance Bennett (1904–1965) shone in the *Topper* movies in the late 1930s, but her best-known comedy at the time of this story was *Bed of Roses* (1933), in which she played a thieving prostitute reformed by the love of Joel McCrea.

47 *"you're not a heel"*: A "heel" refers to an untrustworthy person. Used by mobsters as slang since the 1910s, the word's use goes back before this in the American South and West, as the shorter version of "shitheel." John Steinbeck deploys the long version in *The Grapes of Wrath* (1939) for stuck-up snobs and cheapskates. Throughout, the boy uses gangland slang of the 1920s and 1930s that he has learned from the movies.

47 *"four girls named Meg . . . rabbit hole"*: The boy here conflates Louisa May Alcott's *Little Women* (1868/9) and Lewis Carroll's *Alice's Adventures in Wonderland* (1865). Meg is the eldest of the four March sisters in *Little Women*, and the most beautiful. Alice's adventures in Wonderland begin on the first page of the first chapter, "Down the Rabbit-Hole." These two classics sum up the first, which is to say, the permitted, of the "two kina kinds" of books the boy has.

48 *"not gravement but chronicquement"*: Not gravely ill, but chronically; facing a long-term illness.

51 *rumble seat*: To sit in the rumble seat in this car would be rather like sitting in an open car trunk. The seat was effectively outside the car, a space that could be flipped open above the rear axle (hence the rumble) and accommodate luggage, or, for a short ride, a passenger.

53 *"frails"*: Slang for women, notable here as it came into popular parlance in 1931 via Cab Calloway's smash hit "Minnie the Moocher," with lyrics by Irving Mills and Clarence Gaskill. Minnie is "the roughest, toughest frail." Fitzgerald surely had this song on his mind as he was writing, as it also prominently features a "Gong."

54 *fire-horse harness*: A very heavy, elaborate harness designed for pulling a fire truck full of water. Hardy is clearly doing more of the work in this medical practice.

54 *"in these times . . . it's good to have anything to do at all"*: The Great Depression is on with a vengeance, and millions remain out of work.

"GRACIE AT SEA"

59 *George Burns and Grace Allen*: George Burns (1896–1996) and Gracie Allen (1895–1964) were a popular vaudeville, radio, and movie husband-and-wife team. George played straight man to Gracie's dizzy comedienne.

60 *Augustus Van Grossie*: The America's Cup races of 1934 were dominated by Harold Vanderbilt. After a shaky start, his yacht *Rainbow* bested the British challenger *Endeavour* off Newport, Rhode Island, to defend the Cup.

60 *elder daughter must be married before the younger*: Compare William Shakespeare, *The Taming of the Shrew*. Baptista, who has two daughters, refuses to consider suitors for the younger, Bianca, before someone marries her big sister, Katharina (the shrew).

61 *villa at Newport*: In the 1880s Newport, Rhode Island, began to develop as a summer resort playground for the very rich. Massive mansions, referred to as "cottages," were built on the ocean cliffs. The most celebrated of these Gilded Age villas, many open as museums to the public today, are Cornelius Vanderbilt II's seventy-room The Breakers (1893–1895), the Stanford White–designed Rosecliff (1898–1902), and William Vanderbilt's Marble House (1888–1892).

61 *laundry basket . . . little boy*: The link to Moses in the bulrushes, Exodus 2:3, is explicitly made by Fitzgerald in his revised version of this story, included at the end of these notes. That Fitzgerald names Gracie's favorite goldfish Noah is also an amusing biblical touch.

62 *adopt the child*: Burns and Allen had tried for years to have children and could not. In late 1934, they adopted Sandra Jean Burns, born that August, and in September 1935, they adopted a little boy, Ronnie, who was then three months old. Their wish for children may have disposed them toward the script Fitzgerald offered them in the summer of 1934, or instead made them feel it was too close to home. Did Fitzgerald know of their plans to adopt, and work this theme into the script he offered them?

62 *christen her father's boat*: Launching boats with ceremony is a long-standing tradition. In America, when the U.S.S. *Constitution*, "Old Ironsides," was launched in Boston in October 1797, she was christened with a spill of Madeira wine. Champagne became the liquid of choice during the 1890s; here, its use by Gracie marks the sparkling end of Prohibition.

Fitzgerald's revision

Sometime after the summer of 1937, when he was under contract to Metro-Goldwyn-Mayer, Fitzgerald returned to this scenario and revised it as follows. He retains much from the original, including the most significant moment for a writer: a typewriter, pillowed upon an air cushion, floating out to sea. However, he makes some creative changes, including the introduction of an English upper-class twit, and shifts the setting to Long Island, New York.

F. Scott Fitzgerald
Gracie at Sea

Far at sea off the coast of Long Island, a small passenger steamer has burned to the water's edge. The only living thing saved is a baby who drifts free of the wreckage in a soap-box where she was evidently placed as the last thought of her parents.

Here we begin our story. The rich Mr. Van Grossie is determined to marry off Gracie, the eldest of his three daughters, before allowing the banns to be published for the other two. The two other sisters, a Gail Patrick type and a Mary Carlisle type, are miserable over the situation as each has a man very much in mind—and in hand. However, they have hopes of marrying off Gracie, as the yacht races are at hand and Mr. Van Grossie is entertaining the visiting challenger, Sir Reginald, at their Southampton home.

Sir Reginald, a stupid haw-haw type, has expressed himself as anxious to marry an American girl under three conditions: She must be very talented, a fine sportswoman, and extremely beautiful. Gracie, the eldest sister, is none of these. But the two sisters believe Sir Reginald is so stupid that perhaps with the help of clever exploitation they can convince him that Gracie is what he's looking for. They get in touch with a New York publicity firm who send their representative, George (George Burns), to Southampton on the promise of a large fee if Gracie is put over.

We now pick up Gracie for the first time—in the garden of the great Van Grossie estate—feeding a pool of goldfish. She has just thrown in the last batch of food and is saying goodbye to her favorite goldfish, and as she turns away she hears a sound which is apparently the goldfish thanking her for the food. She turns back.

"What did you say, Noah?" The goldfish doesn't answer.

"Oh, you silly thing," says Gracie and turns away.

But she hears the strange cry a second time, turns back again and follows the sound to a little inlet located in a patch of woods. It is a curious sound, a sound that has been a long time in Gracie's heart, even though she doesn't recognize it. It's something new and fascinating and she stops in her tracks, looking up at the sky for a moment, upon the chance that it may be a bird she has never heard before. She knows in her heart it is not a bird and a minute later traces it to its source.

The source is a dark harbor in the corner of the inlet. The source is the sea. The source seems to be a small, utterly un-seaworthy appearing soap-box, in which is a small, 18-months baby. As the box drifts aground, Gracie snatches him out and cuddles him with awe and enthusiasm. Gracie, whose future is apparently being charted by her two sisters, and the publicity agent they have commandeered, has suddenly found a great interest in life all her own.

What Gracie is going to do with the baby, remains to be seen. For some reason, however, she decides that for the present she shall keep it hidden, like Pharaoh's daughter, and immediately improvises a nursery in the little cove.

We return to the Van Grossie household. George arrives and meets the two sisters. The Gail Patrick type is secretly married to the Butterworth type, and their reason for wanting to get Gracie married is so that they can make their own marriage public. The sweet Mary Carlisle type is engaged to a naval officer, whose ship, floating off shore, is to depart for China at the conclusion of the regatta, so it is to her interest that Gracie get married with no loss of time. George is introduced to the heavy father as a friend of the girls, and immediately starts to work to satisfy Sir Reginald's first requisite for his bride-to-be. He must make Gracie into a sportswoman overnight.

The next scene is one of cross purpose, with Gracie obediently trying to do the sort of things expected of her by Sir Reginald, but being constantly absorbed by her secret care of the baby, she must have it constantly by her side. For example, in the golf tournament, which is arranged for the next day, she is accompanied by an extra caddy carrying a particularly large bag in which is the baby—but this fact does not emerge until the end of the episode. Throughout the game, she tries to teach the baby to count her score. In any case, George soon finds out the secret. He does not give Gracie away, because

Sir Reginald has announced that he does not like children, but he realizes the case is going to be harder than he had imagined. The golfing episode fails to convince Sir Reginald that Gracie is a great sportswoman, but George manages to cover up the truth, which is that she is no sportswoman at all.

His second idea is to put Gracie over as a musical genius. The gag would go somewhat as follows. Evening at the Van Grossie house. George and Gracie enter the music room, she leaning on his arm and sweeping majestically across the room to a raised dais. George is trying to dramatize her talent for the harp and has arranged a claque to applaud her mediocre playing, as well as an expert harpist concealed behind curtains who will fill in with a few finished numbers. He makes a formal speech of presentation which Gracie sweetly acknowledges. He announces the first selection and himself accompanies her on the piano. Gracie starts with a glissonde on the harp strings. Suddenly the baby pops out from behind the piano where Gracie has concealed it, crashes through the harp and becoming wedged, causes Gracie to strike numerous extraordinary notes. The musicale comes to a disastrous end, but again George manages to extricate Gracie from the situation.

George's main coup is the engineering of a beauty contest which Gracie will unquestionably win. It is a fully publicized contest—society reporters from New York are present to make notes and there are photographers in scores. Gracie, with the help of her sisters, has been carefully instructed in her role. The competitors have been chosen from wall flowers in the vicinity, so that they present a stark picture of feminine unattractiveness—there is something wrong with every one of them and apparently Gracie should win with ease. The judges, moreover, are bribed and to make doubly sure there will be no mistake, they are told to give Number 9 the prize. The baby, however, upsets the apple-cart by changing the Number 9 on Gracie's back into a 6 by turning it upside down, and turning another girl's Number 6 into a Number 9, so that the ugliest girl of the lot wins the prize.

While George is working so desperately, the two sisters have been continuing their love affairs—our interest centering upon the affair of Mary Carlisle with the navy officer. We are rather hostile to the Gail Patrick–Butterworth love affair and it is not surprising that this pair discover the baby and decide that its presence is a menace to the whole plan. They kidnap the child with the idea of placing it in an orphanage so that Gracie can concentrate upon the winning of Sir Reginald. But Gracie and George rescue the child in time.

Finally it is the day of the yacht race—the festivities to be opened by the christening of the American Defender by Gracie. From far and near people have gathered upon the dock to watch and applaud. This scene seems to George a sure-fire stunt for pleasing Sir Reginald, but Gracie's talent for going wrong reasserts itself and at the moment when she is about to smash the bottle on the bow, she stops in her swing and holds the bottle aloft to wave at the crowd. The boat begins to move. The swing misses fire, turning Gracie around in acrobatic circles. Not defeated by this, she murmurs "Where am I?" and sets off in a mad run in pursuit of the boat—and overtakes it only by a daring leap through mid-air in an aesthetic pose—and attains her aim at the sacrifice of sinking into the bay. Unfortunately, this great sportswoman can't swim, but Sir Reginald saves her and he is so pleased with himself that things look up.

Meanwhile, the young lovers are apparently going to be tragically parted. Mary Carlisle has gone aboard the battleship to say goodbye to her lover. Gracie has gone out in a launch to watch the yacht race with the baby and coming aboard the battleship manages to postpone its departure because the baby gets lost in a big gun, and the captain cannot fire the salute which is to open the race. Gracie stands with a torch over the powder magazine threatening to blow up the ship unless the baby is found. She succeeds in postponing the ship's departure for China and therefore keeps Mary Carlisle from losing her lover.

The yacht race begins. Gracie misses the official launch and is taken on board a small out-board launch by the faithful George. Gracie sits in the stern, holding the baby with one arm and steering with the other. George sits in the bow, his typewriter resting on an air cushion as he undertakes the double duty of reporting the race and trying to make Gracie look as though she is the heroine of the whole affair. Unfortunately, the launch breaks in half and sinks. George's half sinks very slowly, the typewriter floating off on the air cushion. Gracie's half of the boat contains the motor and the propeller and Gracie and the baby speed in crazy circles round and round George. George, however, picks up a drifting dory and manages to rescue both baby and typewriter. He and Gracie attach their dory to the end of a racing yacht, just as the starting gun is fired and lo and behold, they are an unwilling part of the race. But in the ensuing confusion, as they get from the dory to the yacht, the baby is left behind in the trailing dory.

The yachts are going strong. The American boat is in the lead but Gracie and George are more concerned with effecting the rescue of the baby who sits laughing and clapping his hands as the dory rocks and swerves in the yacht's wake. Gracie wants to pull the dory up to the boat but instead pulls the wrong rope and brings down the mainsail. Sir Reginald sweeps by to victory.

By this time Gracie and George have discovered they are in love and the picture ends with all three couples—and the baby—united and happy. Sir Reginald starts off across the ocean on his yacht with the beauty contest winner.

This is the mere skeleton of the story, first outlined to George Burns by the author in Baltimore in 1935 [1934]. The author is at present under contract to Metro and will be unable to develop the story any further.

The main situations, Gracie as the eldest of three sisters who must be the first one to marry, and Gracie in the position of Pharaoh's daughter hiding Moses in the bulrushes, seem to offer more sympathetic material than she has had of late. It is important to build up some sort of character for Gracie beyond that of a mere nitwit. In this she can be dramatized as a lovable eccentric and the audience will sympathize with her suppressed maternal instinct—as in Chaplin's "The Kid"—and with her ability, in spite of her mistakes, to somehow do well by the baby.

Fitzgerald's cast for the film

The actors Fitzgerald names for this new version of "Gracie at Sea" were Gail Patrick, Mary Carlisle, and Charles Butterworth. Patrick (1911–1980) was an Alabama belle who was at law school at the University of Alabama when she won a trip to Hollywood in 1932. She appeared in *Rumba* with George Raft and Carole Lombard (1935), and notably as Lombard's spoiled big sister in *My Man Godfrey* (1936) and as an opportunistic actress in *Stage Door* (1937). She typically played haughty "bad girls." During the 1950s, Patrick went into television production and used her law-school training to develop a show of which she was executive producer and which was immensely successful for a decade and in reruns, *Perry Mason*.

Carlisle was born in 1914 and raised in Los Angeles, and her blue-eyed, blonde, baby-faced looks made her a rising star by 1930. She was in the racy romp *College Humor* (1933) with Bing Crosby, George Burns, and Gracie

Allen, and retired from movies in 1943 after marrying English actor James Edward Blakeley. Carlisle still lives, as of 2016, in the Rodeo Drive home she shared with Blakeley for sixty-four years.

Butterworth (1896–1946) was a Broadway actor best known in Hollywood for his ad libs during filming, like his line to Charles Winninger in the Mae West vehicle *Every Day's a Holiday* (1937): "You oughta get out of those wet clothes and into a dry martini."

"TRAVEL TOGETHER"

73 *the freight . . . held on to rods all night*: Jumping onto a freight train for a free ride has been done since America's rail system became the chief means of transportation after the Civil War. During the Depression, when people had no money for travel, the cross section of illegal riders became wider. "Riding the rods," lying on the steel rods of the undercarriage of a freight car and holding on just above the train tracks, is the most dangerous way to hop a ride.

73 *Springfield*: This could be the town in either Missouri or Illinois, both reachable in a day's trip by train from Dallas. As this is a slow-moving freight train, it is more likely Springfield, Missouri.

73 *"Slummy"*: Short for "slumgullion," a hobo stew, made of whatever food might be at hand and simmered over a campfire in any available metal container.

76 *"A tec?"*: Short for "detective."

76 *"canned heat"*: Sterno. Used to cook food, but during Prohibition drunk by those who could not find or afford bootleg liquor—such as hoboes. As Sterno is made of denatured alcohol, made so with methanol, drinking it can be fatal.

76 *"Git along, little doggie"*: "Get Along, Little Dogies" is a classic American cowboy ballad, its refrain urging little dogies, or calves, to keep moving on the trail. Recorded in 1928 by Harry "Mac" McClintock, and then by the Beverly Hill Billies, the song was covered by many artists during the 1930s.

76 *green . . . marbles*: Compare Zelda Fitzgerald, *Save Me the Waltz* (1934): "He verified himself in the mirror—pale hair like eighteenth-century moonlight and eyes like grottoes, the blue grotto, the green grotto, stalactites and malachites hanging about the dark pupil—as if he had taken an inventory of himself before leaving and was pleased to find himself complete."

81 *"ten-twenty-thirty"*: Taking their name from the amount of cents one paid for one's seat, these shows were cheap entertainments consisting of short stage melodramas and, eventually, motion picture shorts. Actor-manager Corse Payton pioneered the shows in small midwestern towns in the 1890s, but he soon had a small chain of theaters in New York and Brooklyn, at which he invited regular subscribers to choose the plays and entertainments to be put on that season.

81 *"My blue diamond!"*: The most famous blue diamond in the world is the Hope. Mined in India, and owned by the French royal family until it was stolen during the French Revolution, the diamond resurfaced in 1839 in the possession of London banker Henry Philip Hope. It remained in private hands, the subject of interest and report every time a misfortune befell one of its owners (which was often enough to generate the legend of its being cursed), until New York jeweler Harry Winston donated it to the Smithsonian in 1958.

84 *"Nyask Line . . . He was senile"*: Compare *The Great Gatsby*, Chapter 6, and the story of Dan Cody and Ella Kaye. "The transactions in Montana copper that made him many times a millionaire found him physically robust but on the verge of soft-mindedness, and, suspecting this, an infinite number of women tried to separate him from his money. The none too savory ramifications by which Ella Kaye, the

newspaper woman, played Madame de Maintenon to his weakness and sent him to sea in a yacht, were common knowledge to the turgid sub-journalism of 1902."

"I'D DIE FOR YOU" ("THE LEGEND OF LAKE LURE")

91 *Italianate hotel*: Based on the Lake Lure Inn, in the mountains on the southwestern end of Lake Lure, about twenty-five miles southeast of Asheville, North Carolina. The hotel, next to Chimney Rock State Park, opened in 1927. It retains its Italianate stucco, arches, and tiled roof, and one can stay today in the Fitzgerald Suite, not the room in which he briefly stayed as a visitor, but bearing the memory.

91 *"why they couldn't fake Chimney Rock"*: Chimney Rock is a monolithic granite outcrop that stands 315 feet over Lake Lure and the surrounding Rutherford County, North Carolina. From 1902 until 2007 the rock, the mountain from which it rises, and the restaurant were privately owned and operated as Chimney Rock Park. Today it is part of the North Carolina State Parks system and, though there is an elevator to the top, it is currently closed for maintenance. One must climb the steps.

91 *"Versailles . . . twenty-nine"*: MGM was called in the 1920s and '30s "the Versailles of the movies." *Marie Antoinette* (1938), Irving Thalberg's last project as producer, and incomplete at his death in September 1936, featured an extravagant Versailles built to showcase Marie, played by Thalberg's wife, Norma Shearer.

91 *starlight in them which actually photographed*: Fitzgerald used this phrase in *The Love of the Last Tycoon*: "Her hair was of the color and viscosity of drying blood but there was starlight that actually photographed in her eyes."

91 *Mdvanni*: The Mdivanis were an aristocratic Russian family who left their home in Georgia sometime after the Soviet Russian Red Army invasion of that country in 1921. The five adult Mdivani siblings, all in their late teens and early twenties, and all exceptionally good-looking, arrived in Paris and quickly gained the nickname "the Marrying Mdivanis" for their lucrative alliances. Two married celebrated actresses, Mae Murray and Pola Negri, and one married Woolworth heiress Barbara Hutton (later the wife of, among others, Cary Grant). Nina Mdivani married Arthur Conan Doyle's son Denis. Fitzgerald, writing a story that centers on celebrity, love, death, and suicide, logically has the Mdivanis in mind. The eldest brother, Serge, abandoned Negri after she lost her money in the crash of 1929, married Arkansas-born opera singer Mary McCormic (celebrated in the *New York Times* as "the Cowgirl Soprano" in 1923), left her for his former sister-in-law, and died in a polo accident in Palm Beach, Florida, in 1936. The Associated Press reported on March 15: "The prince, one of the famed 'marrying' Georgia Mdivanis, died 10 minutes after being kicked in the head by his own pony." Serge was thirty-three. Another brother, Alexis, had died in a car wreck in Spain a month earlier. Their sister Rusudan, "Roussie," a gifted sculptor and Parisian socialite, never recovered from the shock of their deaths and died in 1938 in a sanatorium in Switzerland, suffering from tuberculosis and depression. She was just thirty-two.

92 *Great Smokies*: The local name for the Appalachian mountain range as it extends south into North Carolina and Tennessee; the Great Smoky Mountains National Park is on the border of these two states. The Smokies take their name from the clouds often covering their mountaintops and high valleys, as mist rises from the forests on their hillsides.

92 *Blue Ridge*: The local name for the Appalachian mountain range of southwestern Virginia; also, the geographical name of the Appalachians from northern Georgia through southern Pennsylvania. As with the Smokies, the Blue Ridge Mountains

owe their name to the mist and haze caused by the exhalations of primarily decid-uous trees, which, from a distance, give the mountains shades of many blues.

93 *"Dillinger"*: John Dillinger (1903–1934), Chicago-based gangster who planned and led a string of bloody bank robberies in the 1930s. He was killed by the FBI outside a movie theater after Anna Sage, the "woman in red," betrayed him to agents in exchange for their not deporting her for prostitution (she was deported thereafter).

94 *"Atlanta in Calydon"*: Algernon Charles Swinburne (1837–1909) published his long poem *Atalanta in Calydon, A Tragedy*, in 1865. The quotation, from the poem's first chorus, sets Carley Delannux as literate and also a man of times past. Fitzgerald loved this poem in college, and quotes from it in *This Side of Paradise* (1920).

94 *"Pershing and Foch"*: General John J. "Black Jack" Pershing (1860–1948) led the American Expeditionary Forces against Germany in World War I. Marshal Fer-dinand Foch (1851–1929) led the French army, and later the combined Allied forces as Allied Supreme Commander—which appointment annoyed Pershing—in World War I.

95 *winding steps to the restaurant*: The Cliff Dwellers Inn, at the foot of Chimney Rock, had a formal restaurant with bookshelves, wicker chairs around the fire-place, thick granite walls, and long stretches of windows for the view.

95 *"Miss Isabelle Panzer"*: Her surname suggests the war was still on Fitzgerald's mind. *Panzer* is German for "armor," but was in the 1930s already the informal term for a tank. The thirty-ton Sturmpanzerwagen A7V was in use on the Western Front in 1917 and 1918.

96 "I'd climb the high-est mountains": "I'd climb the highest mountain / if I knew that when I climbed that mountain, I'd find you." "I'd Climb the Highest Mountain," Lew Brown, lyrics, and Sidney Clare, composer, 1926. Al Jolson had a hit with the song in August 1926; Dave Fleischer's 1931 animation of the song featured a mouse trying to heave his large wife up the mountain, and things ending badly for him.

96 "I love to climb": "Cheek to Cheek," Irving Berlin, 1935. Written for the Fred Astaire and Ginger Rogers movie *Top Hat* (1935), and sung by Astaire. It was one of the most popular songs of the year and nominated for an Academy Award for Best Song at the 1936 Oscars.

97 *"fly the Atlantic"*: The Atlantic had been flown many times by this point, with the first nonstop flight in 1919 and the first solo nonstop flight by Charles Lindbergh, in *The Spirit of St. Louis*, on May 20 and 21, 1927.

98 *Rhododendron Festival*: Begun in 1928 by the Asheville Chamber of Commerce, the festival lasted until World War II (1942). Craft fairs, mountain and bluegrass music, beauty pageants, livestock shows, and dances culminated in a parade of floats. A king and queen of the festival were crowned at the end of the parade, which fetched up in McCormick Field (completed 1924), Asheville's minor league baseball park and currently the home of the Asheville Tourists. Rhododen-dron festivals are still held in the area in June, most notably in Bakersville, North Carolina, at Roan Mountain, about an hour from Asheville.

99 *"Andy Gump"*: The everyman, long-suffering, average-guy hero of the long-running comic strip *The Gumps*, created by Sidney Smith in 1917 for James Patterson and the *Chicago Tribune*.

99 *"Tillie the Toiler"*: Tillie Jones, heroine of the eponymous comic strip by Russ Westover that ran from 1921 to 1959. A svelte, doe-eyed brunette who initially wore her hair in a flapper's bob, Tillie was a secretary at a women's clothing com-pany, which gave her the opportunity to keep up with styles.

99 *"Moon Mullins"*: Moonshine Mullins, a genial bounder in checkered pants and a derby hat, hero of Frank Willard's *Moon Mullins* comic strip from 1923 to 1991.

Mullins eschewed Prohibition, bet on horses, loved women and gambling almost equally, and managed to be, as the *Chicago Tribune* described him, a "beloved banjo-eyed roughneck."

105 *"fractured arm"*: In July 1936, Fitzgerald broke his shoulder while living at the Grove Park Inn.

107 *evil queen in the* Wizard of Oz: A conflation. The Wicked Witch of the East does not burn, but dries up in the sun. Her sister, the Wicked Witch of the West, dissolves when Dorothy throws water on her. "The feet of the dear Witch had disappeared entirely and nothing was left but the silver shoes. 'She was so old,' explained the Witch of the North, 'that she dried up quickly in the sun.'" L. Frank Baum, *The Wonderful Wizard of Oz* (Chicago and New York: George Hill Co., 1900), p. 25.

107 "Capias ad Respondum": A *capias ad respondendum* (that an individual may be bodily captured in order for them to reply) is a legal writ issued by the court to require a defendant in a civil lawsuit, who has failed to appear or fled the law, to reply to the suit. That writ is served, as we see here, by a process server, whose duty it then is to deliver the defendant in person to an officer of the law unless requisite bail is provided.

107 *"four more hours"* . . . *"Statute of Limitations"*: There are statutes mandating specific periods of time for bringing particular legal actions. Some crimes—murder, for instance—have no statute of limitations. Here, the time period for which Delannux can be made to answer to whatever civil "matter of director's responsibility" he has allegedly miscarried would have expired at midnight on this day.

109 *"like Garbo"*: Greta Garbo (1905–1990) was one of Hollywood's most popular and particular stars of the early 1930s, after Irving Thalberg and Louis B. Mayer championed her through the 1920s. However, from the beginning Garbo avoided studio publicity and public appearances, famously telling *Photoplay* magazine reporter Ruth Biery in 1928, "I have wanted to be alone." When she renegotiated her contract with Metro-Goldwyn-Mayer in 1932, she became entitled to choose her own film projects—which she did sparingly and with care—at a staggering salary of $300,000 per picture.

111 *Sesame of the Lilies*: *Sesame and Lilies* is a collection of John Ruskin's celebrated art-and-culture lectures of 1865, in which the first lecture deals with men ("Of Kings' Treasuries") and the second with women ("Of Queens' Gardens"). Ruskin's rhetoric coupled women and flowers—and men and struggle—in unsurprisingly traditional ways for mid-Victorian times; for example: "This is wonderful—oh, wonderful!—to see her, with very innocent feeling fresh within her, go out in the morning into her garden to play with the fringes of its guarded flowers, and lift their heads when they are drooping, with her happy smile upon her face, and no cloud upon her brow, because there is a little wall around her place of peace: and yet she knows in her heart, if she would only look for its knowledge, that, outside of that little rose-covered wall, the wild grass, to the horizon, is torn up by the agony of men, and beat level by the drift of their life-blood." Fitzgerald seems also to be thinking of Pre-Raphaelite paintings of the sort Ruskin long praised and promoted, like John Everett Millais's *Ophelia* (1851/2), in which Shakespeare's doomed heroine floats on her back in a stream, flowers trailing from her fingers.

111 *at the foot of Chimney Rock*: Despite the railings atop Chimney Rock and along its approach trails, in the 1930s and today, accidental deaths and suicides still occur there.

111 *corruption in its wake* . . . *starlight to so many people*: Two of the many echoes of *The Great Gatsby* in this story. Chapter 1: "it is what preyed on Gatsby, what foul dust floated in the wake of his dreams . . ."; Chapter 4: "He had waited five years and bought a mansion where he dispensed starlight to casual moths—so that he could 'come over' some afternoon to a stranger's garden."

"DAY OFF FROM LOVE"

114 *"Nora"*: In early 1935, in Tryon, North Carolina, Fitzgerald met Nora and Maurice "Lefty" Flynn. Their story would already have been known to him from extensive newspaper coverage for the past two decades. Lefty (1892–1959) was a Yale football star, but was expelled in January 1913 for marrying chorus girl Reba Leary. The young couple divorced less than a year later, and Flynn met Nora Langhorne Phipps (1889–1955). Nora, a sister of Lady Astor and of Irene Langhorne, famous illustrator Charles Dana Gibson's original "Gibson Girl," was married to English architect Paul Phipps at the time. She and Flynn ran away together to Washington State and had a brief affair. They met again seventeen years later, after Flynn had had a career as a movie star and been married twice more—including a short-lived marriage to Viola Dana, who starred in the 1921 silent-film version, now lost, of Fitzgerald's story "The Off-Shore Pirate." Lefty and Nora were married in 1931. That June, when syndicated columnist "Cholly Knickerbocker" (aka Maury Henry Biddle Paul, 1890–1942) asked Nora about the impending wedding, she replied, "I am constrained by legal restrictions not to say much about it, but I admit that my greatest happiness lies just beyond the horizon." Fitzgerald made a flow chart about Nora, Lefty, and their personal lives that survives in the Fitzgerald Papers. His note on this story that "this is Nora, or the world, looking at *me*" puts him in the position of both the weary older man and Mary, the constant observer devoid of jealousy, but with "a big dose of conceit."

115 *"Then she went to Reno"*: In 1931 Nevada had instituted the most liberal divorce laws, providing for speedy dissolutions, in the country. "Going to Reno" was American shorthand for getting a fast divorce.

116 *"X9"*: A spy or secret agent. In 1934, writer Dashiell Hammett (*The Thin Man*; *The Maltese Falcon*) and illustrator Alex Raymond (*Flash Gordon*) began a comic strip called *Secret Agent X-9*. Leslie Charteris, creator of "The Saint," also contributed story lines to the strip in its early days.

116 *silver belt with stars*: In *The Love of the Last Tycoon*, as Monroe Stahr (pronounced "star") is trying to find Kathleen Moore, he provides the following detail to his assistant, Miss Doolan: "'I remember she had a silver belt,' Stahr said, 'with stars cut out of it.'"

116 *Simpson's Folly*: A concrete house built on the beach sands at the foot of Canford Cliffs, between Poole and Bournemouth, England, in the late 1870s. From its completion, if it can ever be said to have been complete, the ocean waves compromised the house and it was unlivable. In 1890 the remains were finally dynamited. Fitzgerald borrows the name from this famously failed construction and applies it to a hotel ruin of his imagination, doubtless based upon one of the many hotel ruins to be found at the time in the Appalachian mountain chain from the Point Hotel in Lookout Mountain, Tennessee (burned in 1908), to the Overlook Mountain House in Woodstock, New York (burned in 1923). The nearest model was the elegant Mountain Park Hotel in Hot Springs, North Carolina, a two-hundred-room resort with bathhouses and a golf club (burned in 1920).

In an early manuscript draft of this fragment, called provisionally "Cheerful Title," the characters' names are different, and their connection before the party more passionate.

(Cheerful Title)
by F. Scott Fitzgerald

The people who gave that party receive a fraction of a mill[ion] from a small article you use every day. It is something that mankind did well enough without until ten years ago—but now finds indispensable. Guess again.

The guest of honor, Liza, wore a silver belt with stars cut out of it. She wore a bright grey woolen dress with a red zipper vest and lips to match. Her hair was dark gold and quiet (dark dull gold) and her voice sounded quiet but all her instincts were rowdy and she functioned in high gear amidst all confusions. She was offered the crown in any gathering but she always mislaid it or wore it rakishly over one [y]ear. Ike Blackford, whom she was to marry in a few months—his first, her second—stopped at the steps of the house and drew her up to him through the cool damp air of the pine grove. Inside an orchestra was playing "Lovely to Look At," molto con brio.

"Don't circulate around," he whispered into her cheek, "Stay beside me—in two hours I'll be on my way." Her arms promised. Then she gathered up all she could of the outdoors in one deep breath as they went in.

"CYCLONE IN SILENT LAND"

124 *"Dr. Craig . . . Dr. Machen"*: Craig House was an expensive private clinic in Beacon, New York, where Zelda Fitzgerald was hospitalized in early 1934. Machen was Zelda's mother Minnie Sayre's maiden name. Either Trouble is getting Dr. Harris's name wrong here, or Fitzgerald made the mistake himself.

124 *cream going into the coffee*: "You're the Cream in My Coffee" was a popular song of 1928, composed by Ray Henderson, with lyrics by Buddy DeSylva and Lew Brown.

125 *"lecture to those probationers"*: A probationer is a student nurse.

125 *"sympathectomy"*: Cutting a nerve chain that parallels the spine. A last-resort operation, with major risks and side effects possible, to control chronic pain, excessive sweating, or hypersensitivity.

126 *echolalia*: Automatic, uncontrollable repetition of vocal sounds made by someone else. This is a clinical word Zelda used often in her own writings, but in 1922, Fitzgerald had written his old Princeton friend the writer and literary critic Edmund Wilson (1895–1972), "How do you like *echolalia* for 'meaningless chatter'?"

126 *rabbit split for dissection*: Rabbits were and are among the most commonly used animals for laboratory demonstration and testing.

127 *a big word*: From the ensuing description is it clear that Dr. Craig has referred to the young women as bitches. It was a prohibited word in films in the 1930s, though widely used in print, and favored by Ernest Hemingway in describing his female characters—see, for example, Brett Ashley in *The Sun Also Rises* (1926) feeling good "deciding not to be a bitch"; Francis Macomber, near the end of his "Short Happy Life" (1938), telling his wife, Margot, "You *are* a bitch."

130 *hoofer on the four-a-day*: Trouble has been a vaudeville variety dancer. Vaudeville bills could be advertised as two-a-day, four-a-day, or more-a-day; four shows a day was serious, hard work for the young woman.

133 *"Bonthron and Venski and Cunningham"*: William Bonthron of Princeton (1912–1983), Eugene Venzke of the University of Pennsylvania (1908–1992), and Glenn Cunningham of the University of Kansas (1909–1988) were American runners, chiefly of the 1,500 meters and the mile. From 1934 to 1936, they traded records in the NCAA championships. Venzke and Cunningham were on the 1936 Olympic team, competing in Berlin that summer. Bonthron did not qualify. Preserved in Fitzgerald's papers is a contemporary clipping from the *Princeton Alumni Weekly* about Bonthron with a perfect cigarette-burn hole in the middle.

133 *"I'll get coffee"*: Coffee, with its caffeine, is a stimulant that increases blood pressure. Coffee and aspirin have long been regarded as emergency home remedies for a person experiencing a heart attack.

135 *hands with wet mud*: A classic palliative for burns caused by chemicals.
136 *"supernumerary toe"*: An extra toe or part thereof.

"THE PEARL AND THE FUR"

141 *"take us to the Rainbow Room"*: The legendary New York nightspot and restaurant opened in the autumn of 1934, on the sixty-fifth floor of the tallest of the Radio City/Rockefeller Plaza buildings. Upon the debut of "Mr. Rockefeller's Rainbow Room," the *Brooklyn Daily Eagle* said, the "glorious interior pales before the magnificent panorama of Manhattan beyond the windows. . . . [A] unique note is the room's indirect lighting arrangement which automatically adjusts itself to fit the mood of the music. If you whistle shrilly into the mike, for instance, bright yellows flood the ceiling. And for soft musical tones, the softer shades of light suffuse the room (romance via robot, huh?)"

143 *"Chinatown"*: In 1907, the *New York Times* gave the popular view of Chinatown, which "has a government of its own, based on terror and graft. Its victims— Chinamen and white men and women of the most depraved types—are drawn from all parts of the city" to its tenements, "where they can sate their thirst for strange vices." By the 1930s, this reputation had given way to the view of Chinatown as more of a stage set for tourists, but Mrs. Tulliver is not about to let Gwen go there.

143 *"the Aquarium"*: At the time of this story, the New York Aquarium had been in Battery Park's Castle Garden (now Castle Clinton) since 1896. New York Parks Commissioner Robert Moses arranged for the destruction of the Aquarium in 1941 so the Brooklyn–Battery Tunnel could be built. Fish and other aquatic life from New York were housed at the Boston Aquarium until the new building at Coney Island opened.

143 *"Empire State . . . flea-circus"*: The girls have truly seen the Manhattan sights, from the Empire State Building (opened in 1931) to the bizarre sideshow world (photographed years later by Diane Arbus) of Hubert's Dime Museum and Flea Circus at 232 West Forty-Second Street. Professor William Heckler's Flea Circus was the highlight of the shows there: fleas pulled chariots in races, juggled, and played football.

143 *"'Ritzy'"*: César Ritz (1850–1918) opened his first luxurious hotel in Paris in 1898. Soon he was managing the Carlton in London (1899); the Ritz-Carlton New York opened in 1911. Fitzgerald wrote a long short story, truly a novella, that he called "The Diamond in the Sky" when he was a young man. Retitled "The Diamond as Big as the Ritz," it was published in 1922 and remains one of his best-known stories.

143 *Southampton . . . and Newport*: Southampton, Long Island, and Newport, Rhode Island, had been since the nineteenth century playgrounds for the rich, and far indeed from Kingsbridge.

144 *beside it was the driver*: New York had no real regulation of taxi drivers at the time of this story; a sixteen-year-old with no experience could walk into a job as one. In 1937, New York instituted official taxi licenses and medallions, the same system its yellow cabs operate under today.

146 *chinchilla cape*: The chinchilla is a small gray rodent native to the western mountain coast of South America. Its very soft, prized fur led to its near-extinction in the late nineteenth and early twentieth centuries.

146 *"Goody-Goody"*: A popular song of 1936, with lyrics by Johnny Mercer and composed by Matty Malneck. A schadenfreude song, in which the singer revels in the fact that a former lover has been in turn rejected: "Hooray and hallelujah / You had it comin' to ya / Goody goody for him / Goody goody for me / And I hope you're satisfied, you rascal you."

146 *"wanted to go to Williams College"*: A small, consistently top-ranked liberal arts college in Williamstown, Massachusetts, founded in 1793.

148 *"my name's Ethan Allen Kennicott"*: The young taxi driver bears one of the oldest names in Vermont; indeed, of its founder, Revolutionary War hero Ethan Allen (1737–1789).

148 *"the TenBroek family"*: One of the oldest and most prominent colonial families in New York, or rather New Netherland, having arrived in America in the 1630s and founded the city of Albany. The Manhattan telephone directory for 1940 lists only one Ten Broeck in the city, in Murray Hill.

150 *"it's the* Dacia*"*: The Roman name for the area in which the Carpathian Mountains and a portion of the Danube River lie, bounded by the Black Sea. In Fitzgerald's lifetime, *Dacia* was the name of a British steamship that laid transoceanic communications cables, and also of a successful racing yacht built in 1892.

150 *"Rhumba dancers"*: In 1935, Paramount released the movie *Rumba*, starring Carole Lombard as a Manhattan socialite and George Raft as a Cuban dancer. Raft, though a professional dancer well before he was typecast as a Hollywood gangster, could not save the film from disaster (though *Bolero*, also starring Raft and Lombard and also a dance picture, had been a hit in 1934). Cuban bolero dance became the basis for a new ballroom dance, the rhumba, that was a rage when this story was written. Gwen is ahead of the curve, having already passed the fad, unlike the English boys.

150 *"Eton"*: Founded in 1440, Eton is one of the oldest and best-known boarding schools, or "public schools," in England. The name still bespeaks aristocratic privilege and social prominence; Peddlar would have been one of the very few American students there at the time.

151 *St. Joseph lilies*: A hybrid amaryllis associated with New Orleans.

"THUMBS UP" AND "DENTIST APPOINTMENT"

165 *bombazine*: A wool blend material, in which wool is mixed with silk or cotton. That Josie's dress is blue is a nod to her Northern sympathies in the Civil War. The family surname, Pilgrim, originating in Massachusetts, comes across as austere, devout, and rigid, as personified by the brother, Ernest; and as adventuresome and in search of new hopes, as embodied in Josie.

165 *"secesh"*: Secessionists, Southerners, Rebels. Confederate sympathizers.

165 *General Early*: In the summer of 1864, Confederate general Jubal A. Early (1816–1894) led the Confederacy's last attempt at Washington, D.C. Without sufficient artillery or troops to take the city, Early managed to reach the outskirts of town just after the 4th of July, sending shock waves through D.C. and Baltimore. He was turned back by Northern troops under Lew Wallace, who would become far better known after the war as the author of *Ben-Hur: A Tale of the Christ* (1880). Early was chased down the Valley of Virginia—the Shenandoah Valley—by Philip Sheridan's army and definitively defeated at the Battle of Cedar Creek on October 19, 1864. During the Valley campaign, the Northern army burned or destroyed the fall harvest, mills, factories, barns, and homes to keep Virginians from supplying the Confederate troops.

166 *verse to the* Lynchburg Courier: A local paper in Lynchburg, Virginia, whose heyday was 1857–1858. In "Thumbs Up" Tib identifies himself as a correspondent for it after the war.

166 *C.S.A.*: Confederate States of America. Announced during the Montgomery Convention, in Montgomery, Alabama, in February 1861; dissolved at the end of the Civil War, April–May 1865.

166 *Pleasanton's cavalry*: Alfred Pleasonton (1824–1897), commander of the Northern cavalry corps, best known for his encounter with the Southern cavalry under

J. E. B. Stuart at the Battle of Brandy Station, Virginia, on June 9, 1863. By the summer of 1864 he was no longer in command in the East, having been sent to Missouri by the time this story takes place.

166 *"Hi there, Yank!"*: The origin of the term "Yankee" in American history is much debated. Applied since at least the mid-1700s by the English to American colonists, it was later variably limited to New Englanders of British origin. During the Civil War, Southerners called Northerners, and particularly Northern soldiers, "Yankees."

166 *"guerrillas"* . . . *"Mosby murderers"*: In 1862, the Confederate Congress passed the Partisan Ranger Act, which legitimated small, commando-style units of soldiers to operate behind enemy lines. These "partisan" groups were regarded as guerillas or "bushwhackers" by the Union army and Northern civilians, and were feared for their unpredictable strikes. John Singleton Mosby, "the Gray Ghost" (1833–1916), was the best-known of the raider leaders, commanding the First Virginia Cavalry and continuing his activities briefly after Confederate commander Robert E. Lee's surrender in April 1865. One of the things in which Mosby's raiders specialized was disrupting Northern communications, including cutting telegraph lines.

166 *"Lee's lines"* . . . *"the Army of Northern Virginia"*: Robert E. Lee (1807–1870), Confederate general and commander of the Army of Northern Virginia.

166 *"clean your . . . face with dandelions"*: The simple meaning is "rub your face in the weeds." The dandelion was not regarded as a weed during Civil War times: hungry Southern soldiers ate the ubiquitous plants, particularly the leaves and roots (from which they made "coffee").

167 *"General Grant's"*: Ulysses S. Grant (1822–1885), then commander of the Northern Army of the Potomac. At this time, Grant was leading the bloody and ultimately triumphant Overland Campaign through Virginia against Lee, incurring heavy casualties at battles like "Bloody Angle" of Spotsylvania and Cold Harbor, near Richmond.

167 *"Jeff Davis"*: Jefferson Davis (1808–1889), formerly a U.S. senator from Mississippi, was named president of the Confederacy in February 1861.

167 *Mine eyes have seen*: Julia Ward Howe (1819–1910) wrote her lyrics to what became one of the most popular Northern songs during the war, "The Battle Hymn of the Republic," in November 1861.

167 *"Cold Harbor"*: One of the bloodiest days of the war was June 3, 1864. The Confederate army under Lee, outnumbered almost two to one, repulsed Grant's troops outside Richmond, Virginia, and inflicted heavy losses. However, the battle set the path for the end of the war: Lee had to devote his army's nearly spent energies to defending Richmond and Petersburg. For Josie to say her brother had been wounded at Cold Harbor is entirely the wrong thing to say to Confederate troops; fortunately for Dr. Pilgrim, the topic goes quickly to teeth instead.

167 *"Maryland, my Maryland"/"Maryland-My-Maryland"*: James Ryder Randall (1839–1908) wrote "Maryland, My Maryland" in 1861 and his poem was quickly set to music. It became the state song of Maryland in 1939, despite its pro-Southern theme and lyrics like "the despot's heel is on thy shore" and "Huzza! She spurns the Northern scum!"

167 *"one of the real Napoleons"/"a real Bonaparte"*: Fitzgerald may have had in mind a prominent Baltimore family, that of Jerome-Napoleon Bonaparte (1805–1870), as he created this character. The cousin of Emperor Napoleon III, "Bo" was a plantation owner and local celebrity, and his son Charles Joseph Bonaparte (1851–1921) was President Theodore Roosevelt's secretary of the navy and attorney general. Scribner published a biography of him by Joseph Bucklin Bishop, *Charles Joseph Bonaparte: His Life and Public Services*, in 1922.

169 *wide white Cordoba*: A *sombrero cordobés*, or sombrero.

169 *"that Libby Prison"*: Occupying an old warehouse space on the banks of the James

River in Richmond, Virginia—the Confederacy's capital—Libby was one of the two principal prisons for Union prisoners of war. It was a horrible, overcrowded, and notorious place by 1864, with a high mortality rate for those incarcerated there.

170 *"'Lynchburg, thy guardsmen'"*: Since its founding in 1757, Lynchburg, which is in the Blue Ridge Mountains of Virginia, has been known alternately as "the Hill City" or—invoking classical Rome—"the City of Seven Hills."

170 *Mason-Dixon line*: Charles Mason (1728–1786) and Jeremiah Dixon (1733–1779), two English-born astronomers and surveyors, agreed in 1763 to assist in a border dispute between the colonies of Pennsylvania and Maryland. The line they surveyed between 1763 and 1767 runs along the bottom of Pennsylvania and the top of Maryland, making a right angle and turning south to mark the boundary line between the counties of Maryland's Eastern Shore and the state of Delaware. The Mason-Dixon Line was an informal boundary during the Civil War indicating the divide between North and South.

172 *"Seventh Virginia Cavalry"*: "Ashby's Cavalry," a large regiment of cavalry, and infantry, commanded by Turner Ashby until his death in battle in 1862. After Ashby's death, Captain, later Colonel, Richard Henry Dulany of Loudon County, Virginia, took command of the Seventh. Fitzgerald gives his surname to Tib.

172 *"hang them up by their thumbs"*: This was indeed done during the Civil War by both sides, and even inflicted by some officers upon their own men as punishment for stealing or attempted desertion.

172 *"follow the feather"*: Confederate cavalry commanders favored a Cavalier-style plume in the hat as well. Mosby could find an ostrich feather for a fancy occasion, like one of his officers' weddings in December 1864, but he customarily wore either a white or a black feather. The song Tib is singing, "Riding a Raid," to the tune of "Bonnie Dundee," initially extolled J. E. B. Stuart. Tib changes the lyrics for his own commander, Mosby.

NOTES SPECIFIC TO "THUMBS UP"

173 *hoop slipped from its seam*: By 1867, hoopskirts, or crinolines, were generally made of rings of cloth-covered steel joined by cloth tapes. Here, one of the lower rings has freed itself of its mooring and tripped Josie.

174 *"Paquebot Rochambeau"*: A packet-boat, originally a ship running a regular route and carrying mail, was by this time a passenger ship. Jean-Baptiste, Comte de Rochambeau (1725–1807), was a French nobleman and military commander who fought with George Washington and the Marquis de Lafayette against the British army during America's Revolutionary War.

176 *"the great Doctor Evans"*: Thomas Evans (1823–1897) was born in Philadelphia, and was one of the first dentists to use gold leaf in filling teeth. In 1848, he moved to Paris under the patronage of the emperor, became extremely wealthy, and was made a grand commander of the Légion d'Honneur, among many titles awarded him. During the Franco-Prussian War, as Paris fell in early September 1870, Evans helped Empress Eugénie, wife of Napoleon III, escape from Paris to Deauville and thence to England.

178 *"here you have For a United Ireland"*: This slogan refers to the United Irishmen movement of the 1790s, which culminated in the French-supported Rising of 1798 and defeat by the British.

178 *"and The Friends of the Freedman"*: Freedmen, which is to say freed slaves, were assisted after the Civil War by the Bureau of Refugees, Freedmen and Abandoned Lands, established in 1865 and commonly called the Freedmen's Bureau. The Bureau lasted only until 1872, when it lost its funding and was closed down in

the backlash to Reconstruction. That this medal is not gold but "a bottle top" is a critical note on the lip service, too infrequently backed up with real help, given to freed slaves after the war.

178 *"Here you've got* United Veterans of the Mexican War*"*: The Mexican War (1846–1848) was fought after the American annexation of the Republic of Texas in 1845.

178 *"This says,* The Legion of Honor, Private George Aiken*"*: Fitzgerald is perhaps conflating here George Aiken, the nineteenth-century dramatist who wrote the stage version of *Uncle Tom's Cabin*, and Wyatt Aiken, a Confederate officer who commanded the Seventh South Carolina Infantry and whose unit suffered heavy losses at Gettysburg. "For Valor Extraordinary" is Fitzgerald's own language, and echoes the words inscribed on the medal Jay Gatsby says he was awarded by Montenegro.

180 *"the* Richmond Times-Dispatch, *the* Danville News *and the* Lynchburg Courier*"*: Three Virginia newspapers.

180 *"Prussian government"*: The Franco-Prussian War began in July 1870. Here we see a preview.

183 *the Empress*: Empress Eugénie of France and wife of Emperor Napoleon III (1826–1920). The daughter of a Spanish count and his half-Scottish wife, she was educated in Paris and married Louis-Napoléon in 1853. After the overthrow of government outlined in this story, during which she did indeed flee Paris from Deauville in the company of Dr. Evans, Eugénie, her husband, and their only child settled in England. Their son, Napoléon, was killed at age twenty-three, in 1879, while serving with British troops in the Anglo-Zulu War in South Africa.

183 *new Marie Antoinette*: Tib has wondered if, as he watched the crowd passing the Tuileries, the empress would be tried by revolutionaries and guillotined, as Marie Antoinette was in 1793. It is not an idle wonder; the fall of the Deuxième Empire after the emperor's defeat in the Franco-Prussian War culminated, in Paris, in street sieges and a second Paris Commune. The Communards set fire to the Tuileries in May 1871 and burned it, and the library of the adjacent Louvre, to the bare walls.

183 *"taking to Trouville"*: A resort town on the sea in Normandy.

183 *Porte Maillot*: One of Paris's ancient city gates, and the route for exiting the city to the northwest, heading for the English Channel.

184 *Ile-de-France*: One of France's eighteen regions, which includes the city of Paris.

184 *belonged to Sir John Burgoyne*: Sir John Fox Burgoyne (1782–1871) was a British army officer. His father was the playwright, bon vivant, and army general "Gentleman Johnny" Burgoyne, who lost the Battles of Saratoga to American troops under Benedict Arnold during the Revolutionary War.

186 *louis d'or*: Gold coins, minted before the French Revolution, though the term was loosely applied to those circulating in France and struck during the Empires.

NOTES SPECIFIC TO "DENTIST APPOINTMENT"

196 *autumn of 1866*: Many people came to Minnesota in 1866, in a boom of settlement that followed a treaty with the Bois Forte Band of the Chippewa tribe. Gold was thought to have been discovered on Native American lands and the treaty was designed to let miners in; the gold proved to be pyrite, but settlers stayed. The capital of the Minnesota Territory since 1849, Saint Paul remained the capital when Minnesota was granted statehood in 1858. After the Civil War, the city's location on the Mississippi River as a northern terminal point for steamships earned it the nickname "The Last City of the East." Minneapolis, the new boom town across the river, began its swift growth in 1867. Minnesota's air is "unpolluted," in Dr. Pilgrim's eyes, because, unlike many northern states in the eighteenth and early nineteenth centuries, it never had slavery.

198 *two red-headed twins*: This recalls directly Margaret Mitchell's Tarleton twins in *Gone With the Wind* (1936), one of Scottie Fitzgerald's—and countless other American girls'—favorite books at the time.

198 *"tear our fences down"*: The ongoing "Dakota conflict" and "Sioux uprising" went on between settlers and these two Native American tribes during and after the Civil War. Cattlemen and farmers fencing land that had been open range for the Indians, who had lived on the plains, was a major point of conflict. In 1862, white settlers were massacred, and Indian warriors hanged in reprisals. In 1863, Congress ordered the removal of all Sioux in Minnesota to reservations downriver. The conflict would not be settled until 1890, if then, at the horrific slaughter of Wounded Knee Creek, South Dakota.

"OFFSIDE PLAY"

209 *Yale Bowl*: The Yale College football stadium opened November 21, 1914, with a game against Harvard. It is literally a bowl, with its top tiers spilling out into a green bank dotted with trees. In October 1915, Fitzgerald took Ginevra King, a wealthy Chicago debutante who was at the Westover School and who was the inspiration for many female characters in his fiction, to the Princeton-Yale game at the Bowl. *The Perfect Hour: The Romance of F. Scott Fitzgerald and Ginevra King, His First Love*, by James L. W. West III, includes entries from Ginevra's diary about their romance—and attending the football game. By 1916, Ginevra was over him; she and a fellow prep-school girl came down to Princeton for the Princeton-Yale game, but then ditched Fitzgerald and another Princeton student, who had escorted them back to New York, for two Yalies in Grand Central Terminal.

209 *"that little guard Van Kamp"*: The name owes a debt to Walter Chauncey Camp (1859–1925), one of the founding fathers of football. He played—as a 156-pound halfback—and coached at Yale, where the Yale Bulldogs had a record of sixty-seven wins and two losses with him at the helm. Hubert Van Kamp is a character in Samuel R. Crockett's novel *Hal O' the Ironsides* (1914), which was popular in Fitzgerald's youth.

212 *the Grand Central*: The Grand Central Terminal station at Forty-Second Street and Park Avenue in New York, the principal terminus for commuter trains arriving in New York from the north and east, opened in 1903. In 1943, Scottie Fitzgerald would become engaged to Princeton graduate and U.S. Navy officer Samuel Jackson "Jack" Lanahan (1918–1998) under the "Biltmore clock" in the Hotel Biltmore, adjoining the station. Zelda painted one of her brightest New York scenes, *Scottie and Jack Grand Central Time*, to commemorate their engagement.

213 *"Gone" or "Lost"*: Both popular songs of 1936. "Gone" was composed by Franz Waxman, with lyrics by Gus Kahn; "Lost" was composed by Phil Ohman, with lyrics by Macy O. Teetor and Johnny Mercer. "Gone" was in part a hit because it was used in the soundtrack of *Love on the Run*, starring Clark Gable and Joan Crawford. In Chapter 1 of *The Love of the Last Tycoon*, a drunken passenger waiting at the Nashville airport "put two nickels in the electric phonograph and lay alcoholically on a bench fighting off sleep. The first song he had chosen, 'Lost,' thundered through the room, followed, after a slight interval, by his other choice, 'Gone,' which was equally dogmatic and final." He is not allowed on the plane, and Cecilia Brady pities him: "The drunk sat up, awful looking, yet discernibly attractive, and I was sorry for him in spite of his passionately ill-chosen music." In Chapter 5, Cecilia and Wylie drive up Laurel Canyon with "either 'Gone' or 'Lost'" on the radio. However, "'Lost' and 'Gone' were the wrong mood, so I turned again and got 'Lovely to Look At,' which was my kind of poetry."

213 *"Goody-Goody"*: See note to "The Pearl and the Fur" on page 342.

216 *"list of names"*: Fitzgerald was making a list of the names of football players, past and present, in the margins of a *Princeton Alumni Weekly* story by Gilbert Lea (1912–2008), a football All-American at Princeton, when he died on December 21, 1940. The very last words he ever wrote are scribbled next to a paragraph of the story he had circled: "good prose."

217 *"the Taft"*: The Hotel Taft opened on New Year's Day, 1912. Former president William Howard Taft was among the notables living, and staying, at the hotel. From 1920 to 1933 (the years of Prohibition), the Taft boasted one of New Haven's most popular speakeasies in its basement. Since the early 1980s, it has been an apartment building.

217 *Little Lord Fauntleroy*: Cedric Errol, the child of an English nobleman and an American woman, is the title character of this children's novel by Frances Hodgson Burnett (1849–1924) serialized from 1885 to 1886 in *St. Nicholas Magazine*. Reginald Birch (1856–1943) created the illustrations that started a fin-de-siècle fad for mothers—clearly including Mr. Gittings', who has given her son Little Lord Fauntleroy's name—curling their sons' hair and dressing them in Renaissance-styled velvet suits with wide lace collars.

219 *expedition in Crete*: Through the 1920s and 1930s the discoveries made at Knossos by Sir Arthur Evans (1851–1941) about Mycenaean civilization made headlines around the world.

219 *the Dartmouth game*: In November 1935, Princeton beat Dartmouth 26–6 in a blizzard at home, in the "Snow Game," on the Tigers' way to an undefeated national championship. That same year, Yale beat Harvard in Cambridge—though the 47,000 fans present sat through only "intermittent snow flurries." When he was on the East Coast during football season, Fitzgerald regularly attended Princeton football games; however, in the fall of 1935 he was in North Carolina.

219 *Sachem Tea House*: Sachem Street in New Haven was in the 1930s a street of little shops and residences, anchored by the Yale Peabody Museum of Natural History.

219 "Philo Vances": Philo Vance is a dapper New York detective who solves murder mysteries in twelve novels by Willard Huntington Wright (1888–1939), writing as S. S. Van Dine. He was created in 1926, and is much akin to his more famous English contemporary Lord Peter Wimsey, Dorothy Sayers's amateur detective, who is also a passionate art historian, polo player, and classicist.

219 "Hercule Poirots": The celebrated Belgian policeman and detective created by Agatha Christie (1890–1976). Poirot has appeared in novels, short stories, a play, and television and film adaptations from 1920 until the present (despite his death in 1949, in *Curtain: Poirot's Last Case*).

221 *parlor car . . . "day coach"*: Parlor cars were popular, particularly on the business routes of the Northeast Corridor, among those who could afford seats there. Day coaches were unreserved, coach-class cars.

223 "Harvard Club": At 27 West Forty-Fourth Street in New York. The main clubhouse, designed by McKim, Mead & White, opened in 1894. A doorman would have had to take Considine a note, as women were not allowed in most rooms of the Club in the 1930s, and long thereafter.

227 A *truck marked* Harvard Crimson: Begun as the Harvard *Magenta* in 1873, the *Crimson* is the oldest continuously published college daily paper in the United States.

228 *"Ted Coy"*: Edward Harris Coy (1888–1935), who died at forty-seven in September 1935, was a three-time All-American fullback for Yale from 1906 to 1909, and a boyhood hero of Fitzgerald's. In 1933, he filed for bankruptcy. After his death, his widow pawned a gold medallion, a gold football, a Yale Skull and Bones Society badge, and a wedding ring set with emeralds. Lottie Coy, who was working in a kitchen, was asked why she had pawned the items. "I haven't any money, that's

the Simon Simple answer to this," was her reply. Skull and Bones redeemed the items and had them sent to New Haven. Ted Fay, in Fitzgerald's story "The Freshest Boy" (1928), is based in part on Coy.

"THE WOMEN IN THE HOUSE" ("TEMPERATURE")

233 *"No reference to any living character"*: This qualifier, or, as Fitzgerald rightly terms it, dodge, came into being in Hollywood. In 1932, the studio for which Fitzgerald would principally work, Metro-Goldwyn-Mayer, released *Rasputin and the Empress*, a vehicle for the three Barrymore siblings, John, Lionel, and Ethel. In it Prince Paul (John Barrymore), based on Prince Felix Yusupov, murders Rasputin, who is intimated to have seduced or sexually assaulted Paul's fiancée, Princess Natasha. Felix did indeed murder Rasputin, and bragged about the fact, but there is no evidence that the movie subplot involving "Natasha" was true. Yusupov and his wife sued MGM for invasion of privacy and libel, and in 1934 were awarded £20,000 by an English court. MGM settled out of court in New York for a further $250,000, and movies—and many novels—have included the disclaimer ever since.

233 *the pictorials*: Magazines and newspapers in which the pictures were of more importance and given more room than text. In the 1930s, major newspapers like the *New York Times* ran "Pictorials" that survive today as weekend magazine sections. The film and celebrity fan magazine *Photoplay* was one of the top pictorials in the world in 1939; Fitzgerald's lover during his last Hollywood days, Sheilah Graham, occasionally wrote for it.

233 *Omigis*: There is no such island chain. However, as Monsen is returning to Los Angeles on a ship with a made-up Japanese name, he may be coming from the Omi-jima (today Oumi or Omi) Island area on the southwestern coast of Japan's Honshu Island.

233 *electro-cardiograph*: Designed to record the heartbeat and cardiovascular disorders. Willem Einthoven (1860–1927) won a Nobel Prize in Medicine in 1924 for his invention of the first practical electrocardiogram machine; by 1937, there were portable ones.

234 *the country estate of young Carlos Davis*: In November 1938, Fitzgerald moved into a cottage on the four-acre Encino, California, estate of the actor Edward Everett Horton (1886–1970). The estate, Belleigh Acres or, locally, "Belly Acres," contained a main house and two guesthouses. Fitzgerald lived in one of these until 1940. Horton was a Brooklyn-born vaudevillian and a character actor who had great success in Hollywood in the 1930s, most notably in a series of Fred Astaire and Ginger Rogers movies, including *The Gay Divorcee* (1934) and *Top Hat* (1935)—movies that Scottie Fitzgerald loved. Horton's partner of many years was the actor Gavin Gordon. Fitzgerald seems to be having fun here with Carlos Davis's sexuality, from the "affectations ascribed to him" and his "extraordinary personal beauty" to his status as "the maiden's prayer," which may come from his observations of Horton and Gordon.

234 *only in flicker form and once in Technicolor*: The flickery quality of an old movie, seen by the light of a primitive carbon arc lamp projector, is why movies are still called "flicks" today. Labor-intensive Technicolor film was still relatively new in Hollywood in 1939, but already the wave of the future. Disney's *Snow White and the Seven Dwarfs*, filmed in Technicolor, was the top box-office movie of 1938.

234 *the sunny May-time*: In April 1939, Scott and Zelda went on a trip to Cuba that was disastrous. He drank so much that she had to oversee his return to a hospital in New York, and then travel alone back to Highlands Hospital, where she was living at the time. Immediately thereafter, upon his arrival back in Los Angeles, Fitzgerald was confined by doctor's orders to his bed for the rest of the spring and

most of the summer. He wrote to Zelda on May 6, "Excuse this being typewritten, but I am supposed to lie in bed for a week or so and look at the ceiling. I objected somewhat to that regime as being drastic, so I am allowed two hours of work a day." He reported to friends and business associates that he was suffering from tuberculosis. During these months, Fitzgerald revised the "Thumbs Up"/"Dentist Appointment" stories, and wrote "The Women in the House." That the doctor introduced here is named Cardiff, is huge, and is also a fraud is a joke to lighten the situation: the "Cardiff Giant," one of the most famous hoaxes in American history, began when the allegedly petrified remains of a man were dug up in October 1869 in Cardiff, New York. One can still see the primitive stone carving that is the Giant in Cooperstown, New York.

235 *two spans of The Grand Coulee*: The massive and controversial dam under construction across the Columbia River in Washington State in the 1930s. Its reservoir provides water for crop irrigation and its hydroelectric capacity makes it still the largest power plant in America. However, it permanently blocked the Columbia River to all migratory aquatic life, and flooded 70,500 acres once occupied by Native American tribes. The spans of the lower portion of the dam had finally met in 1938.

237 *"Rusty's Secretarial Bureau" . . . "Miss Trainor"*: In May 1939, twenty-three-year-old Frances Kroll (1916–2015) was sent by Rusty's Employment Agency to work for Fitzgerald while he was living on the Horton estate in Encino. Kroll spent the next twenty months—until the end of his life—as Fitzgerald's secretary, confidante, gofer, and friend. She typed up "The Women in the House," but, unlike Monsen and Trainor, Fitzgerald and Kroll had no intimation of a romantic relationship. Kroll, later Frances Kroll Ring, subsequently worked as a writer and editor in New York (her hometown) and California. She was loyal to her boss in death as in life, writing letters of comfort to Zelda and to Scottie, sorting out his finances, carefully assembling and sending his papers to his executor, Judge John Biggs of Wilmington, Delaware (a Princeton friend of Fitzgerald's), and selecting the casket in which he was buried. She generously shared her memories of Fitzgerald with scholars and enthusiasts over the rest of her long life.

237 *Dewey and Hoover*: Thomas E. Dewey (1902–1971) was a New York City prosecutor and Manhattan district attorney (and later politician) who prosecuted organized crime figures. J. Edgar Hoover (1895–1972) was from 1924 the director of the Bureau of Investigation, renamed the Federal Bureau of Investigation in 1935. His investigations of mobsters in the early 1930s, and the successful tracking by FBI agent Melvin Purvis (of whom Hoover was envious) of Pretty Boy Floyd, Baby Face Nelson, and John Dillinger—ending in the 1934 deaths of all three—were front-page news.

239 *Queen Elizabeth arriving in Canada*: While Fitzgerald was writing this story, from mid-May until June 17, 1939, George VI and Queen Elizabeth (the Queen Mother) went by train on a royal tour of every Canadian province, with a dip south to visit President Roosevelt in Washington, D.C., and at his home at Hyde Park, New York.

239 *russet, yellow-streaked hair*: Fitzgerald's fiction is full of strawberry blondes, from the title character of "His Russet Witch" (later "O, Russet Witch!") in 1921 onward. That Zelda was a natural redhead is borne out by the lock of her hair preserved in her inscribed copy of *The Beautiful and Damned*, though she liked to lighten her hair from time to time.

239 *"Diplomat"*: After Scott's death, Zelda told Scottie that Scott talked to her about being a diplomat—"he thought that that was what he would most like to do, after writing and being a football hero."

240 *"build these things so jerry"*: Built temporarily and impermanently. Derived from the English navy term "jury-rigged," the phrase gained amplification during World

War I, when "jerry" was a pejorative term applied to Germans. Miss Hapgood is criticizing California itself for these qualities.

240 *"from the East?"* . . . *"Born and raised in Idaho"*: An echo of a celebrated exchange from *The Great Gatsby*. During their trip into Manhattan for lunch, Gatsby tells Nick Carraway that he is "the son of some wealthy people in the Middle West," and Carraway asks him what part of the Middle West. Gatsby replies, "San Francisco."

240 *"Bubonic Plague"*: The bubonic plague pandemic called the "Black Death" killed around a hundred million people in Europe during the mid-fourteenth century. Although the last outbreak of plague in Europe had been in the early eighteenth century, in Fitzgerald's lifetime there had been plague outbreaks in China, Australia, and Hawaii.

242 *"junk addicts"*: "Junk" was a synonym for impure narcotics, including morphine, cocaine, and heroin, as sold on the street, from as early as 1919. Monsen is, revealingly, something behind the times here.

243 *Booth Tarkington*: American novelist (1869–1946). Tarkington attended Princeton University, where he, like Fitzgerald, wrote for the *Nassau Literary Magazine* and the Dramatic Association (renamed the Triangle Club by Fitzgerald's time). As did Fitzgerald, he left Princeton without being awarded a degree—though the school later gave both men diplomas—and, again like Fitzgerald, he was a midwesterner and rather proud of it, using it for the stuff of his fictions. Tarkington won the Pulitzer Prize for the novel twice, for *The Magnificent Ambersons* in 1919 and for *Alice Adams* in 1922, just as Fitzgerald was beginning his literary career. Both *Alice Adams* and Tarkington's popular *Penrod* novels feature junk dealers—as in the sense of antiques dealers—as characters.

243 *"Dope fiends"*: Aleister Crowley's *Diary of a Drug Fiend* (1922) introduced to a shocked world the concept that "nothing means anything any more except dope, and dope itself doesn't really mean anything vital."

243 *"milk toast"*: Toast in warm milk, given to toddlers and invalids throughout the nineteenth century and into the twentieth as comfort food. Consequently, "milquetoast" came to mean someone who was sickly or in some fashion incapable.

243 *"stuff I got in Melbourne"* . . . *"sub-tropical herb"*: Eucalyptus, native to Australia, came to be called "the fever tree" in Europe by the nineteenth century. Its leaves, made into tea or otherwise ingested, calm or cure many types of fevers.

246 *Caesar in his toga*: Fitzgerald's library included two copies of *Plutarch's Lives*, which includes the eyewitnesses' description of the murder of Julius Caesar.

247 *"American Beauties"* . . . *"Talismans . . . Cecile Brunners"*: Varieties of roses. The American Beauty was a deep red-pink French rose brought to America in the late 1800s, and was a best-seller during the 1920s—though its popularity continues today. Talismans were a Jazz Age creation, a hybrid pink-orange rose with coppery petal rims. Cécile Brünner is the now-classic "Sweetheart Rose," a light pink climbing rose developed in France in 1881.

249 *"raw steak for their saddles"*: Ammian (Ammianus Marcellinus, c. 325–391), in his history of Rome, told of the Huns subsisting upon roots and herbs from the fields, and the "half-raw" meat of an animal, warmed between their own bodies and a horse's back.

252 *Priscilla Lane*: Priscilla Mullican (1915–1995), who with her renamed sisters was part of the vaudeville/variety act the Lane Sisters in the early 1930s. Bandleader Fred Waring brought her to Hollywood in 1937, and Lane's rise began—but did not continue after 1939, with the notable exception of her costarring in *Arsenic and Old Lace* with Cary Grant in 1944.

252 *"Juan Gris and Picasso"*: Juan Gris (1887–1927) and Pablo Picasso (1881–1973) were founders of the Cubist movement in art. They were two of the leading artists collected, and befriended, by Gerald and Sara Murphy in France in the early

1920s. The Fitzgeralds, Picasso, and his first wife, Olga, a Russian ballerina, were regular guests at the Murphys' home in Cap d'Antibes, the Villa America.

253 *"we planned to go to Nevada"*: It was, and is, easy to get a marriage license in Nevada. There were no blood tests (for venereal disease) or waiting requirements.

254 *"Cannibal King"*: In May 1939, a horror-comedy movie called *The Gorilla* was released by 20th Century Fox. In it, the maid is terrorized by an escaped gorilla (while an insane killer nicknamed "the Gorilla" terrorizes the Ritz Brothers, and Bela Lugosi is a creepy butler). Fitzgerald would have known the movie because it was made by Allan Dwan (1885–1981), one of his friends from his Great Neck, New York, days. Dwan's parties were one of the inspirations for Gatsby's parties.

255 *"on a bat"*: Carlos Davis's writer is on a drinking spree.

256 *"'Mickey Finn'"*: The use of "Mickey Finn" to mean a doctored drink—generally one into which chloral hydrate or another "knockout" drug has been slipped—dates from the 1910s, and is likely named for a Chicago bartender, Michael "Micky" Finn, who allegedly drugged drinks so he could rob patrons.

261 *"eclusion"*: Fitzgerald means occlusion, a blockage, in this case, of a coronary artery by a blood clot that ensues in a heart attack.

262 *Boris Karloff*: William Pratt (1887–1969) renamed himself Boris Karloff as a stage actor in Canada in the 1910s. He became a Hollywood star in *Frankenstein* (1931), in the role of Dr. Frankenstein's monster.

262 *"One of them hopheads!"*: An opium user. The term was applied by the 1920s to morphine, codeine, and heroin addicts as well.

262 *"G-men"*: Slang for "government men" or U.S. government special agents. The term was commonly used to indicate government agents in gangster films of the 1930s.

263 *"reefers . . . school children"*: On February 23, 1940, the *Los Angeles Times* ran an editorial piece about the plague of "marihuana" sweeping the country, and the madness that resulted from "reefers." When Fitzgerald wrote, in April 1938, to induce his friends Eben "Pete" and Margaret Finney to send their daughter Peaches to Los Angeles for a visit (Peaches was Scottie Fitzgerald's best friend), he made light of Hollywood's perceived perils: "I have a little house on Malibu beach + will arrange for them to meet the stars + go to the studios + keep them so busy that there'll be no time for debauchery nor even to form the marihuana habit which is sweeping the kindergartens. They will come into contact with nothing of which you wouldn't approve, (tho they better not know that)." The Finneys said yes.

265 *Angele Pernets and Cherokees . . . Black Boys*: More types of roses. Angèle Pernets are a pink-orange; Cherokees are the starry white bush roses ubiquitous in the South and the state flower of Georgia; and Black Boys a dark crimson climbing rose from Australia, dating from 1919. Fitzgerald knew a lot about flowers, and in his clippings files preserved cut-out photographs of them, including roses. Zelda knew even more, and loved to paint flowers as much as she loved to grow them. Fitzgerald associated her, always, with flowers and above all the Cherokee rose, the scent she assigned to her autobiographical character Alabama Beggs in *Save Me the Waltz* (1932).

"SALUTE TO LUCY AND ELSIE"

269 *George Lawson Dubarry*: Fitzgerald, a fan of French history all his life, has given the father and son in this story the surname of one of the most celebrated royal mistresses in history, Jeanne Bécu, Madame du Barry (1743–1793). After the death of her lover, Louis XV, she was sent to a nunnery by his successors, Louis XVI and Marie Antoinette. All three died by the guillotine during the French Revolution.

269 *visit his father in Cuba*: Until 1934, America's military occupation of the country after the Spanish-American War (since 1898) meant that American companies held the franchise on extracting Cuba's natural resources, including oil. By 1939, when this story is set, Cuba was under the control of General Batista, and American businessmen, as well as mobsters like Meyer Lansky, were flourishing there.

269 *Pan-American Refining Company*: The Pan American Petroleum and Transport Company was founded in 1916. The company was heavily involved in the "Teapot Dome" scandal of the early 1920s, in which oil production leases on protected oil reserves were obtained, via bribery, on very favorable terms. Fitzgerald's use of a very similar name for Dubarry's company, as well as the Cuba setting, heralds something duplicitous to come.

270 "G. the L.": Get the lay.

270 "being a Catholic": Recall *The Great Gatsby*, chapter 2: "Daisy was not a Catholic, and I was a little shocked at the elaborateness of the lie."

270 "Birth Control . . . Sweet Sixteen": By the time of this story, the age of consent in most, but not all, American states was sixteen. Historically, that age had been much lower. The discussion of birth control is timely, for the Comstock Laws outlawing contraceptives were still on the books, and contraceptives were hard to get in the United States. Infamously, American soldiers were the only troops not supplied with condoms during World War I; resultant cases of syphilis and gonorrhea—together with the condoms readily available in Europe—changed the discussion of contraception in America. In 1932, birth control activist Margaret Sanger had a doctor at one of her clinics order a diaphragm from Japan. It was confiscated, but in 1936 a federal court held in *U.S. v. One Package of Japanese Pessaries* that the Comstock Act could not bar shipment of contraceptives to a licensed doctor. Wardman Evans is also discussing venereal disease here when he says "the doctor said before I left God's Country that I'm O.K.," and he is worried about what he may have now caught in Paris. The only treatment for syphilis at the time was salvarsan (the "magic bullet"); antibiotics were not yet being used to cure it.

270 *Valedero Beach*: Varadero Beach, a resort area on the northwest end of Cuba, about eighty miles from Havana. In the 1930s it was exclusive and expensive; among the Americans who had built vacation homes there were Irénée du Pont, whose mansion Xanadu is now the clubhouse of the Varadero Golf Club.

270 *"Miami clipper"*: The Pan American World Airways service from Miami to Havana.

270 a *"house"*: A brothel; a whorehouse.

272 *El Patio*: Still a top Havana restaurant.

273 *trip to Pinar del Rio*: In the hilly far west of Cuba. At the time, remote farm country—where the best Cuban tobacco is still grown.

274 *into an American past*: One of the terms agreed to by Spain at the end of the Spanish-American War in 1898 was the ceding of territories, including Cuba, to America. The United States received a lease in perpetuity, which it continues to exercise, over the naval base at Guantánamo Bay, and the right to intervene in Cuba's military, economic, and political affairs. Dubarry, here and throughout the story, stands for an archaic, even imagined, American control that had diminished significantly, as far as Cubans were concerned, by 1939.

275 *Elkton, Maryland*: When a wedding was performed in Elkton, Maryland, in 1939, it was a quick one. Neighboring states mandated a forty-eight-hour waiting period before a marriage license could be issued; Maryland did not, and Elkton is just across the Delaware and Pennsylvania state lines. To Fitzgerald's readers, an immediate license and a speedy, easy wedding with no questions asked were what "Elkton" meant. The Maryland Historical Trust marker in front of Elkton's "Little Wedding Chapel" states that, in 1938, a staggering 11,791 marriage licenses were issued in the town.

"LOVE IS A PAIN"

280 *Brenda Joyce*: Graftina Leabo (1917–2009) was renamed as a seventeen-year-old by 20th Century Fox for her first film, *The Rains Came* (which opened in September 1939). Joyce ended her film career as the second Jane to Johnny Weissmuller's Tarzan in the 1940s.

281 *"G man"*: See note to "The Women in the House" on page 352.

281 *the Princeton Prom*: See note to "The I.O.U." on page 328. In the winter of 1939, Scottie Fitzgerald was invited to the event, and received an advice letter from her father: "I hope you enjoy the Princeton Prom—please don't be overwhelmingly—but no, I am done with prophecies—make your own mistakes. Let me only say 'please don't be overwhelmingly anything!', and, if you are, don't give my name as the responsible parent! (And by the way never give out any interview to any newspaperman, formal or informal—this is a most definate [*sic*] and most advised plea."

284 *little woman in the uniform of a trained nurse*: Spies masquerading as nurses were by 1939 an old movie convention; see *I Was a Spy* (1933), starring Madeleine Carroll. Of course, the film fiction was based in fact. Nurses who were also spies, from Harriet Tubman and Sarah Edmonds in the Civil War to Marthe Cnockaert McKenna (whose memoir was the basis for *I Was a Spy*) in World War I, were celebrated for both occupations.

286 *Norman Rockwell hobo*: Norman Rockwell (1894–1978), popular artist and illustrator, did many covers for the *Saturday Evening Post*, the magazine that published most of Fitzgerald's stories during the 1920s and early 1930s. In October 1924, Rockwell used a favorite model of his, James K. Van Brunt, for a cover called *Hobo and Dog* that remains one of his best-known illustrations. Minus the dog, alas, Fitzgerald brings the image of Van Brunt to entertaining life here.

286 *solitaire game*: Fitzgerald's scenario predates Richard Condon's novel *The Manchurian Candidate* (1959) by twenty years, but the use of a game of cards as a game for spies, and lovers, is uncannily similar. Condon was for many years a Hollywood publicity agent and adman, overlapping there with Fitzgerald.

288 *"Glamor O'Hara"*: Scarlett O'Hara is the heroine of Margaret Mitchell's novel *Gone with the Wind* (1936).

"THE COUPLE"

294 *magic of first love*: A well-known quotation, at the time, from *Henrietta Temple: A Love Story* (1837), by English politician and author Benjamin Disraeli (1804–1881): "The magic of first love is our ignorance that it can ever end."

295 *"Mr. Marbleton and Mr. Shafter"*: These gentlemen and their fineness are invoked often by Katy and Reynolds. In a deleted passage, the two servants mock Lou during an argument for not having clothes that are as nice as the Philadelphia gentlemen's.

296 *"grass" . . . looked up in surprise*: Butlers do not cut grass, hence Carrol's surprise.

299 *Yale Club*: In 1915 the Yale Club moved to its present building at 50 Vanderbilt Avenue, on the corner of Forty-Fourth Street next to Grand Central Terminal. In the late 1910s and 1920s, the Princeton Club was renovating a new clubhouse on Park Avenue and Thirty-Ninth Street, and shared space at the Yale Club. In his biography *Scott Fitzgerald* (1962), Andrew Turnbull reported that in 1919, when he was living in New York and working in advertising, "Fitzgerald often ate at the Yale Club . . . and one day, drinking martinis in the upstairs lounge, he announced that he was going to jump out the window." He didn't, but in Chapter 3 of *The Great Gatsby* Nick Carraway reflects, "I took dinner usually at the Yale Club—for

some reason it was the gloomiest event of my day—and then I went up-stairs to the library and studied investments and securities for a conscientious hour. There were generally a few rioters around, but they never came into the library, so it was a good place to work."

301 *"I'm John Bull himself"*: An eighteenth-century personification of England that remains current today. Long popular as a caricature, Bull is usually drawn as a stout man in Regency clothing, sometimes with a Union Jack waistcoat.

303 *"got a Marconi"*: Received a wireless telegraph message. The technology was developed by Guglielmo Marconi (1874–1937), and had been used for ship-to-shore communications since the America's Cup races of 1899.

303 "Mauretania": One of a pair of cruise ships—the other being the ill-fated *Lusitania*—launched in 1906 by the Cunard Line. The world's largest ship until the White Star Line launched its trio of competitors, *Olympic*, *Titanic*, and *Britannic*, *Mauretania* was a transatlantic liner during the 1920s. In 1930, she was switched to a route from New York to Halifax, Nova Scotia, and in 1935, despite much protest, she was broken up.

304 *"saw a revolver"*: The Sullivan Act of 1911 required the licensing in New York State of any firearms small enough to be concealed. The law applied to handguns, razor knives, and brass knuckles.

306 *Twine cooked* à la maître de hotel: A simple sauce of butter, parsley, lemon juice, salt, and pepper.

309 *"typhoid carrier"*: A person who is asymptomatic for typhoid but who can spread the disease to others. The most famous, or infamous, example in history is Mary Mallon (1869–1938), nicknamed "Typhoid Mary." In the first years of the twentieth century, Mallon worked as a cook for a string of New York families, in which every family came down with typhoid fever and several people died. She refused to stop working as a cook, even after she was discovered to be a carrier, and changed her name and place of employment often. From 1915 until her death, Mallon remained in quarantine at Riverside Hospital, on North Brother Island in New York's East River, choosing a life of isolation and incarceration rather than having her gallbladder, which was full of active typhoid bacteria, removed.

309 *the drift of things*: A well-known line from Robert Frost's poem "Reluctance" (1913). It is a poem quite pertinent to this story, and for Fitzgerald to have the dog, as it were, quoting it is a funny touch. Frost did a reading at Princeton in January 1917, sponsored by Fitzgerald's friend John Peale Bishop and his literary club, that Fitzgerald likely attended; surely he knew the poem and the collection from which it comes, *A Boy's Will*.

"BALLET SHOES" ("BALLET SLIPPERS")

317 *arrives at Ellis Island*: Island in New York Bay, from 1892 to 1954 the principal inspection station for immigrants arriving on the East Coast. However, the stream of people went both ways: Ellis Island also had detention facilities, and was a point of deportation for would-be immigrants who were not permitted into the country, as well as "aliens" being sent back to a home country—which is what the dancer daughter in this story initially believes has happened to her family.

317 *Imperial Ballet*: The Imperial Russian Ballet (today the Kirov, or Mariinsky, Ballet) has flourished in St. Petersburg from the early 1700s; under its various names, the ballet and its associated school are among the most celebrated in the world.

317 *young rum runner*: Initially, someone smuggling rum by boat from areas where it was locally and legally made, like Jamaica and the Bahamas, to Florida during Prohibition (1920–1933). By the time Fitzgerald is writing, "rum runner" is a generic

term for any bootlegger bringing illegal alcohol into American cities, though still, as we see here, principally by boat.

318 *The great Pavlova*: Anna Pavlova (1881–1931), the most celebrated prima ballerina of her day. After leaving the Imperial Ballet and Sergei Diaghilev's Ballets Russes, Pavlova formed her own ballet company. She made her American debut at the Metropolitan Opera House in February 1910, and received a rave review from Fitzgerald's friend Carl Van Vechten, then the dance critic for the *New York Times*.

318 *apartment at 125th Street*: 125th Street, Martin Luther King Boulevard today, was in the 1930s the "Main Street" of Harlem. It housed theaters including the New Burlesque Theater, renamed the Apollo in 1934, the Hotel Theresa, and St. Joseph of the Holy Family Church, one of the oldest Catholic churches in New York. When Fitzgerald moved to New York after he took a job with an advertising agency in 1919, he lived in an inexpensive apartment at 200 Claremont Avenue, just off the corner of West 125th Street and Broadway.

318 *St. Saens,* The Swan: Camille Saint-Saëns (1835–1921) wrote the suite *Le carnaval des animaux* (*The Carnival of the Animals*) in 1886. Movement 13 (of 14) is "le cygne," the swan—also known as "the dying swan" since Michel Fokine choreographed a four-minute ballet for Pavlova to perform to the music in 1905. It was her signature solo; a two-minute film clip of Pavlova dancing the Swan survives.

"THANK YOU FOR THE LIGHT"

321 *"the law against it"*: During the 1920s, riding on the coattails of Prohibition, various temperance organizations campaigned against tobacco use, and particularly cigarettes. Fourteen states passed laws against smoking before the public tide turned, and those laws fell—leaving in place only legislation barring minors from buying tobacco products.

321 *"ones that weren't in the war"*: By the end of World War I, organizations, including newspapers, were supplying soldiers with cigarettes, over the protests of state health boards.

322 *"old-fashioned whale-bone"*: The stiffening pieces in old-fashioned corsets, made of bone taken from baleen whales.

322 *Catholic cathedral*: The Cathedral of the Immaculate Conception, on Broadway at Eleventh Street in Kansas City, built in 1882. Its name indicates its dedication to the Virgin Mary, of whom there is much iconography in the building.

323 *the play "The Miracle"*: *Das Mirakel*, a 1911 play by Karl Vollmöller (1878–1948) about a nun who flees her convent with a man, but returns in the end to find that a statue of the Virgin Mary has come to life and taken her place, covering for her in her absence. A film version in English was made in 1912; in 1924, Lady Diana Manners Cooper (1892–1986) starred in a popular Broadway version as the Madonna. Scott and Zelda socialized with Cooper in Hollywood in January 1927, while she was performing in *The Miracle* at the new Shrine Auditorium. Zelda termed her, though cold and unapproachable, "the most lovely, attractive person I ever saw." In *The Love of the Last Tycoon*, Fitzgerald refers to the stage extravaganza, which was directed by Max Reinhardt: "every eight days the company must release a production as complex and costly as Reinhardt's *Miracle*."

Works Consulted

In preparing this collection, I have used all of F. Scott Fitzgerald's novels (*This Side of Paradise, The Beautiful and Damned, The Great Gatsby, Tender Is the Night,* and *The Love of the Last Tycoon*) and also his collections of short stories, from those published during his lifetime (*Flappers and Philosophers, Tales of the Jazz Age, All the Sad Young Men,* and *Taps at Reveille*) to those, including stories written with Zelda Fitzgerald, published since 1940. *F. Scott Fitzgerald's St. Paul Plays, 1911–1914* (ed. Alan Margolies), the scripts of his shows for the Princeton Triangle Club, and his play *The Vegetable* were valuable for responding to Fitzgerald's screenplays and scenarios included here. *Poems 1911–1940* (ed. Matthew J. Bruccoli) shows his touch for light verse. *The Notebooks of F. Scott Fitzgerald* and *The Crack-Up* are essential reading for anyone writing on Fitzgerald. The magisterial Cambridge Edition of the Works of F. Scott Fitzgerald, currently in thirteen volumes, edited by Matthew J. Bruccoli (volumes 1 and 2) and James L. W. West III (volumes 3–13) is invaluable to scholars, and lovers, of Fitzgerald's writing. It has been a chief resource for this book. My explanatory notes are modeled upon those in the Cambridge Fitzgerald.

Seven principal volumes contain all of Fitzgerald's letters published to date: *The Letters of F. Scott Fitzgerald* (ed. Andrew Turnbull); *Correspondence of F. Scott Fitzgerald* (eds. Bruccoli and Margaret W. Duggan); *Letters to His Daughter* (ed. Turnbull); *Dear Scott, Dearest Zelda* (eds. Jackson R. Bryer and Cathy W. Barks); *Dear Scott/Dear Max: The F. Scott Fitzgerald–Maxwell Perkins Correspondence* (eds. John Kuehl and Bryer); *As Ever, Scott Fitz—: Letters Between F. Scott Fitzgerald and His Literary Agent, Harold Ober, 1919–1940* (ed. Bruccoli); and *A Life in Letters* (ed. Bruccoli). Much correspondence from, and most correspondence to, Fitzgerald remains unpublished, however.

My work on this volume draws primarily from the Fitzgerald Papers in the Department of Rare Books and Special Collections at Princeton University: the F. Scott Fitzgerald Papers, including the Additional Papers; the Zelda Fitzgerald Papers; and the John Biggs Jr. Collection of F. Scott Fitzgerald Estate Papers. Fitzgerald remains his own best resource for anyone writing about him, his publications, and his life. He saved everything from scribbled notes on drink coasters and restaurant menus to manuscript drafts to final tearsheets (on which he often wrote further revisions and notes). He kept files of interesting newspaper clippings, illustrations he liked, lists of books he was reading, and very much more. His scrapbooks, now available online, are at once a pleasure and a crucial resource. The *Daily Princetonian* and the *Princeton Alumni Weekly* provide the principal information on Fitzgerald's time on campus, from 1913 to 1917. "The I.O.U." (in manuscript and typescript) is at Yale's Beinecke Library. The typescripts of "Thumbs Up" and "Dentist Appointment," and the only known version of "The Couple" (part typescript and part manuscript), and the *Ledger* of his life and publications (now available online) are at the University of South Carolina's Irvin Department of Rare Books and Special Collections. The original card files of Fitzgerald's story submissions and revisions, still the property of Harold Ober Associates, provided correct dates and in some cases alternate titles, as well as the responses from contemporary magazines to which stories were submitted.

In his scrapbooks, Fitzgerald himself compiled a comprehensive record of the contemporary critical reception of his writings. He kept reviews, columns, and even advertisements that often cannot be recovered in any searches of online newspaper and magazine databases—essential material that would otherwise be lost. Mary Jo Tate's *Critical Companion to F. Scott Fitzgerald*, the entire run of the *Fitzgerald/Hemingway Annual* (1969–1979), and the *F. Scott Fitzgerald Review* (2002–present) are where the ladders start for complex contemporary scholarship on Fitzgerald.

Books about the Fitzgerald family have proliferated in recent years. The standard biography of Fitzgerald himself remains Bruccoli's *Some Sort of Epic Grandeur: The Life of F. Scott Fitzgerald*. Versions of his life as viewed through Zelda's include Nancy Milford's *Zelda* and Sally Cline's *Zelda Fitzgerald: Her Voice in Paradise*. Zelda Fitzgerald's novel *Save Me the Waltz* is a fictionalized account of the Fitzgeralds' lives that has more resonance than biographies of Zelda completed to date. Eleanor Lanahan's *Scottie: The Daughter Of . . .* is a compassionate biography of Scottie Fitzgerald Lanahan Smith, based on primary sources.

About the Author

F. Scott Fitzgerald was born in St. Paul, Minnesota, in 1896. He attended Princeton University, joined the United States Army during World War I, and published his first novel, *This Side of Paradise*, in 1920. That same year he married Zelda Sayre of Montgomery, Alabama, and for the next decade the couple divided their time among New York, Paris, and the Riviera. Fitzgerald was a major new literary voice, and his masterpieces include his short stories, *The Great Gatsby*, and *Tender Is the Night*. He died in 1940 at the age of forty-four of a heart attack in Los Angeles, California, while working on *The Love of the Last Tycoon*. Fitzgerald's fiction has secured his reputation as one of the most important, and beloved, American writers of the twentieth century.

Anne Margaret Daniel teaches literature at the New School University in New York City. She has published extensively on Fitzgerald and on Modernism since 1996. Anne Margaret lives in Manhattan and in upstate New York.